THE GATE BEYOND OBLIVION

RYAN KIRK

WATERSTONE
MEDIA

For Kyle

1

It seemed profoundly unfair that he would die a victim of falling rock.

If Brandt was going to die, he wanted his death to be heroic. A death dealt by an elite Falari commander would be acceptable. He wanted a death where people would speak of his nobility and sacrifice, of the content of his character. Perhaps women who had never known him in life would weep for his passing, bemoaning the loss of a promising warrior taken before his time.

If a falling rock killed him, his own squad, closer to him than blood, might pretend he never existed.

As a stone twice the size of his fist hurtled down the cliff face toward him, he lamented that a betting man's odds were on the falling rock.

Brandt leaped to the side, his hands searching for a new hold, the deadly stone brushing his left arm on its way to the scree below. His hands caught a jagged protrusion and he swung wildly for a moment before planting his feet against the wall. Given the extent of the scree they had to pick their way through just to get here, falling rock wasn't an uncommon occurrence on this cliff.

"Sorry!" Ana called from above him.

Brandt vowed not to climb directly below her anymore. He would rather find his own way up, even if it took longer.

He looked up in time to see her scamper up another section of the wall with ease.

Ana's lightness put his to shame. It didn't help that he was almost twice her size, but even if they had weighed the same, her skill far surpassed his, a fact she seemed eager to remind him of today. She paused on a ledge not much wider than her foot. From the way she stood on it, though, she could have been standing on a wide road in a perfectly flat field.

Brandt looked down. They'd climbed several times his own height. If he fell, he didn't think lightness would prevent an injury. From where Ana stood, a fall meant almost certain death.

She was smiling. She enjoyed the challenge.

"Do you see a trail?" he asked. The locals had said there was a trail. No one had known the exact location of the trailhead, though, and a full morning of searching hadn't revealed it.

Thus, the climb.

"No," Ana replied. "But I think I see the cave above. Maybe forty paces away, if you could walk up the cliff from where I stand."

Brandt muttered a curse. He had never minded heights in the past, but he'd never tried climbing a hundred paces up a vertical wall with a disturbing amount of loose stone, either. A hundred paces didn't seem like much — on the ground he could cover that distance in a handful of heartbeats. On a vertical wall, a hundred paces might as well be the distance to another world.

He took a deep breath and focused his internal energies, feeling gravity relax its relentless hold on his body. He planned his route, then pulled himself up the wall.

Fortunately, though the wall was high, it offered plenty of hand and foot holds. He made himself as light as he could, using the holds to propel himself up. He was just about to lose focus when he reached Ana's ledge.

Brandt wobbled as his feet found purchase. He had forgotten down below that his feet were larger than hers. Where she could stand flat-footed, he had to balance on his toes.

Ana steadied him and pointed. Less than a pace away the ledge was wider. Brandt side-stepped over and finally rested.

From his higher vantage point, he saw the cave Ana had noticed. From below it appeared as a dark smudge on the cliff face. Unfortunately, her estimation of its distance looked accurate.

"What do you think?" he asked.

"It's a good place to hide from the world." She gave him a small shrug. "If I was thieving from the surrounding area, I'd consider it. It's a little hard to reach, though."

Brandt thought the same. A good hideout balanced accessibility with safety. The cave above appeared incredibly safe, but he couldn't imagine making this climb every day. Even a sure-footed gazelle like Ana ran a significant risk with this climb.

Brandt ran his hands over the rock wall, searching for his next hold. His fingers passed over a well-defined edge, barely raised from the surface of the rock wall.

He frowned. Nature rarely made use of straight lines. He

motioned for Ana to approach, then pointed to his discovery.

She came and ran her hand over the same section of stone. The difference was barely visible to the eye. If Brandt hadn't been searching for a hold with his hands, he didn't think he would have noticed it.

"He's got a stone affinity," Ana said. "A strong one."

Brandt agreed, though he hated what that implied. This mission was supposed to be easy.

She gave him a questioning glance. "Keep going?"

Brandt looked up at the cave, then back down. The altered stone was evidence enough their bandit did indeed live in the cave above. No other explanation made sense. They could return tomorrow with the rest of their squad. Five against one sounded much better than two against one.

But Brandt was pretty sure the bandit wasn't home. If their suspect had a strong stone affinity, he would have come down and thrown them off the cliff face by now. They hadn't exactly been sneaking up on the cave.

Besides that, time was against them. The bandit had been striking more frequently. The local governor demanded results.

And strong stone affinity or not, Brandt didn't back down from a challenge.

"Want to risk it?" he asked.

"Against stone?" she paused, more reasoned than him. "Sure."

Brandt agreed. Even if the bandit wasn't home, any information might help them predict his movements.

They made themselves light and climbed the rest of the way.

The cave was bigger than Brandt had envisioned. He'd expected a small space, possibly wide enough for some shelter and storage but little else. Instead, a deep darkness greeted him. The cave went well into the rock face.

Fortunately, Brandt always came prepared to use fire. His small pack carried two small torches, and a moment later he had one of them lit with his own fire affinity. As always, he felt the warmth of the fire calling to him, a seductive, nearly irresistible song.

He ignored it.

All elements were dangerous.

But fire put the others to shame.

They stepped into the cave, Brandt leading the way with his flame.

The darkness retreated before his torch, and he found the end of the cave in short order.

There was no evidence of habitation.

Brandt slowly spun around with the torch. They couldn't have been misled.

"Brandt."

He turned at the sound of fear in Ana's voice. She stood next to a wide crack in the stone. He'd walked right past it without noticing. He stepped closer, thrusting the torch forward.

He immediately took a step back. His legs felt weak.

The crack wasn't a crack, but a tight passage. The stone of the floor, ceiling, and walls was perfectly smooth.

No hammer and chisel could make a hallway so perfect.

But that level of affinity was impossible. The cost was too high.

He heard nothing besides their quick breathing. The cave was empty, and any answers were through that passage. He refused to be cowed, even by a feat as impressive as this. He stepped forward.

Ana put a hand on his arm. Their eyes met. After a moment, she nodded.

Like the rest, she would follow his lead. He hadn't let them down yet.

Brandt went through first. The passage was narrow. He had to turn sideways, and even then either the backs of his shoulders or his chest scraped against the sides. Ana slid through easily.

He wondered if the bandit was closer to Ana's size than to his.

He froze on the other side of the passage, his eyes locked on another impossible scene.

The second chamber was several times larger than the first.

It had been devastated. Rubble lay everywhere, broken boulders larger than his torso.

Behind him, Ana pushed her way through. He stepped to the side to let her in. She froze beside him.

"Oh."

She had a gift for understatement.

Brandt stepped deeper into the second chamber. Ana started to follow, but he waved her back. The light from his torch didn't fill the whole space. He wanted to make sure they were alone.

After picking his way through some of the rubble, he found a flat spot where he didn't have to worry about balance. He closed his eyes and listened to the song of the flame.

Most didn't understand that heat surrounded them, every moment of every day. Even the frigid air of winter contained plenty of heat. The air in this cave, cold and clammy against his bare arms, held more than enough.

He pulled the heat from the air around him, felt the warmth of it as it flowed toward his torch.

He opened his eyes. Held high above him, his torch blazed, several times brighter than it had before. Light reached every corner of the second chamber, if only for a couple of heartbeats. Brandt spun around quickly, just to ensure they were alone.

He saw no one besides Ana.

He released the flow of heat to his torch. He shivered. The air around him had become much colder. It would take a few minutes for the circulation of air to heat the space back to its normal temperature.

Ana stepped closer to him, rubbing her arms to keep them warm. Together, they explored the cave.

Ana focused on the rubble first. She examined a few of the boulders while Brandt swept some of the smaller debris aside with his foot. He frowned when he found a depression in the floor of the cave. It had been partially filled in with loose pebbles, but he could feel the bottom with his toe when he dug it in.

He called to his partner. They stared at the depression.

He shook his head. "Does that look like...?"

She nodded.

"That's not possible, right?"

"I didn't think so."

The depression was an impact crater. Made by a fist or foot of someone with a stone affinity. Each of them had seen plenty.

But it was too large by far.

Even their masters at the academy would have been hard pressed to create one half as wide or deep.

"A new weapon?" she asked.

Brandt wished he knew.

This wasn't a bandit's hideout. The man might be stealing from travelers on the road and hiding here, but this was something more. This was a training ground for an incredibly strong fighter. A place where his training wouldn't be interrupted or discovered.

They continued their exploration. The chamber was filled with damage that shouldn't be possible. Mystery piled on mystery.

As they neared the end of their search, a thought occurred to Brandt. Where was the fire?

If a bandit lived here, he needed to cook his meals. He needed light to see. He needed fire.

But there was no evidence of any. Brandt hadn't seen any wood or ash. He hadn't noticed any scorch marks from fire on stone. The realization hit him hard. "The bandit doesn't live here."

A soft sound, like the scuffing of a shoe on stone, reached their ears. It came from the first chamber. Brandt quickly extinguished the torch.

Had the bandit returned?

With a nod, the two warriors snuck toward the narrow passage, preparing to ambush the man as soon as he came through.

Brandt heard the sound of stone on stone before he saw anything. Whatever moved, it sounded large. His stomach twisted in knots when he identified it.

The passage.

Ana must have reached the conclusion about the same time he did. She sprinted ahead of him, light over the rocks. He followed, but lost ground with every step. Gods, but she was fast.

She was in the passage when he got to the start of it. Sure enough, the narrow passage was closing. Brandt saw the flutter of a dark cloak on the other side of the passage, but his attention was captured by Ana.

She wasn't going to make it.

The passage was going to close around her.

An impossible death, trapped in stone forever.

He reached in and found her hand. Too late, she realized her danger.

He pulled with all his might.

At the same time, she became light. He yanked her off her feet toward him, the two of them crashing down together as the passage sealed shut, as though it had never existed.

2

Alena yelped as her mother pulled the covers off her bed, exposing her to the crisp morning air. Her thin nightgown did little to trap her body's heat.

Even with her eyes closed, Alena knew her mother was shaking her head in disapproval. "You'll be late."

Alena grasped for the covers, but her mother held them elusively out of reach. "There's hot tea for you downstairs. Your brother *might* have left you some food, if you're fortunate."

Alena groaned, but the soft embrace of drowsiness abandoned her. She rubbed at her eyes and pushed herself to sitting. Her mother kissed the top of her head, then left the room, her task complete.

Alena looked longingly at her bed for a few moments before standing and reaching for her clothes. She dressed in the uniform of her academy, a simple blue tunic and dark pants. Dresses were an option, but she preferred the pockets and mobility of her current outfit.

She walked down the stairs of their small home into the dining room, where her younger brother, Jace, ate everything in sight. Alena sat at the table and swiped the last piece of bread before Jace could devour it. He glared at her, but with his cheeks full of food, any chance at intimidation was lost.

The bread was still warm, and Alena said a small prayer of thanks for her mother. Before marrying Dad, she had been the middle daughter of a baker's family, and she still rose early to bake. Alena nibbled on the bread while sipping the cup of tea her mom had prepared.

Breakfast ended too soon, but it was a small price to pay for the extra sleep.

Jace sprinted out of the room to gather what supplies he needed for the day. Alena's mom sat down at the table across from her. "You're working this afternoon?"

Alena nodded. "I shouldn't be long. I just need to finish some of the bookkeeping for the month."

Mom beamed at her, and Alena quelled the now familiar shame in her stomach. "Do you think he'll offer you a position?"

Alena let out an exaggerated sigh. "I told you I would let you know. I'm not sure."

Mom raised her hands in mock surrender. "I know. It just sounds like your apprenticeship is going well. We're both proud of you, you know."

"I know."

Before Alena could say more, Jace burst back into the room. "Let's go! There's supposed to be an instructor from the wolfblades today."

Mom gave Alena a knowing look. Jace dreamed of joining the elite military units with all the enthusiasm a fourteen-year-old scrawny boy who had never been in a street fight could. He didn't have a chance, but it wasn't their parents' manner to crush hopeless dreams. Alena must have picked up the habit, because she said nothing either.

After the customary goodbyes, the two left for the academy.

Jace pestered Alena on the walk. "Did you know that the wolfblades are one of the original units commissioned by Emperor Anders I? They've been active as a unit for over two hundred years!"

"I did not," Alena replied drily. It didn't matter how little enthusiasm she displayed. Jace would continue until they reached the academy. The best she could do was endure it.

Fortunately, their journey to the academy was not a long one. When the squat, two-story structure came into view, Jace quieted. A group of about twenty students had gathered in the street outside.

"What's happening?" her brother asked.

Alena shook her head. She recognized a few of the students. They were drawn to trouble the way Jace was to military history.

Alena was about to pass them by when she caught a glimpse of a student in the middle of the circle. Ren cowered within, overshadowed by a young man who was several heads taller.

She glanced toward the academy, but knew no help would come from that direction. On academy grounds, rules were absolute. On the street in front of the academy, the instructors couldn't be bothered.

Alena took a step toward the academy gates, then stopped. If it had been anyone but Ren she would have walked by.

But Ren didn't deserve his fates. Like most students, Ren was several years younger than Alena, but he was small, even for his age. He attracted tormentors of all stripes.

"Go inside, Jace," she commanded.

Jace looked from her to the group. "Come on—"

"Now!" she interrupted.

He cursed at her, but obeyed. Jace thought he wanted to be like his older sister, but he didn't have the stomach for trouble. Deep down, he enjoyed following the rules. He preferred order over chaos.

Once he was safe on academy property, Alena shouldered her way into the crowd. She received several angry glares, until the students saw who it was. Then they made way for her.

She reached the front of the crowd in time to see the stranger pick Ren up by the front of his tunic.

Alena's first glance revealed all she needed to know. The assailant was as old as her, which meant he, too, was on university track. Between that fact and the quality of his clothing, Alena could imagine his story well enough.

As Ren struggled hopelessly to escape, Alena noticed the crest sewn onto the taller boy's clothing. She made out what looked like a tree, but couldn't catch the rest.

A named family, then.

She didn't recognize the crest, which meant the family wasn't from around here.

So he was from a wealthy and influential family, and he picked on smaller students his first day of class.

Alena didn't think they'd be friends.

But she couldn't help but notice the full coin purse bulging in his front pants pocket.

She stepped into the circle, drawing the new student's attention.

"Who are you?" he asked.

"Who are you?" she echoed.

The new student tossed Ren to the side. Ren, never one

to let an opportunity for escape pass, scrambled out of the circle. No one stopped him. A far more interesting spectacle was developing. Alena felt their attention focus on her. The crowd smelled blood, and no small number probably hoped it was hers.

"I'm Niles." The new student puffed out his chest, displaying his crest for all to see. He clearly expected everyone to recognize it.

Alena shrugged, then turned away. Niles had let Ren go. There was no reason to linger.

She heard his step, felt the pressure of the air change as he lunged toward her, his hand outstretched to stop her. She'd half-expected the move, half-hoped for it.

Alena shifted her stance slightly. Niles missed her arm and stumbled beside her, their bodies colliding awkwardly. Her hand sneaked into his pocket at the moment of impact, then back into hers. Right in front of everyone, and no one noticed.

Niles stumbled as he tripped against her, his face turning crimson. Once he found his balance, he turned on her. "I asked you a question!"

Alena looked up at him, looking bored.

Niles had some martial training. Enough that he believed he was unmatched in an academy fight. She imagined any students who could challenge him lost intentionally. Few interfered willingly with named families.

The air pressure changed again. Alena noted it and turned aside as Niles threw a straight jab at her torso.

She didn't bother to hit him. She carried no weapon, and at best, her punches would annoy him. Far better to let him defeat himself.

He passed her, off balance, and she again made for the edge of the circle.

Niles rushed her, finally desperate enough to make a real mistake. He was expecting her to twist away, his arms extended wide to tackle her.

Alena ducked underneath his hands, extending one of her feet across his shins. Niles fell.

He caught himself well, his training asserting itself.

Alena worried she might have a real fight on her hands. Niles looked angry enough to murder, and she'd just demonstrated the extent of her martial abilities. She was saved by the ringing of the academy bell.

The assembled students released a collective groan, but the circle broke apart and drifted toward the academy. Niles, his audience and his available time vanishing, waved her away as though she was nothing. No one believed he meant it, but no one argued against a named family, either.

Niles joined the others, muttering and laughing with his new friends. She had little doubt they were speaking about her, but she didn't mind. Only a fool sought the approval of academy students.

Alena waited until they were well on their way, then followed them through the academy gate.

She let her fingers brush against the coin purse now resting in her own pockets. She guessed there were at least twenty pieces in there.

She grinned, happy for the first time since she'd been woken up. Today was shaping up to be a good day.

3

B randt stared into the perfect darkness where the passage had once been.

It was impossible that the passage could be closed. That level of affinity didn't exist. How was the cost paid? No one could move that much stone.

Impossible. The thought echoed in his mind.

And yet here they were, sealed inside a mountain.

This darkness had a weight that settled on his shoulders and pressed against his chest. The dark seemed alive as his eyes and mind searched for anything to latch onto. He imagined that they weren't alone, that the perfect dark had spawned creatures of nightmare.

Ana's tentative movement beside him brought him back to reality. He hadn't even checked to see if she was hurt. "Brandt?"

"Yes?"

"I hope the gates reject your soul."

"I know."

He couldn't let despair rule his thoughts. He'd gotten them into this, but he was certain he could get them out.

Sure, the situation looked grim, but they'd been in tight spots before.

Maybe not this tight, though.

The rest of their squad knew their approximate location, but Brandt didn't hold out any hope for a rescue. Even if the squad climbed the cliff and found the first cave, they might not find the sealed passage.

Gates below, even if they found the passage and somehow guessed what had occurred, it wouldn't matter. Kyler had their strongest stone affinity, and he didn't come close to having the power to reopen that passage. No one did.

His thoughts always circled back to the impossibility of their situation. He struggled to accept their predicament, because it couldn't be real.

He shook his head. He needed to think. Impossible or not, here they were. If he wanted to breathe fresh air again, he needed to apply himself. He'd never met a challenge he couldn't overcome.

Brandt reached for his supplies. They needed light.

"What are you doing?" Ana asked.

"Lighting a torch."

"Is that wise? If this cave is sealed, you'll be using up our air."

He hadn't thought of that. His hands stopped before they could spark the flint he carried. "I think it's necessary. No rescue is coming, and we need to see to have any chance of escape."

He waited. He could well imagine her face, scrunched up in thought. How many times had he seen it? He'd been her squad leader for three years now, and it wasn't hard to prove Ana was the most thoughtful of the squad. The rest of them took more after Brandt, jumping in first and sorting out the mess later.

"Fine, but a normal torch only."

Brandt struck the flint. Working in complete darkness, it took him more tries than usual, but eventually the torch caught.

As soon as it did, the darkness no longer pressed against him. He took his first deep breath in what felt like ages and rolled his shoulders back.

Ana wasted no time. As soon as the fire burned, Brandt imagined she had started a timer in her head. He followed her, studying their prison with an eye for escape.

Their initial examination was thorough, but revealed nothing promising.

Brandt swore. "How can this cave not have a second exit?"

If a bandit used this place to hide, they would have had a second way out. No criminal ever voluntarily cornered themselves.

Ana, of course, had an answer. Already she was thinking ahead of him.

"Maybe it does, but it's sealed with stone."

Brandt mentally kicked himself. Of course. If their target was strong enough to seal an entire passage, he was confident enough to seal up his other routes to prevent the accidental discovery of his cave. "If that's true, though, he would want to leave it thin, right?" He was disappointed by the lack of courage in his voice.

Ana shrugged.

Brandt forced himself to hope. The conclusion made sense. If the man had left an escape, he would want to make it as accessible as possible. "Let's look again."

Their second search was slower. They ran their hands

up and down the rock, searching for any clue, any trace of the other exit. Brandt's first torch began sputtering, so he lit the second and extinguished what was left of the first. Once the second burned down, the darkness would return, likely forever.

Brandt didn't think about that. They would find their way out. There had to be a second exit.

"Brandt."

He turned. Ana was farther along the wall, her hands running up and down a section nearly opposite of the passage that had brought them in. He walked over to her.

She pointed at the stone and Brandt ran his hands along it.

There.

Like on the cliffs outside, a slightly raised edge, as straight as a ruler. His heart skipped a beat as he traced the outline of the disturbance.

The second exit was small. Ana would fit easily enough, but it would be a tight squeeze for him.

But how thick was the covering stone?

Brandt took the hilt of one of his daggers and rapped it against the wall. It sounded like solid rock to him.

He wouldn't despair. There had to be a way for them to open this second passage.

Brandt's second torch flickered. They didn't have long. "Any ideas?"

Ana shook her head.

Brandt kicked at the stone a few times, earning a bruised heel for his efforts.

They sat back, staring at the rock. Ana pulled out her small waterskin and took a sip. She handed it over to Brandt. He was about to drink when he had an idea, inspired by the skin. "We could crack it."

Ana looked skeptical. "How?"

"I'll heat it rapidly, then you cool it."

Ana considered the proposal. "Is there enough heat?"

It was Brandt's turn to shrug. "We still have the fire. I would pull all that I can."

Ana considered for a moment. "We won't have more than a chance, maybe two. If it fails, we're out of options."

"True, but I can't think of anything else."

Ana thought for a while. Then she nodded. "Let's try."

They went to work. The majority of the task fell on Brandt. Pulling the heat necessary to crack the stone would require almost everything available. He lit the stave of the first torch with the flames from the second. He placed the burning stave near the hidden passage.

He gave Ana one last look. "I'll give you a signal when I'm ready."

She nodded.

Brandt turned back to the wall. He closed his eyes and listened for the song of the fire. He reached out with his will as far as he could.

Then he pulled.

He caught the heat from the burning stave, some heat from their bodies, and the heat from the air. Goosebumps formed on his skin as the cave air froze around them. He kept pulling, collecting as much as he dared.

The stave burned out, all the heat stolen from it. Their last torch flickered.

When he had pulled as much as he deemed safe, he pushed the heat into the stone, forcing it in like an oversized blanket into a small box. As he pushed, the heat tried to escape, to diffuse throughout the mountain. Brandt grimaced as he held it tight within the rock that sealed the escape. He nodded at Ana.

While he had collected heat, she had gathered water.

She pushed the water at the stone, the liquid turning into steam on contact.

Brandt lost his focus when he heard the stone crack. He opened his eyes.

The torch flickered wildly, barely holding on to its remaining flame. In the dim torchlight, Brandt saw deep gouges in the stone.

But no light.

Ana leaned in closer. After a moment, she sat back. "It worked, but not enough. The wall is thicker than I hoped."

She left their other fears unspoken. They were only guessing the altered stone was a passage. If it wasn't, they were wasting their efforts. Brandt picked at the gouges with the tip of his dagger, but the stone resisted the blade.

"I want to try again," Brandt said.

"The effort alone might kill us. I can probably collect enough water, but what about heat?"

"I can do it."

Ana sighed. She didn't believe him, but she would follow him. "All or nothing, right?"

"Always."

"If you freeze me to death, I *will* haunt you for the rest of your life."

"That's fair."

They collected themselves. Brandt closed his eyes and felt around the cave. He had gathered everything he considered safe last time. Now he would have to pull more. But he supposed a quick death was preferable to a slow one.

All or nothing. Always.

Brandt pulled heat again. He pulled the last of the heat from the dying stave, the warmth still stored in the cracked stone, and the heat from their own bodies. He began shivering uncontrollably, but he kept pulling from the air around them, scraping every last bit of heat together that he could.

He pulled the last of the heat from the lit torch, casting them into permanent darkness. At the same time, he could feel moisture pulled from his body. They were both at their limit.

He pushed the heat into the stone, focusing it. "Now."

There was a splash, followed by a wave of steam.

For a moment, nothing happened.

Then the stone cracked, echoing loudly in the small chamber.

Light shone through.

Brandt whooped with joy, crawling forward as fast as his cold limbs would allow. He banged the hilt of his dagger against the stone, breaking it into pieces he then pulled into the cave. Warm air flowed in from the small passage on the other side of the rock. The wolfblades had revealed a small tunnel just large enough to slither through.

He returned to Anna. She was so cold she could barely move. Brandt had nothing to give, but he pushed her gently toward the passage. The air flowing in felt tropical compared to the frozen air of the cave.

Ana lay on her belly and crawled forward. Brandt followed suit, exhaling deeply to fit through the initial gap.

The farther they went, the faster Ana climbed, the tunnel angling upward. Like the opening that had led them here, the surface was unnaturally smooth. Occasional depressions in the stone served as holds. Her body was warming up again, and the passage opened up until they were standing in a vertical crack. They walked toward the light, coming out into a thickly wooded deciduous forest.

Ana laughed, her relief finally finding expression. Brandt laughed, too.

They had done it.

He'd never had a doubt.

They began their journey back to Landow, where they would meet the rest of the squad. Now that his survival was certain, at least for a while, his mind returned to his previous concerns.

They had escaped with their lives, but they still had a bandit to catch.

And he was impossibly strong.

Brandt looked forward to the challenge.

He would show the bandit what the wolfblades could do.

4

Alena left the academy before the last class of the day began. She studied history last, but the instructor was a doddering, absentminded fool who read from a book out loud to the class. He didn't teach her anything she couldn't learn on her own. So why waste precious time?

Wisdom also dictated that she leave early. She had crossed paths with Niles three times that day, and his glares were unmistakable. Throughout the day he'd gathered a following of students eager to ingratiate themselves with a named family. She guessed he planned on waiting for her outside the academy, this time with a more supportive entourage. She refused to grant him an easy opportunity.

The streets outside the academy were quiet as she walked out the gates. The city guard at the gate nodded as she passed. She was beyond the age of compulsory education. University-tracked students attended of their own choice, so the guard had no reason to stop her.

Alena chose streets more or less at random. Landow had been one of many cities redesigned by Emperor Anders I, so all the streets were set out on a grid. So long as Alena continued either north or east and paid some attention to her surroundings, she would eventually end up at her destination.

She glanced behind her periodically. She didn't believe anyone would try to follow her, but one couldn't be too cautious.

Her checks revealed nothing suspicious. A handful of wage earners cleaned the streets. A few merchants stood talking outside a shop. The sameness of it all bored her, much the same as her classes.

The walk to the shop didn't take long. Landow's academy was near the center of town, where most of the government buildings stood. Bayt's shop was located among a small group of other shops, surrounded by nice houses.

From the outside, Bayt's shop appeared pristine. Alena knew he paid more than was necessary on upkeep. He knew well the value of appearances. The shop inside was equally clean.

To most people, Bayt was a merchant who specialized in the spice trade.

And to be fair to him, Bayt *was* a successful spice trader. Caravans never passed through Landow without a visit to Bayt's shop. Alena noticed a cart sitting outside as she approached. A young man, looking thoroughly bored, rested in the cart, a large brimmed hat pulled over his eyes.

Alena ignored him and stepped into the shop.

Bayt glanced at her, smiled, then returned to his conversation with the visitor. They spoke in a language Alena didn't understand. It sounded like one of the southern dialects, but Alena didn't have her master's ear for tongues. He frequently criticized her lack of interest in language.

She was about to start cleaning when Bayt called out to her. "Alena, could you fetch the caraway and the fennel?"

Alena nodded and stepped into the back, where the stores of spices were collected. Bayt's organization was impeccable, and she found the spices with ease. She brought them to the front, then cleaned until Bayt finished his meeting.

It wasn't long before Bayt said his farewells with a smile and a wave. Alena noted that no small amount of coin had changed hands. Much more than the spices were worth.

He turned his attention to Alena. "You're early today."

She smiled. "I brought something."

Bayt glanced around, then nodded for her to go into the back room. He ordered another apprentice to watch the shop, then followed Alena. He locked the door between the shop and the back room, then gestured toward the floor. Alena found a recessed button within the floor by memory and pushed it. There was a click and a section of the flooring popped up. Alena lifted the section and descended some steep steps into the small room below.

Bayt followed, latching the flooring closed behind him.

Her master might be a successful spice trader, but this room was where his true wealth was built.

Most of the cramped space was filled with papers and scrolls. They were all encoded in a script Bayt had invented. He had promised to teach it to her one day, but until that day, she was welcome to break it herself. It had been a pet project of hers for almost a year now, but she still hadn't broken it.

She didn't know what made Bayt more proud: the fact that she had been trying for over a year, or that his script had resisted her persistent efforts. She might not possess his ear for language, but there were few codes she couldn't unravel.

A small table stood in the center of the room. Alena took Niles' coin purse out of her pocket and set it on the table with a satisfying thunk. Bayt took one glance at the crest. She thought she saw a flash of worry in his eyes. "Where did you find this?"

"From a new student at our school. He didn't seem like he deserved it."

"You should get rid of it."

Alena blinked. "What?"

"Some money isn't worth the trouble it brings." He pointed at the crest. "Do you know who this is?"

Alena shook her head.

"This is House Arrowood. They're a newer named family, and one you had best steer clear of."

She crossed her arms. "Why?"

Bayt looked around the small room, as though worried someone might overhear. "If half the rumors I've heard are true, they earned their name solving problems for the emperor. Problems no one else could. Extortion, bribery, even assassination. Nothing is beyond them."

Alena frowned. She tried to reconcile her image of Niles with the description Bayt provided. She couldn't get them to match.

Bayt's real income and real power came through the information that flowed through his shop along with the spices. If he believed something, odds were it was true. But Niles? He'd been well-trained, but an angry fool.

Still, ignoring Bayt's warnings was even more foolish.

"If they are so dangerous, why are they in Landow?"

Bayt shook his head. "I don't know. I haven't heard even a whisper of their arrival. This," he pointed to the purse, "is the first I've heard of them. If they arrived here this quietly, it's even more cause for concern."

"What should I do?"

"Dispose of the money. Throw the purse someplace that it can never be tracked to you. Pray to the gods that young man doesn't figure out who stole from him."

Bayt wasn't given to dramatics. Alena had seen him deal with belligerent investigators with a cool and easy grace. But that crest frightened him more than threats of a life imprisoned.

"Don't you want the money?" Normally, he would fence her goods for her in exchange for a sizable share of the profit. Alena never complained. He paid well enough, and her real reward wasn't in coin, but in knowledge. Bayt had taught her most of what she knew.

"No, and you shouldn't either. When you get rid of it, make sure no one can trace it to you."

"Don't you think you're overreacting?"

"If anything, I'm remaining remarkably calm. If anyone but you had brought that, I'd be turning them in myself."

That stopped her in her tracks. Bayt's primary income was illegal, but he held to his own sense of honor. Alena could never quite pin down the rules he followed, but she had never distrusted him. For him to turn on his own associates was unlike him.

"Fine. I'll do it."

"Thank you. And Alena?"

"Yes?"

"Could you talk to your mother about coming by here all the time?"

"I'm not sure it would do much good. She is set on you offering me a full position here."

"I thought you told her you were going to university."

Alena shrugged. "Maybe? She would be excited to have me stay in town."

Bayt put his hand on her shoulder. She tore her gaze from the crest on the purse and met his. "You're going to need to decide soon, you know. University exams are only a few months away, and you won't be able to play both sides then."

She glared at him, and he held up his hands in mock surrender. "I know I'm not telling you anything you don't already know. But sometimes it's good to be reminded."

"Thanks." Alena scooped up the coins that had fallen from the purse, then put the purse back in her pocket. She would have to leave soon if she planned on dumping the coins and purse somewhere safe and still be home in time for the evening meal.

She went to the steep staircase, where she went to work on the latch of the hidden entrance. Bayt mumbled and she looked at him. "What?"

"You would need to be *very* careful, but if you could find out what the Arrowood family is doing here, that is information I'd pay quite a bit for."

——————

5

B randt watched Kyler half-place, half-drop five large mugs of beer on top of the table. Only the giant man's meaty fists could possibly hold so many handles at once. Kyler's delivery was greeted with a chorus of thanks, and the wolfblades each jostled one another for the nearest mug.

Brandt waited until the others had taken long pulls before sipping at his own beer. The brew tasted more bitter than usual. He made a face, but the others didn't seem to suffer the same problem. He was pretty sure Kyler was half out of beer before he finished sitting down.

He barely noticed when Lola reached out, took his beer from him, and took a long pull. She placed the mug back in front of him, now more empty than full.

Kyler looked between Lola and Brandt, tensed for conflict. When none erupted, he looked even more concerned. "That doesn't bode well."

"Relax. The sergeant's had a rough day. It's not every day you almost get yourself and your best warrior killed," Ana said. "Still, if that's how he's going to be—" She reached over, snatched his mug, and finished what little beer Lola had left. Then she slid the empty mug back at him.

Kyler and Lola chuckled. Ryder, taciturn as always, barely reacted.

Brandt stared at his empty mug for a moment before looking up.

"What was worse?" Lola taunted. "Almost getting buried alive, or meeting with the governor and telling him your foolishness almost got you buried alive?"

"Do I have to choose?" Brandt asked.

The five wolfblades sat in a corner booth at one of the local taverns, huddled around a round table that comfortably seated three. The tavern was doing brisk business tonight, though, and the table was all that was available. Brandt imagined if they flashed their unit crests, space would clear for them, but they preferred the relative anonymity.

Brandt leaned back in the booth, willing himself to relax.

"You going to tell us about it, or are we just going to keep drinking your beers for you?" Lola asked.

Brandt ran a hand through his short hair and sighed. "The governor wasn't upset."

"Then what's the problem?" Kyler asked.

"He ordered us to return to the mountains to find the man who trapped Ana and me."

"And that's a problem because..." Kyler prompted.

"It's the wrong decision."

"Of course it is," Lola said, the sarcasm dripping from her words. "Only you would know better than the governor."

"I do," Brandt replied.

Despite the good-natured ribbing, when Brandt made

the claim, the others listened. His wolfblades weren't ones to show outward respect to their sergeant, but they didn't need to. Brandt knew they would follow him to the gates and back.

"*If*," Brandt emphasized the possibility, "this bandit is still in the mountains, hiding among the cliffs, we would be doomed if we found him. Given the strength of his affinity, even we aren't good enough. The mountains are a battleground he controls."

"But that's not all, is it?" Ana, as usual, seemed like she could read into his thoughts.

"Nothing about this bandit makes sense. Look at the testimonies of the merchants that brought us here. By all accounts, we were supposed to be dealing with a weakly talented bandit, probably self-taught. He never took more than coin and left the merchants unharmed. None of that lines up with the man we encountered in the mountains."

Brandt paused, wishing now he had that beer at hand. His throat was parched. "If he possesses this kind of power, why isn't he using it? Why is he stealing petty amounts of money from merchants?"

"Maybe it's not the same person?" Lola suggested.

"Possibly," Brandt admitted. Something was getting under his skin, but he couldn't figure out exactly what it was. The details didn't line up.

"There's something else," Brandt continued. "As I was leaving the governor's mansion today I ran into Zane Arrowood."

Even Ryder cursed at that.

"What's that snake doing here?" Ana asked.

Brandt shrugged. "He didn't even acknowledge my presence, and I didn't ask. But his being here worries me."

Ana didn't mind speculating. "Maybe he's here about the bandit, too?"

Lola shot that idea down. "The Arrowoods don't have any affinities in their family. They'd have no chance. And they don't leave the capital for mere bandits."

Kyler glanced from one woman to the other. "A lack of affinities has never stopped Zane Arrowood's enemies from passing through the gates. He's a dangerous man."

Brandt cut off the speculation. "We could guess all night and never come close to the truth. That family has enough secrets to fill a library. I would like to believe that if we were both chasing the bandit the governor would have told me, though."

Brandt didn't need to explain his distrust of coincidences to the others. His fellow wolfblades had served together long enough. True coincidences were rare. Finding Zane Arrowood and an impossibly strong bandit in the same region wasn't one.

"So, what's tomorrow's plan?" Kyler asked. He grounded the group and kept them focused on their next steps.

"Well," began Brandt, "you still have to go to the academy."

Kyler swore. "I hate children."

"And yet you're the best with them." Brandt leaned forward. "I had an idea about the bandit, though."

Lola shook her head. "Against orders, I assume?"

Brandt managed to look offended. "The governor's orders don't make any sense. Even if we could find him, he'd just send us all to the gates without a second thought. Besides, from what Ana and I saw, I don't think he's living up there. I think he's only using the isolation for training."

Brandt paused to ensure he had everyone's attention. "I want us to focus on the road south of town. It's where the bandit has been striking, and that is where we'll find him. If we fight there, perhaps we'll have an opportunity."

Brandt's confidence convinced most of his wolfblades. They nodded, agreeing with his logic. Despite their orders, they'd follow him.

Ana alone didn't look convinced. He understood. The depth of the man's affinity beggared belief. Even on flat ground, against a power like they had encountered in the mountains, they might not have a fighting chance. But without a better suggestion, she capitulated.

Brandt turned to Ryder. "Send a message to the captain. Request reinforcements. I'll include what Ana and I saw."

"Should I also inform him you're disobeying a direct order from the governor?" Ryder asked.

"I was hoping you would leave that part out."

A grim smile flashed over Ryder's face.

"Also, I don't want anyone wandering around town alone. As much as possible, *all* of us stay together. If you do encounter the bandit, don't engage alone."

Kyler looked hopeful. "Does that mean you'll come help at the academy?"

Brandt laughed. "No. If you can't survive a room full of children, you deserve your fate."

Kyler swore as the others chuckled. The large man stood up. "Well, if I have to be in front of children tomorrow, I'd like to get drunk tonight. Another round?"

A round of agreement answered his question. Kyler glanced to Brandt for approval. Brandt nodded. He knew the tolerances of his wolfblades. "One more round, then we're done."

As Kyler left, Lola leaned close to Brandt. "When the captain finds out you've disobeyed direct orders again, I was wondering if you could do me a favor?"

"What's that?"

"Could you recommend me for your position? I think I'd be better at it than you."

Brandt grinned. "You're welcome to my third stripe whenever the captain rips it off me. I'd hate to deprive you."

Lola smiled. "You're a good man, sir."

Ana overheard the exchange. "If the captain didn't take his stripe after Tinsworth, he never will."

Brandt tried to look hurt. "That wasn't my fault!"

"You led us straight into the enemy encampment," Ana replied.

"Because I was sure we could win!"

"Because you forgot how to count?" Ana asked, a smile on her face.

"We won!"

Ana was about to reply, but mercifully, Kyler ended the conversation when he brought the next round of beers to the table, the mugs laughably small in his large hands.

Brandt leaned back after he grabbed his mug. This time, he guarded his beer zealously. Conversation quickly turned to other matters. Kyler wondered if anyone had heard any local ghost stories, and Lola asked if any well-regarded warriors lived here she could train with.

Brandt sipped his beer and relaxed.

The wolfblades were loud and obnoxious.

But they were his, and that was enough for him.

6

Alena worried she might run into Niles in the street before class. She tensed as she turned the corner to the academy, then relaxed when she saw no one waiting.

The entire day passed without event. Bayt's warnings unnerved her, but if Niles missed the coin purse, he made no public show of it. Thankfully, he also seemed to have forgotten about their small confrontation. Though they shared several classes, he didn't so much as spare her a glance.

She did have to sit through a wolfblade's visit. The man was a giant, standing two heads over their martial arts instructor. He carried a hammer taller than her and gave the usual speech about duty to the empire and the benefits of service. No doubt, Jace was swooning on the other side of the room with the younger students.

Alena *was* interested in the man's forms. Despite his size, he moved gracefully, his oversized hammer whistling through the air with ease. She didn't know much about the wolfblades, but Alena was certain this man was the strongest warrior she had ever met. Even their instructor looked impressed.

Dozens of questions followed, and Alena's attention quickly drifted. The wolfblade looked like he wanted to be in the academy about as much as she did.

Most of her thoughts focused on Niles Arrowood. Bayt had offered good money for more information about the family, which had piqued Alena's interest. Bayt rarely parted with money without good reason. Alena glanced over at Niles several times during the presentation, wondering what could possibly be so worrying about the boy or his family.

The presentation ended with the wolfblade sparring empty-handed with some of the students in the class. Even though the outcome was inevitable, Alena still found her attention drawn to the fights. She wasn't sure she would ever be an expert martial artist, but she loved the exchanges, the subtle movements of balance and power that could win or lose a fight.

A number of the students in the class had developed their martial arts to a high level, at least for their age. Jace was among the first students to fight the wolfblade, and although he was flat on his back within a few heartbeats, he came away beaming. Alena couldn't help but chuckle to herself as she shook her head. Her brother was hopeless.

She wanted to see Niles fight the wolfblade, but he didn't volunteer himself. Was he scared of being beaten? Or did he possess a secret family technique? Alena had heard many named families did, but she didn't know one way or the other.

The presentation ended and classes resumed as normal. Being as both Alena and Niles were on the university track, their schedules collided throughout the day. Every class she had with him, she found her gaze drawn to the boy.

She didn't like that there were two stories about him in her head. In the first he was a spoiled, wealthy child who enjoyed lording his named status over others. But Bayt's reaction indicated something more. The second story was more sinister, filled with conspiracies and secrets. Alena knew she wouldn't be able to rest until she'd resolved the difference.

Alena left class early again, but she didn't travel far. She changed out of her academy uniform into a faded tunic and pants. She tied her hair up tightly and threw a hat on. Unless he was supernaturally observant, Niles wouldn't recognize her when he left.

Her wait didn't take long. The streets were busy at this time of day, so she had no fear of being spotted. A group of Etari traders in their red cloaks attracted most of the attention in the area.

If Bayt's warnings were accurate, she was taking on more risk than was healthy. But she didn't believe Bayt. Perhaps Niles' family was one to worry about. Crossing a named family was never wise. But perhaps Niles was the weak link. He certainly hadn't shown her any skill worthy of concern yet.

She promised herself she would be careful, but she planned on getting answers.

Niles left the academy with the rest of the students. He walked for a few blocks with a group of his new friends, then peeled off. Alena followed, leaving plenty of distance between her and Niles.

After another two blocks, Niles turned right into a narrow alley. Alena didn't follow. The alley was empty except for the academy student. She waited away from the entrance, watching her peer.

At the end of the alley Niles turned right again, walking back the direction he had come.

The hairs stood up on the back of Alena's neck.

Niles was trying to lose a tail.

Did he know that she was following him, or was this something he did every day?

Following someone who didn't want to be tailed was difficult, especially when working alone.

Far from being discouraged, Alena turned around and paralleled Niles on her current street. When she reached the cross street she had just passed, she looked left and saw Niles coming straight toward her.

She didn't see any flash of recognition in his eyes, so she blended into a group of customers outside a food stall and waited for him to pass. After a few moments, she picked up his trail again.

They walked another two blocks, and Alena found herself grateful the weather was nice outside, encouraging crowded streets. Alena was a bit shorter than most girls her age, so she was hard to spot in a group.

Niles ducked into a shop and Alena walked past, glancing in as she did. Niles bowed to the owner, then stepped into a small room behind the main shop.

This wasn't the Niles she expected. His face didn't have any of the pride he'd displayed so openly at the academy.

Bayt's worries seemed more likely than ever, but Alena couldn't shy away from the challenge. Was this new student finally a match for the skills she'd developed over the years? Her heart beat a little faster at the possibility.

Alena went into a shop across the street, keeping an eye on the room Niles had ducked into. When he emerged, she almost dropped the fruit she pretended to examine.

Niles' well-made clothes were gone. In their place he wore a tunic even more ragged than her own. He bowed to the shopkeeper one more time, then stepped back onto the street.

Alena remembered the fear in Bayt's eyes when he had spoken of the Arrowoods. Reason told her it was wisest to leave Niles alone. He had training she hadn't expected and was clearly trying to lose any pursuers. But it had the feeling of a daily routine. She didn't think he was aware of her. He just didn't want to be followed.

She didn't care much about Bayt's offer of a reward. She had plenty of money.

But she hadn't had a challenge in months.

Alena put the fruit down and followed Niles.

He was good.

Niles took several unnecessary turns, sometimes walking around the block and sometimes just doubling back on his path. Alena hung far back from her classmate. She didn't take risks. If she lost Niles today, she could try again tomorrow. Patience rewarded victory.

As near as she could tell, Niles never noticed her.

It was the most difficult task she'd attempted in recent memory. Her heart beat faster and her palms were damp. She had a smile on her face.

This was fun.

Niles' path led him to a section of town Alena hadn't expected to visit. It wasn't the worst part of town, which was far to the west, but it was a rundown section. The buildings here were in various states of disrepair, and most of the citizens who lived in the area were the empire's wage earners, the citizens who did the work required of them by law and earned just enough to live.

Their lives could be worse. Everyone had food on the table and a shelter over their heads, but little else.

As evening approached, the streets became quieter. Workers returned home from their day of service and families sat down to eat.

Fortunately, Niles found his destination before the streets emptied too much for Alena to follow him.

He looked both ways before entering, and Alena's gut told her this had been his destination the entire time.

Alena looked up to the rooftops. With the streets emptying out, she couldn't stay on the streets unobserved much longer. If she wanted to watch the building, the rooftops were her best bet. Better to hide out of sight than try to blend in.

Alena found a potential spot on a house across the street from the small one Niles had entered. She made herself light and climbed up the wall with ease. Once she was on top she settled in to watch.

She didn't know exactly what she was looking for. Bayt had been willing to pay for any information. Perhaps the location of this place would be enough. But she figured she could watch for a while, see if she saw anything interesting, then report to Bayt on her way home.

Alena had been waiting for a while when she saw the door to the building open. A man stepped out, slightly taller than Niles. The family resemblance was easy to see, though. Alena guessed she was looking at Niles' father.

She felt a chill go down her spine as she looked at him. Niles had been a mystery, but there were no questions about this man. He moved with a cold precision, every movement calculated. After a single heartbeat, Alena knew there wasn't a chance she could follow him successfully. Niles was the student, but this was the master.

The man stood outside his door for some time. Alena slowed her breath, wondering if he was listening for the presence of observers. No normal person could have heard her from so far away, but she had heard stories of martial artists who had honed their senses to an incredible degree. Just looking at this man made her believe those stories.

Eventually, he left, so silent and quick Alena almost didn't believe he'd ever been there.

Alena made no movement. Something about that man had frightened her, and she didn't plan on leaving the safety of her rooftop until she was absolutely sure he was gone. And when she left, she fully planned on heading out in a different direction. She didn't want to risk even a chance encounter.

She watched for a while longer, but there was no further activity from the house. Alena could see silhouettes moving inside. One was probably Niles, and another looked to be his mother. Based on what she could see, it looked like this was where the Arrowoods lived.

Why had Niles worked so hard to disguise his movements? And why did a named family live in a living-wage part of town? They could have had a house anywhere in the city.

She figured she wasn't going to learn the answers that night, so she climbed down the wall and made her way back to Bayt and to home.

She knew one thing, though. Niles had just become the most interesting person in her life.

7

Brandt walked beside the merchant's wagon as it creaked and groaned its way south of town. The wagon protested this journey almost as much as his legs did. He forced back a yawn. The sun would be setting shortly, and his feet ached.

For three days the road had been peaceful. Brandt's squad woke early every morning to escort merchants for the first league of their journey. If the wolfblades had received the governor's blessing, the task would have been much simpler. Brandt could have ordered the merchants into a single morning and afternoon departure.

Two trips.

Easy to protect.

He had tried convincing the governor again, but the man hadn't budged a hair. He continued to insist Brandt and his wolfblades search the mountains. Brandt hated appointees like the governor, so full of themselves they didn't even listen to those who served them.

A warrior serving such a leader was no better than a sword frozen in its sheath.

So his group waited beyond the sight of the walls, rendezvousing with merchants as they were already on the road. The merchants were almost always skeptical at first, but the wolfblade insignias on their uniforms, and their insistence, eventually convinced most traders.

Still, their days boiled down to escorting merchants for a league, returning, and repeating the process for the next merchant. Brandt figured they were walking somewhere between six and eight leagues a day. It wore on a person. They hadn't even felt like drinking most nights.

And nothing called his wolfblades to attention faster than a mug of beer.

If there was something worthwhile in their efforts, it was the fact the bandit hadn't attacked again. Brandt wondered if it was because of his wolfblades, or if another factor was at play he didn't understand.

He had spent the past days and leagues turning the problem over in his mind, but he hadn't come to any conclusions.

Brandt still didn't understand their experience in the mountains that day. That passage couldn't have closed. No power like that was possible. The cost was higher than anybody could pay. So the feat was impossible, yet it had happened.

The events in the cave offered one tantalizing possibility: What if the cost could be bypassed? What if the strength Brandt believed to be an upper limit was just the beginning of what those gifted with affinities could achieve?

The sound of the breeze through the branches brought his attention to his surroundings. Landow was located near the edge of an expansive evergreen forest, and tall pines loomed overhead. The wolfblades escorted the merchants until they cleared the dense woods, about a league from the walls. From there the road traveled through leagues of lightly wooded grasslands.

Brandt didn't notice anything suspicious, beyond the merchant they escorted. The man's eyes darted back and forth, but he wasn't watching the trees. He was watching the wolfblades as though they might attack at any moment.

Outside of town, when they had first crossed paths, the man had insisted he didn't need an escort. He wasn't the first merchant to say so, but he had been the most adamant. It wasn't until Brandt made it crystal clear they were escorting every merchant, regardless of desire, that the man capitulated.

Ana stepped up beside him. "You look troubled."

Brandt glanced at the merchant to ensure he wouldn't be overheard, then kept his voice low. "I suspect he's a smuggler."

Ana laughed. "You just figured it out?"

He arched an eyebrow at her.

"If the scene when we met wasn't enough, you should have at least noticed his wife has been constantly rearranging the goods in the wagon. Ryder is pretty sure he's identified at least three hidden compartments."

"And you didn't inform me?"

Her grin was sly. "We might have had a bet on when you would figure it out."

"Who won?"

"Ryder, of course."

Of the group, Ryder's intuition was the sharpest. He possessed some combination of skills that made him seem almost telepathic at times. Brandt had never figured the man's means, but his results were beyond question.

"Out of curiosity, what was your bet?"

"That you would never notice."

"Your confidence is flattering. When were you going to tell me?"

"Near the edge of the forest. We figured it would only distract you from the larger objective."

They had the authority to search the wagon. No citizen could disobey the request of a soldier. But Ana was right. If they stopped the wagon and arrested the smuggler, it would probably occupy them for the rest of the afternoon and evening.

It was probably worth the small risk. The bandit hadn't struck in days, and the odds of him attacking today felt slim.

Before he could order the wagon to stop, though, Ryder ran up to him. In a low voice, he said, "Stop the wagon, now."

Brandt didn't hesitate. He yelled for the merchant to stop. The man obeyed, eyeing the wolfblades warily. Brandt ignored him for the moment. He turned to Ryder, who had separated from the group, eyes fixed on the road behind them. "Someone's coming. I think."

Brandt frowned. The man was never unsure. "Weapons out! Close together!"

The smuggler must have seen his chance, because he snapped his reins and urged his wagon forward. The hefty contraption had just started rolling when a short wall burst from the road just ahead. It only stood a few hands high, but it was more than enough. Harnessed as they were, the horses couldn't jump over, and the wagon didn't have a chance of clearing it. Brandt was a little surprised the rickety contraption didn't break at the mere sight of the wall.

Only one man could move so much stone at once, though.

Kyler swore, then pointed into the woods with his hammer. "There."

Brandt spotted the dark cloak as the bandit rushed toward them, weaving between pine trees with sure footsteps. Brandt squinted. It looked like a swarm of large bugs floated in front of the bandit.

He also swore when he realized what they were.

Stones.

"Find cover!"

His warning came just in time. Stones zipped toward them, launched with blinding velocity.

Against lesser warriors, the attack would have been devastating. Kyler used his own affinity to bend the rocks aimed at him harmlessly away.

Ana dodged, dropping to the ground gracefully as the stones passed overhead. Ryder put the wagon between him and the bandit, and Lola and Brandt used their swords to protect themselves, slapping the projectiles out of the way.

The bandit burst into the open. He was clothed from head to toe in dark fabric, with only his eyes and hands visible. He carried two long knives, already drawn.

The bandit's first attack focused on Brandt. He led with one long knife, almost wielding it like a sword.

Brandt used the longer reach of his own sword to deflect the knife, then stabbed at the bandit's chest. His enemy might have an inhuman affinity for stone, but Brandt was clearly superior with the blade.

Or so he thought.

The bandit's attack proved to be a feint. The ground under Brandt shifted as a slab of stone rose underneath his feet. Brandt's stab missed high as he was thrown up and back.

Brandt became light, but he knew, in a moment of

terrible clarity, he'd been bested. The bandit darted in with the same knife Brandt had just been so proud of deflecting.

Lola's blade flashed in the late afternoon sunlight, and the bandit was forced to use his second knife to defend. Steel rang against steel and the bandit was knocked sideways.

Right at Ryder, who had leaped over the wagon and joined the fight with his own two knives, shorter even than the bandit's.

Brandt's opinion of the bandit's skill quickly changed. Ryder was one of the fastest two-handed fighters Brandt had ever found in the empire.

The bandit matched him strike for strike, even with the longer weapons.

Lola, Brandt, Ana, and Kyler moved in. No matter how strong a warrior the bandit might be, the difference in numbers couldn't be overcome. It was only a matter of time. Brandt was eager to bring this villain to justice.

Kyler sounded a warning. "Brandt!"

It wasn't in time. Brandt steeled himself, but the large stone that had been underfoot a moment ago crashed into his back. He landed flat on his stomach, gasping for a breath that refused to come.

Brandt struggled to his feet, the world twisting violently around him. How could the man focus enough to use his affinity while fighting off five wolfblades?

The sound of wood creaking against wood was his only answer.

Brandt turned to see the wagon leaning over, threatening to crash on top of them all. Stone rose underneath it from the other side.

Ryder had already disengaged, and Ana and Kyler were moving away.

Only Lola hadn't noticed the danger. She'd be crushed under the wagon in less than two heartbeats, but she only had eyes for the bandit's retreating back.

Brandt sprinted and tackled her, getting both her and him out of danger just as the wagon crashed over on its side.

Screams came both from within the wagon and from the horses harnessed to it. Brandt looked up, ignoring the noise, just in time to see Ryder get pinned under the same stone that had slammed into his own back just moments ago.

It was the first time Brandt could remember seeing Ryder stuck in place. The man was a human tornado in a sword fight.

Brandt guessed he wouldn't have a chance at lifting the stone with the bandit forcing it down, so he attacked the bandit directly. Kyler, with his stone affinity and sheer physical strength, was Ryder's best hope for a physical rescue. Brandt just needed to give Kyler the time and space to work.

Ana entered the fray from another side, a thin sliver of water under her control. She lashed at the bandit's face, hoping to distract him while Brandt made a fatal cut. Ana wasn't a strong sword compared to the others, but her water manipulation made her powerful support in combat.

The bandit sent two small stones toward Ana. She dodged, but the attack broke her own focus, giving the bandit time to meet Brandt.

Brandt had the advantage of reach, but the bandit willingly gave up ground, and with the two long knives, his defense was impenetrable. Brandt kept waiting for the bandit to make a mistake, for the heat of battle to carry him away, but his opponent remained unflappable.

In a moment, Brandt was joined by Lola and Ana. They pressed the bandit back, but even the three of them couldn't execute a killing blow. It was only when Kyler came in with his giant hammer that the bandit seemed to consider them a threat. Whoever he was, his affinity and his martial arts were beyond anything Brandt had ever seen.

The bandit threw up a wave of small stones. The act of affinity lacked the bandit's earlier control, but made up for that lack with sheer intensity. Brandt and the others were forced to defend themselves, providing the bandit with enough time to turn and run deeper into the woods.

Brandt looked back at the wagon. Its goods had been strewn over the road, but both merchant and wife appeared unharmed. Ryder grimaced as he moved, but the wolfblades looked healthy otherwise.

His choice was simple. He had no particular desire to help the smuggler more than was necessary, and he refused to be beaten by anyone. "After him."

The five wolfblades gave chase. The bandit ran straight to the west. Brandt guessed he was heading for the mountains a league away. Once there, the wolfblades' slim advantage would melt like snow under a burning sun.

They couldn't let him reach the mountains.

The bandit moved lightly through the forest, his feet barely tapping against the ground. The wolfblades followed suit.

Brandt fell behind. Lightness required a calm manipulation of internal energies, and at the moment, he was anything but calm. That bandit had sealed him and Ana in a mountain, condemning them to a slow death. He had tried to crush Ryder.

Brandt's blood boiled.

"Ryder, cut him off!"

Ryder nodded, but Brandt noticed him grimace as he

darted ahead of the rest of them. He was hurt worse than he had first appeared.

Brandt yelled ahead. "Ana, assist Ryder."

She darted farther ahead of the group, trailing Ryder as best she could. Ryder's lightness was unmatched, but Ana's came close.

Brandt continued to lose ground to the rest of the group. His sword and his affinity were strong, but lightness had never been a technique that came easily to him.

Ryder and Ana caught up with the bandit in less than thirty heartbeats. Brandt could just see the initial exchange, which his friends took the worse of.

But it gave the other wolfblades time to catch up, and soon the battle was again five against one. The bandit's capture was only a matter of time. Brandt burned to know the identity of the man who possessed such an affinity. How had this skill come to be?

Lola collapsed beside him. In the shade of the trees, Brandt wasn't sure what felled her.

Brandt caught a glimpse of a fist-sized stone as it struck Ryder in the back of the head. Ryder folded over, his eyes blank.

He couldn't track the single stone. It was moving too fast, its direction changing moment after moment. The remaining wolfblades had also caught on to what was happening, and they looked around warily.

It didn't save Kyler. The rock caught him in the stomach, then lifted him high into the air. Brandt couldn't believe his eyes.

He focused on the bandit. He couldn't stop the stone, but he could kill the man controlling it.

Kyler crashed to the ground, the only warning Brandt

had that the stone was no longer occupied with the giant warrior.

Then the stone smashed into his side. Brandt only caught a glimpse of it before it picked him off his feet, just as it had Kyler.

Brandt kicked his legs, clawing for the ground no longer beneath them. His flight only lasted for a moment before it ended with him slamming up against a tree. The stone flew away, and Brandt collapsed to the ground, clutching at his stomach, unable to breathe.

The sounds of battle only lasted another few heartbeats. The thump of another unconscious body against the ground signaled the end of the wolfblades.

Brandt fought to stand. Rage burned within him, but all the hate in the world wasn't going to make his legs move.

He slammed his fist into the ground as the forest went quiet around him.

He didn't know how much time passed, but the groans of his squad brought him to his feet. His breath came in ragged gasps, but it came. Maybe he'd cracked a few ribs. He couldn't be sure.

Brandt stumbled over to Lola, who had dug her sword into the ground and was using it to stand up. "You okay?"

She inhaled sharply. "I will be."

Together, they checked on the others. Kyler and Ana both responded well, but Ryder took some time to recover. Blood flowed freely from a wound to his scalp.

Miraculously, none of them had died. As Brandt watched his friends recover from the various blows they had taken, he understood a truth.

The bandit had intentionally left them alive. Several of the blows could have killed them. If the man had the ability to lift Kyler in the air with a single stone, the blow to Ryder's head could have easily sent him to the gates.

The bandit had pulled his punches.

Brandt wished he knew why.

Once everyone was back on their feet, they returned to where the wagon had tipped over. When they arrived, they found another surprise. One surprise too many, in Brandt's opinion.

The merchant and his wife appeared to be dead.

Ana approached and kneeled down beside them. She put her hand next to the merchant's face. "He's alive."

She moved to the wife and confirmed she lived, too. Ana examined the woman more closely. She squinted as she brushed some of the long dark hair away from the woman's neck. "There's a small puncture wound here."

Brandt examined the merchant, finding a matching wound.

"The bandit?" Lola asked.

Brandt shook his head. "I can't imagine him using poisoned darts."

"The walls are gone," Kyler observed.

Brandt hadn't noticed, but once Kyler pointed it out, he couldn't believe he had missed the detail. The short wall that had stopped the wagon during the ambush was gone. The taller wall that had toppled the wagon was, too. The road looked clear as far as the eye could see. "Could you have fixed that?"

Kyler rubbed at his chin. "Not in less than a full afternoon's worth of work and two full meals."

"So the bandit returned and repaired the road?"

"That would be my guess."

Brandt shook his head. Who else had been after the

merchant? Why had the bandit fixed the road when he returned?

He had no answers. "Let's arrest these two and search through what's left. We can question them back in Landow."

They went to work, hoping to find answers to the questions that plagued them.

8

Alena helped serve the meal her mother had prepared. Tonight's meal was simple, if hearty. Mother had roasted a whole chicken and boiled potatoes, a celebration of a project her father recently finished.

One advantage of Alena's position with Bayt was that she had access to more spices every day than most people saw in a month. Often, in lieu of accepting gold for her activities, she took her payments in spice. Her mother was an excellent cook and used the herbs and seasonings to great effect. Tonight's chicken and potatoes were no exception.

Their father was home this evening. He owned one of the best smithies in town, thanks in large part to his long history of hard work and uncompromising standards. Many years ago he had started out as an apprentice smith, but the quality of his work slowly became known throughout the area. When his master became too old to lift the hammer, he had inherited the smithy and built its reputation further.

Now the smithy employed four well-regarded apprentices, and the forges were in almost constant use.

Father was best known for his blades, but he gave the same attention to a farmer's horseshoe that he did an official's sword. It made him the best in the area, but it also meant long absences from his family.

The four of them sat down to eat. The chicken was moist and savory, and the potatoes filled the small spaces in Alena's stomach. The fireplace warmed the room, and Alena wished she could sit at the table forever. She was eager to explore the world, but less enthused about leaving her family.

Father gave her a pointed glance in between bites. "How are your studies?"

"Good."

He gave her a knowing glance. "I hear you haven't been attending your history lessons very often."

Alena knew where that rumor would have come from. Jace did everything he could to curry favor with their father. Little did he realize their father looked down on a tattletale.

It wouldn't stop Father from using the information, though.

"I've been using the extra time in the shop."

"You believe you will still pass the exams?"

"Yes, Father."

He held her gaze for a moment, then smiled. "Very well."

"Luc!" Mother sounded indignant.

Father chuckled, a low soft sound that put Alena instantly at ease. "She's nearly an adult, and she's a bright girl. I choose to trust her." He grinned at his wife's glare. "Anyway, if she fails to pass the exams, she knows she's stuck in this town for the rest of her life, and then you won't have to worry about her leaving."

His indirect threat struck uncomfortably close to her heart. She loved her family, but the continent was vast, and she wanted to see as much of it as possible. University was her only legitimate way out. She had been studying history, just not under the tutelage of that old fool at the academy. She wouldn't miss her chance to escape Landow.

After the meal was over, Alena went to help Mother with the cleanup, but Father stopped her. "Jace, help your mother tonight, please."

Jace, always eager to please Father, jumped to it.

Alena followed her father and sat next to him near the fireplace. He spoke low, so as not to be overheard.

"You're not being a fool about your classes, are you?"

"I don't think so. Our instructor does little more than read from a text. I can do that on my own, and faster."

"You understand what you risk? History is a key component of the exam."

She nodded. "I do. I've been borrowing additional history texts from the academy library. I will be prepared."

"Very well. Just remember, Alena, your intelligence is a double-edged sword. With it, you can accomplish great deeds. But left unchecked, it will get you into trouble. It must be balanced with hard work and wisdom."

"I know, Father." She meant it, too. He had hammered that teaching into her with the same intensity he hammered imperfections out of steel.

"Good." He reached into one of his deep pockets, pulling out a hide-wrapped object and handing it to her. "I have something for you."

She recognized his handiwork immediately. It was a long knife, and it had all the hallmarks of his craft. The blade was simple and unadorned, with a hilt that didn't draw attention to itself. Her father created the best blades, not the best-looking ones.

She put the knife down and leaped at him, wrapping her

arms around his thick neck. He embraced her tightly, his strong arms threatening to crush the breath out of her.

"Thank you, Dad."

"You're welcome, girl. I'm proud of you."

They broke apart and she studied the knife for some time. They were shortly joined by Jace and Mother, and the family exchanged stories of their past few days. Alena went to her bedroom that night warm and full of cheer.

But she didn't remain there long. As soon as she was certain her family was asleep, she threw on dark clothes and slipped out the window of her room, using lightness to skip across the neighboring roofs. She landed on a street a block away and made her way toward Niles' house, the same way she had for the past three nights.

After the first night, Bayt had told her to stay far away. Though he'd tried to hide the fact, he had been supremely interested in where the Arrowoods were living. The very spices her mother had used tonight had been a direct result of that information.

Nothing encouraged Alena more than telling her that something shouldn't be done, though. For the past few nights she had watched the house. She had no specific purpose. She just wanted to learn more about the new named student and his mysterious family. Her curiosity had always been insatiable.

Alena reached her usual observation point without difficulty. She settled in, allowing the shadows to embrace her.

Waiting had never been challenging for Alena. Even as a young girl, she had found the world rich in sensory details. As she watched, she let her senses wander. She traced the smoke rising into the sky from the chimneys, listened to the sounds of people walking on the streets below. Someone in the house beneath her must be cooking, because the scents of roasted meat filled her nose.

It was very late when a now-familiar figure appeared in the darkness of the streets below. Every step landed without a sound, and his head swiveled back and forth at regular intervals.

Zane Arrowood had arrived.

Most nights, Zane walked straight to his house. Tonight, though, he was more circumspect. He doubled back, then walked around a block twice. He even used lightness to reach a nearby rooftop.

Alena pushed herself deeper into the shadows.

Eventually, he came to the door of his house, but he didn't go inside. He looked around one more time.

Then he climbed to the roof of his own house. He crouched down behind the chimney, and Alena heard the soft sound of brick scraping against brick, barely loud enough to reach her ears.

A few moments later, Zane was back on the street, opening his door as though nothing unusual had just occurred.

Alena bit her lower lip. Zane had hidden something. Given his precautions, she had no doubt that whatever was hidden was particularly valuable. She wiped a bit of sweat from her palms.

Bayt would *kill* her.

But she would never have a better opportunity.

She could hear her heart thundering in her chest.

She had pulled some foolish tricks before.

But this, this was a whole different level of foolish.

She imagined the look on Bayt's face.

Perhaps she could earn enough to buy her way into university. It was possible for some. The exam was the only way in for those who couldn't afford better. Her father would be proud of her admission, even if he could never learn the method she'd used.

She wrung her hands. She wanted to pace, because pacing always helped her think.

Alena cursed. What could Zane have hidden?

Sure, Zane seemed frightening enough, but there was no connection for them to draw to her. No one besides Bayt even knew she had been here. The Arrowoods didn't even know she existed.

She leaped from roof to roof, using all the lightness she possessed to land on the Arrowoods' roof.

Alena stepped slowly, testing her weight on every step. Every soft sound echoed like thunder in her ears.

She loved this feeling. Every sense was sharp. Colors, sounds, and smells were all more vivid. When she reached the chimney, she had little difficulty seeing what brick had been removed.

Alena crouched down, listening for any sign her presence had been detected. Then she dug her fingers into the crack and began gently prying at the brick.

She forced herself to be patient. The brick moved, one hair's width at a time.

Then it was out. Alena reached her hand in and found a small package, wrapped in hide. She pulled it out, then replaced the brick. Remaining close to the scene was a risk, but if it delayed the discovery of her theft, she figured it was worth it.

Then she reversed her path, leaping back onto safe rooftops. As soon as she was clear, she dropped back to the ground, pulling a hood over her head. She walked away, putting as much distance between her and the scene of the crime as she could.

9

B randt paced outside the governor's residence. He still felt the aches and bruises from the battle the day before, but he counted himself lucky for surviving a fight of such intensity with as few wounds as he did. None of the wounds hurt as much as his pride. In the whole history of his command, he'd never suffered a defeat.

The bandit would suffer for the humiliation he had caused. Brandt planned on ensuring it.

The rest of the wolfblades recuperated at the inn. Ryder, in particular, required quiet rest. Brandt couldn't wait for answers, though. The governor had to know more than he was letting on. A bandit that powerful left traces of his existence. Powers that strong left a path to follow, like an army marching across a field.

A man dressed as a servant stepped out and motioned to Brandt. "The governor can see you now."

Brandt took the stairs up to the house three at a time. He'd been politely but firmly rebuffed when he tried to force his way in earlier.

The building wasn't nearly as ostentatious as some

governor's residences Brandt had seen in his travels. Landow wasn't a frontier by any means, but it did rest within a week's journey of the northern edge of the continent. Given the abundant wealth of natural resources and the booming trade, no doubt the governor could have afforded something more.

The house was large, but it was only a third the size of some closer to the interior, where the power and wealth of the empire were concentrated.

The servant led him through a long hallway to a single door. They walked past the main receiving room. Brandt took that as a promising sign. He hated the pretense of proper receptions.

The servant knocked lightly on the door. From the way the servant fussed about his tasks, Brandt guessed the man was privately paid help. No wage earner took his work so seriously.

At his master's response, the servant opened the door and gestured for Brandt to enter. Brandt did, then stopped short, surprised by the room.

The servant had led him into what appeared to be the governor's private study. Several shelves of scrolls, all labeled and neatly organized, stood on the wall to Brandt's right. A window on Brandt's left let in the afternoon sun. The room smelled like old paper.

He approved.

The governor's desk also impressed him. Instead of the tall desk with a chair most preferred, the governor's desk was designed for sitting on the floor, a traditional style in some parts of the country, but considered far out of date now.

Brandt's previous interactions with the governor had been by appointment, at the government offices near the center of the city. There, the governor had been formal, almost condescending.

Brandt received a distinctly different impression now. As the governor stood to greet his guest, Brandt's eyes tracked the smooth motion. The governor was young, as far as such positions went. He couldn't be much more than thirty. But he stood in a single motion, rising to his feet in a manner that demonstrated a care for his body most government officials lacked.

This man was determined, and ambitious. He greeted Brandt politely, then motioned for him to sit. Brandt did, ashamed the governor made the motion look easier than he did. His body still ached from yesterday's beating.

"Governor, thank you for seeing me on such short notice."

"Call me Kye, please. There is no need for formality here. The short letter you sent left me in disbelief. Had the words come from anyone other than a wolfblade, I'm not sure I would have taken them seriously. Tell me everything, from the beginning."

Brandt wondered for a moment at the change. His prior visits with the governor hadn't earned him nearly this level of respect and attention.

Brandt told his story. Kye leaned forward as he listened, his whole body involved. At times, he scribbled notes to himself on a sheet of paper. Other times he stopped Brandt, asking a clarifying question.

"And you're sure your men don't need further medical attention? I can put them in touch with some of the best private doctors in town."

"Thank you, but they should all fully recover."

The governor looked over his notes, then looked out the window. Brandt couldn't guess where the governor's considerations wandered, but the intensity of his thought wasn't in question.

The moment stretched out, silence settling between the two men. Brandt fought his body's urge to fidget.

"Do you know what was stolen from the merchant?"

Brandt did. He had spent most of the day interrogating the man. It hadn't been difficult. The man was a smuggler, so he understood his options. He could cooperate and suffer a lesser punishment or refuse and die. Brandt had all the authority to take the man's life under any pretense, and they both knew it. The man confessed right away, the words pouring out of him. The smuggler possessed no regrets beyond the fact that he had been caught. The questioning had only taken so long because Brandt had been certain the man knew more than he said. Only after most of the day had passed was Brandt convinced by the man's lack of knowledge. "A diamond."

Kye sighed and his shoulders slumped. He gazed out the window. "That's what I feared."

Brandt frowned. "Why?"

Kye didn't answer for several long moments. "The emperor himself has been looking for that diamond for almost a year now. He just received information that a smuggler's network had brought it here. It was thought they hoped to carry it to the coast and onto a boat traveling to an Etari port."

Brandt absorbed the new information, then made a connection. "That's why the Arrowoods are here."

Kye raised an eyebrow, as though he was surprised the wolfblade was so well-informed. "Indeed. Their methods are unique, but the family has been known for its success in such delicate endeavors."

"Why is the diamond so special? It can't be about money. He leaves most valuables alone."

"An astute observation. It is rumored that the diamond can focus and increase one's personal affinity." Kye met Brandt's gaze, watching his reaction.

Brandt blinked rapidly. "Truly?"

Kye shrugged. "I cannot speak to the veracity of the rumors. But I suspect it is those very rumors that have attracted so much attention to our corner of the world."

Brandt had never heard of a diamond being able to increase a person's affinity. Ever since the empire had been founded by Anders I, hopefuls had searched for ways to artificially increase their affinity, but all such attempts had failed. Some still searched, but most sensible people considered it the modern equivalent of alchemical gold.

If it was true, though, the consequences were staggering. Affinities could be useful, but they were rarely strong enough to defeat a talented martial artist.

The bandit was an exception. He was strong enough to destroy all five of Brandt's warriors at once. Did he already possess a diamond like the governor spoke of?

Brandt's mind spun at the possibilities.

One worried him more than the others.

What if the diamond worked, and the bandit just now got his hands on it? The man's power was already inhuman. To amplify it further seemed impossible, but what if?

Brandt shuddered.

Kye noticed. "You can well understand why this diamond is so important. Most likely, the rumors amount to nothing, but the emperor can't take a chance on such an item. It must be retrieved. All of us must turn our efforts toward this cause, now."

"What would you have of my wolfblades?"

"Search for the diamond."

"You believe it is here?"

Kye appeared genuinely concerned. "I do not know, but I hope so. Between your squad, the Arrowoods, and the city watch, we have a chance to retrieve the diamond if it's here. If it's beyond our grasp, I fear the consequences."

Brandt wasn't sure how much help his wolfblades could be. They were soldiers, not investigators. But disobeying a governor's orders came with a cost, and this time he had no better ideas. He bowed and accepted the charge. Kye dismissed him, immediately returning to the stack of papers at his desk.

One thought worried Brandt as he walked from the governor's house. Kye had known about the strength of the bandit and the Arrowoods' search for the diamond before the attack on the smuggler yesterday. Yet he hadn't put the pieces together.

Perhaps the governor hadn't believed Brandt's outlandish story from the mountains. Perhaps the governor just hadn't put the two strings of events together. It seemed unlikely. His impression was that the governor was sharp. It seemed like a connection he should have made.

There was no telling, though. All Brandt was certain of was that he felt a deep unease as he walked toward the inn to give the wolfblades their new orders.

10

Academy crawled by. To Alena's sense, every class was at least twice as long as usual, every instructor endlessly lecturing on meaningless topics. She couldn't care less about Emperor Anders I's establishment of the monasteries, or the battles he fought to unify the continent after declaring himself emperor.

The diamond felt heavy in her pocket, weighing her down whenever she moved.

She had considered skipping the whole day and going straight to Bayt's. Only two obstructions kept her from doing so.

The first was Jace. Perhaps she could convince him to keep her absence a secret, but she doubted it. He might try, for her sake, but secrets leaked out of him like water through a sieve. He simply couldn't do it. She didn't want another lecture from Father, especially so soon after the last one.

Alena felt in her other pocket for her new knife. The hilt of the blade was cool against her palm, but the thought of the gift warmed her.

Bayt was the second obstruction. He had told her, early on, how important it was to maintain a normal lifestyle. His own routine served as an example. He didn't need to trade in spices. The information he collected and sold more than paid for his simple life. But the facade was important. It prevented people from becoming curious and asking questions there were no easy answers to.

He had taught her never to run from the scene of a crime unless she was chased. Running attracted attention. Likewise, she didn't skip a full day of classes the day after she had stolen a fist-sized chunk of diamond from a named family. People were too talented at making connections.

So she sat in class, tapping her foot and trying not to run her hand down to her pocket every other heartbeat to ensure the diamond was still secure.

She skipped history, but that was routine enough that no one noticed. She worked her way toward Bayt's shop, using many of the same techniques Niles had attempted just a few days ago. Hopefully her skill exceeded his.

Alena took far more extensive precautions than usual. Only when she was absolutely sure she was safe did she approach the shop.

She was probably paranoid. There was no connection between her and the diamond. Neither Niles nor his father had ever noticed her. She'd taken advantage of chance encounters.

There was no way they could suspect her.

Bayt's shop was quiet when she stepped in. The hairs on the back of her neck rose and she stopped just inside the door. No one stood in the front of the shop.

Bayt always kept an apprentice out front. It was one of the primary rules of the place, drilled into all new apprentices on day one.

The practice wasn't just about having someone present for customers. The apprentices up front acted as the first line of defense when imperial investigators appeared.

She almost ran.

But there was nowhere to run to. She didn't know what to do with an enormous uncut diamond. Bayt fenced everything for her.

She looked behind the counter. Nothing was out of place. The spices were well-organized, every container where it belonged.

Alena stepped into the back room.

She found Bayt.

Or what was left of him.

Alena gagged and rushed out of the room. She ran to the front door, then stopped. What if someone was watching? She had looked for people tailing her, but spotting someone watching a building was often far more challenging. It was how she'd found the diamond in the first place.

She breathed deep through her nose, calming her heart. There wasn't much stink, yet. Definitely not enough to overwhelm the various scents of the spices. Bayt hadn't been dead long.

She'd never seen a body disfigured like that.

She needed to go back. If there were any answers, they were in the back room.

With a deep breath, she steeled herself. She returned and forced herself to look at Bayt.

The bruises that covered his face and body told Alena Bayt's last hours had been anything but pleasant.

Part of her had always known Bayt's work ran this risk. But it had never felt real. Bayt had been too smart. He always knew just how far to push people. Far enough to profit, but never enough to bring this down on him. What had he done?

Alena studied the trap door in the floor. There were unbroken blood clots across it. Bayt hadn't spilled his secrets, even at the end.

Who would do this, though, and why?

Alena wished she knew more of Bayt's business. She had no idea who would wish such harm on him.

Would they go after his apprentices, too?

As her eye studied the floor, she noticed writing she hadn't before. The letters had been written in blood. Her breath caught in her throat.

Return it.

She sank to her knees, her breath coming in gasps.

Those two words told her all she needed to know.

She was the reason Bayt had been tortured and killed.

That thought ran through her head, repeating itself over and over. She lost track of time and her surroundings.

When her awareness returned, she realized she was vulnerable as long as she remained here. She knocked the palm of her hand against her forehead, forcing herself to think.

Bayt's voice echoed in her head. "Think! Then act."

She needed to leave. Being here implicated her. If a customer came in, they would link her to the body when the murder was discovered.

She stood up and left the store. Her eyes searched the streets and the rooftops, looking for a hidden observer.

She saw none, but that meant little. There were too many places to hide.

She needed to move, to flush out anyone who might follow her.

Alena chose directions randomly, her eyes always

looking back and forth. She turned left, then right, then turned back and walked the way she came. A few passersby glanced at her curiously, but no one followed.

She stepped into a teahouse and sat down. When the tea arrived, Alena sipped at it greedily. A little spilled down her chin. As she brought the cup down, she saw that her hands were shaking.

She placed the cup down gently, then put her palms on the oak table, spreading her fingers out and forcing them to relax. She closed her eyes, then worked her attention down her body, relaxing her tongue, her shoulders, and her back.

A calm mind followed a calm body. Bayt had taught her that.

He had taught her more than she realized.

She needed to think.

Bayt's trap door hadn't been opened. Granted, Zane Arrowood hadn't been searching for the information. He had been searching for her.

She thought of the message, left in her mentor's blood. Why leave it? If Bayt had given her up, Zane wouldn't have left the message. He'd be on her trail, sniffing her out.

Bayt hadn't talked.

She grimaced. She knew she was grasping for hope, but the story fit.

So how had Zane found Bayt?

That was easy enough, she supposed. Everyone on the wrong side of the law knew Bayt. He'd carved out a niche for himself, and among the locals, his reputation protected him. Bayt didn't intimidate with physicality, but with connections and information.

Alena realized the next few days would be complete chaos within the city. No doubt, Bayt had put plans in place if something happened to him. Zane had just inadvertently released dozens of pieces of compromising information on city and government officials.

But Zane wouldn't care about any of that. Alena suspected he only cared about the diamond.

And he had tortured and killed Bayt, who had been innocent enough of the crime, without a second thought.

She understood well enough what had happened to her master. Only one question remained: what did she do next?

If Zane had found Bayt within a day of the theft, he would quickly make his way through the underworld here. He would learn that Bayt's apprentices knew about more than just spices. Soon Zane would be coming after her, seeking information. He wouldn't know she had the diamond, but he'd get lucky all the same.

She sipped at the tea, fighting desperately against the tightness in her stomach, the bile rising in her throat.

She just had to test herself, didn't she? She couldn't leave well enough alone. Bayt's death landed squarely on her shoulders. Her breathing came fast and shallow as further consequences unfolded in her imagination.

She couldn't stay at the academy. Her family would be in danger.

Her only hope was to return the diamond. She wouldn't be able to do anything with it anyway. Bayt had been her only fence.

If she returned the diamond, maybe Zane would stop the hunt before it reached her.

She bit her tongue. It was a slim hope, but the only one she had.

She finished the whole pot of tea, the warm liquid calming her a little. The sun fell on the horizon, and she figured there was no point wasting time. She placed a few coins on the table and left the teahouse.

Alena used most of the remaining sunlight to ensure she wasn't being followed. By the time it was dark, she was certain no one was behind her.

She made her way toward the Arrowoods' house, stopping about a block away to climb to the roofs.

Alena watched every rooftop, looking for shadows out of place, or a hint of movement in the dim light of the stars. The moon wasn't up yet, and there wouldn't be a better time.

She waited. She almost convinced herself it was because she was checking for traps, but she fooled no one.

Her heart raced and her palms sweat. In so many ways, tonight was like the night past.

Last night, though, she had welcomed the nerves. Tonight she wished them away.

Thoughts of her family in danger forced her feet forward, but she almost didn't make the jump across the first roof gap. Lightness was difficult to summon with her internal energies all awash with torn thoughts.

She had to pause. Any hope she had depended on her abilities, and her abilities required a calm mind. She ran through the same practice as she had at the teahouse. She sat in the darkness and closed her eyes. She breathed deeply and relaxed the tight muscles throughout her body.

Her family needed her to return the diamond.

She focused on that one thought, pushing out all others.

Her heart slowed.

Alena stood up and ran her eyes over the roofs one more time. The city was quiet. She leaped from roof to roof, each jump bringing her closer to the house and the chimney where she had taken out the package. Soon only two gaps remained.

She looked one last time for hidden warriors, then

leaped across the gaps to the Arrowoods' house, making her steps as light as possible. Once there, she waited for ten heartbeats, listening for any sounds that signaled danger.

Alena took the hide-wrapped package from her pocket and placed it next to the chimney. She didn't want to be on the roof long enough to wiggle the loose brick out and replace it exactly where she had found it.

She leaped off the rooftop just in time to see the tall silhouette of Zane Arrowood dash up the other side, rush to the package, and pick it up.

"Halt!" he yelled.

The tone of command in his voice almost gave her pause. But she had seen Zane's handiwork up close. She wouldn't stop for him. She had left the diamond. That had to be enough.

In an instant, Alena learned firsthand how the Arrowood family had earned their name. Zane Arrowood leaped across the roof with ease, landing only a few paces behind her. His hand whipped out and Alena's heightened senses caught the slim displacement of air as a needle threaded its way toward her.

Alena ducked, and the needle passed overhead.

Poison?

She didn't want to find out. Alena sprinted. What little martial skill she possessed paled in comparison to Zane. Her only hope was in escape.

Alena kept to the roofs. There were fewer obstructions up here. Streets and alleys passed below. Every so often, Zane would whip a needle at her, but every time she felt it approach and avoided it.

Unfortunately, the needles kept her from escaping Zane. He was the stronger fighter, but her lightness was superior to his. If she could just open a gap between them, she might have a chance.

Just as the thought crossed her mind, a brick at the edge of a roof crumbled as she stepped on it. Even as light as she was, she couldn't clear the gap. She fell, landing lightly on her feet. But before she could move, the ground gave way under her. She swore, unable to dodge as a stone slammed into her stomach, knocking the wind from her lungs.

A shadow emerged from an alley just as Zane dropped from the roof. In a moment, Alena was forgotten as the two men focused on one another.

"Where is it?" asked the shadow.

"Out of your reach. Now, will you take off the mask, or will I take it off for you?"

Alena swore again as the city watch bells began ringing.

This street was not where she wanted to be right now.

The frantic ringing of a city watch bell drew Brandt's attention.

The wolfblades stood as a pack in the street. They had been patrolling the city, looking for some clue as to the diamond's whereabouts.

They hadn't even known where to start, and they'd made no progress. How did one find a single stone inside a city?

A sudden premonition caused Brandt to shudder.

More bells joined the first, a chorus of need, playing for all who would listen.

They shouldn't respond.

They were still recovering from their fight the day before. By all accounts, Ryder should still be on bedrest. Ryder, though, refused to let the wolfblades leave without him.

Glances passed between members of the group. They all thought the same as him, Brandt suspected.

There were no coincidences.

Brandt listened to the bells, his concerns mounting. The five of them hadn't defeated the bandit in their last encounter, when the conditions were nearly ideal. In Landow, there would be watchmen and civilians to worry about.

His stomach twisted at the thought.

Their duty was clear. The bandit was a threat, regardless of whether he possessed the diamond. Brandt didn't believe in the diamond's powers, but even the chance of truth was enough to warrant action.

Brandt focused on Ryder, the question unspoken.

Ryder nodded.

Brandt didn't share the other man's assessment, but he trusted his wolfblades. And they owed the bandit a rematch to prove once and for all who possessed superior skills. "Stay close."

Brandt became light, speeding toward the sound of the bells. No doubt, the city watch was doing the same.

The sound abruptly ended.

Brandt ran faster, checking behind him to ensure everyone kept pace.

It wasn't long before they could hear the battle. Steel rang against steel. Men yelled as they attacked, then screamed as they fell.

A moment later they saw the fight.

Brandt skidded to a stop, surprised by the extent of the damage. Men and women clothed in the uniforms of the city watch lay motionless in the street.

Ryder, sensitive to the currents of air that swirled around them, gave him a better idea of what he observed. "Most of them still live. Three are dead."

Farther up the street, the bandit and another man passed one another with a furious exchange of blows. In the darkness, Brandt barely tracked the exchange. A closer glance revealed the other man was Zane Arrowood.

Brandt understood, after watching the warriors for a few moments, why Zane Arrowood was favored by the emperor.

His wolfblades were some of the best warriors in the army. Each of them possessed an affinity. And none of them alone would last more than a few heartbeats against either of the warriors in the street. They fought as if they were warriors of legend.

Zane didn't possess an affinity, but his martial skills were clearly second to none. He was a living spiral, his body in constant, circular motion. His sword spun, deflecting stone after stone while still threatening the bandit.

Stepping into that fight was suicide.

The sight of a young girl in the street froze the order to retreat in his throat. She possessed some small amount of martial skill herself, although it appeared relatively untrained. She tried to escape the battle, but deadly stones darting around her locked her in place. Only her quick reflexes kept her alive and uninjured.

It took Brandt a few moments to understand.

The bandit was intentionally pinning her in. He wanted her there.

Brandt couldn't guess why, but he knew the bandit had to be stopped.

He felt the eagerness of his warriors behind him. Wolfblades didn't take defeat well. He held out his hand, restraining them for a moment.

Desire or no, charging haphazardly helped no one.

Brandt watched Zane move and assessed his skills. For tonight, at least, they shared a purpose. The wolfblades needed to support the master swordsman.

"Ana, Kyler, and I will use our affinities from a distance. Our goal is only to distract the bandit. We'll give Zane an opening. Lola, Ryder, get that girl out of here, but keep her close. She knows something."

A chorus of affirmations followed his order and the wolfblades sprinted down the street. Brandt listened for the song of the fire, hearing it as he passed an alley lit by a torch. He pulled the fire to him, splitting it in two. He fed it with some of his own energy, flinging one ball of fire at the bandit as soon as an opening presented itself.

The bandit stepped back, giving up ground in exchange for safety. Zane pressed into the opening, refusing to give the bandit even a moment to recover.

Ana pulled a string of water from the skin at her hip, whipping it at the bandit just as Kyler flung a rock at the bandit's head.

The tide of the battle turned in a heartbeat. Zane and the bandit had been well-matched, but the addition of the wolfblades overwhelmed the thief. The man in black retreated, surrounding himself with a wall of swirling stones.

Brandt flung his last ball of flame at the bandit, the fire passing through the storm of stone without problem. It struck the bandit on the left shoulder, burning through his clothes, but he uttered no cry of pain.

The stones spinning around the bandit launched away from him.

Brandt could do nothing but raise his arms to shield his face as stones blasted into him. They cut into his skin and bruised his arms and torso, but thankfully, he avoided taking any worse damage.

When he brought his arms down, he saw the bandit lunge at Zane.

The movement was desperate, and Zane rewarded it by stabbing his sword into the bandit's side.

It didn't look to be a fatal cut. The bandit's move had been too unexpected and too fast.

The two men grappled. Zane looked like he was trying to throw the bandit, but the bandit stood rooted, his footing firm. The bandit drove quick strikes into Zane using hands and elbows.

Across the street, Lola and Ryder reached the girl. In a few moments they would have her to safety.

Zane cursed loudly enough for Brandt to hear.

He turned back to the fight in time to see the bandit pull a small leather-wrapped package out of Zane's pockets.

The bandit stumbled backward, as though realizing for the first time a sword was embedded in him. But he unwrapped the package as Zane lunged for him.

Brandt wasn't sure what happened next.

Zane flew backward, and his body slammed into a brick wall across the street. He impacted with a sickening *thud*, the sounds of bones cracking easily audible down the block.

Zane's eyes went blank.

The bandit turned his attention to the wolfblades.

Off to Brandt's side, the bricks cracked in the building next to him. What little light the stars provided disappeared as the whole building leaned over him.

Brandt looked up, frozen in place.

Then Kyler was there, pushing him aside. The giant man's muscles bulged, tense with the effort of supporting the building, and he grunted a single word. "Go!"

Brandt looked up at the building, hovering above them.

Brandt ran, hating that he ran, but knowing there was no other way to honor Kyler's sacrifice. He grabbed at Ana's wrist as he passed her. The building resumed its descent well before they were clear.

Kyler screamed.

Brandt flung Ana forward, then leaped himself.

The building crashed down, a cloud of choking dust filling the street.

The sound of footsteps running echoed in the gloom, followed by a shuffling step. Brandt pulled at Ana, who resisted his efforts.

"Kyler's back there!"

He didn't have time to argue, to tell her Kyler wasn't going to follow them. Their friend led the way, now, to the gates that awaited them all.

So he pulled, overpowering her objections with physical strength. After a faltering step or two, she followed.

It didn't take long to come out of the dust. Brandt wiped his eyes. Ahead of them, Lola stood her ground against the shuffling bandit, sword in hand. Beyond that scene, Ryder and the girl ran.

Ryder stumbled, holding his head. Brandt couldn't see clearly, but it looked as though he had been hit with something. Then he straightened and continued.

At least they saved one life tonight.

A stone as large as Brandt's head sped from the rubble straight at Lola. She saw it coming and dodged, moving in close, hoping to find protection right next to the bandit.

Brandt summoned what little strength remained to join the fight, his sword leaping from its sheath. As the stone turned and raced toward Lola, he kicked at it, the power of his kick shattering the stone into pieces.

The bandit growled, "Pathetic."

It was the first time Brandt had heard the bandit speak.

More bricks flew from the collapsed building.

Brandt cut through one with his sword, but the bandit caught the two pieces and circled them around. His control and strength still surprised Brandt, even after all this time.

He needed to get close enough to use his sword. The bandit was injured and relied on his affinity to win this battle.

In the moment of his distraction, a handful of bricks crashed into Lola from different directions. She grunted, then fell to the ground.

Brandt jumped into the swirling storm of stone surrounding the thief, driving his blade straight forward.

Brandt never had a chance. He was caught by several stones at once, and his blade never made it close. The power of the defense threw him off to the side, resting against the side of a building. Brandt looked up, uncomfortably aware of how dangerous buildings were now.

He tried to sit up taller, but his body refused to obey his commands. He looked around, finally finding Lola. She lay still on the street.

He couldn't find Ana either. Had she also died in the attacks? Everything had happened so fast.

The bandit stepped toward Brandt. He growled, disguising his voice. "You shouldn't have been here, fool."

Brandt couldn't fight. The bandit remained out of reach.

His team was dead. Thoughts of Kyler, Lola, and Ana filled his head. Hopefully Ryder would escape. He'd always been the most clever of them.

Brandt gritted his teeth. Their deaths had to mean something.

He searched for the bandit's warmth. It was there, a quiet song, barely audible over the rampaging beat of his own heart.

Brandt imagined entwining his fingers in that heat, finding a hold deep within that couldn't be broken. He might die, but he would die together with this man.

"Why?" he croaked.

He didn't care much. No reason was worth the death of his friends. But an explanation would distract the man in those crucial first moments.

The bandit didn't answer. A single rock, not much larger than Brandt's index finger, floated between them. As Brandt watched, the rock fractured, flakes of stone fluttering to the ground like heavy leaves. The stone became a thick needle, pointed at his heart.

Brandt clutched the bandit's heat in his will and pulled. He yanked as hard as his affinity allowed. A sweat broke on his brow as the heat came into his own body.

But nothing happened.

Brandt pulled and pulled until sweat poured from his forehead and armpits. The bandit should have died. He should have crumpled in agony as his blood froze in his veins.

But the bandit just shook his head. With a wave of his hand, the stone needle darted at Brandt. Brandt twisted, but the projectile pierced his chest, embedding deeply there.

A burning white agony blackened his vision. His body no longer obeyed its orders, and darkness swallowed him whole.

12

The wolfblade who called himself Ryder pulled her along. For the moment, she followed, the direction a welcome relief from having to solve her problems on her own.

Alena knew she was fast. She didn't have many martial skills, but she had developed her lightness as far as she could. Of all the martial abilities, it was the one that came most easily to her. Had Ryder been healthy, though, she suspected he was even faster.

Despite the pounding of her heart, she studied him as he moved. She noticed the novel ways he changed directions, using walls, carts, and benches to alter his momentum.

It wasn't just sheer physical ability. It was technique and imagination.

She feared the consequences of the gash across his forehead. It was bleeding freely, and his footsteps didn't always land exactly where she thought they should.

Ryder pulled her into an alley. They rested for a few moments. More accurately, Ryder rested. He grimaced as he explored his wound with his fingers. He leaned back against the wall, using his left hand on his knee to brace himself.

"What happened?"

"I got hit by a sharp rock. It probably should have killed me, but I sensed it coming in time." He gasped between his sentences.

"You sensed it?" Her curiosity was piqued. Sometimes, she believed her experience of the world was different than most people's. She was sensitive to the movements, much more than anyone she had met. She could feel a ball speeding toward her, or a punch. It had only been a few years ago she realized few people shared that skill.

Ryder nodded. "Air affinity."

The revelation struck her like a slap. Did she have an affinity? The idea had never occurred to her outside of daydreams. Affinities allowed one to manipulate elements, and she couldn't do any of that. They had tested her just a few years ago.

"If you sensed the rock, why not use air to deflect it?"

Ryder's chuckle was grim. "Wish I could. But air's not helpful that way. Can you imagine how much wind it would take to deflect a thrown rock?" He straightened up. "We need to keep moving." He stumbled as he took his first step. She reached out to support him.

He waved away her help. "Let's go."

They kept running, but Alena quickly realized he was now slowing her down. He shouldn't be running, or fighting. After a couple of blocks, he came to the same conclusion. He stopped again. "Do you know of a good place to hide?"

Before Alena could answer, she sensed the projectile.

She dodged out of the way, her lightness keeping her safe.

Ryder wasn't so fast. He grunted as a razor-sharp stone sliced through his shoulder.

Alena turned to see the bandit, not more than a block away. How had he followed them?

Then she noticed the blood on the ground, the constant drip from Ryder's forehead.

The sight of the bandit deflated Ryder. Whatever hope he had held onto was gone. He turned to her. "Run."

"What?"

"I can't stop him, but I can hold him off. Go."

Alena wanted to protest, but she didn't. Ryder was right. Her only chance at safety was to run. So she did.

Behind her, she heard Ryder shout. She didn't waste even a heartbeat to turn around. She knew the result. Air against stone was no contest.

Alena ran, her body as light as possible. She used the tricks she had picked up from Ryder, changing her momentum at will.

She sensed the stone flying for her, but dodged as it cut into the wall of a house. Before the bandit could send another her way, she broke line of sight by jumping into an alley.

She didn't take to the roofs. The ground level was filled with hiding spots. Up high she might move faster, but she would be seen for hundreds of paces.

She turned and turned, never running straight for more than two blocks. Landow's gridded system of streets would protect her.

Her hair blew behind her as she ran.

Despite the danger, Ryder's tricks unlocked a new freedom.

Another stone or two followed her, but soon even those fell away. She was faster than the bandit.

Alena slid into a narrow gap between two houses, burying herself between two stacks of logs and an old sheet. She calmed her breathing.

She didn't know how long she hid there. Every sense tingled as she waited for any sign she had been discovered. As her heartbeat returned to normal, her perspective shifted.

She had escaped. But at what cost?

She knew, now that she had a moment to reflect, why Ryder had given up all hope at the end of the chase. If the bandit had followed them that far, it meant he had killed Ryder's other wolfblades.

Memories of the giant man who had presented at their academy came unbidden to her mind. He had been so strong.

And Alena had watched a building come down on top of him, snuffing his life with the same ease as when she stepped on an ant.

All because of her.

She hugged her knees tightly to her chest, rocking back and forth.

Before tonight, she had always wanted to be big. She wanted to be noticed. She wanted people to pay attention to her, to see what she was capable of. Born and raised in Landow, near the edges of the empire, attention promised her a future outside the walls of the city.

Now she saw her foolishness under reality's harsh glare. She regretted any time she had been noticed or remarked on. Every moment of attention she had worked so hard to earn was now a threat to her safety.

The bandit had killed Zane Arrowood. He had killed the wolfblades.

Would he kill her?

Would he even make an effort to find her?

She squeezed her eyes shut and bounced the back of her head against the wall she hid against.

She had to focus.

How much danger was she in?

The bandit had seen her face. By itself, that meant little. Landow was big enough to hide in. A face alone wasn't enough to cause her to worry.

But Zane had been tracking her down quickly enough, and he hadn't known her face.

She shook her head, then buried it in her knees.

She could guess at probabilities all day, but she didn't know enough. If the bandit considered her a threat, he would come after her. But she was no threat. There had been other members of the city watch left alive by the bandit. Surely he wouldn't track everyone down?

There was no way of telling.

Bayt's advice had been to stick to routine whenever possible.

So she would go home, and in the morning, she would return to academy. She wouldn't even skip history.

Thoughts of academy made her stomach churn.

She would have to face Niles, who had lost his father this night.

But it had to be done.

She sighed and stood up, looking both ways to ensure she was truly alone. The barest hints of sunlight were starting to show on the horizon.

As she walked, a new determination settled on her. She *could* do this.

Perhaps this life of thieving wasn't for her. It had been a fun game for a time, and she had learned enough to fill a library of books, but it wasn't reality.

People didn't steal out of boredom. They did so out of necessity, and in this empire, where was the necessity? Everyone worked enough to eat. If they didn't, the empire disposed of them.

She had been a fool, protected by Bayt and his unique position. He had created an illusion, a dream world for her to play in.

Reality was raw, though, and dangerous.

In just a while, she would be home, and she would wake up on time and pretend nothing was different. She would make her parents proud, and they wouldn't be proud of the lie she had created around her life. They would be proud of her true achievements. She would never steal again, nor even think of breaking the law. From this night forward, she would be a loyal servant of the empire.

The sacrifice of the wolfblades wouldn't be for nothing.

13

B randt opened his eyes, the stabbing pain in his skull evidence enough that he still lived.

His gaze darted around, searching for clues. He lay on a bed, as did many others. Individuals wearing the white uniforms of healers moved from bed to bed. The atmosphere was quiet, an unspoken recognition of the nearness of the gate that separated the living from the dead.

He'd seen the gate himself, once. Years ago as an infantryman, before joining the ranks of the wolfblades. He had been stationed near the Falari border, involved in a small skirmish, one of the endless border conflicts the southern lands were involved in. Brandt had taken a spear through the side. The strike hadn't hit any vital organs, but nearly a full day passed before he was discovered by his fellow soldiers. By then infection had set in and he was weak with fever.

He didn't remember much from the following days, but he remembered the gate.

Less a gate, perhaps, and more an arch. Made of smooth stone, eroded until it was almost as smooth as glass. Yet somehow every stone fit perfectly, held together by an invisible mortar.

He had been walking toward that gate when a force had pulled him back.

And he had lived, and gone on to join the wolfblades.

Was it truth, a vision of his eventual destiny? The destiny that waited for all?

Or was it a figment of his mind, created out of the myths and legends of his people?

He considered himself fortunate to return once. He still had days where he wondered about the veracity of his vision. Unfortunately, the only way to discover the truth was to make a journey from which there was no return.

He had seen no gate this time. There had only been the pain of the stone blade through his chest and the sweet blackness that followed. Then now.

Brandt lifted his right hand, grimacing against the pain. He brought his hand into sight and flexed his fingers. They moved as expected. Gingerly, he touched his left chest, the slightest touch sending a flare of agony down his spine.

Alive, then, but not well.

One of the healers, a middle-aged woman, noticed his movement. She approached him, her eyes missing nothing as they examined him. "I'd tell you to be careful, but judging from the scars on your body, this isn't your first time under a healer's care."

Her voice was rough, but concerned. Like a disapproving mother.

The edge of Brandt's lips turned up in a smile. "I've seen one or two."

"Closer to a dozen, would be my guess."

"It's easy to lose track."

She made a sound that might have been a chuckle, or a grunt. Brandt liked her.

"How bad is it?"

"Not fatal. The stone pierced almost directly over your heart, but entered at a shallow angle. Your chest is a mess that the healers have been trying to fix, but some of it is just going to require time to heal. You can count yourself lucky."

"Other survivors?"

"The city guard was luckier than they should have been. About twenty injured, but only four dead."

Brandt didn't want to ask the question, but he had to. He clenched his left fist, already suspecting the answer. "The other wolfblades?"

"You're the only one we found alive."

Her tone was direct but compassionate, the voice of one used to giving terrible news to worried families.

A chasm opened within him.

He had known, of course. Only a fool would hope. But he had hoped anyway.

He lay there in mute shock. The healer reached out and grabbed his right hand, gently moving it away from the wound he had been exploring a moment before. She squeezed it before she let go.

Understanding his needs better than him, she offered him a short bow and then moved away, giving him the space to breathe.

Brandt stared upwards, looking at nothing in particular.

Just two nights ago they had been drinking together.

He'd lost friends in combat before, but not since becoming a wolfblade. They were among the best. For over two years the five of them had spent almost every day from sunrise to sunset together. They fought as one.

And now only one remained.

Brandt lay there, unmoving, even as the healers came to check on him. In the back of his mind, he heard the soft songs of the torches scattered around the hall of healing. Fire still called to him, but he didn't respond.

The world felt empty and cold. He had no desire to move through it, to be a part of it.

He slept, then woke, then slept again. Time meant nothing. Sometimes light shone through the windows of the hall, other times it did not. He endured the healing process, and forced himself to eat.

Every time he awoke, he felt something new growing inside of him. A stone that sat in his stomach and grew with every waking.

Rage.

At himself, for surviving.

And at the bandit, for taking away those he loved.

Rage bred purpose.

He began stretching, running through what exercises he could. His wounds closed up on his chest, thanks in no small part to the constant ministrations of the healers.

After eight days, he stood up, put on his bloody wolfblade uniform, and walked out of the hall of healing, ignoring the protests behind him. He could clean and dress his own wounds, and they had done little else for him the past day. Rest could come later.

Brandt ignored the stares as he walked down the street toward the center of Landow. When people saw his uniform, they moved out of his way. A few brave souls offered to help, but were silenced when they glanced into his eyes.

The city guard was headquartered in a small fortified building near the center of town. Watchmen came and went regularly, but Brandt felt a sense of unease over the place, a grief that hadn't yet found a home.

When Brandt passed through the open gate, activity in the courtyard came to a stop. Several of the watch turned and bowed to him. Brandt returned the bow, unsure of where to proceed.

A young officer saved him from embarrassment. He approached, gave a quick bow, and asked, "How can I help you, sir?"

"Is your commander here?"

The officer nodded. "He hasn't left much since the incident. I'll take you to him."

The young man led Brandt through the narrow halls of the building, escorting him to a room nestled deep within. "This is Commander Scot."

Brandt and Scot exchanged introductions and the commander motioned Brandt to a seat.

Brandt respected the commander after only a glance. He sat tall, and his head was shaved. Everything in his command post was clean and orderly. He looked the part of a warrior, and from the way he moved, Brandt imagined it wasn't a false pretense.

"I'm sorry for your loss," Scot began.

"Thank you." Brandt noticed the bags under the commander's eyes and the disheveled uniform. Scot had lost warriors, too. "And I'm sorry for yours."

The commander nodded. "It would have been much worse if you and the other wolfblades hadn't shown up. There's not a man or woman in the watch that isn't thanking you in their heart right now."

The words lifted Brandt's spirits. His friends deserved the recognition, little as it would mean to them now. But hearing accolades wasn't why he had come. "What can you tell me about that night?"

Scot looked down at his desk in disgust. "Not enough.

We haven't been able to track down the bandit or the missing wolfblade."

Brandt's eyes shot up. "What did you say?"

"We haven't been able to find—"

Brandt cut him off with a snap of his hand. "There's a missing wolfblade?"

"Yes. A woman, of average height, with long dark hair. She might have a water affinity."

"Ana."

Scot made a note on a sheet of paper. "You didn't know?"

"The healers told me I was the only one found alive." Brandt raged at the healer until he realized his mistake. She hadn't lied. It had only been the day after the battle. They probably hadn't realized a body was missing yet.

Ana was alive.

She had to be. Brandt hadn't seen her near the end of the fight. But what happened? Where had she gone?

Brandt shook his head to clear it. Ana lived. He would find her, but that still wasn't why he had sought the commander. "Have you come any closer to learning the criminal's identity?"

"No." Scot's anger reflected Brandt's own. "With the strength of the man's martial arts and the power of his affinity, it makes sense to assume a man of at least some wealth or power. That level of skill takes years of dedicated training. We've been interviewing possible leads, but nothing has come of it, yet."

"Can you give me writ to investigate on my own?"

Scot frowned. "Do you need it?"

"Probably not, but if someone challenges my authority, it'll be much faster to turn to you than my own commander."

Scot considered. Brandt could decipher his uncertainty

easily enough. Wolfblades were military. On paper, their authority exceeded that of the city guard, but the reality was often far more tangled. Local officials could tie up Brandt's investigation for weeks if they challenged him and required letters from his commander, stationed hundreds of leagues away.

Scot looked up, studying him. "Very well." He took out a sheet of paper, wrote his orders on it with a neat hand, then pressed his seal near the bottom. He held out the paper. "If you find anything, let me know. We'll offer whatever help we can. The watch is always at your call."

Brandt nodded and took the paper.

It was time for him to find the man who had killed his friends.

14

Alena woke to the sound of Jace pounding on her door, yelling at her to wake up. She blinked rapidly, her mind struggling to stitch together two very different realities.

She was a student at Landow Academy. And she was a thief who had watched brave warriors die the night before.

The worlds collided, making her head spin. Jace's pounding on the door didn't help.

"I'm up." When the banging didn't stop, she yelled, "I'm up!"

The cacophony ceased and she heard Jace's quick footsteps down the stairs. Alena rubbed at her eyes. She'd feared she wouldn't sleep well, but as soon as her head had hit the pillow she had fallen into a deep slumber. Exhaustion overtook fear.

The morning had come far too soon. She closed her eyes, the world spinning around her. She was Alena, an overtired and ambitious student. A glint of morning sunlight caught the blade of the knife her father had given her. She reached over and grabbed it, taking strength in the solidity of the weapon.

She would bring it to academy today. Weapons were strictly forbidden, but so long as she kept it hidden, it wouldn't be a problem. They never searched students. She slid her finger over the side of the blade. It wouldn't break, and neither would she.

She ran through her usual morning routine, taking comfort in the normalcy of a morning with her family. Whenever she lost focus, her mind returned to the scenes from the night before. So she threw herself into everything, from brushing her hair to dressing.

But her focus failed often. At breakfast, her mind wandered, and her food remained untouched. Mom caught her staring off in the distance. "Alena, is everything all right?"

She nodded, hating the lie. She should tell her parents. They deserved the truth. Perhaps they would have some guidance for her.

But the truth endangered her and them. Lying to them kept them safe.

The two siblings finished preparing for the day and stepped into the streets on their way to academy.

It didn't take long to hear about the events of last night. The news was on every tongue. Everyone in town had an idea, a theory, or a rumor to spread. By the time they had walked five blocks, Alena had learned that the wolfblades had fought the city guard. That Zane had been a thief pursued by the emperor. That the wolfblades had torn a building from its foundation. The only fact everyone could agree on was the truth: three wolfblades, four city guards, and Zane Arrowood had died violently.

Alena watched Jace. His first reaction was disbelief. The

wolfblades couldn't be killed, not by anything happening in Landow. She guided him forward before he could raise a scene in a square where a particularly bold young man was claiming the wolfblades hadn't been that strong to begin with.

For once, she understood how her brother felt. The wolfblades had saved her life. They deserved nothing but respect.

Brother and sister walked in silence. With every step, Jace's disbelief turned into acceptance. But acceptance grew into something darker. When they came in sight of the academy, Jace turned to Alena.

"He deserves to die."

The vehement statement, uttered after so long a period of silence, made her jump. "Who?"

"Whoever killed the wolfblades."

"I agree."

"People like him, they don't deserve to live." Jace grabbed onto Alena's hand. "I'm going to make sure of it. I'll make sure that people who hurt others get what they deserve."

Alena's heart broke a little at that. Her brother was still so kind, because she heard the hurt underneath his threats. Would he be the same as he grew into a man? She was tempted to poke fun at him, but when she saw the seriousness on his face, she withheld her comments. Let the world crush his dreams. She, for one, would support him. "That's noble of you," she said. "I hope you still feel that way as you get older."

"I will," he vowed. "The wolfblades shouldn't have died."

Was it only yesterday that she had felt something similar? That she lived in a world where "should" mattered? Zane Arrowood, the city guard, and the wolfblades should be alive. Bayt should be alive. And she should have known to stay well enough alone.

As they approached the academy's gate, Alena's legs grew heavy.

This was her fault.

She was the one who had put the pieces in motion.

If she had never stolen the diamond, none of this would have happened.

She watched Jace walk in front of her, the picture of young justice. If the bandit did seek her out, Jace would put himself between her and the criminal, just like Ryder had.

She should run. Running kept her family safe. It guaranteed that Jace could grow up to become the warrior he dreamed of. She imagined turning right there, running away from Jace and Landow until everyone she loved was safe.

Then they turned the corner and the familiar walls of the academy reassured her. She was scared. She had let her emotions start to dictate her behaviors.

The bandit wouldn't come after her. He had no reason to. So long as she kept her head down, she had no reason to worry. She needed to stay calm.

A small crowd had gathered inside the academy gates. With a sinking feeling, Alena guessed the cause.

She was right.

Niles stood there, surrounded by friends and those who wanted to be his friend. His eyes were rimmed with red, but he stood tall.

She studied him, drawing her conclusions quickly.

He knew his father was dead. But he had come to academy anyway. He wasn't the same boy he had been yesterday. He was the head of the Arrowood family now. The sudden responsibility stiffened his back. She stopped to listen. One younger girl was asking him what he would do next.

He looked out over the crowd, meeting many of them by eye. Alena cast her eyes down, unable to meet his gaze.

"My family was given a task by the emperor himself. I plan to follow the orders of my liege. My father was investigating illegal activity in Landow. I will do the same."

Had Niles said those words a week ago, Alena would have classified them as an empty boast. Now she heard the determination in his voice. Last week he had been a spoiled child. This morning he was a young man with a purpose. Could the transformation last?

The crowd also noticed the determination, in their own way. They leaned in, drawn toward the power of his belief.

"Won't that be dangerous?" one girl asked.

Niles nodded. "My father was a far stronger martial artist than me. But I will train to meet the challenge. I have the notes from his investigation, so I can pick up where he left off."

The others kept drawing closer, wanting to know more about what had happened. Alena snuck away, ashamed to even be near Niles.

And his words worried her. He presented a new challenge. If what he said about the notes was true, it wouldn't be long before he was following the same thread of investigation his father had, an investigation that led straight to Alena.

The bandit might decide she wasn't worth the trouble, but she didn't imagine Niles would feel the same.

The question of his transformation became more vital now. If Niles' boast was empty, she had little to worry about. But if this transformation was something deeper, something more meaningful, she had a problem.

Her first class passed by in a blur. Alena tried to focus, but compared to the issues of life and death that faced her, ancient literature about flying dragons held little interest.

She doodled in her notes. She had two problems: the bandit and Niles. If she was going to survive, she needed to know how much of a threat each was. She needed to know more.

Every time a student shifted, she startled, expecting to see Niles standing over her, unanswered questions written on his face. But he didn't even notice her.

By the time the students were summoned for lunch, Alena had reached a decision. The only way to keep her family safe was to learn more. She needed to know who the bandit was and if they would seek her out. And she needed to know how dangerous Niles truly was.

But how would she answer those questions?

15

Brandt's next visit was to the governor. Before the attack, Kye had known more than anyone about the events transpiring in his region. He was sharp and well-informed. If there was a lead to find, Brandt's best hope was with him. The wolfblade hoped he wasn't wrong. He didn't know where else he could turn.

The journey from the barracks to town hall was blissfully short. Every step caused Brandt's chest to burn, tendrils of pain branching through his entire body. By the time he arrived at the governor's workplace he was sweating and out of breath. Perhaps he wasn't as healed as he thought he was.

His blood-soaked uniform attracted significantly more attention than he would've received under normal circumstances. Within moments an aide appeared, and a few moments after that the same aide disappeared into the halls of power, seeking the governor.

Brandt rested on a bench, closed his eyes, and focused on calm breathing. The pain in his chest faded, at least a bit.

It wasn't long before he heard the soft footsteps of another man on the polished wood floors.

He opened his eyes to see the governor standing before him. Kye looked about the same as Brandt felt. His hair was disheveled, he moved slowly, and his eyes didn't possess the same sharpness Brandt had noticed when they had met just a few days ago. The governor looked like he hadn't slept for several nights.

Which, Brandt supposed, might actually be the case. The bandit had proven to be no ordinary criminal. Brandt remembered the building toppling on top of Kyler. Such a feat wasn't possible, just as the cave mouth closing hadn't been possible. The rumors of the diamond had to be true, as it was the only explanation. And if the rumors were true, Kye had failed the emperor. Brandt wouldn't be sleeping well, either.

Without a word, the governor beckoned for Brandt to follow. Brandt grimaced as he stood and tailed the governor down the long hallway. The building was surprisingly quiet. Kye wasn't moving quickly, and to Brandt's eye, it looked like the governor was injured.

Or just very tired.

Brandt was grateful for the pace. If Kye required him to move any faster than a shuffle, he wasn't sure he'd remain upright.

After a long journey down a never-ending hallway, they sat in a small, quiet study. This wasn't a room where the governor usually received guests. Kye's desk here looked far less organized than the one in his mansion. Papers were scattered all over, and a pot of tea sat off to the side. The governor reached for it and poured two cups. Kye passed one over and the two of them sipped their tea in silence. The drink was colder than it should have been, but the lukewarm liquid still provided a welcome relief from Brandt's misery. He needed to rest, and soon.

"I — I was very saddened to hear about the loss of the wolfblades." The governor's voice was hoarse, as though he had been talking for hours on end. "I'm sorry."

Brandt couldn't get the governor to meet his eyes. Kye either stared down at his desk or off into a corner of the room, his eyes unfocused.

Guilt?

But why? Did he feel somehow responsible for the battle that had taken place in his city? "Are you all right?"

Kye gave a grim smile, gesturing to the papers on his desk. "Even after the fight, the bandit isn't my only problem. Another criminal was killed the day of your fight. Apparently he had no small amount of blackmail on many officials throughout town. His death caused many officials to resign, and the town is barely functioning. So I need to perform tasks others would have done, taking up my time, when all I want is to find who killed my guard and your wolfblades."

There was a silence as Brandt absorbed the outburst.

What he heard was guilt, some flavor of the same guilt he felt.

Brandt knew those emotions intimately. They had haunted him when he first took command and he questioned every decision. Regardless of the result, he always believed he could have done better. Before this mission he had never lost a soldier, but he had given orders which had injured others, and it had taken him no small amount of time to process even that small guilt.

He couldn't think about the loss of his friends. If he did, he wasn't sure he would function at all.

"It's not your fault," he said.

Kye shook his head. "I think the bandit was pushed too far. Few of the city guard were killed. It was only when your soldiers and Arrowood attacked that his violence reached its peak."

The thought hadn't occurred to Brandt. He supposed it made sense. The bandit hadn't harmed them in their first exchange. "Well-intentioned or not, his crime remains the same."

The governor grimaced. "I don't suppose there's any chance you will turn aside from this? So many have already been lost."

Brandt shook his head. His direction was clear. "Do you have any leads?"

This time it was the governor's turn to shake his head. "The bandit has left no trace. He's a master swordsman with a powerful stone affinity. Nothing else is known."

"And what about Zane?"

"He, too, is dead. Why?"

"He knew something, or else he wouldn't have been there. Perhaps he left papers."

The governor leaned back. "I suspect whatever knowledge he had died with him. More so, I do not even know where he resided. He was a man of mysterious ways."

Brandt frowned at that. "Did he have a family?"

"I believe so, a son. I know the line has not been ended, at least."

It wasn't much, but it was better than nothing. The governor gave him a place to start. "Thank you for your time, governor."

"Of course. Please, let me know if you find anything. You are not the only one who wants justice for the fallen."

Brandt nodded and stepped out of the room, leaving the governor to his problems.

. . .

BRANDT SAT on a stone bench near the edge of the town center. Here the government buildings and large commercial properties began to give way to homes and small businesses. This bench was well-positioned in a corner formed by two adjoining buildings. At this time of the day the sun beat down, but the spot was protected from the chilly breeze. Brandt closed his eyes and enjoyed the feeling of the sun warming his body, a seeping warmth penetrating all the way to his bones.

If Zane had a son, where would he be?

Brandt thought it odd that the governor hadn't known where in town a named family lived. For a man who seemed otherwise so well-informed, it seemed like an egregious oversight. Kye didn't seem like a governor who let such things slip by him.

Brandt could still find the son, though. When hunting anyone, Brandt found it easy to put himself in another's position, especially if he knew something about them.

He imagined himself as Zane. The man was named, which implied that he had some small amount of pride, at least. Most named families found the most ostentatious houses they could when they moved. If Zane kept his location a secret, it probably had more to do with his assigned task from the emperor than anything else. But secrecy wouldn't diminish his pride.

So if the boy was still in Landow, where would he be?

One idea came to mind.

The academy.

There were several schools in the area. Landow was certainly big enough to have more than one. But there would only be one academy, where the best and the brightest would gather. He couldn't imagine Zane not sending his child to the very best that was available.

Brandt figured there was no better place to start. It took him most of the afternoon to find the academy. Within its walls there was a hushed feeling, the same oppressive atmosphere that followed so many disasters. Brandt was taken to the headmaster, who eyed his uniform skeptically. "How can I help you, Sergeant?"

"I am looking for the son of Zane Arrowood. Is he here?"

The headmaster hesitated for a moment, which only confirmed Brandt's suspicion.

"I mean the boy no harm. But my questions must be answered."

"Whether or not you mean harm is irrelevant. The boy has just suffered the loss of his father and everything he knows. As gentle as you intend to be, you will still reopen wounds that are just barely closed."

"I understand, but that does not change the necessity."

The headmaster gave him a long, hard look, but there was nothing he could do to stop Brandt. The wolfblade's authority superseded all in this region except the governor's. More than anything, the headmaster just wanted to ensure that his feelings on the matter were known. Brandt understood. He even respected the headmaster. But it didn't alter his course of action.

The headmaster summoned an assistant, who then ran to find the boy.

"What is his name?" asked Brandt.

"Niles."

A few minutes later the assistant reappeared with a student in tow.

Brandt studied the young man, curious. There was a hint of haughtiness to his demeanor, a slight upturn of the nose that couldn't be hidden. This was a boy who had grown up named, a status he had lived with for his entire life. No matter how well-intentioned the parent, status changed a person's outlook.

But Brandt didn't think he should underestimate the young man. The boy had spirit, a backbone of steel that had probably only appeared in the past few days. For the first time he understood hardship, and he looked as though he would respond with strength. There was something of the father in the son, it seemed.

Brandt offered the young man a short bow, which was not returned. He saw the way Niles looked at his uniform, though, caught the flicker of recognition in the widening of his eyes. The reaction was only of a moment, but it gave Brandt hope. He turned to the headmaster. "Is there someplace that Master Arrowood and I can speak in private?"

The headmaster nodded. "Feel free to use this space. I shall wait outside."

The headmaster looked chagrined that he had to leave his own office and forfeit his protection of his prize student, but there was one very tangible benefit to being a wolfblade in the empire.

When Brandt gave an order, people obeyed.

Niles sat before Brandt could even offer him a seat.

Brandt watched him with interest. This was a young man who was still used to getting everything he wanted. The power of his name no doubt caused him to think he was superior to most adults. Brandt had already appealed to the young man's vanity by titling him master. Now it was time for something harsher. "Who killed your father?"

The boy's eyes narrowed at that. He'd been expecting sympathy or gentleness. But if he wanted to be the head of the Arrowoods, he needed to earn it. His father had died a warrior.

Niles' response was defensive. "How should I know?"

Brandt's reply was sharp. "Because you are master of the Arrowood name, a house known for its intelligence and ability to gather information. Your father died pursuing his mission, and you'd be a poor son indeed if you didn't at least have an idea of who murdered him."

The boy leaped to his feet. "You can't speak to me like that!"

Brandt kept pushing, acting nonchalant. "I'll talk to children however I choose."

He hadn't been sure it would happen, but Niles swung at him. Even injured, Brandt had no problem countering the attack. With a quick movement of his right arm he redirected the boy's attack away and down, causing Niles to stumble to the floor. The pain in his chest seared even at that small movement, but the boy was too caught up in his own shame to notice.

"I mean no disrespect, Master Arrowood. But you *are* Master Arrowood now, and the cheap intimidation you used to engage in as a boy has no meaning in my world. There are plenty of people who won't cower at a name, and it is up to you to convince them the name has meaning. Your father died in front of me, right next to my own warriors."

Niles' face was a mix of emotions. Brandt saw anger, pain, and loneliness. The boy was a seething cauldron of emotions that needed a direction. Brandt could supply it.

"I will have vengeance for my wolfblades, and for your father, but I need your help."

Niles looked up and met Brandt's gaze. Brandt could almost see the transformation right before him. It was challenging to overcome a lifetime of habit, but Niles succeeded. He put the past behind him and stood up tall, dusting himself off.

He bowed.

His father's son indeed.

"Let's get started, then," Niles said.

Questions.

There were too many questions, and not enough answers.

When she listened to Niles the day after the incident, Alena had worried he would track her down in a day or two. But then nothing happened. Niles went to class, and after that he returned home, just as he had before his father's death. Alena knew because she followed him. He made no effort to hide his destination anymore.

After a few days, Alena began to believe she was safe. Niles had been boasting. He didn't have the character to follow through on his claims. She still felt for her knife several times a day just to reassure herself that it was still there, but she didn't feel the same need for it she once had.

Days passed, and nightmares faded into memories.

Then the wolfblade, still wearing the bloody uniform he had fought in, appeared and spoke with Niles.

The academy wasn't that large, and news traveled through the student body within an afternoon of the wolfblade's appearance. No doubt some of Niles' new friends were all too eager to spread the rumor. Their champion had been summoned by a wolfblade.

Alena's stomach twisted into knots then. The hunt would be on for her.

The wolfblade had seen her. There would be no hiding from him, and if he joined with Niles and learned what Zane had been investigating, it was only a matter of days before she was discovered.

So what options did she have?

She searched her mind for any advice that Bayt might have given her, but nothing came to mind. She wasn't sure that her former mentor had ever found himself in a situation as dire as this.

The one time he had, it ended with his death.

The problem that haunted her the most was the same as it was over a week ago. She didn't know enough to make an informed decision. She lacked enough information to predict anyone's next actions. Any choice she made was just as likely to harm her as it was to work.

When a good idea finally hit her, it seemed so obvious she was ashamed she hadn't thought of it earlier. This whole time she was complaining about a lack of information, yet she had worked for the town's most well-known supplier of exactly that commodity.

The evidence was everywhere. News of the attack faded quickly as scandal after scandal enveloped the town. The governor had to replace nearly every official of note. Bayt had set up a system to protect himself, and when Zane killed him, that system fell into place.

On one hand, she laughed at the thought of so many officials with their secrets revealed. If the governor acted wisely, Landow could become the jewel of the empire in the next few years as corrupt officials were replaced. On the other, the knowledge that it was her theft that had set this chain of events in motion haunted her. How many people's lives had been destroyed in the past week?

Her best opportunity to stop the ripples from spreading further was to visit Bayt's shop and uncover the rest of his information.

The thought of returning to her former workplace worried her, but she saw no better way forward.

That afternoon, Alena skipped history, the mere act bringing a brief smile to her face. She hadn't skipped since the incident. There had been no point.

But it did cause her to reflect. Even though there had been no consequences to her routine of skipping history, she was ashamed that she had felt so daring as she had done it.

Now her past behavior just seemed childish.

She didn't have much of a plan for her return to Bayt's shop, but she figured she didn't need one. All she needed was to make sure that she was unobserved, and the rest would take care of itself.

She used lightness to reach the top of a roof across the street from Bayt's shop. She watched and she waited, searching for anyone with an unnatural interest in the building.

When she was certain that the shop was unobserved, she entered through the front door. The door had been locked, probably by the city watch, but her key still provided easy enough access.

When she entered, she was surprised that the room didn't smell worse than it did. The scent of the various spices was still strong enough to overpower most other smells. She could just barely detect a hint of a foreign stench, a metallic odor that did not belong.

The details, as they often did, caught her attention. Some of the jars of spices had been opened and not returned quite correctly. Out of curiosity, Alena approached one of those jars and peeked inside. She couldn't be absolutely certain, but she suspected there was far less of the cinnamon in here than there had been a week ago. The city watch appeared to have helped themselves while they were investigating the crime.

She shook her head. The behavior didn't surprise her. People would take what they could get whenever they had a chance to do so, but she was still disappointed. She had hoped, perhaps, that it would be different with the people whose duty it was to protect the citizens.

But people were people no matter what profession they claimed.

Replacing the cinnamon how she had found it, Alena walked into the back room. Even now, all she could think about was how much blood painted the floor. The human body, it seemed, held far more than she had suspected.

The blood had soaked deep into the wood. Whoever purchased this building would most likely have to tear up the floor and replace the boards.

They would be in for quite a surprise when they did.

Alena forced herself to examine the rest of the room. With the blood such a prominent feature, it was easy to think that was all that mattered. But there were more spices back here, as well as the ledgers for the legitimate business. Alena looked around, noticing that the ledgers were gone. No doubt the city watch would be looking for some motive to explain the grisly murder. But they would find no answers there.

Eventually she turned her attention back to the floor and to the bloodstain. She kneeled down and studied the edges of the floorboards that formed the trap door. There were three places where pools of blood had coagulated across the boards. They were still unbroken.

Alena pushed the switch, opened the trap door, and stepped down. As she descended, she closed the door from below. If anybody happened to come into the shop, it would be far safer to be hidden below than have the trap door hanging open.

She glanced around the small room, already confident that she wouldn't notice anything that she hadn't seen before. The place was untouched since her and Bayt had been below. There wasn't much point in being discriminate. She didn't know what was valuable and what wasn't, so she took as much as she could. She loaded up the sack that she had brought, filling it with papers and gold and anything else that might prove valuable. There were a few knives that she passed over. She was no martial artist and even a quick glance told her that every blade was of inferior quality to the one she carried as a gift from her father.

It didn't take long to clear the small space. It seemed a shame that a man's life amounted to so little when it was over. She still had room left in her sack.

But it would be enough to get her started. Information was a currency more valuable than gold. If she had learned one lesson from Bayt's tutelage, it was that.

It was time to put his knowledge to good use.

17

B randt couldn't decide how he felt about young Niles Arrowood. When Niles said they would begin immediately, it wasn't a figure of speech. He stood up and left the headmaster's office, forcing Brandt to follow.

Outside the door, the headmaster waited for them. Niles took command before Brandt could even open his mouth. "Sergeant Brandt and I are leaving for the day. There's a matter that requires our urgent attention."

Niles spoke as though he expected the headmaster to obey without question. No doubt, the expectation had only been reinforced through a lifetime of permission.

Brandt respected Niles' willingness to jump right to work, but the way he treated others grated on him.

Brandt hadn't grown up with the privileges that Niles enjoyed. His father and mother had both been wage earners, and while Brandt never needed anything more to survive, thanks to the empire's policies, he also never received anything beyond the essentials. That lack of wealth was the primary reason he had joined the military as soon as he was old enough.

The young man had character, but it was buried under years of affluence.

Brandt didn't need to make friends. He only needed information. And who was to say? Perhaps in time the young man would make the Arrowood name synonymous with honor. It hadn't been his father's way, but perhaps Niles could chart a new course.

Brandt shook his head softly, wondering who he was trying to convince.

A few blocks after leaving the academy grounds, Niles came to a sudden stop and turned to face Brandt. Brandt had struggled to keep up with Niles and was grateful for the pause. There was a wary look in the youth's eyes, as though a suspicion had just occurred to him. "How do I know I can trust you?"

Brandt could have given half a dozen reasons, from the blood of his friends on his uniform to the gaping hole that had been in his chest just a week ago. But as he looked at Niles he saw more than simple wariness. He caught a hint of paranoia. "There's nothing I can say that would convince you. You can only decide for yourself. You have enough information to choose."

They stood there, facing each other, as Niles debated with himself. Finally, he gave a small nod. "My father wished for the location of our house to remain a secret. But I believe this action is justified. Follow me, and do as I say."

Brandt bristled at being commanded by a boy, but he held his tongue and followed.

That afternoon was one of the most torturous of Brandt's life. He had been on long marches before, and the wound in his chest was certainly not his first injury. But between having to follow the boy's instructions, the never-ending agony of the still-healing wound, and the ridiculous route they took to their destination, Brandt was surprised he hadn't either passed out from pain or attacked an innocent bystander.

They had walked, then doubled back on themselves. They circled around blocks and stopped at shops for no discernible reason. Brandt caught Niles trying to detect pursuit, but the whole routine felt amateur. Eventually they reached a section of town where Brandt felt right at home, the part of town he would've grown up in had he been born in Landow. This was where the wage earners lived. Simple, small houses clustered closely together.

No wonder Kye had never figured out where the named family lived. It never would've occurred to him to search somewhere like here.

The house Niles led him to was nondescript, with no distinguishing features that Brandt could observe. All in all, it was exactly the sort of house he expected would appeal to a man who did not want to be noticed.

Niles opened the front door and gestured for Brandt to enter. They weren't more than a few steps in when they encountered a woman coming to investigate the visitors. At one point she might have been pretty, but it looked like the years hadn't been kind to her. Brandt figured she wasn't much more than ten years his senior, but she seemed far older.

Brandt offered a small bow. Niles jumped in before the woman could ask a question. He seemed to enjoy speaking first. "Mother, this is Sergeant Brandt of the wolfblades. He was with Father the night he was murdered."

Niles' mother didn't react.

Whatever emotion the woman might have possessed was buried deep.

She didn't even reply. She gave the two of them a small

bow, then turned and retreated into the shadows. For a moment, Brandt wondered if he had imagined the whole encounter.

Brandt turned to Niles. "She has taken the death of your father hard. Does she have friends or family to help her?"

Niles shook his head. "She was like that before Father died. He was not an easy man to live with."

Brandt stared at the space where the woman had stood. The more time he spent around Niles, the better he understood this family. It had all focused on Zane, an overbearing master. What shape would the family take now that Zane was dead? Would Niles make it something more than it had been, or would he let the pull of the past set his course?

Brandt admitted that he was curious, and vowed to do what he might to help the two surviving Arrowoods, little as that might be.

The two of them went deeper into the house into a small study. Papers were scattered all over, and a few books were open to various pages. Brandt took an initial survey of the room, seeing that most of the books had to deal with the lineages of wealthy families in the area.

So Zane had believed much the same as the commander of the city watch. Any warrior with the skill that the bandit possessed had to come from a well-off family. That level of skill didn't develop naturally, but through years of dedicated training. And beyond that, Brandt suspected that the bandit also had a military background. There was a difference between a fighter who had simply trained for battle and a fighter who had experienced the real thing. The bandit fought like one of the latter.

"Your father suspected a wealthy family."

Niles nodded. "He didn't discuss much of the

investigation with me. But I have come to believe that was his suspicion. He had been searching through the houses to find candidates. Unfortunately, he found too many leads. Landow is a wealthy enough city that even with his criteria there were too many suspects to be useful."

Brandt released a small sigh of disappointment. He supposed it would've been too easy to figure the mystery out immediately. But surely Zane had discovered something that would lead Brandt to his next steps.

"Do you know what your father was investigating the day he was murdered?"

Niles nodded. "I do, actually. We spoke that night, not long before he left. When he didn't find a useful lead among the wealthy, he focused on the criminal element within town. My father was searching for a diamond, and he believed that talking to Landow's local smugglers might point him in the right direction."

"And he found something?"

Niles shrugged. "The day he was murdered he found someone who he thought could provide a lead, but he never gave me the name."

Brandt swore softly. "Your father was a paranoid man."

"Apparently not enough, though." Niles shrugged. "But you are right. My father was secretive, and very difficult to work with. He was happiest when he was out on his own, in the middle of the night."

Brandt looked around the room again. He didn't think his answers were in the books or papers. "Can you think of anything that might help me figure out who killed the wolfblades?"

Niles looked thoughtful. "I can't, unfortunately. I would say that we could interview whatever criminal my father spoke to, but I suspect that person is dead, leaving us without a lead."

Brandt frowned. "Why do you say that?"

"Because when my father returned that day, before night fell and he left again, he was more relaxed than usual. The only time he acted like that was after he had taken out his aggression on someone."

Brandt heard the weight of the confession in Niles' voice. The truth was unspoken, but obvious now that Brandt knew to look for it. Niles had been the victim of that aggression more often than not.

Niles was named, and had nearly all the privileges that society could offer. And yet Brandt suspected that his own meager childhood had been far happier than Niles'.

They spent the rest of the afternoon going through Zane's records, but there was little for them to find. Zane had kept plenty of notes, but they appeared to be aids for his memory more than explanations. Without the core set of knowledge that Zane had possessed, the notes were nothing but vague hints.

Brandt hadn't learned as much as he had hoped, but perhaps it would be enough.

Zane had suspected somebody wealthy or noble. He had been so certain of his belief that he had hidden his family in town, rather than permitting them the privileges they were due.

But the most useful clue he possessed when he left was the one that Niles himself had given. The night he died, Zane had already killed someone else.

18

F amily dinners were always a boisterous affair.

Alena blamed Jace. For all his faults, her younger brother was a never-ending fountain of energy, and even though no one in the family could match her brother's outgoing spirit or joyful attitude, there was something about him that rubbed off on the rest of them. They were happiest when Jace entertained them all.

No one in the family was a slouch. Jace and Alena's studies occupied many of their waking hours, and their father hammered away in the smithy almost all day, every day. But at least twice a week, suppers were considered sacrosanct, and nothing short of the gates themselves was permitted as an excuse for missing those meals. Even Father took the time to join, no matter how pressing the projects at the smithy were.

Of the four of them, Alena sometimes thought that her mother was the hardest worker. It wasn't as obvious as with her father and his long absences, but she often ran deliveries for the smithy while maintaining the household.

She was an excellent cook, and there were few experiences as pleasant as stepping through the front door and smelling the warm aromas of that day's culinary efforts.

Their meals tended to pass by quickly. Only Jace didn't pile food into his face, and that was because he was usually too busy regaling them all with some dramatic tale from the academy.

In the past few days, Alena had developed a much deeper appreciation for family meals. She had been reminded, in the most brutal way possible, that life was not an activity that went on forever. In her usual day-to-day, obsessed with her studies and her work out of Bayt's shop, it was sometimes easy to forget that the only resource that mattered was time.

Alena swore she would never take her time for granted again.

She drank deeply of these moments of relaxed and unrestrained pleasure with her family. Some part of her knew that as much as Jace's antics might frustrate her on occasion, if she ever had to live without them her life would be much bleaker.

So she threw herself into meals, laughing at Jace and soaking in her father's stories from the smithy. The apprentices that worked under her father were a fascinating collection of individuals, and Alena was in turn impressed by their skill and horrified by their incompetence, at least as told by her father.

She learned something about her father, though, as she paid more attention to him. He was a demanding man, who asked for nothing less than the best metalwork in town. Even though his apprentices were a source of unending grief, she didn't miss the affectionate smile that he flashed after telling a story. The apprentices failed or succeeded on their own merits, as was their father's way, but he loved them like children.

After one particular meal ended, Alena noticed a silent signal pass between her mother and father. Her mother nodded briefly and asked Jace to help with the cleanup.

Alena saw her father's gaze, and she realized that Mother's request had been planned since before the beginning of the meal. The corner of her father's mouth turned up in a smile. He saw that she noticed. "Let's go to the other room."

Alena followed her father, sitting on the floor as her father took the giant rocking chair that was his own. Her father's father had made it by hand, many decades ago.

"Sometimes you are so observant that it frightens me," her father began.

Alena smiled at that, flush with pride. "Why?"

"Because parents are supposed to know more than their children, and with the way you study the world, I'm afraid it won't be long before you know more than I do."

"Maybe I already do."

Her father laughed at that, a deep-throated chuckle that warmed Alena's heart. "I'm not sure about *that*, but your wits may very well be quicker."

The smile faded from his face and he leaned forward. Alena knew they were about to dive into whatever was worrying him."

"How are you, Alena, truly?"

She'd finally had to break the news about Bayt. She told them her former master was found dead in his shop. No doubt they had heard more from local gossip, but she couldn't be sure. Between the resignations of so many officials and the demise of the wolfblade unit, perhaps the news had never become public.

Either way, she pretended that all she knew was that Bayt had died.

Since then, they had been worried about her, even though she reassured them that she would simply spend more time studying for the upcoming exams. But that didn't stop their fretting, or such meetings with her father.

Alena knew that she couldn't just tell him that everything was fine. His eyes were too sharp, and clearly both he and her mother had sensed something. She didn't know exactly what her father had observed, so she wasn't sure how to ease his mind. "It's been a struggle," she admitted.

Her father waited silently, giving her the space to tell him more.

And how could she not, under that close but loving gaze?

"I think that I've made some mistakes, Father. And it makes me doubt my decisions now. The future... it worries me. At times I think I'm ready to leave this house, but other days I'm not nearly so sure."

She wasn't sure what to say. How else could she frame her problems so that she could benefit from her father's advice, without getting him mixed up in her problems? Her father nodded, as though he understood. "You know, I think sometimes that it is harder for you than it ever was for me," he admitted.

"Really?"

Her father scratched at his beard. "Your grandfather was a smith, and I grew up in his workshop. Blacksmithing was all I knew as a child, even with the education from the empire. I was never as smart as you or Jace, but more importantly, I always knew where my path would lead. What was the point of learning history or philosophy? I knew from the day I first held a hammer that smithing was all I wanted to do."

Alena nodded. Her father worked hard and put in long hours, but she didn't think she had ever seen him happier than when putting the finishing touches on one of his pieces, or presenting them as a gift to someone in the family. He might complain about the long hours and the occasionally terrible conditions, but he was also a man who loved the craft he pursued. Alena suspected it was one of the reasons he was as good at it as he was.

"Jace shares something of that same focus, although his craft will be different. He wants to go into the military, and I'm not sure anything will dissuade him. And honestly, I believe it will be a good place for him. He's young and energetic and quick, and the instructors at the academy tell me that he pursues his physical lessons with diligence. He may not do as well with books as you do, but his gifts lie in a different domain. You are different. I've seen the way that you watch the world since you were a small child, and there is one thing that I have known ever since you were little."

Alena realized that she was leaning forward to catch every word. "What's that?"

"That someday, you were going to leave us. Landow is a decent-sized city, and I'm glad that you and Jace had the opportunity to go to the academy and receive some of the finest learning in the region. But you'll never be satisfied here. You were born for the world."

"But what if I don't pass the university exams?"

"Then you will find another way out. The how does not

worry me. I know that given enough time, you will always solve your problems."

Alena nodded to hide the fact her eyes were watering. "Thank you."

Her father smiled. "No matter what happens, Alena, just know that we always trust in you and believe in you. And you can always come to me if you don't mind the sound of your father going on and on."

Alena nodded, and a sudden thought occurred to her.

Sound. Her father's word stuck in her mind.

She had tried hundreds of ways to break Bayt's code, but she had never thought of sounds.

"You've given me an idea, Father. Thank you."

He grinned, some fatherly pride showing. "Go on, then. I'll distract the others."

Alena went to her room and pulled out a long sample of Bayt's currently unsolvable cipher.

She had tried all sorts of mathematical substitutions, but nothing ever worked. However, she had never tried phonetic decryption.

She started with a simple premise: what if Bayt's cipher wasn't some fancy code, but was instead just a system where he had substituted different symbols for the sounds that they made?

The more she considered it, the more the idea made sense. In written imperial, the same letter could often make different sounds. Assigning a different symbol to each sound would ruin any substitution she tried. She started by highlighting the most common words in the code, matching them to the most common words in imperial. Then she matched the symbols to the phonemes in the imperial words. It required a lot of guesswork, and more than once she had to backtrack and try again. But her premise was quickly proven as she decrypted phrase after phrase.

After that it was just a matter of time.

It was late in the night and she had burned down two candles when she finally finished creating her key.

Now it was time to see what Bayt knew before he died.

19

S ometimes, all it took to unravel a mystery was to find
one thread and pull until the whole shroud fell apart.

Niles' hint, as inconsequential as the youth had
considered it, ended up being the piece of information that
gave Brandt the rest of what he needed. He returned to the
city watch, digging through their records of the past two
weeks. He found the bloody murder of a spice merchant
without problem.

A quick interview with Commander Scot confirmed
Brandt's assumptions. The city watch had long suspected
that Bayt was a key figure involved in illegal smuggling and
other nefarious deeds. But they'd never been able to gather
conclusive proof, and Scot implied the man knew enough to
remain out of sight.

The death of Bayt also coincided with the scandals and
resignations of many officials. It wasn't hard to assume the
events might be linked. Bayt didn't just trade in spices. He
traded in information.

Brandt found Bayt's ledgers and spent the better part of
a day paging through them. The man had worked with

three apprentices, and one name stuck out among them: Alena, the only girl.

Brandt had a clear memory of the girl from the night of the fight. Perhaps it was coincidence, but he didn't think so. There were no coincidences, not in his life.

The next question was how to find her. The city kept no official records of its citizens. But the girl had been young, perhaps young enough to still be attending academy. She might be at another school, or make her living as an apprentice, but Brandt didn't think so.

His assumption was nothing more than a hunch, but it felt right.

After all, there were no coincidences.

He returned to Landow Academy and asked to meet the headmaster. Ignoring the man's angry glares, Brandt asked if he could see the student roster. The headmaster complained but complied.

Sure enough, there she was. An Alena, on university track.

Brandt thanked the headmaster and left without another word. That afternoon he waited outside the academy as it let out. He had dressed in inconspicuous clothes to better blend in with the crowds.

He spotted her without a problem, the mere sight of her causing his fist to clench. It was the girl from his memory. She had been involved, and he would find out the truth of what had happened that night.

He waited until she walked past him, then turned and followed. He had no specific plan. All he knew was that he wanted to question her. He tailed her as she walked toward one of the nicer neighborhoods in town.

Then she disappeared.

He blinked, trying to understand what had happened.

A cart had passed between them, and after, she was gone, as though she'd never existed. He spun around, but couldn't see her anywhere.

Then he heard a voice behind him. She was trying to sound tough, but a slight tremble in her voice gave her away. "It's rude to follow someone."

She had long, dark hair and full lips. But Brandt was drawn immediately to her eyes. They were as sharp as his sword, and they missed nothing. He could see the fear within them, though. Alena *was* tough, but the events of the last two weeks had strained her. They weren't the eyes of a killer.

His gut told him that she was innocent of the worst of the crimes. "I want to know what happened the night my wolfblades were killed."

Those sharp eyes studied him for a moment. Most days, Brandt realized he expected the authority inherent in his position to be enough. It worked with the headmaster, as well as Commander Scot. This girl didn't seem to hold the same respect for authority, though. She would choose to trust him based on her own assessment.

She gestured toward a nearby teahouse. "You're buying."

Not long after they sat at a table in the corner of the teahouse, partially hidden from most of the other patrons. Brandt noticed that Alena's eyes never rested long in one place. No wonder he hadn't been able to follow her without being discovered. She possessed the skills Niles someday hoped to have.

Alena poured herself a cup of tea, her hands only betraying a slight tremor. It was some of the most expensive there. She took a deep sip, then met his gaze. "How much do you know?"

"Assume I know nothing."

"An easy assumption."

The words were biting, but the tone was not. The girl was quick-witted and probably couldn't help it. Her blush of embarrassment was proof enough of that.

Suddenly, Brandt missed his fellow wolfblades. Their banter had drawn them together. Once a warrior reached a certain status, others tended to treat them with deference. The military thrived on the system, but without peers to keep one in check, the deference could go to one's head.

Alena eased that burden, just a little. Without further prompting, she launched into her story, beginning with her apprenticeship with Bayt.

Another full pot of tea later, she finished. Her head was down, her gaze focused on the table between them. "Ryder saved my life."

Brandt fought the storm of emotions battering his calm facade. Ryder could be a pain, but he had always had his heart in the right place. Like everyone else, he was gone now, in no small part due to the actions of this girl.

Brandt wanted to hit her and comfort her at the same time. She was a thief, yes, but perhaps it was more accurate to say that she had been playing at being a thief. She was foolish, but wise enough to recognize her own foolishness.

He was so distracted he didn't realize that he hadn't responded to her. He'd let the silence stretch between them.

"What will you do?" she asked.

He wasn't sure. He was well within his rights to kill her and be done with the matter. She had freely confessed to crimes punishable by death.

But he didn't think she had told him everything.

More than that, his people had died trying to save her life. To kill her now seemed disrespectful to their memories.

Uncertain, he turned the question back on the girl. "What will *you* do?"

She looked up. "If you allow me to live, I plan on finding out who the bandit is. If Niles finds out about my involvement, he will kill me. The only way to save myself is to uncover the truth."

"And how will you accomplish that?" The girl might be clever, but why would she succeed where so many others had failed?

"Bayt wasn't just a thief and a smuggler. He collected information, as well. I'm hoping that some of that information will guide me."

Brandt leaned back and sipped at his tea. He decided he didn't want to kill the girl. It was nothing but noting the feelings in his body. His wolfblades had died for her. Mistaken or not, their fates had been set before this meeting even began. "How can I help?"

"What do you know? Right now, I have a pile of information, but without context, I don't know what to search for."

"Not enough. I suspect that he comes from wealth. His martial skill must have required years of dedicated training."

"Why not just a soldier?"

"I think he *has* served. But his skill goes far beyond what the military provides. I'd also like to believe I would have heard of such skill if he was still in the military. He's more than talented enough to join the ranks of the wolfblades. I imagine he served for a year or two, then left."

"And he has a stone affinity."

"Beyond compare."

Alena chewed on her lower lip. "That can't leave too many people in town."

"But hard to find."

"Maybe. I'll begin searching. How can I find you?"

"Meet here? Every afternoon after academy?"

Alena thought about it for a moment, then nodded. "I'll start looking tonight, and I'll tell you what I find."

"Thank you."

She gave him a wry smile. "You're the one letting me live. I should be thanking you."

She stood up and gave him a sloppy bow. "So thank you."

Brandt watched her walk down the street and vanish in the crowd.

An interesting young woman indeed.

20

A lena's heart pounded as she walked away from the teahouse. With every breath she had taken near the wolfblade, she had expected to feel the burning agony of cold steel through her chest.

She was the reason Brandt's closest friends were dead. They both knew it. She swore she could see the knowledge haunting his decisions, a darkness deep behind his gaze.

The death blow had never come. As she retreated from the teahouse she kept checking behind her, trying to see if she was being followed. He hadn't been very good at it the first time, but perhaps he had intended for her to notice him.

She didn't observe anyone following, and in time, she gradually relaxed.

When she was completely sure she was out of his sight, she collapsed onto a bench and closed her eyes. She heard concerned murmurs from passersby, but she ignored them. She took deep breaths in through her nose, wishing for a chance to go back a few weeks and make different decisions.

In time, the feeling of being overwhelmed receded.

What was done was done. The past couldn't be changed. She opened her eyes and stood up, rejuvenated by a fresh burst of determination.

She took a long route home, making sure, once again, that she wasn't being followed. Perhaps she was too cautious, but right now, no amount of caution seemed unreasonable.

Once home, Alena went straight to her room and pulled out all the papers she had acquired from Bayt's shop. She had cracked the cypher, and was gradually becoming able to read it.

Reading and writing languages came easily to her. Her memory was excellent, and memorizing the cypher proved to be little problem. She still got stuck on occasion, but her progress was quick.

Bayt's papers had been far more organized than she had first imagined. On her desk she had sorted them into piles. The largest pile, by far, was focused on various people, unofficial biographies that Bayt had collected over time. Other stacks dealt with resources, locations, and legends. As Alena categorized the papers, she learned more about the man she had called master.

Bayt had apparently never met a piece of information he wasn't interested in. His notes were well-organized, with small, neat handwriting. She hadn't thought Bayt possessed much, but as she organized her stash, she came to understand Bayt had collected an enormous amount of information over the years. Not a single word was wasted in the notes, making each paper a literal treasure trove.

Alena turned her attention to the pile of papers that dealt with people. Within the stack, the papers were organized by location, so it didn't take long for her to find the stack of papers dealing with citizens of Landow.

She began to read, separating the papers into new, smaller piles. One was for people meeting one of Brandt's criteria. Another was for people meeting more than one.

The sun went down, and Alena lit a candle to work by. She heard her father come home from the smithy. On his way to bed he paused outside her door, no doubt wondering why she was still awake. He didn't knock, though, and eventually continued on to his room.

Alena took some of her own notes to pass on to Brandt, then went to bed and fell immediately asleep.

The next morning, Jace gave her a strange look as he saw the piles of paper with bizarre scribbles across them. She rolled her eyes at his questions, though, which silenced them quickly enough.

She struggled to keep her mind on her studies all day. The far more interesting problem was the identity of the masked bandit. Alena forced herself to sit through history, leaving only when the others did.

Like her, Niles still attended academy. He had many of the same classes as her, and he didn't seem to be struggling with his studies. In fact, he appeared more focused than ever. His father's death had motivated him, more than Alena gave him credit for. His focus reminded her she needed to work just as hard to avoid him. It hadn't taken Brandt long to find her. How long would it be until Niles was in front of her, demanding justice for his father?

After the final session of the day, Alena made her way to the teahouse, once again ensuring that she wasn't being followed. Brandt was already there.

She didn't feel the same fear she had yesterday. He didn't seem to be duplicitous. His actions reflected his words. For now, at least, she was safe.

One troubling thought passed through her mind,

though. What would happen when the bandit was unmasked and she was no longer useful to him?

He didn't seem like the type of man to exact such a coldhearted revenge, but there wasn't any way to tell. Not until it was too late.

Alena pushed her concerns aside. She handed Brandt her notes. "I'm about halfway through the citizens of Landow. I don't think anyone here is who we are looking for, but these are the closest matches I've found so far. I wanted you to have them, in case something stood out."

Brandt looked through the papers. His eyebrows rose as he read. "This is... thorough."

"Bayt's systems were more impressive than even I realized."

Brandt nodded. "I see."

There wasn't much else to discuss. Alena wanted to return to her research, eager to solve the problem. From the way Brandt kept looking out the window of the teahouse, he wanted to pursue some of the new leads she'd just handed him. She left as soon as their first pot of tea was finished.

Back at home, she returned to her papers, losing herself in the task. She didn't even realize the sun was setting until she noticed she was having trouble making out the words of Bayt's notes. She lit a candle and once again lost herself in focus.

Alena didn't stir again until she heard a knock on her door. She turned around to see the shadows of a pair of feet underneath her door. "Come in," she said.

She made no move to hide her work. The easiest way to arouse suspicion was to act as though there was something to hide.

Her father stepped in, a candle in his hand. His eyes

took in the piles of papers on her desk. "You've been up late."

Alena nodded. "There's been a lot to do, lately."

Her father's smile told her that he recognized the evasion for what it was. He came into her room and sat on the edge of her bed, the frame creaking as he rested on it. He put his candle off to the side and looked at her. Alena could tell he had something on his mind, but wasn't quite sure how to say it.

Finally, he spoke. "I'm not a fool, you know."

Alena grinned, even though her heart was beating faster. "Trust me, I know."

"I know Bayt was up to something, something that probably ended up getting him killed. And I don't believe for a moment you don't know something about it. I haven't said anything because I don't want your mother to worry, but I'm afraid for you."

He had guessed far more than she suspected. Alena closed her eyes and took a deep breath. Everywhere she turned, the walls were closing in on her. How long would it be before one collapsed with her underneath?

She forced herself to open her eyes and meet his gaze.

"Alena. You know how much I love you, right?"

She nodded, surprised by the sudden appearance of tears coming down her cheek.

"You know that I would do anything for you?"

She nodded again, then stepped over to the bed, sitting next to him and burying her head in his chest. His strong arms wrapped around her, holding her tight, protecting her against the world.

Alena realized then she hadn't cried, not really. Everything she had been holding in suddenly exploded out of her. She sobbed silently, her tears soaking through her father's thick shirt.

He said nothing, just holding her there. She could hear his heart in his chest, slow and steady like the falling of his smith's hammer. She felt his strength, not just in his arms but in the tempo of his pulse.

Their candles had burned low by the time Alena's distress finally eased. She rubbed her face in her father's chest, causing him to chuckle. Then she finally leaned away from him.

As tempted as she was, she didn't dare tell him what had happened. The more he knew, he more he and others were at risk.

"Thank you," she said.

He laid his hand on her shoulder, missing nothing. "Are you in danger?"

"Maybe. I'm trying to get out of it."

"Is there anything I can do?"

"Don't let Mother and Jace know."

He stiffened at that, and she spoke quickly to reassure him. "It's safer for you all the less you know. I couldn't live, knowing anyone else got hurt because of a mistake I made."

Her father thought about it for a moment. "Your mother thinks you are stressed because of the upcoming tests. Jace hasn't noticed a thing, nor do I think he will."

"Thank you."

Her father stood up and moved toward the door. Alena started. "That's it?"

He gave a small shrug. "You're nearly an adult, and smarter than most. If there's anything else you want me to know, now's the time. But as I said, I trust you, no matter how afraid for you I am."

His trust felt completely unearned. After all that she had

done, how could he still trust her? Yet he was willing to walk away, even knowing the depth of trouble his oldest child faced. Her tears started again. "You know that no matter what happens, I love you, right?"

He grinned. "I know. And I know you'll figure it out. If there's anything you need, just let me know."

He closed the door behind him, leaving Alena alone once again. She looked over to her desk, where the knife he had given her rested.

His visit and his trust renewed her focus. She returned to her desk, determined to see if the answers they sought were in Bayt's papers.

Near the bottom of the pile, she found an interesting candidate. He had grown up heir to a fortune, although it looked as though that fortune had been lost when the man was young. There was a long gap of time in Bayt's notes — her former master had been unable to discover much until the young man had joined the military. In the military, he had been commended many times, more than any of the other soldiers Alena had studied over the past two days. Had the man remained in the military, Alena suspected he would be far up the chain of command.

There was no mention of an affinity, but there were plenty of rumors. Bayt had put question marks all around the man's notes.

Her eyes traveled upward, searching for the name.

Despite his exemplary service, the emperor had never granted the man's family a name. And yet, Alena recognized the individual in an instant.

It was Kye, the governor of the region.

21

Brandt set aside the papers Alena had given him and rubbed his eyes. She had provided him with nearly a dozen names, and he had tracked down two on the list that seemed like potential matches.

He'd ruled both men out quickly. One limped from an old injury, and the other was far shorter than the criminal had been.

He didn't despair. He hadn't found the murderer yet, but he was closing in. Bayt's information was good. Both of the men Brandt interviewed were former soldiers with stone affinities.

Brandt was no stranger to patience. The life of a wolfblade was often one that demanded both haste and prolonged waiting. If he investigated just a few names on the list every day, he was confident he would uncover the bandit.

He glanced at the papers again. The information within was powerful. Leveraged correctly, it could make its owner both wealthy and influential. When all this was over, it made sense to confiscate everything from Alena.

He rolled his head in a circle, loosening the tight muscles in his neck. He was putting off the other task he had to do today, and he knew it. Delay wouldn't make it any easier.

Brandt threw on a cloak and stepped out into the streets, heading in the direction of the academy.

His wound continued to heal. Thanks to plenty of rest and light movement, he was nearly back to full health. His chest still bothered him at times, but he was almost ready for another fight.

Like his body, life in Landow slowly returned to normal. The streets were filling up with people again, and every day that passed without incident helped citizens to delude themselves into thinking they were safe.

Safety was an illusion, though. Waking up was a risk. Accidents, illness, and age threatened everyone with every step. But most willfully ignored the fact.

Brandt envied them. He had seen the gates, and thought about them nearly every day. He often imagined what it would be like to enjoy the simplicity of most people's lives, worrying about trivial matters.

Brandt reached the academy just before it let out for the day. He waited as students filed past him, most of them even more carefree than the adults he'd so recently been jealous of.

He watched Alena walk by, but although she no doubt noticed him, she gave no indication of having recognized him. He was here looking for another student.

Niles saw him as he left the academy. The young man's face seemed set in a perpetual frown.

"May I walk with you for a few moments?" Brandt asked.

Niles nodded. "What progress has been made?"

Brandt was relieved that he had something to report. "I

believe that I am getting closer. I've been able to narrow down a list of suspects, and it will only be a matter of time."

Niles couldn't hide the edge of desperation in his voice. "Let me help you. I want to be there when you capture him."

Brandt shook his head. He understood the boy's desire, but he couldn't allow it.

Niles looked like he was about to argue, but he backed down. Brandt was disappointed, in a way. He suspected Niles had been beaten down so often by his father he wasn't quite used to standing up to authority, yet.

Brandt stopped and turned to face him. "You'll have vengeance. I won't stop until I've found him."

He could tell Niles wanted to believe him, but didn't want to get his hopes up too high. If he was in the boy's shoes, he'd feel the same, he supposed.

Brandt looked around and noticed they weren't even walking in the direction of Niles' house. "Did you move?"

Niles shook his head. "I have an appointment with the governor this afternoon. He wants to speak about the investigation, and about what he can do for my family. He's been very supportive."

Brandt felt a pang of regret. Kye had asked him to report back with any findings, but he'd held off until he had something solid. "Will you pass on what I told you? I want him to know that I think I'm getting close."

Niles nodded. "I will."

Niles made to leave, but Brandt held him back for a moment. "There's something else." He handed Niles a sealed letter.

"What's this?"

"A letter of acceptance into the wolfblade training cadre. I wrote to my commanding officer, and this just came in reply."

Niles looked at the letter like he wasn't sure what to make of it.

"The choice is yours," Brandt said. "Training and acceptance are two different accomplishments. But if you want the best martial training in the empire, it's found here. And it will give you a reason to leave the horrors of this town behind."

Niles nodded. He offered Brandt a short bow. "Thank you for everything you have done."

Brandt offered an even deeper bow. "I lost my own friends. It's the least I could do."

He watched Niles as the young man continued down the street alone. Niles' meeting looked to be at the governor's personal mansion, given the direction he was traveling.

After a few moments, Brandt turned and began his daily trip to the teahouse.

Alena had beaten him there, but he hadn't expected much else. From the look on her face, though, he immediately realized something was wrong.

He didn't even have to ask. She launched right in. "How loyal of a servant of the empire are you, Brandt?"

His answer was immediate. "I would give my life for the empire."

It wasn't an empty phrase. The empire had made him into the warrior he was. Everything he owned or had earned was a result of the empire. Its rules were strict, but those who obeyed lived contented lives.

"I think I know who the bandit is."

"Who?"

She didn't answer, her eyes darting anywhere in the room except to him. She took deep sips of her tea, but she couldn't be thirsty after all that she had consumed already.

The serving staff hadn't even had time to remove the first pot yet.

"Alena, you can tell me."

Anger built inside him. His friends had died, and now his loyalty was being questioned?

She finally looked straight at him. "It's Kye."

Brandt shook his head. "He's been nothing but helpful since I got here."

Alena pulled a sheet of paper from her pocket, unfolded it, and spun it so that it was facing him. "I copied everything from Bayt's notes, word for word. This isn't my summary."

Brandt read through the page. Kye had been the third son of a wealthy family. Some rumors indicated the family was on the verge of being named. But then a disaster had befallen them. Bayt hadn't been able to find out what it was. Whatever the case, it was well-hidden, and over two decades ago. No one knew. Kye disappeared from the public's attention for a long time, only showing up again when he began his military service.

Brandt glanced through the notes Bayt had made. The man's information was extensive.

He wasn't surprised Kye had a history of military service. Most governors did. Military service proved an individual's dedication to the empire and served as a proving ground for leadership skills. Kye had been appointed governor of the region after a series of particularly nasty border encounters with the Falari. Brandt had actually been at one of the battles described, near the beginning of his service. Those were memories he'd rather forget.

"There's no mention of a stone affinity."

"Keep reading."

Brandt read down to the bottom of the page. There were

a few quotes from fellow officers within. As he read, he understood Alena's concern.

Kye had never done anything to attract much attention in regards to affinities. It was, instead, a series of small events at crucial moments. An enemy soldier losing his footing as he was about to strike. A stone rockslide giving away the position of an opponent. Nothing that by itself would raise an eyebrow.

But put together, the way Bayt had here, the conclusion was inescapable.

Kye possessed a strong stone affinity.

And he had hidden it.

Brandt passed the paper back. He had seen enough.

The evidence was there, but he still wasn't sure that he believed. There was another question that didn't have an answer. "Why go to all this trouble? He's the governor, and the only one in this region who could order the wolfblades about."

Alena shrugged. "I only know what Bayt wrote. But if I had to guess, Kye wanted the diamond for himself, not for the empire."

They sat in silence.

"What do we do?" Alena asked softly.

Brandt didn't know the answer to that. If her research was right, then what could he do? He couldn't arrest the governor without better evidence than this.

He wasn't even sure he could arrest the governor. The man was substantially stronger than him, both in terms of stature and martial ability.

Then another thought turned over in his head. Niles. Right now, he was meeting with Kye, reporting that Brandt was close to finding the bandit.

Kye knew they were coming.

Alena, missing nothing, noticed the change in his demeanor. "What?"

He didn't want to worry her, but she would recognize a lie. "I think Kye will know he's almost been discovered."

"So if we're going to act, it needs to be now."

Brandt nodded, his decision made. "I will call him out, outside of the city. And I will kill him."

"Even if it costs your life?" There was no concern in her tone, just a statement of fact.

"Yes. It will end the search for you, and I'll be able to join my friends on the other side of the gate. They deserve as much."

She shook her head. "I can't believe you have faith in that foolishness."

"It's not foolishness. I've seen the gate. Death doesn't frighten me anymore."

Her glare was hard. Brandt couldn't tell if she wanted to call him a fool or if she wanted to share in his belief. His tone gave her pause, though.

"It's time for you to leave, Alena. This is my burden to carry from here." He bowed deeply, his head nearing the table they sat at. "Thank you for helping me find who was responsible."

Alena appeared torn for a few moments. No doubt, she had hoped for some different ending. He hoped she would find a new purpose to her life.

Finally, she stood, casting another uncertain look back at him. With a final shake of her head, she left the teahouse without another word.

Brandt watched her go, wishing her the best.

He would find some paper and send the governor a message.

It was time to end this.

22

She should be overjoyed.

In a single stroke, Brandt had volunteered to lift the burden from her shoulders. If he killed Kye, her problems would be over. Even Niles would end his search if the bandit was unmasked. The wolfblade had solved all her problems for her.

She couldn't accept it, though. She had done nothing useful for him. Despite his kind words, all she had done was steal Bayt's information and decipher it. It was hardly the sort of effort that deserved such a sacrifice.

She thought she understood Brandt. Those he cared about had been taken from him. He didn't hold the attachment to life that bound so many. He probably saw this as a way to finish everything cleanly.

And he was right. He just had to kill Kye in the process.

The problem was, she couldn't believe it would work.

She didn't believe in any solution that she wasn't involved in. It wasn't that she didn't trust Brandt, it was just that the only way to guarantee that a task got done the right way was to do it yourself. How many times had each of her parents hammered home that lesson? If she wasn't involved, it would all go wrong.

At the very least, she could see everything through to the end, she supposed. Then she would know her living nightmare was over.

The simplest method forward would be to follow Brandt. The wolfblade paid attention to his surroundings, but not the same way she had been trained to. Brandt looked for threats, for problems on the horizon. He wouldn't notice her.

After she passed out of sight of the teahouse, she quickly turned and ran, circling the block and coming at it from a different direction. She found a shadowed alcove where she could watch the entrance and she melted into it.

She didn't have long to wait for Brandt. She followed at a respectable distance, trailing him into a nicer, more commercial area of town. He stepped into an inn, and Alena again found a quiet place to stand and watch.

She was in luck. Brandt had a room that opened out onto the street, and she was able to watch him sit down and begin to write.

So he would be sending a letter, then. A smart decision. It forced Kye to react. Brandt could choose the time and the place of the fight.

He would fight at night, away from civilians. It provided the best opportunity to minimize interference.

In other words, she had time. She could sit and watch him all afternoon and into the evening, but she suspected he would stay put. He seemed like a man who had no problem waiting in one place, like a predator silently preparing to spring on its prey.

If that was the case, she planned on spending the time

with her family. Missing any supper would raise questions, so it was better to be present.

She returned home, surprised to find that even Jace's antics upon her return didn't bother her quite as much. He meant well, even if he couldn't control himself.

Her mother's stew was excellent, and her father had come home as well. Jace spent most of the meal regaling them all with the tale of how he outsmarted his writing instructor. Alena sometimes secretly envied her brother's stories. In her world, she went to class, learned what she needed to know, and prepared for university exams.

In Jace's world, school was an epic battlefield, where friendships were made and lost, and knowledge was only gained after literal blood was shed. Comparing their retellings of their day would lead most to believe they attended completely different academies.

If the military rejected Jace, Alena supposed he could always be one of the oral storytellers that graced taverns and street corners. In Jace's world, even a trip to the market became a tale straight out of legend.

Most days she found Jace obnoxious. Alena preferred simple facts. Storytelling, especially the way Jace engaged in it, somehow seemed less honest to her.

Tonight, Jace's stories moved her. She cheered as he finally won over the student a level ahead of him. She worried what his instructor would do when she found out one of Jace's closest friends had cheated on an exam. Jace's stories carried her away, at least for a while, into a different world.

And she loved him for it.

She helped clean after the meal while her father and brother went to go play a game of stones in the other room. Jace always got handily defeated by Father, who didn't play down to any opponent. But the defeats only encouraged him further. Jace could be obnoxious, but even Alena had to admit that when he set his sights on a goal, he never wavered.

She tried to memorize everything, from the look on her mom's face as she spoke about her own day, to the knowing grin her father flashed as Jace made a foolish move on the board. She even tried to imprint the smell of the stew.

This was home, and it was good.

She was resolved. Tonight she would watch Brandt's final act, because she knew it couldn't be anything else. Then she would return home and throw herself into studying for the university exams. They were only three weeks away, but she would be the most prepared any student had ever been.

She bid her family goodnight, then walked to her room. The night was young, but between her father and mother, the rest of the family had a practice of waking up before the rising of the sun.

While she waited for her family to fall safely asleep, Alena prepared for the night ahead. She wanted to be ready for anything. Her father's knife was strapped to her hip, hidden by her clothing but easy to reach. She brought a set of lockpicks Bayt had given her early on in her apprenticeship. A mask covered most of her face, except for her eyes.

She was as ready as she ever would be.

When she was sure her family was asleep, she snuck out the window and onto the streets below. She pulled her mask down, so as not to arouse suspicion.

It didn't take her long to reach the inn where Brandt lived. She breathed a short sigh of relief to see that he was still within. The window had been covered, but she could see light and movement inside. She suspected he prepared for the fight ahead. She settled in to wait.

Eventually the light winked out with surprising quickness, and a few moments later, Brandt left the building. Alena pulled up her mask and melted into the shadows.

Following him turned out to be an easy task. He never once looked behind him. His eyes and his steps were focused forward, to the battle ahead.

She'd never seen this side of the wolfblade. Given who he was, she'd never doubted his strength or ability, but it was something different to see it with her own eyes. Despite his kindness, Brandt was a man who killed for a living, and he planned to do so tonight, even if it cost him his life.

They left town. Brandt passed through the gates, his uniform allowing him to exit without question. Alena used her lightness to climb over the wall about a hundred paces away from the gate, passing just behind a couple of sentries as they made their rounds. She landed softly outside the walls, a sense of exhilaration coursing through her. She rarely left Landow, and never for reasons as compelling as this.

Alena followed Brandt into the woods.

23

B randt paused outside the town, bending down to light a torch from his pack. He didn't have any problem walking through the woods at night. Both moons were high in the sky, reflecting plenty of light to see by. The fire was for him to fight with.

He held the torch close to his face, hearing the song clearly. Perhaps it was just his imagination, but he thought the song was sharper than it had been in the past, the flickering notes more distinct.

He pulled a bit of the flame away from the torch, letting it dance in the air. He flicked it from side to side in front of him, testing his control. The flame was his element, obeying even the slightest whim of his will. He returned the ball of flame to the torch. No point in wasting any of it, he supposed.

He walked on, deeper into the woods. He had asked for the meeting at the place where they had first fought, when Zane Arrowood had stolen the diamond from the smugglers on the road.

His heartbeat was steady as he walked, even though he

suspected it was to his doom. For weeks now, he had considered how he might beat the bandit if it came to another fight. He had only come up with one thought, and he had no idea if it would work in practice. But he wouldn't fail to kill Kye. He needed to, both for his wolfblades and for Alena. Perhaps she would make something meaningful with her second chance.

He looked forward to seeing his friends again. He would give everything he had tonight, if only to avenge them. Surely that would be enough to put their spirits to rest.

Brandt's chest ached as he walked. He'd pushed himself hard in his room, testing the limits of his mobility and strength. He could move well enough, but he was doomed in a sword fight.

He didn't think that would matter. Against Kye, it would turn into a battle of affinities. Brandt already knew he couldn't fight Kye with a sword.

It didn't take him much longer to reach the meeting ground he had chosen. The spot was only half a league outside of town, and easy enough to reach. He was early, so he jammed the torch into the ground next to the road, sat down, closed his eyes, and meditated, listening to the sounds of the world around him.

He didn't know how much time passed before he heard someone approach. A single pair of feet, walking confidently towards him. Brandt opened his eyes and saw Kye step into the circle of fire left by the torch.

The governor looked at the torch with disdain. When he glanced back at Brandt, there was a knowledge in his eyes. But he didn't try to snuff out the torch, as he might have.

Brandt wasn't sure why Kye didn't try to seize every possible advantage, but he didn't question his good fortune.

"Your commander told me that you were stubborn, but I never expected this," Kye said.

"Why did you kill them?" It was the only question Brandt cared about. "If you wanted the diamond, all you had to do was ask."

Kye shook his head and studied the forest around them, as though suspicious of a trap. "I tried to keep you away. I sent you into the mountains, even though I knew they would try to smuggle it past Zane. If you'd listened to my orders, your friends would still be alive."

The words pierced him, sharper even than Kye's stone blade.

That was why Kye's orders had made no sense.

Brandt's perspective of the last couple of weeks shifted. Kye had been trying to protect them.

"But why kill them?"

"You left me no choice. I'm strong, and I could have fought off the guards and Zane, but when you ordered the wolfblades to attack, what else could I do? There's far more at stake here than you can possibly imagine."

"Then tell me."

Kye shook his head. "You can't help my cause, so there is no point."

"You betrayed the empire!"

Kye chuckled then, a soft sound that carried more sadness than humor in it. It caught Brandt off guard. "Far from it, actually. But I suppose it means little."

A stone floated in the air between them. Shards flaked away until it became as sharp as a blade. It turned until it was pointed at Brandt's chest. "For what it's worth, I am sorry," Kye said. "Please let your friends know when you pass the gate."

The rock shot at Brandt, but he twisted, letting the rock fly past him.

There was no point in testing Kye, trying to find the extent of his skill. Brandt already knew he was far outclassed. He only hoped his last idea would work.

It had been inspired by some of his earliest grappling lessons as a child.

How did you submit an opponent much stronger than you?

You turned their strength against them.

Brandt remembered trying to pull the heat from Kye's body in their last encounter. He remembered how it had been like drinking from a bottomless well.

While they had been speaking, Brandt had focused on Kye's heat, hearing the whisper of it within.

He suspected the bladed stone would stop and make another pass soon. He couldn't dodge for long.

So he pulled, as hard as he could, with every bit of his will.

It worked. Sweat dripped from Brandt's forehead, and the moisture dripping into the wound on his chest caused it to burn with agony.

Kye shook his head, as though disappointed Brandt would try the same technique twice.

Then Brandt pushed Kye's stolen heat into the torch.

The whole clearing lit up as the flame expanded. The torch had been propped up between them, and a wall of fire now separated them.

Brandt looked at the fire in awe. He heard its song, loud and clear and joyful. The flame was unleashed and powerful. It wanted more, but fire always wanted more.

Distracted, he didn't notice the stone until it struck him

in the back. But the strike was weak, the stone not even hitting him with the sharp end.

Brandt's trick had distracted Kye as well.

He focused, pushing the wall of fire at Kye. He couldn't let the governor recover.

Brandt couldn't see the governor's reaction thanks to the flame, but he heard the shifting of what sounded like a massive amount of stone, and he felt the rumble beneath his feet.

The wall of fire split as it ran into two slabs of stone, lifted from deep below the trail. As the fire passed over the stone, the stones separated and Kye stepped through.

Brandt grimaced. Kye's clothing smoked, but he was otherwise unharmed. "Clever," the governor observed.

Brandt kept pulling. He couldn't have sustained a wall of fire like that for more than a heartbeat on his own. But he used Kye's strength. Perhaps he could find the bottom of this endless well and freeze Kye in place. But lacking that, he would steal every scrap of power he could.

Brandt focused the wall of energy, creating two balls of flame. He sent one overhead while another flew straight at Kye.

Kye responded by moving the slabs, walls of stone as tall as he was. He lifted one overhead while the other blocked the ball of flame coming at him.

Fire was one of the strongest elements, but it wasn't enough to destroy such a massive amount of stone. Given enough time and focus, Brandt could melt those slabs, but he didn't think he would have that much time.

His guess was confirmed when Kye threw the slab of stone that had been hovering above him. Brandt's only option was to dive, rolling to the side.

The slab crashed into the spot where Brandt had stood,

a thunderous crack that shook the surrounding area. Brandt hit the ground hard, another wave of agony emanating from his chest.

Brandt held onto his focus, barely. But it required all his attention.

He slammed the second ball of fire down, but the first stone slab snapped overhead, faster than Brandt could believe. The fireball broke apart, and Brandt desperately seized at one of the flaming chunks, funneling all the stolen energy he could into it, building yet another fireball.

He couldn't comprehend Kye's strength. Even as he pulled, Kye had enough power to hold enormous stones in the air using only his will. It was so far beyond anything that should be possible he didn't even try to find an explanation. He just kept pulling, building another fireball, growing it in the sky as fast as he could.

He would reach a limit soon. Fire could be sustained with energy, but the bigger it became, the more energy it required. Brandt was still the weak link. The heat had to pass through him, and there was only so much his body could handle.

But he wouldn't allow Kye to win this fight.

He was so distracted by the creation of his fireball that it took him a few heartbeats to realize a stone blade was held at his neck.

Kye's voice was soft. "Stop this, now."

"I'm going to kill you."

"No, you won't. All you'll do is set the forest on fire and endanger the town. You can't control a blast that size. You're already near your limit."

Brandt screamed. The amount of heat coursing through his body was all he could think about. It was so much.

But some part of him knew Kye was right. He had been doomed from the start.

He stared at the fire, a huge inferno raging high above the tree tops. If it came down, Kye's prediction would certainly come true. He might avenge his friends, but they wouldn't welcome him if it came at the cost of the town.

He hated himself, but he let go.

The raging fire, suddenly deprived of the energy it used as fuel, vanished in the blink of an eye, casting them into darkness. Brandt slumped over, defeated in more ways than one.

He was surprised when Kye lit Brandt's torch without a fire starter. That was a fire affinity, and a fairly advanced one at that.

Kye sat down beside the defeated warrior, placing the torch between them. The governor studied Brandt, as though deciding something. Brandt couldn't imagine what. The stone knife remained pressed against his neck, his death one sudden movement away.

Something had changed in the governor's demeanor. He'd been ready to kill Brandt a moment ago, but now, something stayed his hand.

"Which one of Bayt's apprentices helped you?"

Brandt couldn't hide the surprise on his face.

Kye sighed. "It's the only explanation. The man was better at gathering information than anyone I've ever met. I've hired his services on occasion myself. It makes sense he would have trained some or all of the apprentices. It's the only way you could have figured out as much as you did so quickly."

Brandt opened his mouth to answer, then shut it. He frowned. For a moment, he had *wanted* to answer. Why would he? "Leave them out of this. They made a mistake they don't deserve punishment for."

An unreadable expression passed over Kye's face. "My secrets can't be allowed to escape. Not yet. Who is it? I'll find out soon enough."

More than anything, Brandt wanted to tell Kye everything. He wanted to explain how Alena was innocent enough, and how she wouldn't tell anyone if she was just given the chance. Kye seemed terribly understanding, and there wasn't any doubt he would accept Brandt's word on the matter.

He grimaced, shaking his head. That didn't make sense, either. If he gave Kye Alena's name she would be dead before the sun rose. What was he thinking? "I won't tell you."

Kye's eyes narrowed at that. "You have an impressive will."

Kye pulled a stone from his pocket.

The diamond.

It was so close, but Brandt had no desire for it.

"These are remarkable, you know. Do you even know what it is?"

Brandt shook his head.

"A pity. They're going to change the world someday. They'll burn the empire, but the nation that rises from the ashes will be so much stronger, so much better prepared for the future."

Brandt was suddenly tired, a bone-deep exhaustion far beyond the rigors of the battle he'd just endured. Kye sat next to him, but Brandt couldn't even summon the energy to draw his sword and send them both to the gates. He didn't want to.

Kye put the stone back. "It's taught me, too. More is possible than we even dream."

Kye stood up and brushed off his clothes. "The guard will be here soon, no doubt drawn by your impressive display." He gave Brandt a curious look. "I've heard you once fought the fever after battle. Tell me, did you see the gate?"

Brandt thought the question strange, but he wanted to answer. "Yes."

"Did you touch it?"

Brandt shook his head.

"Pity." Kye studied Brandt. "I'm going to let you live. I think she would approve."

Questions swirled in Brandt's mind, but he didn't want to ask them. He found that all he really wanted to do was listen to Kye. The governor spoke, authority ringing in his voice. "You need time for healing, and time to find understanding. You're strong and talented, but not yet enough for our purposes. There is a monastery to the south, called Highkeep, that could use a man of your skills. You will train there until you are ready. You must leave tonight, and tell no one."

The plan made perfect sense to Brandt. He did need rest and healing. Kye was giving him a wonderful opportunity. "Thank you, sir."

The blade dropped from Brandt's throat, but he barely noticed it.

"Ah, and Sergeant Brandt?"

"Yes."

"One more thing."

Then there was nothing. He was standing in the road, all by himself.

Why was he here?

And where did the other wolfblades go?

All he remembered were his final orders. He needed to go to a monastery where he could heal and train. It was vital he do so. He looked out along the road. It was dark, but he was a wolfblade, and the orders needed to be carried out quickly.

Without hesitation, he set off down the road, eager to complete his new assignment.

24

A lena couldn't believe her eyes. She wasn't sure she could believe any of her senses. What had she just witnessed? The scene before her made no sense, and had not made sense for some time. She felt as though she was in a play, or a dream, because this wasn't the reality she knew and understood.

She was familiar with affinities. Everyone was. But affinities were small things, skills that were closer to tricks than world-ending powers. The strongest affinities made a minimal difference in most people's lives. But now she had seen Kye knock down a building with his will, and that was just a prelude to the quick but furious battle she had just witnessed.

Brandt was several orders of magnitude stronger than she had suspected. His wall of flame had surprised her so much she had almost fallen out of the tree she hid in. Why had he not used that same power in the fight the week before? Had he been too nervous about harming civilians?

The wall had been impressive, but she expected that no matter how long she lived she would never forget the sight of the enormous fireball hanging over her head in the sky above. Had it fallen, it would have burned her and the tree she sat on to ashes. She thought she had been far enough away to be safe, but she had never anticipated such a display.

She'd seen walls of fire and slabs of stone that danced with the speed and agility of children at play. And they had changed her life. But she wasn't sure they compared to the conversation she'd witnessed afterward. That conversation challenged her perception of everything.

Alena understood that she didn't know Brandt all that well, but everything she knew about him indicated that he was a man of honor, a man on a mission to avenge the death of his friends. He had fought with ferocity, but with a few quiet words from Kye, he stopped. She swore he had intended to fight to the death.

Alena was too far away to clearly hear what the two men spoke about, but she could read their body language well enough.

Not only had Brandt stopped, but he then took orders without question. It was almost as if Brandt was two separate people. Her one-time ally now behaved as though he was one of her enemies.

Kye stood up, then gave one more order to Brandt. Then he left, barely winded after the enormous energies he'd expended.

Brandt stood up, still as a statue for some time. Alena watched, waiting to see what he would do.

His first movement was to shake his head, as though waking from a long sleep. Then he turned and walked south on the road, his stride purposeful.

Alena didn't understand. What had happened? Had Brandt betrayed her?

Her first problem was her most serious. Kye would search for her. Given how easy it had been for others to find her, it certainly wouldn't take him long to figure out her identity.

She didn't think there was anything she could do to stop him. No matter what steps she took, Landow wasn't safe for her. She didn't know or understand how Brandt had survived the battle. Something happened at the end that was beyond her comprehension, but she didn't think that Kye's attitude toward her would change so abruptly.

She needed to run.

She tested the idea, trying to find an alternative. She didn't want to leave her family behind, not so soon after she resolved to be diligent in her studies and make them proud. Leaving would break their hearts.

But it was also the only way to protect them.

No matter how hard she considered other options, running away was the only solution she could come up with. She could sit in the tree all night and debate it, or she could take actions to make sure her family was safe.

Once she was sure that it was safe to move, Alena dropped down from her tree and ran toward Landow. Again, she used her lightness to climb up the wall and dart behind a pair of unsuspecting guards. Within moments she was back in her city, walking the dark streets at night.

She made it to her house without incident. She climbed into her room without being noticed and stood there, seeing the place with fresh eyes.

Her room had always been her own space. She kept it clean and meticulously organized, a harsh contrast to Jace's room. Some simple calligraphic prints were the only decorations she had allowed herself, and her room almost had a barren feeling to it.

But it was hers, and she was leaving it all behind. She wasn't sure what to make of that. What did she take into her new life? She searched through her room, looking for answers.

Bayt's papers were a given. They were without a doubt the most valuable items she possessed, and would help her land on her feet wherever in the empire she ended up.

She grabbed all the papers, making sure that they were organized, and threw them into her sack. She took a variety of clothes, ranging from some of her winter wear to her lighter summer outfits. She didn't pack more than a few spares of anything. She would need to travel light, and it made more sense to wash than overpack. It didn't take her long to gather everything she needed. She was surprised to find that all she needed to live fit within a moderately-sized pack.

The pack would carry everything she needed, but not everything she wanted. She couldn't bring her family. That was the one thing she would have to leave behind for good.

Her last act in the house was to write a letter. She was limited in how much she felt she could say. It wouldn't be long before the governor's investigation reached this house, and when it did it would no doubt uncover this letter. So she couldn't give her family any clue as to where she was going.

She said all she could in the letter. She apologized for leaving them behind, but explained that it was necessary for their safety. She tried to reassure them that she would be fine. And she ended by telling them that she loved them.

When she finished, she was crying.

She wiped the tears away with an angry swipe.

She was angry at herself. Her family was in danger, and it was no one's fault but her own. This was the least she could do for them.

She hoped it was enough.

Alena took small comfort in the fact that her father would believe her. That trust meant the world to her now. She left the letter, lying open, on her bed. There was nothing else she could do. She wanted to be away from the city before the sun rose. Any longer could prove to be too dangerous. She took one final look at her room and then slipped out the window, leaving her home and her family forever.

25

B randt's days passed in a blur of half-remembered experiences. There were long days of walking, leagues of road passing underfoot. He only ate and slept when he needed to. Otherwise he walked, putting Landow behind him.

Whenever he tried to think of his orders, he couldn't. He remembered traveling to Landow, then nothing until he was alone in a forest in the middle of the night. All he knew was that he had to get to Highkeep. Nothing else mattered.

He held onto that order like a drowning man holding onto floating debris. He needed to get to Highkeep. He would find answers there.

Days and nights passed, and they were all the same to him. He ate when his hunger overwhelmed him and slept when he could no longer keep his eyes open. Beyond that, he walked. When needed, he asked for directions.

When Brandt saw Highkeep for the first time, he stopped in his tracks. For as many stories as he had heard about the monasteries, he'd never seen one in person. Guesses about what happened within were more rumor than fact. Shrouded in secrecy by order of the emperor, the only way to learn about them was to become a monk. Those that took the monastic vows rarely spoke about their lives.

Brandt had heard plenty of idle speculation. He'd heard the monasteries were places where soldiers driven mad by their affinities were cared for. Or that they served to advance a secret agenda set by the emperor. Or even less likely, that Anders I was still alive, moving from monastery to monastery. There were as many theories as there were soldiers to create them.

Brandt had his own suspicions, never voiced. He believed the monasteries were places where broken but powerful soldiers went to live out the remainder of their lives in peace. The mysterious institutions didn't accept just anybody, but when the rumors involved a warrior of known ability, or a soldier who had distinguished themselves through service, Brandt had always been a bit more inclined to believe.

He supposed he would find out for himself soon enough.

The complex itself was imposing. He stood on a mountain path that hugged the edge of a precipice. The monastery had been carved into the mountain, and even from a distance Brandt thought he could see evidence of a mason with a strong stone affinity. The buildings beyond the wall were squat, but he saw three separate rooftops protruding over the wall.

He started forward, his breathing heavier than normal thanks to the thin air of the higher elevations. A constant headache bothered him. His blood pounded in his head, making him feel like a child was sitting on his shoulders, constantly hammering at the back of his skull with a thick pair of sticks. The headaches had been a nearly constant companion ever since Landow.

The last half league to the monastery passed quickly. Despite the fact that he had not seen a soul on this path since turning onto it, the road itself was impeccably maintained. He stopped a little way in front of the gates.

There was something in his head, something bothering him, a whisper he couldn't shake. He wanted to be here, and yet, he didn't. Why was he here? He knew this was where he needed to be, but there was something else, a memory that eluded him every time he tried to pull it into his consciousness.

He gave up after a few moments. He had been feeling the same ever since he began walking. No matter how long or hard he thought on the problem, answers evaded him.

He knocked on the gate of the monastery, surprised when a viewhole in the gate opened immediately. A pair of sharp eyes glanced out at him. "What do you want?"

"I'm supposed to be here."

"On whose orders?"

"I don't remember. But I'm supposed to be here."

The man on the other side stared hard at him. Brandt saw his eyes narrow. "You'll be wanting to see the abbot, then," he said. The viewhole shut and a few moments later the gate swung open.

He stepped in and was treated to his first real view of the monastery.

Most of his initial impressions were reinforced. The monastery consisted of four squat buildings, one just a single level that couldn't be seen from the other side of the walls. The stonework throughout was simple, but executed so well as to nearly be art. A small courtyard stood just inside the gate, but there was little activity at the current moment. Brandt saw several people going about their daily tasks, but a single glance didn't reveal any common threads. He saw young and old, man and woman, with skin tones providing evidence enough that people had come from throughout the empire to be here.

The man who had been guarding the gate motioned for Brandt to follow. "Name's Kurl."

"Brandt."

Kurl nodded, and that was the end of that discussion. The guard took him to the smallest of the four buildings, the one that couldn't be seen from beyond the walls. He led Brandt through barren hallways to a large office where he knocked on the door. When he heard the answering call, he opened it and announced the visitor. "This here is Brandt. Says he is supposed to be here."

Brandt wasn't sure what to make of the abbot at first glance. She seemed unremarkable, the sort of woman he would have passed on the street without a second glance. And yet she led this secretive outpost, and her gaze was piercing. His curiosity was intense.

The woman looked up at Brandt. She studied him for a moment through narrowed eyes.

"Who told you to come here?"

Brandt looked down. "I don't remember. I just know I'm supposed to be here."

The abbot looked to Kurl. "A compulsion, then, and a sloppy one."

"I'd wondered as much," agreed Kurl.

Brandt didn't know what they were talking about. The woman waved Kurl away. "Summon a group. A strong one. Have them wait in the courtyard."

Kurl nodded and left them, closing the door behind him as he did.

Brandt couldn't shake the feeling there was more happening here than he knew.

The abbot addressed him directly. "Why are you here?"

Brandt opened his mouth to answer, but the words somehow caught in his throat. He tried again. "I'm supposed to be here."

The abbot shook her head, as though he hadn't answered her question. "What happened to you before you were ordered to come here?"

"I was on the way to Landow with my unit of wolfblades. We were supposed to find and apprehend a bandit."

"Where are your wolfblades?"

"I don't know." The confession shamed him. He wanted to find them, but he needed to be here.

An expression passed over the abbot's face too quickly for him to decipher. "Interesting."

Brandt felt a certain desperation creep through him, like an unsatisfied desire. "Can you help me?"

"We'll see." The abbot took a key from within her robes and unlocked a compartment in her desk. She reached inside and grabbed an item, then stood up, as though she had finally decided something. "Come with me."

Brandt followed. As they walked, the abbot spoke over her shoulder. "You are about to experience something profoundly disturbing. Do I have your word that you will not attack us here?"

Brandt's confusion only deepened. "Of course. Why would I attack you?"

The abbot gave a bitter laugh at that.

They entered the courtyard, but this time it was filled with more people. There was a whole ring of monks, all apparently waiting for him. His old instincts warned him of danger, yet he couldn't quite bring himself to react. The pieces in his mind just didn't match up, no matter how hard he tried to make them. He shook his head, following the lead of the abbot. She seemed to be the only way out of this confusion.

They walked to the center of the circle. The abbot looked around the group and spoke loudly enough for all to hear. "This man has been placed under a compulsion, which I am about to remove. Be prepared."

There were nods around the circle, and people took various fighting stances. Brandt almost drew his sword in response, but couldn't convince himself it was the right idea. He'd just promised he wouldn't attack them.

But he had to defend himself.

Before he could understand, something in his mind suddenly shifted, like sand being pulled back into the ocean by a receding wave. His head felt as though it had imploded in on itself.

Why had he come here?

He needed to find his wolfblades. He hadn't seen his friends in some time, and now this group of strangers surrounded him.

Recent memories returned, but this time they carried a different weight. They mattered now. A compulsion.

What had happened to him?

The abbot's voice spoke behind him. "Brandt, sheath your sword. No one here is going to hurt you."

He looked down at his hands, surprised to see his sword in hand. He looked around at the surrounding monks. They were prepared to fight, but he saw no willingness to do so.

Through an act of sheer will, he sheathed his sword. He turned and faced the abbot, who smiled at him. "Welcome to Highkeep."

26

S urvival was easy, but it wasn't enough.

Alena had taken all the money she kept in her bedroom, which hadn't amounted to much, but it was more than many lived on. She thought nothing of sleeping under the stars and eating simple, cheap, but filling food. Her days were long as she put leagues of road behind her, but there was a startling simplicity to travel that she grew to appreciate.

At home, every day had been filled with tasks. She attended academy, studied, and performed countless chores around the house. There had never been enough time in the day for everything she wanted to do.

On the road, all she needed was food and occasional shelter.

Food only cost a few coppers a day. Thanks to her mother's insistence that Alena help with purchasing food for the family, Alena knew how much food should cost, and haggled until she was paying what she considered an acceptable price. She avoided the inns, where she would end up spending far more. According to her rough estimate, she could survive another four weeks of travel without problem.

It was deciding what to do that took up most of her attention.

Before, her options had always been limited. She could have pursued more active employment through Bayt, or she could have gone to university, where her chosen field of study would naturally lead her to a few specific opportunities.

Now her options were limitless. She could do whatever she wished.

So what would she do? Where should she even travel to? For now she walked south, but that was only because most of the empire was south of Landow.

Some nights, after finding a secluded place far off the road, she would light a small fire and read through Bayt's notes. She'd broken the code, and it was easy enough for her to read without consulting her key now. She'd even taken to jotting down her own notes using the same cypher.

Part of her considered vanishing into the background of a new city. She could find employment with some time and effort, then maybe hunt down a nice man and build a family with him. She couldn't deny the appeal of a simple life.

But when that future played out in her imagination, she found that she couldn't summon any lasting enthusiasm. It left her feeling cold and empty. What she really wanted, more than anything, was a chance to reunite with her family.

Doing so meant taking Kye down, though.

She didn't know how, yet, but the challenge of it excited her. Kye held every advantage, and he possessed a strength she could never match.

Just thinking of ways to bring his rising star plummeting into the abyss made her heart sing.

As she flipped through Bayt's information, she began keeping an eye out for anything that might be related or helpful in destroying the governor. She kept her mind open, uncertain of what path would lead to his downfall.

Her first decision was her destination. There were several towns and cities near Landow, but none of them called to her. She wanted to be close enough to Landow that she could hear rumors and influence events, but far enough away that her own actions wouldn't draw any suspicion back home.

After several nights on the road, she settled on the city of Tonno. It was a bit farther from Landow than she would have preferred, but it had the advantage of being the largest city near the Etari border. From everything she had heard, it was a busy, bustling place where she could make her mark. And Bayt's papers detailed quite a few men and women in positions of power there. It was as good a place as any to begin her revenge.

It took her nearly three weeks to reach Tonno, but not because it took her that long to walk the distance. Once her destination was chosen, she focused on acquiring the information and skills she would need to be successful outside Landow. Her days became not just about travel, but learning.

Alena resolved to never forget the most valuable lesson that Bayt had taught her. Information, when wielded correctly, yielded power. She knew now that Bayt had made some errors. He had become too big and too public among those who lived on the wrong side of the law. When trouble had come, no doubt his name had been among the first to arise.

She could do better, and she would. So she rested when she didn't need to, especially at the junctions where travelers gathered. As she listened, she realized that what she didn't know about the world could fill entire libraries. She had been happy in Landow, but she had never realized how small one town could be against the backdrop of the empire.

News that never would have mattered to her in Landow was important out here. The emperor was raising taxes on goods entering the empire's borders, causing no end of grumbling among the traders. They made their profit from buying goods cheaply in neighboring lands and selling them within the empire. The emperor's actions cut into their profits.

She began to understand, in a very real sense, how complex the empire was. She knew it spanned almost all of the continent, and thus the world, but for the first time she learned more of how it worked firsthand. There were military units tasked exclusively with the protection of the roads. Any crime upon the roads most likely resulted in a death sentence. The units rode up and down the road, often in groups of four or eight. Alena tried to discover a pattern to their movements but failed.

When she finally came upon Tonno, she stopped for a moment to admire it. The town sat on a river that made it a popular trading destination. The river, the Alna, if Alena remembered correctly, traveled down to Etar and then to the limitless ocean beyond.

She bit her lower lip as she looked over the trading city from a small rise in the road. She wouldn't be able to sleep out in the open, which meant she would have to find an inn.

An inn would eat through her remaining money in just a few days.

So she had to find more.

How could she go about it, quickly and quietly?

She thought back to Landow and some of the petty scams that people ran there. No doubt, some of the same would have developed here. She smiled as she considered each in turn.

Alena went down to the town, passing through the main gates without a question. The streets seemed a little busier than Landow, but otherwise, there was a familiarity to everything that she found disheartening.

In her imagination, every town was an adventure, a new place to explore. And there were differences. The market specialized in different kinds of food, and of course the shops themselves were unfamiliar.

But everything else was much the same. Merchants hawked their wares, the city watch patrolled the streets with vigilant eyes, and people went about their days much the same as they had in Landow.

While she might be disappointed by the lack of difference between the towns, it made her more confident in her chances of sudden riches appearing in the near future. She wandered until she came upon a more commercial area of town, where well-kept shops stretched for several blocks.

Alena stopped by one shop to purchase some bread and butter. Then she sat, ate, and watched.

It didn't take long to spot a group of wage earners coming through. Just like in Landow, the group numbered four with one supervisor. They swept the street and picked up whatever garbage they saw.

In theory, they should have walked down the street, picking up as they went. When they didn't, instead following their master's orders and going from shop to shop, she knew she had found what she was looking for.

Wage earners were supposed to help everyone in the community equally, but that was rarely the reality.

If Tonno was like Landow, the supervisor would have private deals with the shop owners. Their properties would be cleaned by the wage earners first, and more thoroughly, giving them an advantage over the competition. Alena watched the supervisor accept money from one of the shop owners, confirming her suspicion. Wage earners were paid out of taxes, not collections from the supervisor.

The supervisor's actions weren't illegal, technically, but Alena doubted he shared the extra earnings with the men he supervised. Making it worse, the supervisor role was already a higher-paid position.

She watched as the supervisor slipped the extra coin in his pocket.

Alena smiled.

It would be easy enough to take that off him.

As they moved on, Alena followed.

Her moment came not long later. The group was moving from shop to shop when they encountered a small crowd of people moving through the market. Alena seized the opportunity. She slipped into the crowd, her knife flashing along the bottom edge of the supervisor's pocket.

The coinbag fell into her waiting hand and she melted into the crowd. She suspected the supervisor hadn't even felt a thing.

With a smile, she decided to go searching for an inn.

27

B randt looked at the tea in his hands as though it might somehow be used against him.

Ever since having the compulsion removed, he struggled to trust that the world was as it appeared. Everything he thought he knew had been tumbled about, and for the moment, he held onto the abbot's presence as his only anchor. She sipped her tea silently, waiting for the barrage of questions she no doubt expected.

"What is compulsion?"

She set her tea down. "There are more affinities than just the elemental ones you are familiar with. About two years ago a monk in another monastery discovered a fifth affinity by chance. That affinity is best described as mental, and can involve the manipulation of memories and thoughts. It can, to some degree, be used to convince people to act in ways they normally wouldn't. We call it compulsion, although that's simplifying a complex concept. It's one of the most closely guarded monastic secrets."

"So someone forced me to come here?"

The abbot grimaced. "Not exactly. It's true you wouldn't

have come here of your own choice, but at the same time, we've never seen a compulsion that can force someone to act completely against their will. I have little doubt that someone seized on some deeper desire of yours, whether that be to get stronger, or to save lives, or to simply stay alive yourself."

Brandt's hand tightened on his teacup. "Are you implying that I'm a coward?"

The question was unfair, and he knew it as soon as the words left his mouth. He was a warrior. He lived under the constant threat of death, and was ready for it.

But the abbot couldn't know any of that. She had just been listing possibilities.

Even so, a small whisper of doubt creeped into his mind. What if he hadn't been as ready to die as he thought?

He shook the thoughts away. He knew his own mind, no matter what the abbot implied.

Through his internal debate, the abbot sat silently, watching him closely.

Brandt didn't believe his answers were here. "How long does it take to get to Landow?"

"A couple of weeks."

Brandt let out a frustrated sigh. Whatever had happened was done. He couldn't reach Landow in time to change the course of anything.

The abbot had sent out birds to learn news from Landow. They would return soon, but every day that passed here would be a nightmare. He wanted to ask about his wolfblades, but knew the abbot knew no more than him. Waiting had never been half so challenging.

He forced himself to return to the matter at hand. "So why would someone compel me?"

The abbot steepled her fingers. "I wish to know that

myself. Until you arrived, it was believed that only three people in the world were capable of compulsion, and all of them are monks. The fact that someone else is aware of the affinity, and can use it, albeit clumsily, worries me."

"And my memories?"

The abbot grimaced. "I do not know. I am skilled enough to recognize the compulsion, and given how poorly it was implemented, it was easy to remove. But your memories are beyond me. It's possible they are gone for good."

Brandt swore. The answers to so many of his questions were locked in his head. He was sure of it. He just couldn't access them.

"What should I do?" He hated the question, and he hated the tone of voice he asked it in. But he was lost. Ever since he was young he had known his next steps, but now all he had were questions.

"I can't tell you that," the abbot replied, "but I can extend my welcome to you. I know much of your decision will rest on what you learn when Landow replies, but you are more than welcome to join our community. I have little doubt your commander will allow it."

He supposed he would never have a better opportunity to ask his question. "What is it, exactly, that you do here?"

"We work to extend the empire's knowledge both of martial arts and affinities. The best come here to study. The more we learn, the more we realize how little we know. The emperor works alongside our ranks to strip away the mysteries surrounding affinities."

"Why the secrecy?"

The abbot rapped on her desk. "Reality, as we know it, seems to be a thin veneer over much deeper truths. When we discover even a portion of these truths, the implications can be staggering. Imagine, if you will, the public learning that a skill like compulsion even exists."

Brandt considered such a world. No doubt, people would claim they had been compelled whenever they made mistakes or committed a crime. And if memories could be changed, or altered, the consequences would ripple throughout society.

The abbot nodded, seeing that he understood. "Our secrecy isn't malicious, nor is it a conspiracy. Many of our discoveries eventually make it out into the world. Some of the masonry techniques used to build this monastery are now being used throughout the empire, as an example. But we must help the emperor guide the empire. You are welcome to be a part of that."

Brandt sipped at his tea, already cool. He funneled some of his body heat into the cup, finding the task remarkably simple. Whatever had happened in Landow, it had made his affinity stronger.

He sat in silence for some time, and the abbot gave him ample silence to think, which he appreciated. The way he saw it, he only had two options. He could stay here and train, or return to the capital, where the commander of all wolfblades was stationed.

Brandt had been a soldier his entire life, but the thought of returning to his commander grated against him. The abbot had sent a bird that direction as well. If he received new orders, so be it. But some instinct told him he had a better chance finding answers here than he did if he returned to active service.

"If I chose to stay here, what would happen?"

"You would have to take a series of exams. You're a bit of a special case, so you wouldn't have to worry about not passing. But the exams will help us understand both your strengths and your weaknesses. Then you may join our community. Our lives are simple, and our days are spent in training. If you join us, you'll have access to some of the best warriors and strongest affinities in the empire."

She made a convincing argument.

The monastery, at least for now, seemed the safer option, the path that provided him the most opportunities.

He looked up and met the abbot's cool gaze. "I'll take the tests."

28

When Alena woke from her sleep, the sun already burned high in the sky, the buildings in the street casting short shadows. She yawned and stretched, relaxing the sore muscles that groaned after her weeks on the road.

Her room was nothing special, but after weeks of sleeping on hard ground under a cold sky, it was luxurious. Thanks to the supervisor's involuntary donation, she had enough coin to remain cozy under blankets for a few days.

Alena rolled out of bed, walking to the window and looking out at Tonno. The inn sat near the edge of Tonno's main market and the shops and stalls below were busy. Alena watched for anyone who seemed out of place, but she detected nothing to worry about.

She let herself relax. Tonno was far from Landow. Here she could make a new start for herself. Both she and her family were safe. Here she could rebuild and begin her quest against Kye.

For now, life was pleasant. She had enough money for a few days of comfortable living, and in that time she had little doubt she could find more. If possible, she would

rather avoid thieving. At worst, she could report as a wage-
earner. The work wouldn't be pleasant, but she would gain
access to the city dormitories and be able to save some coin.
So long as you were willing and able to work, the empire
took care of its citizens.

She changed into different clothes, wrinkling her nose at
the smell coming from her travel bag. Perhaps one of her
first tasks would be to wash her clothes.

Alena broke her fast while other patrons ate their lunch.
She hadn't intended to sleep as long as she had, but she
must have been exhausted.

After a full night of sleep and an even fuller belly, she
felt ready to take on the world. Alena stepped from the inn
and into the market. The sun warmed her face and hands
and she began to wander.

Alena wasn't looking for anything in particular. She just
watched and took notes in her mind. Anything could be
important and form the seed of her new life.

She listened to the prices haggled between buyers and
sellers, mapping out the rough state of Tonno's economy.
Food was a little cheaper here, it seemed, but iron more
expensive. Spices were substantially cheaper, but she
supposed that was to be expected. Traders delivered the
spices along the Alna River. No one needed to be paid to
deliver the spices to towns like Landow, far from the river
itself.

Intrigued by thoughts of the river, Alena made her way
toward the southern edge of town, where Tonno met the
water.

Her first sight of the river up close caused her jaw to
drop. Father had taken her up into the mountains outside
Landow a few times to see the streams and waterfalls. She

had thought those features beautiful, but that was the most running water she had ever seen.

The Alna was something else entirely. It stretched out forever, nearly as wide and as placid as a lake. Boats of various sizes traveled both up and downstream. Alena stared at the river in wonder, barely believing it could be real.

She passed some of the largest estates she had ever seen, enormous houses built overlooking the river.

As she continued on, she left the expensive neighborhoods, passing through a commercial area to finally reach the docks. She found it hard to believe the huge estates and the docks were both part of the same town. The docks were grimy, filled with wage earners hauling supplies to and from boats. The docks were loud, everyone shouting over everyone else in an attempt to be heard.

Alena found the chaos comforting. All sorts of trade originated at these docks, and she spent most of the afternoon watching. All of it, from the boats coming in to dock, to the unloading, to the bargaining that happened directly on the docks, fascinated her.

One downside of sleeping in so late was that she had lost much of the day for her observations. Eventually the falling sun reminded her to return to the inn, where she ate a hearty supper and fell asleep early.

The next morning her schedule returned to normal. She broke her fast with the other guests, then resumed her exploration of the town. In so many ways, Tonno and Landow were indistinguishable. They operated on the same principles. If she recalled her history correctly, both had essentially been built from small outposts to the towns they were by Anders I following his final conquests. As she thought about it, she realized there were even similarities to how the towns were laid out.

But they weren't the same. Tonno had a different feel to it, one she struggled to name. Tonno was more connected, thanks to the Alna, than Landow was. Landow was the last town of any import before one reached the Northern Sea, but there were very few boats sailing those treacherous waters. There was a small port on the sea, but it saw little traffic. As such, Landow felt like the end of the road. It didn't connect people like Tonno did.

Alena noticed the influence everywhere, from the variety of goods sold to the food on the street.

The variety of people was greater, too. Alena saw people from throughout the empire, but she also noticed an Etari trading clan, too, the first time she had seen one in years. Their distinctive red dyed clothing made them easy to spot.

By the third day of her exploration she felt like she had a basic understanding of the town. She began to understand how trade worked here, and she saw a few opportunities to begin a business. She could take advantage of the price difference in materials between here and Landow, and hopefully offer superior goods for cheaper prices.

She was sitting on a bench in a square, jotting down some notes to herself, when a city guard came and nailed a notice to a board. Alena noticed but didn't much care.

A while later, when she stood up to stretch, she wandered over to the board. The notice was a wanted poster. Her eyes wandered lazily over it, stopping when they saw her name.

Alena swore under her breath. Their description of her was perfect, and she saw that she was accused of treason against the empire. Her eyebrow rose at that, but she didn't stand to wonder about it.

Alena left the square. She needed to leave Tonno, but she needed to be smart about it. Tonno was a good-sized town, and she hadn't attracted any attention, yet.

The inn was her biggest problem. If the guard in Tonno was actively looking for her, they'd check with the inns, and they'd soon find her. There weren't many women traveling alone.

Even returning to the inn was a risk. But everything she owned was there, and she would rather not leave it behind. She decided the inn was worth the risk. Odds were good she could beat the city guard there.

Alena hurried to the inn. A quick examination of the surroundings led her to believe it was safe. She didn't see anyone moving in her room, and the inn itself was quiet. She walked in the front door and nodded to the owner, who gave no indication that Alena's presence had raised any suspicions.

Alena took the stairs three at a time, reaching her room in just a moment. Most of her clothes were still packed, so it only took a few heartbeats to gather the rest of her belongings and pack them up.

As she did, she saw movement in the corner of her vision, out through the window. She looked out and saw a pair of city guards approaching the inn.

She swore, watched them for a moment, then swore again. If she'd had just a little more time, she would have been out without a problem. The guards didn't seem too concerned, though. From their walk, she guessed they didn't know she was here.

But they would soon.

Alena tied her pack shut, then took out her purse and pulled out enough money to cover what she owed the innkeeper. She opened the window and glanced out. The guards had come inside.

Alena placed the money on the bed, then slipped out the window as she heard heavy footsteps on the stairs outside her room. She made herself light and climbed to the roof of the inn.

She hadn't climbed a single roof in her time in Tonno, but the sight of rooftops stretching off into the distance was surprisingly reassuring.

Below, shouts came from the room, the guards quickly realizing what had happened.

Alena secured her pack tightly and ran.

29

B randt had little trouble fitting into the daily life of the monastery. Daily routines were strictly regimented, much like they had been when Brandt was an infantry soldier. The days were filled with physical training, meals, chores, and lessons. All of it felt eerily familiar to Brandt.

Except for the affinity training. What little he had received in the military had come near the end of his training, and it had been little more than basic lessons on controlling the ability.

Here, the training was deep and varied. He observed exercises far beyond the simple practices the military employed. Though he hadn't yet tested, the abbot, Kyla, had allowed him to participate. He suspected the permission was a kindness on her part.

After a few days had passed, he was summoned for his test. Most of the other monks had been kind and welcoming, inviting him to join them during meals and for training, but none of them spoke about the test. He understood whatever was to come was for him to discover alone.

He liked the monks that he met. Much of the day was spent in relative silence. Brandt had never been around a group of individuals so focused on their own development. Only in the evening did they gather around fires to share their learnings from the day. Every monk was unique, but they all ran toward the same goal.

He'd been willing to test right away, but Kyla had insisted he rest for a few days. She claimed she wanted him to be at his best when he tested, but he suspected a different motive. Though no one said anything aloud, he could feel the eyes on him throughout the day.

Brandt suspected they were searching for lingering effects of compulsion.

He didn't feel any, though. As near as he could tell, he was wholly himself, and grateful for that. When he thought about what had been done to him, he imagined the pleasure he would enjoy when he found the one who had done it. It was one thing to fight and die, but to strip the will from another warrior was beyond excuse.

On his fourth day at the monastery, Kyla summoned him.

"How are you finding life at the monastery?"

"Comfortable. Thank you for all you have done."

She waved away his gratitude. "Your presence serves us, too. I would like to test you today. Are you ready?"

"I am." Brandt had watched many of the other monks closely while he'd been here. They had affinities more finely developed than his own, but he didn't think he'd seen anything beyond his capability. He felt confident enough.

"Very well. You may use the flame from the torch behind you. Please create a small ball of flame and run it around the room, twice in one direction and once in another."

Brandt didn't even need to close his eyes. He heard the

torch and pulled a small amount of fire from it. He kept the ball small. The energy was easier to manipulate, and she hadn't specified a particular size. He completed her task with ease.

"Now add another ball and juggle them between us."

Brandt did.

"And a third, the same."

Brandt pulled more fire from the torch, almost enough to cause it to flicker out. He took a deep breath to center himself. The task by itself wasn't hard, but he'd been supporting the flames for a bit now, and he couldn't relax his focus at all.

"Can you do a fourth?"

Brandt wasn't sure, but it was a test, so he tried. He managed to pull the flame away from the torch, extinguishing it completely. He could only hold all four for a few heartbeats before he knew he was about to lose focus. He let the flames burn out before he caused an accident.

Kyla's face remained expressionless. Brandt couldn't tell if she was impressed or not. But she passed over some tea. "Drink and take a few moments. When you are ready for the next task, please let me know."

The warm liquid tasted like sunshine to Brandt. After he finished the cup, he told Kyla he was ready to continue.

"Put as much heat as you can into a ball of fire no larger than your fist. You may pull whatever heat you wish that doesn't endanger your life or mine." The abbot gestured toward a candle on her desk.

That was an interesting task. Brandt had just seen focused fire done for the first time the day before. He was grateful he'd had the opportunity to try it once before the test. He pulled the flame from the candle and fed the fire with heat from his own body and from the surrounding air.

His natural inclination was to allow the heat to expand, but he forced it tighter, trying to keep it to the size Kyla had wished.

The challenge was greater than juggling fireballs, and he could only hold his final product for a heartbeat before letting it dissolve, the heat spreading back through the chilly room.

Kyla nodded, the first indication that she was satisfied with his performance. "You're gifted, and are naturally stronger than many I've met. I have only one final test."

Kyla put her hand to her desk and Brandt heard the shifting of heavy stones within. From the outside, the desk appeared rather unimpressive. But from the sound of it, the interior was quite the opposite. From the desk she removed a stone.

Brandt was no expert in rocks, but it appeared to be an uncut diamond.

"This is the final part of the test. I would like you to hold this diamond."

Even though obedience had been a part of his life for as long as he could remember, it slipped at the moment. "Why?"

"This stone has unique properties. I cannot say more at the moment. I will promise you, though, that it will do you no harm."

Brandt hesitated. Something about the stone worried him. But he'd never backed down from a challenge. He reached out and took the stone from her hand.

He'd been expecting something more dramatic, but he felt nothing. It was just a stone.

"Push some heat into it, but just a little. Then pay attention."

Brandt did. He pulled some heat from his own body and pushed it into the stone. Then he closed his eyes.

There was only one flame left in the room, another candle on Kyla's desk. He heard its song first, the same staccato rhythm he knew so well. The song was louder than he expected, though.

And it wasn't the only song.

Brandt twisted his head, trying to hear the other songs, faint and unfamiliar. One was a low hum, deeper than any male voice he had ever heard. It was solid and reassuring. Another song whistled a higher tune, while yet another sat somewhere in between the others, a calming sound that reminded him almost of the gentle roll of waves against a beach.

The whole world was alive with music, and it was more than he could handle.

He dropped the diamond on Kyla's desk.

"What was that?"

She didn't answer, but instead asked him, "What did you experience, just now?"

"Songs, of all different types. More than I've ever heard before."

"You hear the fire as music?"

Brandt nodded.

Kyla picked up the diamond and extended it to him again. "Hold on to it."

Brandt didn't want to. It was like jumping into a pool of muddy water, with no idea where the ground was beneath him. He didn't know what he would find if he touched that stone again. But he reached out and held it. He channeled some of his affinity into it.

The songs returned, soft, but distinct. When Kyla spoke,

her voice sounded loud in his ears. "What song, besides the fire, is loudest?"

Brandt listened. It was the low hum he recognized most easily. "Stone."

He didn't know exactly how he knew it was stone, but some part of his mind or body was confident in the knowledge. Kyla picked up a rock, no bigger than her thumb, and placed it on the middle of her desk. "Pull it toward you."

"I can't."

"Pull, the same way you would a flame."

Brandt concentrated, recognizing the song of stone. He pulled, and the stone moved toward him. He dropped the diamond again, his eyes wide.

This time, Kyla smiled wide. "Congratulations. As of today, Brandt, you are an official monk of Highkeep."

30

The guards didn't give chase. Alena wondered if it was because they lacked the skill, or if they just weren't that interested in a supposed traitor from Landow. Whatever the reason, she was grateful that escape was easier than she had expected.

Unfortunately, escape was only the beginning of her problems.

She hadn't thought Kye would extend his search for her so far. The fact he was willing to accuse her of treason and hunt her down as far as Tonno frightened her. Was the knowledge she possessed so worrying to him?

Her initial assumption had been that once she left Landow he would give up looking for her. That assumption wasn't true. Now, she had to expect that he would search until the ends of the empire for her.

Which meant living her entire life as a fugitive. She wouldn't be able to run a normal business, or even apply as a wage-earner. Every time she did, it would only be a matter of time before she was discovered. Every day she would have to look constantly over her shoulder.

She also had more immediate concerns. She would eventually need food and shelter. Tonight wasn't a problem, but tonight was just the first night of many.

By the time the first moon had risen, Alena's heart had stopped racing and the nervous energy dancing within her body had subsided. In the wake of the excitement, she felt exhausted. She found a sheltered corner of a roof where she was reasonably certain she wouldn't be found. She pulled a blanket over herself and fell promptly asleep.

The next morning she woke up before the sun. She came to awareness slowly, her mind unwilling to face her new set of problems. Her stomach, however, reminded her she needed to eat.

She wasn't sure how dangerous the streets would be, but she couldn't imagine everyone in town would be looking for her. The notices had just gone up yesterday. So long as she was careful around the city guards, she figured she didn't need to worry overmuch.

Alena waited for the sun to rise, then went down to a market. She kept close to groups and acted as though she wasn't a wanted criminal. As she had expected, most people weren't looking for her. She purchased food without a problem, and without having to pay for another night at the inn, she had enough money to last for a while yet.

She still wasn't sure what to do next, though. Tonno wasn't safe for her, so she needed to leave.

Before she could work on the problem, she heard the sounds of a commotion in an alley off to the side of the market. She walked past the entrance, glancing in and seeing three city guards kicking a young boy.

Alena shook her head.

She'd seen the same plenty in Landow. Crime was punished violently throughout the empire, with the punishment for most offenses being death. But it was slightly different with children. Killing a child was within the authority of any member of the city guard, but it was frowned upon. Instead, beatings were used to encourage proper behavior, with the enthusiasm for such beating varying widely among the guards. Back in Landow, Alena knew exactly which faces among the guards to avoid even looking at the wrong way.

These guards were laughing as they kicked, their attacks slamming the boy against a wall. They were the type of guards who enjoyed their duty a little much.

Most days, Alena would have walked past the scene without a second glance. Everyone else in the market did. Far wiser to avoid the attention of the city guard. One of the guards in the alley had a crossbow strapped to his back, identifying him as a ranking officer, too.

Alena's fists clenched. Perhaps it was because the empire was chasing her, too, but she wanted to help that boy. Or at the least, she wanted to make the guards look like fools.

But getting involved was risky even when one wasn't a wanted criminal. Doing so now was a fool's errand.

And it didn't matter to her in the least. Her confusion, loss, and worry all found a focus in those guards.

She couldn't fight them. Her limited martial training in the academy wouldn't count for anything here. But in her experience, most guards weren't too bright.

"Um... excuse me?" She made her voice meek and she hunched a bit, the better to allow them to loom over her.

The officer with the crossbow grunted with one final kick and turned to look at her. "What do you want?"

Alena had her head down, her eyes pointed at their boots. She desperately wanted to look up, to see if there was any hint of recognition in their eyes. But she didn't dare.

"I'm sorry, sirs, but the baker on the corner, he said he wanted to see you right away. Something about a thief."

Her statement was met with silence, and she imagined the two soldiers looking at each other.

When the officer spoke, she heard the doubt in his voice. No doubt, similar tricks had been played on them in the past. "Go, check it out. I'll stay here with the boy and the girl."

The other guards left and Alena cursed. She had hoped all of them would leave. It would only take the soldiers a few moments to go to the baker and find out she'd been lying. Then they would both be on the receiving end of those boots.

She'd put herself in a corner.

Alena glanced at the boy. His face was bruised and starting to swell, but he recovered quickly. His eyes were already darting around, wary. He looked to be a few years younger than her.

Then she noticed that his features were different. It was his ears, just slightly larger and shaped differently than she considered normal.

The boy was Etari.

But he wasn't wearing the red clothing that identified him as part of a merchant clan.

Those were questions that could wait. In just a few moments, the other guards would be coming back.

The boy looked ready to run, and Alena's anger was enough to turn her foolish decision into a mad one. In one quick motion she stepped forward and kicked, her foot sliding between the guard's legs and striking the soft target she had aimed for.

A gasp of air escaped from the officer's lungs as he fell,

and Alena darted past him, helping the boy to his feet. "Can you run?"

The boy did something with his hands. Alena didn't know what it meant.

Alena turned around just in time to see the other guards come running back into the alley. She swore out loud.

She launched herself up, making herself light and reaching the roof with a single jump.

A moment later she saw a pair of hands reach over the roof, and the boy soon followed. He had his own lightness, even if it wasn't quite as developed as hers.

Below, the soldiers yelled at them to stop. Alena risked a glance to see the officer rolling over, bringing his crossbow to bear.

The two of them ran, Alena certain they wouldn't have enough time to get out of the way.

She felt the bolt the moment it left the crossbow. She shoved against the boy and they separated, the bolt slicing through the air between them. The boy gave her a sharp glance, but they kept running and were out of line of sight in a moment.

Alena led them across the rooftops. The guards who hadn't been injured tried to chase for a while, but the two younger people were much faster and agile. It wasn't long before they had escaped.

They ducked down into another alley and curled up in a corner. Alena rummaged through her pack until she found some food. She pulled it out and shared with the Etari, who nodded his appreciation.

"You're welcome."

A while later, after the food was finished, the younger boy stood up. Alena noticed his eyes, constantly roving back and forth. She knew very little about the Etari except for the basics everyone learned in class, but she was impressed by his awareness. He gave her a short bow.

Under other circumstances, Alena would have found him to be a delightful mystery. Now that she had a chance to study him, his Etari features were more pronounced. A quick glance probably wouldn't reveal his race to most people, but the signs were there. He wasn't wearing red, though, so why was he here?

But she didn't have time to dig into the mystery. She had her own health and wellbeing to worry about. "Take care."

He gave her a long, questioning look, then was off, leaving her with the problem of escaping the city now that every guard would be looking for her.

31

B randt had never deluded himself into thinking that he knew everything. Throughout his years of service, he'd come to realize that the world was a far more mysterious place than he believed. And yet, he still thought he had some basic grasp of how the world worked.

Until he began the real training at the monastery.

Day after day, he felt as though he was learning how to walk all over again. Truths he had once considered as obvious as the sun and moons were cast into doubt. It all began with his testing, holding that cursed stone in his hand.

If he hadn't heard the songs with his own ears, he wouldn't have believed. He would have scoffed. But he had moved the stone with his will, a feat he long believed impossible.

And it hadn't been much harder than using his fire affinity.

It turned out the training he'd participated in before the tests was but a taste of the training the monks actually engaged in. Once he passed the tests, the flavor of their training changed. Before, he had compared the training to his routines in the military. What he discovered was that it was anything but.

Brandt had always enjoyed a strong fire affinity. He'd always known he could do more than most. Even here among the best in the empire, his strength was only slightly less than the others. His control, though, lagged far behind. In their sparring matches, no one pulled punches, and Brandt discovered a dozen different ways to lose every day.

The monks didn't just have superior control. Their imagination was far beyond his experience. When he fought against a water affinity, his opponent would keep a globe of water around his head, ruining his vision, interfering with his breathing, and frustrating him to no end. Against an air affinity the breath would be pulled from his lungs, or a gust would blow straight up his nose, giving him a pounding headache.

But he learned. The other monks were patient, a trait developed throughout the monastery. Most monks trained primarily in a single element, but everyone had at least some ability with another element. What Brandt had considered impossible a month ago was day-to-day life here.

Some part of his learning came from just being around the other monks. Their unique abilities demonstrated a long history of experimentation and practice. In a sense, he was learning how to learn in an entirely new way. The military had trained him to become a soldier, but here, no one knew where the limits were.

His single greatest initial achievement was focusing flame. He was used to pouring more energy into a fire and watching it grow, but pushing more energy into the flame and keeping the ball contained created spectacular results.

After less than a fortnight he could create little balls of flame that burned through armor.

The other elements didn't come so easily. Brandt would sit for an entire afternoon in front of a pile of stones, but he couldn't be sure he heard their song again. Memory and reality mixed, confusing him terribly.

Fortunately, he had just enough success to stay motivated. One day he got a pebble to roll over without touching it. Another day he succeeded in cleaning up a small puddle without a rag.

He had a template, though, memories of his own training in fire. Learning to control flame had been a long and arduous process. There was no reason why learning other elements would be any easier.

The martial training was no less enlightening. Brandt was an excellent sword, but here he studied under true masters. Much of their focus centered on manipulation of their internal energies. The practices benefitted both affinity and martial skills. They made him fight, switching between being light and not in less than a heartbeat.

The training demanded a focus he'd never summoned outside of combat, but the rewards were immediate. Even after his initial sessions he was convinced he was a stronger fighter. And the masters were evidence enough that he had much left to learn.

In many ways, those first weeks were a nearly idyllic existence.

Except for the hole in his memory, tormenting him with the passing of every day.

Then one day he was summoned to the abbot's study.

He was welcomed in and given tea. After checking in with him she came to the reason why he was summoned. "Have any of your memories returned yet?"

Brandt shook his head. "None."

Kyla looked disappointed, but not surprised. "The others report that your skills are considerable, but your techniques are limited."

He wasn't sure how to respond. He considered his techniques sufficient, but he had seen how varied the others' were.

Kyla gave a slim smile. "It's nothing to be concerned about. We see it often with those who were active warriors before they arrived. When your life depends on your skills, it's better to master a few skills than be decent at many."

Brandt sensed something behind Kyla's words, an undercurrent he couldn't quite place. "What is it?"

"We've received word back from the wolfblades and Landow, Brandt. I know what happened to your squad."

The look on her face said enough. He had suspected, already. If they had been alive and well, they would have found him. Some part of him had already known.

But it all hit him like a boulder rolling down a hill. How had his entire squad been killed, and why was he still alive? Tears trickled down his cheek, but he ignored them. Kyla knew he had guessed. "What happened?"

"Your last assignment was in Landow. As you've said, you were responsible for pursuing and capturing a bandit that had been a nuisance in the area. Your squad was involved in several conflicts. Witnesses report a fight in the forest south of town and another within the town. It was the fight within the town that killed three of your soldiers. One is missing and presumed dead. It's where you received the wound on your chest as well."

Brandt stood up, unable to contain his emotion. The memories had to be somewhere in his mind. He was sure of it, like a name on the tip of his tongue that refused to be spoken. But no matter how hard he pounded on the doors of his memories, they remained locked to him. He remembered setting out for Landow, and then walking here, with blackness in between.

"Does any of this sound familiar?"

"Yes, but I still don't remember anything. Did the wolfblades send orders along?"

Kyla nodded. "In my letter I mentioned that you had passed the tests. Your commander wishes to let you know the choice is yours alone. The wolfblades will welcome you back, but you are welcome to stay here with us." She held out a piece of paper in his direction.

Brandt took it and read it. He recognized the neat handwriting. It was, indeed, his commander. There was a very straightforward, rational tone to his words that Brandt found familiar. The tone of the letter said enough. Brandt could still call himself a wolfblade, and could return if he chose, but his commander wanted him gone. His squad had been killed. Who would want to serve with him now?

He was surprised to find the idea didn't bother him as much as he expected. For much of his life, all he had wanted was to be a wolfblade. Now, all he wanted was to find who had done this to him, and make them suffer. The best way of doing that was by staying here and learning all he could. It was what everybody wanted anyway. "You don't mind if I stay here?"

"On the contrary, I'd be excited to have you with us," Kyla replied. "It's been a while since we've had a warrior of your skill and potential here, and you might be needed now more than ever."

Brandt frowned. "How so?"

Kyla waved another paper in front of him, but didn't pass it over. "We've gotten word from the emperor. Our studies have always had a martial focus, but he's exhorting us to ever greater levels. He wants us to be the finest elemental warriors the world has ever seen."

"Aren't you already? What does the emperor need strong warriors for?" An answer came to him as soon as he asked the question. One of two conquests that had eluded the empire since Anders I. "He's finally planning on attacking the Etari, isn't he?'

Kyla shrugged. "I can't guess the minds of most people, and the emperor least of all. But I doubt it. What I can say is that he wants strong warriors, and you are the best sword to come through those gates in many, many years. I'm very interested in learning what you are capable of."

"I'm honored."

"Good. We have a few months."

Brandt frowned. "Why so little time?"

"Because after that, the emperor is visiting, to see our progress himself."

32

Alena's recent life demonstrated a terrible tendency to go from bad to worse.

It didn't take the city guard long to connect the new wanted posters with the young woman who had helped the Etari boy. In the space of an afternoon, she became the town's most wanted. They knew she was in town, and assaulting a guard had been added to treason, making her tremendously unpopular.

Making her problems worse, the city guard within Tonno was far stronger than Landow. Landow was a quiet city. Tonno shared the quality of being near the frontier, but instead of a sea, Tonno bordered Etar, one of the last stretches of land resistant to the empire's expansion. Because of the location and the amount of trade coming up and down the river, the city guard numbered almost three times that of Landow.

And they were all looking for her.

Alena felt the noose tightening around her neck.

First she had gone to the wall, but lightness wasn't going to save her here. The wall was filled with guards, most of them looking in on the city. She didn't think she could sneak over, even in the dark of night. Attempting it would be a last-ditch effort.

Guards within the city patrolled the streets and the roofs. She chose her hiding places with care. The first night she squeezed in between a line of barrels and a wall in an alley, the space so narrow she had to lie on her side with barely enough room to breathe.

She had hoped perhaps the search would die down a little by the next day.

Instead, it had intensified.

They knew she was still in town, and they were searching for her, going from house to house and searching every nook and cranny. She kept moving, doing everything she could to avoid them.

Was the attention because of her attack on the guard?

She couldn't imagine it. No doubt other guards got attacked in the course of their duty. She hadn't done any permanent damage except to the man's pride.

This was too much.

Which meant the trouble originated in Landow. Kye was pushing to find her, and pushing hard.

She considered going to the local governor and telling them everything. Perhaps the truth would set her free of all this.

The idea was naive. It would be her word against a governor's. Even a fool would know that future ended with a quick trip to the local headsman.

She had to run, but she was at a loss on how to get out of the city. She watched the docks, studying the loading and unloading of the boats. There were possibilities there, but most of them required a willing accomplice. With only a few coins left to her name, she couldn't afford to buy the help of a stranger. The reward for turning her in was much more lucrative.

That night, the neighborhood she hid in was searched by the guard. She avoided detection, but it was like playing a drawn-out game of hide and seek with deadly stakes. By the time the morning rose, Alena's desperation was as high as it had ever been.

And her situation continued deteriorating. The city guard seemed more active than ever, determined to find her.

Their behavior didn't match her expectations. It had been days since she attacked the guard. Their enthusiasm, even for catching a treasonous citizen, should have wavered a little by now.

Then she overheard a pair of guards speaking as she lay flat on a roof above them. She heard them rummaging behind a stack of crates she had considered using for cover before choosing the roof.

"What do *you* think she did?" a female voice asked, the tone indicating a conversation happening throughout the ranks.

"Don't know, don't care," replied a gruff male voice. "But if the reward is doubled for finding her, I'll spend every moment of my duty looking for her."

"You're no fun. You've got to have some guess. Maybe she stole something valuable? Or maybe she's the governor's ex-lover. Her description makes her seem pretty enough."

"Jealous?"

"Not now. But I've never heard of a governor traveling so fast just to help lead the search for a single person. Whatever she's wanted for, it's gathered more attention than I've ever seen."

"Maybe she kicked the governor the same way she

kicked Laren. I heard he went to sit on a block of ice all afternoon after she was done with him."

Alena heard the female guard chortle. "He had it coming."

Their voices faded as they turned the corner, continuing their search.

Alena wiped the sweat from her palms. Kye was coming here? With fresh horses, she wondered how long the journey would take. Safely, she couldn't assume that she had more than a day or so left.

She came down from the roof, landing as softly as her lightness would allow. Her heart pounded in her chest, distracting her.

There had to be a way out of town. The more she considered the problem, the more she understood she would probably need to take a risk she wasn't comfortable with. The town was locked down too tight for anything else.

Distracted by her own thoughts, she didn't notice the guards on the street. But they noticed her.

She heard their shouts.

Eyes wide, Alena took to the roofs. Up high, she could put distance between her and her pursuers. Then she would drop back down to the streets to find a place to hide.

Behind her, a bell began sounding. She cursed, but heard the shouts of surprise below her.

In the middle of the day, the rooftops weren't providing her enough advantages. The guards chasing her could see her every move. Glancing around, she could see other guards on the roof converging on her. She dropped down to the street, landing lightly on someone's shoulder and changing direction.

Two more corners, and for a moment she was out of sight of the guards.

She didn't even notice when a pair of thin hands reached out for her.

They locked on her wrist and pulled her down.

Alena stopped, more confused than scared. A younger boy had been crouching in a corner. He was out of breath and sweat beaded down his forehead. He handed her a red cloak.

She stared at it, not understanding.

The boy thrust it at her again.

Then she understood. It was a cloak of the Etari merchant clan.

She would never find a better disguise in town. She pulled it on and let herself be pulled into the street by the boy.

It was the first piece of luck she'd had in days. An Etari merchant in the street wouldn't attract a second glance. Hiding in the alley, she might as well have painted a target on her back.

Her rescue didn't come a moment too soon, either. Guards rushed around the corner, searching every alley for her. The boy gestured that she should pull the hood of the cloak over her head.

Normally, Alena avoided doing so. A raised hood on a nice day aroused suspicion. But the Etari often wore the hoods, now that she thought of it. She pulled it up, grateful for the relative anonymity it provided.

She was led through a combination of enthusiastic gestures and pulling. She felt uncomfortable at the idea of trusting this stranger, but without any other options, she wasn't sure what else to do. Once she made the decision to follow, her world narrowed until all that mattered was the boy.

The last part of the chase was far different than the first.

For all the boy's enthusiasm, they walked at a normal pace, following a winding path that led down to the docks. The boy led her to a large building two blocks away from the river. He gestured at the door.

Though she had trusted him thus far, taking the final step made her hesitate.

Her lack of options made her ultimate decision easy. She followed, her eyes needing a moment to adjust to the darkness of the room that she entered.

As she could make out more details, she saw that she was in a functioning warehouse. Several people who appeared to be wage earners hauled crates and barrels back and forth, supervised by red-cloaked figures. The boy indicated she should keep the hood up, then led her toward a smaller, separate room near the rear of the warehouse.

The boy knocked on the door and gestured for Alena to enter. She did, the boy closing the door behind her.

She found herself in a small but tidy office, looking into the eyes of an Etari woman of about forty years. Alena tried to remember her lessons in Etari etiquette but failed.

The woman flashed a hand sign at her which Alena couldn't interpret. Not sure what to do, she bowed deeply. "Thank you for helping me."

The woman's answering smile warmed Alena's heart. How long had it been since someone had shown her kindness? Too many days to count. Of that she was sure.

Alena thought of her parents, the pain of their separation sharp in her chest.

"Please, sit. Perhaps we should be thanking you, for rescuing Azaleth."

The woman's imperial speech was nearly flawless, with just a small trace of an accent.

"You're welcome."

If Alena had been dealing with one of her own people, she would have expected an exchange of courtesies, but the Etari were different. The woman got straight to the point. "Azaleth tells us that you are being pursued by your own kind. The signs say for treason. Why?"

Alena almost answered, then stopped. There were consequences to her actions here. "I've learned a secret about the empire, and the individual whose secret it is wants to silence me."

"Governor Kye."

Alena wished she could have hidden her surprise at the woman's knowledge.

The Etari made another hand gesture. "The guards talk. Too much. It couldn't be a coincidence the governor is making all haste toward us."

Alena looked back at the door. She had learned enough to know when she was in well over her head. "I should leave. Just being here puts you in danger."

Another hand sign, different than the first two. "That is our choice, not yours, to make. Do you wish to trade this secret for passage out of town?"

Alena's racing mind froze. Passage out of town?

The offer was so tempting she almost accepted it right there. But she didn't know enough. "Where to?"

"Wherever you wish to be dropped off on our route."

"Which leads?"

"Back to Etar. I lead my family back tomorrow."

Alena licked her lips, thinking quickly. She didn't have any better options. She'd been trying to come up with one for days, and now this had fallen in her lap.

She would be a fool not to accept.

And yet, she hesitated.

If she traded the secret, the Etari would be in danger.

Kye was willing to go to extreme lengths to protect himself. If she joined with the Etari, would he continue to push? She saw the escalation playing out in her mind. She refused to be the cause of a war.

As much as it pained her, she would have to find another way. She shook her head. "I appreciate the offer, but I can't. I don't want to put your people at risk for my sake."

Alena made to leave, but a sudden hand gesture from the woman stopped her. "You have not interacted much with us, I think."

Alena nodded, wondering what the woman meant.

"You have saved one of our young from his own mistakes. For that, there is a debt my family owes you. You have told me the risk of your secret, and I have still offered you aid. You have no responsibility for the consequences of my decision. I respect the kindness you attempt to show me, but it is misplaced."

Alena frowned. "If they attack you because of me…"

"Then it is my fault for offering you aid."

Alena wasn't sure what to make of the reasoning. It didn't quite ring true to her, but she didn't doubt the conviction in the woman's voice.

And in a moment, Alena's decision was made, her final objections pushed aside. She wanted to leave Tonno.

"I will join you, then."

The woman stood and bowed in imperial fashion. "Be ready to leave in the morning. We must make haste before the governor arrives."

33

"**A**gain!" Kurl shouted.

In unison, two dozen wooden swords sliced down. Brandt's was just one of many.

"Again!"

As Kurl came by he nodded at Brandt. "Your tip is coming too far down as you cut. You're losing control of your energy and focus."

Brandt nodded, taking a slow breath and focusing on internal energies. He was tired, but that was when focus was needed most.

In his mind, swordplay was a constant pursuit of unattainable perfection. Brandt now lived among some of the strongest swords in the empire, and even they still had room to grow. Small adjustments led to tremendous changes. Strength, balance, and control all had their roles to play in the art.

He lost himself in training. When he was here, in the courtyard, all that mattered was his sword and his movement. The troubles of the world slipped away.

He saw the same on the faces of the other monks. They

didn't train because of orders, or because they had some ultimate goal in mind. They trained for training's sake, to constantly improve themselves.

He was pleased to be among them.

The hole in his memory still existed. Kyla had hoped that perhaps they would return on their own in time, but every passing day strangled that hope.

But if there was one truth about life, it was that time covered all wounds, slowly drowning them with new experiences. His days were filled with mind-numbing effort, and in the months he had spent here, he had developed new friendships. He had always been welcomed, but now he was valued.

The session ended and Brandt collected the swords. He had just finished putting them away when a soft bell rang in the courtyard. It wasn't an alarm, but a notice. Given the day, everyone knew what that bell meant.

The emperor had finally arrived.

Brandt had seen the emperor once before, back when he had completed his wolfblade's training. The emperor had given a short speech welcoming Brandt and the other graduates to the ranks of the empire's elite soldiers.

Brandt climbed the wall of the monastery, along with quite a few others. The monastery was positioned so that it was nearly impossible to approach unobserved. The road to the monastery could be carefully studied for over half a league.

The emperor's retinue was smaller than Brandt had expected. He wondered if it was usual for the emperor to travel so lightly guarded, or if most of his protection had been left at the beginning of the trail, where it was easier for an army to camp.

Brandt returned to the courtyard as the monks

assembled. He joined the line, just another face in the line of monks.

The gates opened, and the first line of the emperor's personal guard came through. Four riders sat tall on enormous warhorses. Both rider and horse were armored with heavy plate. Brandt pitied any enemy who stood in their way. Another four warriors entered next. They wore nothing but light armor, similar in design to that of the wolfblades. A single glance was enough to evaluate their quality. They didn't appear as intimidating as the armored warriors, but were every bit as dangerous.

Then the emperor entered. Once past the wall, he removed his helmet and took the monks in with a sharp eye. He rode between the lines, giving each of his subjects a clear view.

Brandt recognized the martial skill in the emperor's riding. Like every emperor named Anders before him, he had risen through the ranks of the military. Rumor among the warriors of the empire was that the man was an excellent sword but an even better strategist. He looked to be about fifty, but held himself with the steadiness of a much younger man. Streaks of gray cut through his hair, but most of it remained dark despite his age. His hair was cut short, a military cut similar to many others.

Then the emperor passed by, and another four lightly-armored guards followed. The procession ended with another four heavy cavalry, the horses glaring almost as fiercely as their riders.

The emperor dismounted and approached Kyla, offering her a short bow. She returned the gesture more deeply and led him into her study.

The monks had been assigned tasks prior to the arrival, and now that the ceremony was complete, they moved to complete them. The guards were shown to their guest quarters, while other monks helped with the horses and gear. Brandt had been assigned horse duty for the day.

The rest of the day passed much like any other. They resumed their training, always aware of their guests. The guards watched, and occasionally were joined by the emperor himself. There was little formality otherwise, which surprised Brandt. Any visit by the emperor in the military ruined routines for days on either side.

As the sun set, Brandt noticed a quiet commotion on the wall. Several monks were arguing quietly to one another. Curious, Brandt climbed the stairs to join them. They welcomed him in eagerly. "Brandt, have you noticed anything unusual today?"

"The emperor showed up?"

The other monks waved away his answer as though they believed he was joking. "No, with the air."

Brandt frowned, then realized that the monks gathered all possessed strong air affinities. He shook his head. "No."

Was it his imagination, set off by the suggestion, or did the air feel thicker, and warmer than it should? He thought so, but dismissed it as a trick of the mind started by the monks' question.

"We should tell the abbot," one monk declared.

"Tell her what?" Brandt asked.

The monks glanced at each other, as though debating whether to tell him. "Something unnatural is happening with the weather. We've never felt anything like this."

Brandt left them with more questions than answers. The air *did* seem to have a different quality to it, but he didn't trust his own senses. They were too easily led astray by suggestions. He put the incident aside as one of the small but odd experiences he'd had since joining the monks.

That night, a storm struck.

Brandt had spent the vast majority of his life in cities. He had undergone some mountain maneuvers as part of his training, but he'd never experienced a true mountain storm. He woke to the sound of thunder echoing between the stone walls of the valley, louder than any storm he'd ever heard.

Another rolling echo caused the ground to rumble. The air seemed heavy and damp, like he was in the middle of a jungle instead of on a mountainside. Through the window, lightning lit the valley, the blinding light of multiple strikes casting pure white light over the monastery and the path below.

Brandt squinted and left his room. The first monk he crossed paths with had a look of fear frozen on her face. Brandt tried to make light of the situation. "This is quite the storm."

She shook her head. "This is no storm!"

Then she ran off, toward the abbot's quarters.

Belatedly, Brandt realized she possessed an air affinity, too.

The realization sent a shiver down his spine. He glanced in the direction of the emperor's quarters. At the least, he could go check to ensure the emperor and his guards were fine.

More lightning flashed, the strikes blinding him for several heartbeats. The thunder followed almost instantly after, indicating how close the strikes were hitting.

Most of the monks gathered in their shared dormitories, hiding from the storm. Even those without air affinities realized something was wrong. Brandt ran faster towards the emperor's quarters.

There were no coincidences.

He first ran into the lightly armored guards who had

walked closest to the emperor on his arrival. Four of them formed a loose blockade, their eyes wary as the lightning crashed around them.

The frequency and intensity of the lightning strikes beggared belief. As soon as one flash died another was there. The thunder rolled continually, the ground rumbling as though the earth itself threatened to split apart under the assault.

Speaking was difficult. Brandt had to shout in between blasts, but he made himself clear. He had come to help. After only a moment of hesitation, the guards shooed him past.

He came to a small lobby, an open space for receiving visitors before one reached the main guest room. The four heavy guards stood in a loose semicircle around the room, their backs to the emperor's door. The remaining eight guards knelt in a circle, sweat pouring from their brows.

Brandt told the guards he wished to help. One of the heavy cavalry asked, "What is your affinity?"

"Fire."

"Any others?"

"Stone." It was still the element he had the second-best luck with.

The guard nodded and pointed to the circle. "Join them."

As Brandt approached, one of the guards opened her eyes. Brandt asked, "What's going on?"

Thunder drowned out most of her words, but Brandt heard, "Attack."

How could a storm, no matter how severe it was, be an attack? Was another group using the storm for cover?

Brandt didn't understand.

The woman motioned him closer, asking for his affinity. Brandt repeated his answer. The woman nodded. "Help us."

Brandt didn't know exactly what was expected, but he kneeled down next to the others and closed his eyes, using the song of the fire as a gateway to the other elements. He could hear the song of the stone, a low rumble near the edge of his awareness.

He couldn't describe all the sensations that washed over him in those moments. Between the storm and the affinity of the emperor's guards, there was more energy here than Brandt had ever felt.

The songs increased in volume, deafening him to the world outside. He listened to the familiar songs of the flames, surprised to find them quieter than the song of stone, now dominating his attention.

The building that protected them from the wrath of the storm was mostly stone, with wood forming the interior. Brandt heard the stone, solid against the tempest raging around them.

Then he felt a spike of heat, a moment before the backs of his eyelids lit up and an earth-shattering crack broke over him like a wave.

It must have been a lightning strike, exceptionally close to the building.

It was the last thought he had before the stone screamed around him.

A sudden infusion of heat burned against his will. The whole world rang, as though he was standing underneath the world's loudest bell.

There was too much heat in the stone. The low rumble stuttered.

Some instinct deep within him pulled at the heat. He didn't do so alone. Others pulled and pushed, transferring the sudden energy from the stone to the room they sat in. Brandt found himself drenched in sweat, the room beginning to feel like an inferno. He thought he heard someone next to him grunt, but his senses were frayed and raw. He wasn't sure what was real and what was false.

The lightning attacked again, and Brandt could think of nothing else as his world went white.

34

Alena fell asleep easily that night. Now that the Etari had promised her protection, she could finally allow her exhaustion to claim her. She didn't even have the energy to pull out a blanket. A small cot was in the corner of the office. In moments she was drifting off to sleep. Her last thought was wondering if the secret would be less dangerous to her if more people knew it. Kye couldn't kill everyone.

She didn't wake until the sun was well overhead. When she woke she saw someone had thrown a blanket on top of her overnight. Alena went to see the woman she had negotiated with the day before.

The woman's name was Sooni, and she led with some authority among the Etari here. Alena tried to remember what lessons she had learned about the Etari. She knew they were a nomadic people who had never been conquered, but that was all that came to mind.

Alena supposed she'd be learning more firsthand.

When Sooni saw Alena, she flashed a perfunctory smile. "We'll be leaving soon. Are you ready?"

Alena almost laughed. Everything she owned was in the bag she'd been carrying around for weeks. Getting ready was simply a matter of picking the bag up. She barely managed to keep a straight face. "I am."

"Good. When the time comes, I'll discuss how we'll smuggle you out of town. Be ready."

For what little remained of the morning, Alena had little to do. She found an isolated corner where she wouldn't attract attention and watched as the Etari worked, curious about their culture. The warehouse was busy with wage earners loading and unloading crates under their supervisors' watchful eyes. The Etari didn't speak as much as Alena was used to. She realized, though, that much of their communication happened through hand signs.

As early afternoon rolled around, the Etari dismissed their wage-earners for the day, promising a full day's wages for less than a full day's work. Alena narrowed her eyes as the Etari started hauling crates down to the docks, work that should have fallen under the wage-earner's purview.

Sooni gestured for her to approach. She stood next to a long crate, more than large enough for Alena. A layer of straw coated the bottom of the crate. Sooni gestured. "Get in."

Alena did, lying down. The Etari had bundled more straw near one end of the crate, which served almost as a pillow. Alena wasn't too cramped, even with her pack by her side. Sooni bent over the crate, holding out a tube and a cloth. "You can put the cloth over your face. We're going to cover you with straw and pack goods on top of you. They'll be light, but it won't be comfortable. Use the tube to breathe, and focus on taking slow, even breaths."

Alena felt a twisting in her stomach, fear threatening to

turn her insides into jam. But this was the way out of Tonno. Getting her past the guards wouldn't be easy. She forced herself to nod, and pulled the cloth over most of her face. She put the tube in her mouth.

Then the Etari buried her.

The straw was hot and scratchy. Sweat dampened her clothes, but she couldn't do anything about it. For a moment she hyperventilated. The tube was the only thing preventing her from suffocating under the straw. Just the thought of it terrified her.

They placed objects on top of the straw. Sooni had spoken true. They weren't heavy, but it was uncomfortable. Alena was pretty certain that she could free herself from the layers of straw and trading goods that covered her. But the constant weight against her chest and legs made her fight panic.

The crate began to move, the faint stirrings of air through the straw a minor but welcome relief.

With her senses restricted, Alena became disoriented. She couldn't see or feel anything besides the straw scratching at her exposed skin. She didn't dare try to breathe through her nose, and her hearing was muffled by the layers of straw.

Alena focused on her breath. It was all she had in this confined space.

Deep breath in.

Slow breath out.

The crate paused and resumed its journey several times. Then it stopped and Alena thought she could hear conversation above her. The crate was jostled, and she imagined that the lid had been pulled off for inspection.

She slowed her breath, sipping from the tube while

trying to remain as still as possible. Her exhalations were similarly gentle.

Muffled words were exchanged, and she thought she felt a shifting of the straw around her body.

She could well imagine a nosy guard, digging his hand through the crate to ensure everything was as it appeared.

Alena despaired. She waited for the discovery to come.

But the guard's hand never made contact.

More words were exchanged overhead.

Alena would have given half the papers in her bag to learn what was being said above her. She couldn't make anything out clearly.

Then she felt a repeated jolting through the crate. It took her a few moments to understand what was happening.

They were nailing the lid of the crate shut.

It had passed inspection.

She smiled to herself

She might be blind, deaf, and forced to breathe through a tube.

But soon she would be outside of Tonno, and hopefully beyond Kye's grasp.

THEY RELEASED her from her prison later that day. She felt the vibrations as the nails were pulled out and the lid lifted away. As the Etari began pulling the objects out of the crate, Alena's breath came easier. Not long after, hands lifted the straw off of her. Once they began, she sat up, spitting out the tube and taking her first full breath of air in ages. She'd never before thought about how wonderful it was just to breathe.

She needed a few moments to find her bearings. She was on a boat, larger than she had expected. Nearly a half dozen Etari stood in silence near the crate, Azaleth among them. He handed her a red cloak, which she donned and threw the hood up.

Far off in the distance, she thought she could see the faint outlines of Tonno. She had escaped the city, but now she once again needed to decide where to travel.

She stepped out of the crate and gingerly tested her mobility. She was stiff, but didn't suffer from anything that couldn't be fixed with a bit of stretching and movement. Sooni watched her from the back of the boat. Once Alena felt comfortable enough to walk, she approached the leader. "Thank you, again."

Sooni made a hand gesture. "Where would you like us to drop you off?"

Alena had spent some time considering that very question. Her problem was largely the same wherever she chose, though. Kye clearly had no qualms about spending enormous sums to track her down. Wherever she ran, he would be there.

She could only think of one solution, as much as she disliked it. This was a direction she'd never imagined her journey would take. "Would you take me with you to Etar?"

Several Etari around the boat muttered, but Sooni flashed a hand sign and they all quieted down. Sooni struck her as a wise leader. She would have suspected Alena had few other reasonable choices. Which also meant she would agree to Alena's request.

"Etar is open to you," Sooni proclaimed. Alena suspected the simple sentence held more importance than the words alone expressed.

The decision made, Alena found a certain sense of peace. If there was any place in the world she could be safe, it was in one of the only areas the empire had never conquered.

After three days of downstream travel, the boat came to a small dock, built in the middle of the plains. Alena had never seen a dock without an accompanying town, but the reasoning became clear soon enough. A large collection of carts and horses waited there, more Etari in their red cloaks gesturing at the incoming boat.

"Why are we docking here? Are we already in Etar?" she asked.

One of the young men next to her replied, "No, but there are rapids up ahead. We will dock and unload while another family from our clan will load new supplies."

Soon enough the process began. Alena helped, carrying crates and placing them onto carts. She received a few questioning looks, but when Sooni flashed a series of hand signs the rest of the Etari relaxed around her.

She was going to need to learn that hand language, she supposed.

There was little talk and even less delay. Once the boat was unloaded, it was immediately loaded up with new crates, then it drifted back into the river again, a set of long oars emerging from below deck. With steady sweeps, the boat began the long journey back upstream toward Tonno.

Alena watched the boat with mixed feelings. It had taken her away from Tonno, and for that she would always be grateful. But it was also her last link to her homeland. She had little doubt they had sailed to near the edge of the empire. From here, it was an entirely new journey.

Alena shrugged to herself. What else was there for her to do? As far as she knew, this was the only way forward.

It still hurt to watch the boat sail away.

The Etari left her little time to mope. The now empty

carts were reloaded and they began journeying further west, into a new land.

The ride proved to be more boring than the boat. The lands here were flat plains that stretched as far as the eye could see. The rest of the day passed with only small copses of trees to break the monotony.

After another day of travel, they came to a creek. A short but sturdy bridge spanned the water, and Alena thought little of it until she saw the looks on the faces of those around her. They were looking upon the nondescript bridge with undisguised eagerness. She didn't understand.

She was sharing a cart with Azaleth, whom she had still never heard speak. She assumed he was mute, but after spending time with the other Etari, she wasn't so sure. They weren't a very vocal people, standing in stark contrast to everyone Alena had grown up with. Jace, in particular, would have been endlessly frustrated by the lack of conversation among the family.

As soon as they passed over the bridge, though, Azaleth looked at her. "Welcome to Etar." His voice was deeper than she expected.

He must have noticed her surprise, because he laughed. "I can speak. I was forced to take a vow of silence after my failure in Tonno. It lasted until we returned to Etar."

Alena turned to her now vocal companion. "How did getting beaten in Tonno make you a failure?"

Azaleth waved away her question, as though he could explain but she wouldn't understand. Alena overcame her irritation at the dismissal by looking around. Beyond the small creek, now fading into the distance, she couldn't tell any difference between Etar and the empire.

She had expected more.

What little she knew about the Etari came from basic

civics lessons. The Etari were supposed to be fierce warriors who eked out their living in a harsh land. Looking around, though, the land looked no harsher than the empire's lands. And if that creek was the border, it was mostly a joke. She could have gotten off the cart and passed through on foot anywhere in that creek.

"That was the border?"

Azaleth laughed and nodded. He seemed more lighthearted now, as though a burden had been lifted from him. "It doesn't look like much, but can't you feel the difference in the air?"

She frowned. Now that he mentioned it, the air did seem different. Lighter, maybe. She looked around and saw smiles on the faces of her traveling companions. Were they just excited to be home, or did they experience the same sense of change that Alena felt?

Alena had no answers, but she also found that for once in her life, she had no questions, either. Her shoulders relaxed and she slumped deeper into the seat in the cart. Perhaps it was the air, but she knew why she was relaxed. For the first time in weeks, she was safe.

Two days passed without incident. Alena noted that there were no small farmhouses dotting the landscape, the way they did in the empire. Wild grass was far more common than wheat, and more animals seemed to roam the plains than back home. Otherwise, the journey was as monotonous as ever.

Until one of the Etari came and whispered into Sooni's ear.

Sooni raised her hand, making yet more signs. The caravan increased its speed.

Sooni waited until Alena's cart passed, then pulled her

horse up beside them. "Someone broke the border, not long ago. We're being pursued by a large group."

The leader of the clan stared at Alena, the message clear. Kye was prepared to wage war for the information Alena knew.

35

B randt woke up with a splitting headache. The world seemed brighter than it should, light stabbing at his eyes as though it had a vendetta.

He closed his eyes and breathed deeply, focusing on the familiar sensation of breath moving down his throat and into his lungs. He was alive. The pain left no doubt of that. His last memories had been of the lightning striking the building, the incredible energies at play.

What had happened?

When he opened his eyes again, he saw that he was in his own room within the monastery. A tall cup of water sat near his bedside, which he eagerly sipped from.

The headache didn't fade, but his vision returned to normal. He sat up, slowly, searching for the signals his body provided. Besides the drum pounding in his head, he felt fine. His limbs were a little stiff, but it felt more like the stiffness of a long sleep than the body trying to protect itself from injury.

He stood up, pleased to learn that he didn't feel dizzy or otherwise unwell. He dressed in a fresh pair of monastic robes and slipped out into the day. The storm had passed, but it had left plenty of evidence of its passing. Several of the monastery's buildings had sustained visible damage, from shattered walls to blackened stone. In all his life, Brandt had never seen anything like it.

He walked into the courtyard, surveying the damage. Most of the stone had been cleared, but the destruction hadn't been repaired yet.

One of the other monks approached him. She gestured toward the main hall of the monastery. "The abbot requested we send you to her as soon as you awoke."

Brandt nodded, taking one last look around. This wasn't natural. He knew well the power of storms, but this was too focused, too intense.

"Is the emperor alive?" he asked.

The monk nodded. "And well. He will probably also want to see you when he learns you are awake."

Brandt wasn't sure what to make of that, but he wasn't able to think too deeply about anything at the moment. He walked to the abbot's study, knocking softly on her door and entering when invited.

Kyla looked haggard, as though she hadn't slept in days.

"How do you feel?" she asked, ignoring the customary formalities.

"Well enough. I have a pounding headache."

"Have one of the healers take another look at you after this."

"I will. How long have I slept?"

"Not long, actually. It's the morning after."

That surprised him. Kyla must have made clearing the debris a priority if it was completed after a single morning. "What happened?"

"I could guess, but I'm not sure. The emperor knows

more, but he isn't saying. He's been in meditation all morning."

He frowned, confused by that.

Kyla noticed. "I don't know how, exactly, but the line of Anders possesses gifts beyond my understanding. I'd heard rumors before, but this is the first I've seen of it. I hope to find out more soon."

Brandt heard the edge in her voice. "What's wrong?"

"Three monks died last night."

The news struck Brandt like a hammer fist to the chest. "How?"

"One was hit on the head with a falling rock. Two others were struck by lightning as they raced across the courtyard. It's the worst disaster the monasteries have ever experienced."

Brandt didn't know what to say. Words were empty.

He was saved by another knock on the door. Kyla welcomed the visitor, then stood abruptly when she saw who it was. Brandt turned to find the emperor standing there, and he stood up as well. Anders VI was accompanied by two guards, one of whom started when she found Kyla accompanied by another. But a flash of recognition soon followed, and the guard relaxed, even going so far as to offer Brandt a slight bow.

The emperor stepped inside and Brandt bowed deeply. He'd never been so close to the emperor in his life. Few in the empire had.

"This is the wolfblade who assisted my guards?"

Face to the floor, Brandt couldn't see Kyla's reaction.

"Sit down, then, and join us."

Brandt froze for a moment. The offer broke every rule of etiquette drilled into him from the first day he entered the military. But even a polite suggestion from the emperor couldn't be refused. Brandt came out of his bow, surprised to see the wry grin on the emperor's face.

"How are you, soldier?"

Brandt stuttered. The emperor himself was speaking to him. "Fine, your imperial majesty."

The emperor laughed. "In here, you can call me Hanns. There is no need for formality between us, in this moment."

The emperor turned and focused on Kyla, giving Brandt the time to process this sudden familiarity. No one dared call the emperor by his given name. Such a breach of etiquette was an immediate death sentence.

It took Brandt a few moments to realize the discussion had advanced without him. He focused his attention and sat down.

"So it was an attack?" Kyla asked.

The emperor, Hanns, nodded. "The skills required are beyond my own comprehension, but I am certain. I can feel the trace of will the storm left behind, and that lightning didn't obey nature's laws."

Kyla shook her head, clearly in as much disbelief as Brandt. "How is such a thing possible?"

"I cannot fathom the method, but I understand the theory. A small change, given enough time, can create a large effect. Imagine, if you will, making a tiny crack in the foundation of a building, the sort even the weakest affinities can produce. By itself, it does little, but if every day a person comes back and expands on that crack, it can eventually send a building crashing to the ground."

"You believe they can control storms?"

"Not perfectly. But they could add some heat when needed, move moisture. With enough knowledge, patience, and skill, they could direct the storm."

The abbot intuited something from Hanns' tone. "This isn't the first time."

Hanns shook his head sadly. "It is by far the worst, but no, it isn't the first attempt. They don't come frequently, but when they do, they are unmistakable."

Hanns turned to Brandt. "I wanted to thank you for your actions during the assassination attempt. Your quick actions saved the lives of several of my guards." He paused. "Kyla has told me of your situation. I am sorry for your loss. If you wish, I can try to retrieve your memories."

Brandt's surprise overwhelmed his propriety. "You can do that?"

"I can try."

"Hanns has a strong mental affinity," Kyla said, and Brandt thought he heard a bit of envy in her voice. "If anyone in the empire can unlock your memories, it's him."

A lump formed in Brandt's throat. He wanted to know what had happened in Landow, but he was suddenly uncertain of reliving the memories of his team's deaths.

It would be easy to refuse, to continue to hide.

But what kind of friend would that make him?

"Do it, please," he said.

The emperor nodded and closed his eyes. For a moment, Brandt wondered if the emperor had fallen asleep. But then he felt a presence, ghostly, near the back of his mind.

"Can you focus on your breath, please?" Hanns asked.

Brandt closed his own eyes, falling into the meditative state he was most familiar with. The presence in his mind increased, and the headache that had bothered him vanished. The presence was gentle and kind, and Brandt thought of a grandmother holding a child, the image seemingly random.

He lost track of time, but then his awareness returned sharply, the presence fading away.

He opened his eyes and looked at the emperor, who shook his head. "I'm sorry, they're gone."

"What do you mean, gone?"

The emperor fluttered his hands, like a bird taking flight. "I thought that perhaps your memories had been covered up, the mental equivalent of being hidden under a blanket. But they've been destroyed. Some fragments might remain, but nothing either of us could make sense of. They are gone for good."

Brandt swore and stood, pacing the small room back and forth for a heartbeat before remembering whose presence he was in. He stopped and returned to sitting, barely able to control himself. His friends were dead and he would never be able to remember them properly.

The emperor turned back to Kyla. "You've said your training is proceeding well. How soon can they be ready if they are needed?"

Kyla gave a small shrug. "We're ready now, but we haven't made any meaningful advances. Our knowledge grows bit by bit, but it's not enough to complete the tasks you've set for us."

The emperor nodded. "Maintain your readiness, Kyla. She's getting more bold, and I'm not sure how much longer I can keep her at bay. There may be a need for the monks soon."

Kyla said that she would, and Brandt's thoughts finally caught up with the discussion. "What's happening? Who has the sort of power that can unleash a lightning storm upon a monastery? Why are you pushing so hard for monks ready to fight?"

Hanns gave Kyla a questioning glance.

She nodded.

Hanns let out a deep exhalation of exhaustion. "There is a power, stronger than anything I've ever felt before, making moves against us."

"The Etari?" Brandt asked.

Hanns gave him a grim chuckle. "Not even close. I do not know exactly who or what is at the heart of the disturbance. They are beyond even my sight. But I suspect it is an affinity from Palagia."

"Palagia?"

"The other continent on the planet."

Brandt was more confused than ever. "There's only one continent."

A glance at the emperor revealed the truth. Brandt's headache returned. "Why does no one know about the existence of an entire continent?"

"That is a story for another day, but please accept the truth of the matter. There are two continents we know of, and although we've been protected here for hundreds of years, the barrier is wearing thin. Already they strike at me, hoping to cripple us before the legacy of Anders can be passed on to another. Something is coming, and I mean for us to be prepared."

Brandt's head spun. "What do we need to do?"

"I know very little, Brandt," Hanns said. "I know that as a people, they seem to have mastered affinities in a manner that I can't comprehend. But I do not know how many there are, or what they intend. But I prepare for the worst."

"How long do we have?"

"I don't know. It could be tomorrow, or it could be three generations from now. All I can say is that our barriers are being weakened. The sooner we are prepared, the better."

"Why have you kept this a secret?"

The emperor grimaced. "I am an inheritor of a legacy, Brandt. There are days where I wished I could tell the truth, but doing so risks so much more."

"So you need us to prepare the monks for an attack from an unknown enemy, arriving in unknown numbers, at an unknown time, with unknown abilities?"

The emperor nodded. "And I want you to do it quickly."

36

For almost a full day, Alena thought the Etari would avoid their pursuit. The group made good time, pushing their mounts hard. Surely whoever Kye had sent would turn away.

But her hope was in vain.

The next day, she saw a plume of dust rising into the air. Not long later, Sooni ordered the Etari to a halt. In the wide-open plains, the Etari carts had no way of outrunning the pursuit.

As the distance between the forces closed, Alena realized they were a large unit of cavalry.

She guessed there were close to a hundred horses approaching.

She glanced over at Sooni, who watched the approaching soldiers with an impassive eye. Could the secret she carried be worth so much to Kye that he would provoke a war? Or had she stumbled upon something larger between the Etari and the empire?

Either way, the Etari couldn't protect her from this.

"Mercenaries." Sooni glanced at Alena. "That must be some secret," she said, her tone dry.

"It seems that way." Alena didn't know how to respond. She wasn't worth this much effort. She couldn't be.

Yet the evidence grew closer with every passing moment.

Alena turned to Sooni. "You have to surrender me. My life isn't worth your family's."

Sooni frowned. "Of course it isn't." She continued studying the riders. "But they have entered our land without permission. They have sealed their fates."

Alena watched as her doom approached.

Maybe if she jumped out of the cart and ran toward the charging mercenaries she could save the Etari lives. She didn't want to die, but she refused to have the blood of more people on her hands, especially that of people who helped her in a time of need.

Alena glanced back to take one last look at the caravan, to imprint their faces on her memory. She saw Sooni flashing hand signs too fast for her to follow.

What did they expect to accomplish? The Etari were outnumbered. Less than two dozen Etari accompanied the caravan, making the odds almost four to one. On the plains, there was no terrain to use to hide or to set an ambush. The battle would be on a level playing field, dooming the Etari.

But from the looks on her companions' faces, they didn't feel the same. Those riding horses dismounted, tethering them to carts. Every cart came to a complete halt as the Etari formed a loose line between the caravan and the approaching riders.

Sooni glanced at Alena, suddenly alone on the carts. Even Azaleth, the youngest among the Etari, had joined the line. The family leader's gaze hardened. "Are you not going to join us?"

"I don't know how." Shame flushed her cheeks.

Alena supposed that wasn't exactly true. She had received the same martial training as everyone else in the academy. She'd never taken to it the same way Jace had, though. Running, hiding, and outsmarting were her methods.

Sooni shook her head. "It doesn't matter. Fight, or your welcome is rescinded. In Etar, everyone participates."

Alena frowned, not understanding quite what Sooni meant. But the part about having her welcome rescinded stuck. If they wouldn't let her surrender herself, they were all going to die. She might as well die standing. "You don't have to do this," she said as she climbed down from the cart.

"We do," was all Sooni said.

Her knees shook. The riders were still a ways away, but every instinct Alena possessed told her to run. It was the reasonable reaction when charged by an entire unit of cavalry.

Sooni made a gesture even Alena could guess. She held her hand flat as a blade and swiped it quickly across her neck. In response, everyone else flashed a sign Alena knew represented an agreement.

Several of the Etari dug into pouches at their hip, pulling out what appeared to be small stones. Next to her, Azaleth pulled one out, allowing her to examine it more closely. It was a small stone, sleek but narrowed to a point on one end. Azaleth held the stone in front of him, where it floated and began to spin rapidly.

For a moment, Alena forgot her fear. What was this? It was a stone affinity, without doubt, but she had never seen such a technique before. And how did everyone possess a stone affinity? The odds of that were inconceivable.

Azaleth's actions were mirrored down the line. Alena saw nearly a dozen stones, floating and spinning.

The riders charged, slowly becoming individual shapes.

Sooni made a gesture with her hand, and the stones disappeared.

Alena blinked, her attention drawn to the approaching line of riders, thrown into sudden disarray. At least a dozen riders, if not more, fell from their mounts, life ripped from their limp bodies.

When she looked back at the line, everyone was floating more stones in the air. They disappeared as well, but Alena saw the streak of darkness this time, zipping toward the enemy charge. More men fell, then more again.

The charge began to break up, and they were still several hundred paces away. A handful of arrows floated through the air, arcing toward the line of Etari.

Each arrow suddenly spun in the air, as though a hand had come through and swiped at them all. They fell harmlessly to the ground.

By the time the riders were within two hundred paces of the Etari, their numbers were more than halved.

By the time the charge was a hundred paces away, there were maybe only three dozen riders left. Their commander ordered them forward.

From the confident tone of his voice, Alena wondered if he had even looked behind him to see how few men remained.

Between the riders and the Etari a spark flashed, erupting quickly into a conflagration, a wall of fire that burned between the two forces.

About ten paces after the fire, a short wall of earth and stone rose. It wasn't higher than Alena's waist, and she wondered what good it would do.

A few moments later, she understood.

The cavalry leaped through the flames, but the fire and smoke obscured their view. The horses ran into the wall, seeing the obstacle too late. Horses and riders went down, terrified screams and cries of agony echoing in Alena's ears.

All the while, stones continued spinning and disappearing, a relentless onslaught.

As destructive as the attacks were, a handful of cavalry made it through to the Etari line, long swords drawn.

Then Alena watched the Etari display their martial prowess.

She had seen better at the academy. The empire had created some true masters over the years. But she'd never seen such a consistent display of skill among a group of people.

Imperial-style swords sliced down from up high, but all they cut was air and grass. The Etari were quick. Though their swords were shorter, their agility was unmatched. Alena thought of Ryder, and wondered if he had trained with the Etari. Their styles of movement were very similar.

One rider came close to Alena, although her focus was on Azaleth. The rider cut down, but Azaleth dodged her sword, then darted back, scoring a cut along the horse's back leg. The animal lost its balance, throwing the rider from the saddle.

The empire soldier had the wind knocked out of her, but she recovered quickly and got to her knees, raising her sword to duel Azaleth.

For the moment, the woman's attention was focused straight ahead, her back to Alena.

Alena wasn't sure what came over her, but she became light and approached, wrapping herself around the warrior's arms, preventing her from moving easily.

She realized in a heartbeat it was a terrible move. But it distracted the woman and slowed her down. Azaleth stepped forward, the point of his blade aimed straight at the woman, and Alena behind.

Alena grimaced, expecting the point of a sword to pierce her flesh in a moment.

But it didn't come.

She felt the woman's body go limp under her grip. Alena let go and the body fell forward. She shivered as she realized that for a moment she'd been holding onto a corpse.

Alena looked around and realized that the battle was over. Ahead of them, the flames were snuffed out and the berm of dirt and stone disappeared into the land it came from.

The plains were too quiet then. Alena counted the Etari. Impossibly, none of them had been killed. One had a nasty gash on his forehead, but that seemed to be the extent of the injuries.

The trail of corpses stretched out for hundreds of paces.

Alena shivered again, wrapping her arms tightly around herself. Sooni was watching her, nodding in approval.

She had helped to kill a warrior.

Nothing made sense, but her mind was blank.

Sooni made another gesture, and the Etari began to strip the corpses.

Alena watched with horror as the bodies were tossed and pulled. Clothes and weapons were collected, leaving the bodies naked beneath the sun.

Not wanting to be heard by all, Alena approached Sooni and whispered, "What are you doing?"

Sooni gave her a look, as though the answer was obvious to anyone with eyes.

"You can't desecrate bodies like that!" Alena protested.

Sooni frowned. "We're not desecrating them. We're taking their supplies, which will help protect our people. They are dead and beyond care, and they can't use the material anymore. Besides, the bodies must be burned. The skills we used today can't be learned by the empire. The evidence must disappear."

Alena shook her head, unable to wrap her mind around the reasoning.

She had never felt so far from home in her life.

37

The emperor left two days later. He attended the death ceremonies of the monks and sent birds requesting aid. But the duties of the empire weighed on him, and he could not remain in any one place for long. Ostensibly, thought Brandt, he had been here to examine the martial progress of the monks. Now, though, Brandt realized the monasteries were the keystone to a much larger battle the emperor expected.

Brandt wandered in a daze for the next few days. He attended all the usual trainings, but neither his mind nor his heart was in the routine.

The emperor's visit had reminded him of his wolfblades. The emperor's failure to restore his memories troubled him, more than he revealed to Kyla or the monks. He had always hoped, had always believed the memories would return.

Then Hanns had told him it would never be possible. In all likelihood, he had watched his friends die and would never remember their final moments.

That inability to remember gnawed at him and denied him true grief. He couldn't accept that they were truly dead.

Every time he passed the gate to the monastery, he glanced toward it, halfway expecting Lola to come through the door, yelling at him for his prolonged absence.

But the monastery received few visitors, and Brandt's wolfblades were certainly not among them. They were dead, whether or not he could accept the fact.

His training also suffered. He had seen firsthand the power arrayed against them. Such strength made his own abilities seem pointless in comparison. He sought answers, but none came.

He kept running up against an impossible foe: reality. The laws of the world could not be broken. One evening, desperate for answers, he turned to the abbot.

He caught her walking after the evening meal, wandering the wall as she often did at night. After engaging in the customary formalities, he got to the heart of his problem. "Do you know of any way to negate the cost?"

She raised one eyebrow. "The short answer is no."

Brandt had hoped for a different answer. Still, her answer suggested she had more to say. "But?"

"But I am increasingly convinced there must be a way to bypass the cost. The storm is one example, but others have reached my ears." She hesitated for a moment. "One of your own wolfblades was killed in Landow by a building falling on top of them."

"We fought someone who could ignore the cost?"

Kyla gave a small shrug. "It appears that way. But we know little."

Brandt looked up into the night sky. "Sometimes I think I should return to Landow and try to find my answers there."

"An understandable desire, but foolish. There is no

guarantee that the one who compelled you is still there. There has been no further violence since you left. It's been months since the incident, and no new information has emerged."

Brandt acknowledged her point but hated it anyway. He returned to the question that had no answer he would accept.

"So, what do you know about avoiding the cost?"

Kyla spoke slowly. "I believe that avoiding the cost requires the use of specific stones."

"Like the one in your office?"

Kyla nodded. "Some of us have made it our life's work to study them. The monasteries are only in possession of four, each a fragment of the same stone discovered some years ago in Falar. There are far more questions about them than answers, but they have effects that defy what we understand about affinities."

"Like being able to hear more than one element?"

"Exactly. Although perhaps 'defy' isn't the correct term. They make us question everything we believe is true."

She gave Brandt a moment to understand her meaning. When he did, he stopped walking. "You're saying anyone with an affinity actually possesses all affinities?"

Kyla looked both ways, appearing as though she was making sure they wouldn't be overheard. "I believe an idea even more outlandish. I believe that all people possess all affinities."

"What?" Brandt couldn't imagine that being true. It went against everything they knew.

"Do you know when the first affinities were recorded?"

Brandt searched his memory. "About the time of Anders I." It was said that Anders I had a stone affinity, a fact others with the affinity held as proof of their superiority. In the stories of his ascension to the throne, he had often used the affinity to prove his right to rule.

Brandt, and most people, believed the stories of Anders I to be exaggerations of the truth. No man could crush dozens of soldiers at a time with a flying boulder, a commonly held myth.

"Exactly," Kyla replied. "We don't know of any affinities before Anders I. Don't you think, if there had been affinities throughout our history, we would have heard of them?"

"But there isn't much left of the time before." Anders I's conquest of the continent had destroyed much of the history that had come before. The order of the empire had come at a cost.

"But there is enough we would have heard something. At least, that is what I believe."

"You think affinities only began when Anders I was alive?"

"Or that it was the first time they were strong enough to observe. I don't know. But I do know there isn't anything about affinities prior to the founding of the empire."

"That proves little."

"Did you know that every year, more people with affinities are discovered?"

Brandt grunted in surprise.

"The numbers of those with affinities are growing. The emperor keeps lists, and the evidence is there for anyone willing to look."

"What are you saying?"

"That as a people, I believe our affinities are getting stronger. That's my theory. I can't prove it yet, but it's a story that fits the facts."

They walked in silence, Brandt digesting the idea. He didn't believe it. There were too many other possible explanations. They were getting better at identifying those with affinities and training them. Their record keeping was improving. There was no need for Kyla's odd ideas.

"How does this help me?"

"You know what I think when I look at that stone in my desk?"

Brandt gave her a blank look.

"I think that what we don't know about these powers is far greater than what we do. Right now, the cost seems real, but there are these small pieces of evidence that suggest that maybe we're wrong. Start with our assumptions. Question them all."

"Easier said than done."

"True. Keep working at the problem, though. It's a worthy one. It might be the only one that matters."

They were coming off the wall for the night when a lone figure appeared on the road, walking toward them. Brandt and Kyla both stopped to watch. Brandt thought there was something familiar about the figure, but he couldn't be sure.

They kept their watch as the figure continued to approach with sure steps.

Eventually, the visitor was close enough that Brandt could make out her face. He almost fell to his knees at the sight.

"Ana?"

38

E very day Alena looked over her shoulder, expecting to find an even larger force bearing down on them. But the plains remained empty.

She supposed that wasn't true. Thanks to Azaleth's patient instruction, Alena came to understand that what looked empty was in fact full of life. He pointed out deer hiding in tall grass, their coats nearly invisible to the untrained eye. Enormous birds flocked overhead, and he introduced her to a wide menagerie of small critters who called the grasslands their home.

But the only humans she saw were the Etari, bringing her more deeply into their land and their lives.

Alena spent most of her waking hours with Azaleth. The two of them drove a cart together, and she suspected the young man considered her some sort of hero. His patience with her ignorance went far beyond what she expected. She had tried a bird call for an entire morning, causing the rest of the Etari to gradually pull away. But he remained, helping her develop the technique.

She didn't deserve his kindness, even if she'd helped him in Tonno.

She was a fool tossed about by the winds of fate. Her choices drove her from her own home and haunted her across the empire and beyond. She was lost, following whatever path presented itself to her.

But Azaleth was one of the kindest young men she had ever met, and she tried hard to be a worthy student. For the first time, the skills that had served her well throughout life failed her. She was given nothing to memorize, no rules to follow. A life among the Etari lacked the structure she was used to. Without Azaleth's kindness, she wasn't sure what she would have done. He was her guide, explaining the hand signs and showing her the dangers hidden in the plains. For a young man, he knew more about their world than she could have imagined. He possessed a level of knowledge she would have expected in someone much older.

Every day among her new companions shifted her worldview. The physical differences between the Etari and imperials weren't great, but the difference in how they lived was tremendous.

The first difference she noticed was their attitude toward responsibility. The family, as this traveling group called themselves, looked out for one another. But at the same time, everyone was expected to contribute their effort and skills. If an individual failed at a task, they always accepted responsibility. Alena started to understand what Sooni had said back in Tonno. She took all responsibility for her decision to have Alena join them. Likewise, if a hunter came back without food for the group, they voluntarily fasted through the evening and into the next day.

No one slept in, and no one shirked duties. Even Alena,

as she gained the skills necessary to help the family, was expected to take part.

And they were a very physical people.

They embraced upon greeting and danced at night. When they paused throughout the day, the younger Etari raced one another or kicked a small ball of hide around.

And at night, they kept Alena awake.

The sounds of coupling made it difficult to rest, especially when the sounds came from less than two paces away. Others went about their work as though nothing unusual was happening.

In the empire, the traditions of courtship were well-established.

Here, most days ended in coupling, and Alena noted that the couples were usually different. She wanted to ask Azaleth about the practices and expectations, but worried she might send him the wrong idea. The longer she spent with him, the more she worried his kindness wasn't entirely altruistic.

She never felt at risk, though. It appeared as though women initiated most, if not all, of the liaisons. At least, Alena thought so. She still struggled to understand the hand-signing language. Gestures didn't represent words so much as they did ideas, with a nuance Alena couldn't quite pick up on.

They traveled alone for a week before they saw anyone else. It was a collection of shelters, round homes with wooden frames and leather stretched around. Alena counted more than a dozen when they came into view.

The caravan was welcomed with open arms by the residents of the shelters. Alena wasn't sure what to call the place. Was it a settlement, or a village? Even a glance told her that this new family could easily pick up their belongings and move within a day.

Hugs were exchanged all around, with Alena being the sole exception. Words passed back and forth between the Etari, Alena picking up small snippets from what Azaleth had taught her.

She had been warned that most Etari couldn't understand her. The merchant clans studied the imperial tongue as children, but few others bothered. Until she learned Etari, navigating daily life would be a difficult process.

Alena detached from the scene and observed. The other clan dressed in a wide variety of clothing, but Alena didn't see a scrap of red anywhere that wasn't on one of Sooni's clan. There were other commonalities, though. The Etari, in general, seemed to wear less than imperials. What clothes they wore were often loose fitting, providing ease of movement.

The whole area buzzed with activity as the two groups came together. Several Etari approached the carts the merchants had brought this far, sifting through the goods from Tonno as well as the spoils of the battle.

Alena still hadn't made peace with the desecration of the imperial bodies. Sooni insisted the Etari burned their dead as well, but it seemed convenient that the burning destroyed all evidence of the mercenary company. The Etari clearly didn't fear bringing the wrath of the dead upon them. Even Alena, who found most superstitions about the gates foolish, was discomfited by the lack of respect afforded to the dead.

She hadn't known what to do in response, except to stay far away from the stolen armor.

The clan they met shared Sooni's clan's lack of respect

for the dead. They rifled through armor, weapons, and clothes as though they were everyday items, not stripped from corpses. Alena couldn't follow the language, but she recognized haggling when she saw it.

The bartering for the goods of dead soldiers broke through her enforced separation. She couldn't stand to watch, so she went off to find something else to observe. She hadn't gotten far before Sooni stopped her with a hand gesture, signaling that Alena should approach.

Alena obeyed. Sooni stood next to another man, probably in his fifties. Physically, he didn't seem like much, but there was an air of menace about him. He intimidated Alena, though he gave no outward sign of violence.

"Rotger, this is Alena. She has been with us since Tonno, and the reason we were attacked. Alena, this is Rotger. He is the head of this family."

Alena bowed, not knowing how else to show the man respect.

He laughed, a low rumble from deep in his belly.

Somehow, even his laughter frightened her.

He led the three of them into one of the structures near the center of the village. Alena's eyes took a moment to adjust, and she was surprised by the interior.

Furs were scattered throughout the space, with a clearing made in the middle for a fire. The day outside was warm, but it was cool inside. Rotger settled on the furs with a grace Alena's father would have envied. Sooni and Alena followed suit.

"You may tell your story now, Alena. What is the secret that has made you such powerful enemies?" Sooni glanced at Rotger. "And please speak slowly. Rotger understands your imperial tongue somewhat well, but it would be a kindness to him."

Alena nodded, wondering where to start.

"I used to live in a town called Landow, far to the north. Are you familiar with it?"

Rotger gave a hand sign. Sooni smiled. "By name only. I have done most of my trading at Tonno."

Alena shrugged, realizing it didn't matter much. "In Landow I learned that the governor of the region, a man named Kye, was a bandit in search of a particular stone."

Sooni gestured for a stop. Her entire expression changed. "Can you describe the stone?"

"An uncut diamond, about so large." She traced the shape with her hands.

Sooni gestured for her to continue. Alena suspected Sooni knew something, though.

Alena spoke about the battles she had observed, about the murder of the wolfblades and the battle with Brandt out in the forest. Sooni and Rotger were an attentive audience, and Alena walked through the entire journey that led to their meeting.

When she finished, a combination of words and hand signs passed between the two leaders.

Rotger turned to her. "How are you involved?"

Alena hadn't said. Some part of her suspected her past could come back to haunt her here. The empire was strict about thieving, but they were considered gentle compared to the Etari. She took a deep breath. They had protected her thus far. "I was a thief."

"Was?" Sooni asked.

Alena shrugged again. "I'm trying to stop."

Rotger asked. "Thief?"

Sooni turned to the other clan leader, explaining. Rotger laughed.

"What's funny?"

Sooni replied. "All possessions within the Etari are communal. You couldn't steal anything from this home until you took it over the border. He finds the idea of individual property absurd."

Alena searched her memory. Had they ever taught her that about the Etari in the academy? She supposed even if someone had told her, she didn't remember. She would have laughed at communal ownership the way Rotger laughed at her imperial customs.

"How does that work?" Alena's curiosity overwhelmed any sense of propriety she possessed.

Sooni waved the question away. "There are more important matters to discuss. Do you know why Kye values this secret so much?"

"No. I don't know why he needed to adopt the disguise of a bandit in the first place. He's been hiding his affinity from the world, but he could have just asked for the stone. The wolfblades would have given it to him."

Rotger's deep voice rumbled.

Sooni translated. "He wanted the stone, but he didn't want anyone to know he has it."

That was as far as Alena's logic had taken her, too.

Rotger looked around the house, as though he might find answers written upon its blank walls. When he spoke again, his words were slow and soft. Sooni nodded, but didn't translate.

She looked to Alena. "The time has come for you to make a choice. Rotger is the head of this family, part of a clan that stretches for dozens of leagues both to the north and to the south. His people roam closest to the border of the empire. He has given his permission, so if you would like to settle with them, you may. If you wish or think that you might someday return to the empire, they will be closest."

Alena was surprised. Even though they'd done nothing but travel for many days, she had worked hard at not thinking about her future. She hadn't thought Sooni would just leave her behind, especially after all she had risked to save her. "You're leaving me?"

Sooni didn't respond right away, studying Alena's face. "I had planned to offer you a place within my family. Your past, though, concerns me."

Alena bowed her head, properly chastised. How would Sooni's family react if they all knew the truth? "I understand."

Sooni made a hand gesture. "I don't think that you do. It is difficult to steal among our people, but your actions reflect a lack of respect for others. I have seen you fight, and you have a spirit we admire. Others share my opinion. But if you wish to join us, you must confess your crimes to the whole family. There are no secrets among us."

Alena didn't understand. "You would take me with you, if I wished?"

"The choice is yours. But it is a hard road we travel. From here we head toward the center of our land, and after that our destination is unknown. Trade with the empire is our purpose, but we will not be able to safely return for some time. I do not know where the winds will take us. Either way, our bargain is now complete. You have given us the information you possess, and Rotger will make sure the word spreads. You may remain with Rotger's family, join us, or go your own way."

The idea of living on these plains alone frightened Alena. That option, at least, was out. Sooni's family still confused her, but they were the closest she came to familiarity these days. Her decision, then, was easy enough to make. "I would stay with you."

Sooni signed her acknowledgement, then stood up. A flash of hand signs passed between her and Rotger. She motioned for Alena to leave the tent.

Alena glanced between the two of them, but saved her question until she and Sooni left the tent. "You know something about Kye, or about that stone, don't you?"

Sooni's sharp intake of breath was answer enough. "No knowledge. Just guesses, but they are most likely accurate."

"Why is that stone so important?"

"I believe it is a gatestone stolen from one of our clans almost a year ago."

"A what?"

Sooni made the negative gesture, cutting off Alena's line of questioning. "You will learn more soon enough. There is much I must do, now that I know more."

"What do you mean?" Alena was tired of always being confused, of not knowing what was going on.

Sooni stopped. She was clearly eager to be rid of Alena, but also unwilling to abandon her without an explanation. "If it is what I believe it is, your story affects all Etari. We must make haste so that this story may spread, and a decision can be made. We leave at dawn."

39

B randt barely slept, despite Kyla's orders that he do so. Kyla hadn't let him speak to Ana the night before, insisting on interrogating her first.

Brandt understood his abbot's reasons, but they didn't ease his anguish. Ana had somehow survived. Against all hope, she had found him.

He held onto the memories from the night. He had jumped off the wall, Kyla's warning fading behind him. She had run to him, recognizing him as well.

Their embrace, short-lived as it was, told him all he needed to know. She had come here looking for him and was every bit as excited to see him as he was her.

Kyla had intervened then. Brandt had acquiesced, though it pained him to do so. So soon after the attack on the emperor, Ana's arrival seemed too coincidental. Ana's last words to him were that she would see him in the morning.

His world, already on edge, tilted even further, tossing his thoughts around like a farmer tosses hay. He couldn't hold on to any thought for more than a few moments. No doubt, Kyla evaluated Ana, tested her to ensure she wasn't under some form of compulsion.

He drifted in and out of sleep all evening, finally giving up when he thought sunrise was near. Now he paced the wall, watching the first pinks of morning brightening the dark sky. Every few moments he would glance behind him, looking down into the courtyard to see if she had woken.

The sun was barely over the horizon when Ana finally emerged.

Brandt ran to her, wrapping her up in his arms.

She was solid, and just the way he remembered her. Her long dark hair was loose, flowing down to below her shoulder blades. Her dark eyes found his, tears welling up in them. "I'm so sorry."

He just held her tightly, not sure what to say. She had nothing to apologize for. She was alive and that was all that mattered. After a few moments, she pushed him away. "I need to say this."

Brandt stood there, confused, a war of emotions tearing through him.

"That night, Brandt, I ran."

Brandt frowned. His lips formed a question, but no words came out.

"I know you don't remember, but I saw that building come down on top of Kyler, and in that moment, I knew we were up against someone we couldn't beat. I'd seen what we discovered in those caves, and Kyler's death confirmed my worst fears. So I ran. I should have stayed. I should have fought and died with the others. But I ran."

Ana kneeled down in front of him, baring the back of her neck, offering her life in exchange for her cowardice.

Brandt stood there, mouth agape.

He was delighted to see her. It didn't matter to him what

she'd done. She was alive. How couldn't she see that was all that mattered?

And he had survived, too. He hadn't completed his own fight. Compulsion had taken him and he had run when provided the opportunity. He was as much a coward as her.

But his words wouldn't come.

He kneeled down beside her and wrapped his arms around her again, holding her close. She had to understand that it didn't matter.

It couldn't matter.

Her composure cracked, and he felt her body convulse as sobs wracked her. In time, they faded. She eventually broke away, looking at him with red-rimmed eyes. "You really don't remember?"

Brandt shook his head. "I want to, but I don't."

"You're fortunate, not to carry those memories."

Brandt wasn't sure he agreed. He understood her meaning, but without knowing the ending, he wasn't sure how he could honor the memory of his friends. "Will you tell me what happened?"

"I can tell you what I know."

They stood, ignoring the questioning glances of the monks just coming out for their morning training. They went to the dining hall, where Brandt prepared tea for both of them.

By the time he poured the cups, Ana had calmed herself. "How much do you remember?"

"We were traveling to Landow. The last memory I can recall was Lola losing three games of dice in a row to Ryder. After that, it's empty."

"That was a day outside of Landow."

So Ana began there, retelling the story of their discovery

up in the mountains and the decisions that had led to the end of Brandt's wolfblades.

He found it strange, listening to Ana recount events that he had been present for. She kept looking at him, as though expecting her retelling of the story might spark something in him. He hoped the same, but the emperor's assessment was far too accurate. He remembered nothing.

Ana struggled when she came to the final battle, but she recounted what little she had seen, which ended with Kyler's death.

It occurred to him then that the honor they held so tightly to as a society was a foolish notion. His friend, a woman he had fought side-by-side with for years, was alive. And she feared he would hate her because she had run.

The thought troubled him. That same commitment to honor had gotten him through much of his life.

Would he have detested her for her moment of cowardice if he could remember more?

He was glad he didn't have the answer to that question.

She quieted as she neared the end of her story. They sat together, drinking tea in companionable silence.

"How did you find me?"

"I didn't try, not for some time. I figured that I would be tried and killed as a deserter for what happened. I hid, taking wage-earning jobs in small towns, moving from place to place, not really sure of what I was doing. Then, at some point, I heard the news of what happened in Landow. It said that three wolfblades had died. Your name wasn't listed."

She took a sip of her tea. "After that, you actually weren't hard to find. I sent a letter to central command, claiming I was a relative worried about you. I asked for your whereabouts. Three weeks later I got a reply."

"How long ago was that?"

"Two months."

So she hadn't come immediately, even after learning where he was. He understood, though. "You were that uncertain?"

She nodded.

He took a deep breath. "I'm glad that you're alive."

She reached out and took his hand. "You too."

He felt the warmth in her hand and treasured it.

"What will you do next?" he asked.

She looked at him sheepishly. "I didn't really think beyond this. I was sure you would kill me for abandoning you during the fight."

Even as she said it, he felt the flicker of anger within. His whole adult life revolved around the idea of fighting beside others, trusting that they would protect you at all times. But he couldn't be mad, not with Ana.

She bowed her head slightly, sipping at her tea while she thought. "What do you think I should do?"

The answer was out before he could think about it. "You could stay here."

"I deserted my post. The empire will kill me when they find out. Your abbot already knows."

"I don't think you need to worry." The more the idea sat in his thoughts, the more he approved. "You possess a strong affinity, which is exactly what the empire needs right now. Together, we can convince Kyla to let you stay. I think the empire will see the wisdom of the choice."

Ana looked around the barren dining room. "It's not exactly the life we were used to."

"No, but it's a way to serve the empire, even after what happened."

Ana gave him a quizzical look. "The abbot told me some

of what happened to you, but you've changed. You're... calmer."

Brandt retold his own story, detailing the struggles he had being a monk. By the time he finished, Ana was leaning in, eager to hear every word.

He could tell from her posture she was convinced. Now it was only a matter of letting her thoughts catch up.

"I'll stay," she declared.

He smiled. A few weeks of his memory might have disappeared, but he still knew his soldiers. "Let's get to work, then."

40

S ooni's family left Rotger's village the next day. From what Alena could observe, it looked as though Rotger was planning on moving soon, too. His family was beginning to pack their belongings into the carts scattered throughout the village.

Sooni had been the one who introduced her to the Etari concept of family. Family wasn't blood, but some other relationship, a subset of a larger clan. Rotger's family was much larger than Sooni's, and Alena understood they were parts of different clans.

None of which stopped the previous night from being particularly loud. The meeting of different families was a very — physical — affair, Alena had learned.

Azaleth climbed nimbly onto the cart beside her, a spring in his step that she'd never seen before. The bruises on his face from his beating in Tonno had faded completely, and he had attracted the attention of two young women the night before.

Even among a new family, Alena was left alone. She

noticed the stares and the obvious interest, but all she wanted to do at night was sleep.

Azaleth started the cart, flashing hand signs behind him as he did. Alena noticed Azaleth's focus on one of the young women, and was surprised to feel a flash of jealousy.

Soon, though, Rotger's village was gone and out of sight, and Azaleth was more talkative than usual. He spoke at length about any question she asked, which she appreciated.

Every morning she felt as though she was waking to a new mystery. If she closed her eyes, everything almost seemed familiar. She had ridden in carts before, and a horse smelled like a horse, no matter where in the world one was.

But when she opened her eyes, her whole world shifted. She found that she was beginning to get a taste for it.

Azaleth flashed her a smile that stretched from ear to ear. Alena had seen him use that same smile to great effect last night.

Still, it was an infectious smile. She'd seen him fight, but he still struck her as one of the most lighthearted souls she'd ever met. She returned the smile.

"Sooni says I'm supposed to teach you our language, and teach you how to fight."

Alena gave Azaleth a doubting look. "Really?"

Yes, flashed his hands. Then he pointed at himself. "Azaleth." He laughed.

She rolled her eyes.

Despite his inability to focus, Alena found Azaleth to be an effective tutor. He spoke imperial fluently, and learning the name for objects was a simple practice of memorization. Alena enjoyed Azaleth's quizzes, and she figured that after a few days she had learned a few hundred words.

There wasn't much else to do as the caravan trudged along.

The Etari language was easier to grasp than Alena expected. The structure was different than imperial. In Alena's world, most sentences began with a noun followed by a verb. There were plenty of complications, of course, but the general rule held.

The Etari led with verbs, followed by the objects of the verbs. Unlike imperial, though, which had dozens of exceptions, the Etari language was strict.

The Etari also lacked some of the more abstract concepts Alena considered necessary. They didn't have a word for honor, or family, as near as Alena could tell. The Etari "family" was a division of a clan, but as Alena had guessed, they weren't formed around blood ties. They had a word for birth mother, but that was it.

At random times throughout the day, Azaleth would switch to speaking Etari with her. He spoke slowly, so she could make out the words easily enough, but it took her time to decipher them.

She thought she learned quickly, though. After just a few days she could hold a basic conversation with him.

But knowing the language and being able to communicate were two very different tasks. She figured over half of Etari communication was nonverbal, and that was the hardest barrier for her to cross.

In imperial culture, it was considered rude to meet the gaze of a superior. As such, Alena realized she had developed a habit of glancing down or to the side when she spoke. The practice complicated her learning of the hand signs that made up so much of the Etari language.

The Etari tended to be very physical and very expressive. As she had already learned, different hand signs represented different ideas, but what she hadn't realized was that there was a tone to the signs as well. Sharp motions indicated anger or frustration. A gentle sign meant that all was well, or that one didn't need to worry.

Worse, there was no standard guide. After one particularly frustrating afternoon, Azaleth switched from tutoring to making fun of her. "You want a rule for everything!"

"Are you saying there are no rules?"

He made a sign for idiocy, but the motion of his hand was slow and easy. He wasn't upset about her question. "There are rules, but not written rules like what you want. You need to feel it! How can you talk to one another when all you have is your words?"

Alena opened her mouth to respond, then stopped. The idea made her head hurt. Words were the best way to transmit ideas. Writing was practically the foundation of civilization!

But Bayt had often told her that when she didn't understand something, the smartest thing she could do was close her mouth and watch.

So she did. She begged off lessons for the rest of the day and just observed her new family.

It was easier as an observer than as a participant. As an observer she could keep her eyes focused on the conversation without feeling like she should be looking down or away.

By the time they stopped for the evening, she thought that perhaps she understood. Etari communication wasn't just in the language, or even in the hand signs. She was looking for a direct correlation with her own language where none existed. Their communication was a combination of facial expressions, gestures, posture, and the words that they used.

As the family pitched their one large shelter for the evening, Alena pulled Azaleth aside. She smiled, performed the sign for gratitude slowly, and kept her other arm loose to her side.

Azaleth's laugh came easy. He spoke in imperial. "I think you begin to understand. But don't think about it so hard. Relax into it."

He turned to brag about his accomplishment to whoever would listen. Alena was just grateful they could break eye contact.

After the tent was set up, she and Azaleth practiced their martial skills. It was another area for Alena to learn humility. Azaleth was smaller and weaker, but that didn't seem to stop him from besting her in every fight they had.

The conclusion was inescapable. The martial training taught at the academy was inferior to what the Etari learned as children.

Sometimes the duels were close. Alena learned fast, and Azaleth tended to show off when he could, trying more complex techniques when simple ones would do. Every time she thought she had him, though, he would overcome her.

Some of it was through his sheer doggedness. He never gave up, no matter what position she had him in.

Azaleth provided most of the instruction. They would spar, and after he won they would break down what happened. Sometimes an adult would watch, providing suggestions if they found it appropriate.

The only time she didn't embarrass herself was with a knife. It had always been her favorite weapon at the academy, and only Azaleth's quick speed saved him from the wooden edge of her practice weapon.

Azaleth made her work with many different types of weapons. When she said that she preferred knives, he replied that a knife was great if you had one in hand, but that wasn't always the case. She needed to be prepared to fight with whatever was nearby.

That phrase, more than any other, seemed imprinted into Etari philosophy. They valued preparedness, almost to the exclusion of all else. After only a few weeks among them, she found the attitude seeping into her own thoughts as well.

Where martial skills were a struggle, their training with affinities was disastrous. No matter the amount of encouragement Azaleth offered, Alena couldn't summon any display of aptitude. Among a family in which every member could display multiple affinities at will, Alena's shame grew deep. Once, when a small gust of wind blew dirt into Azaleth's face, she claimed it as her own.

No one believed her lie.

Today's training was no different. Azaleth ran through the same exercises they practiced every day, hoping for a different result. She hated how he looked at her during those sessions, as though he was trying to puzzle out why she was broken.

Whenever she saw that look on his face she wanted to shout at him, to tell him that she wasn't damaged. She just wasn't capable. Perhaps Ryder's guess was accurate and she did have some small air affinity. But it meant nothing, especially here among the Etari, where affinities manifested differently.

They were about to end the training one evening when

Sooni came to them. She tossed a leather bracer on the ground between them. "Use this."

Azaleth looked up at his leader, surprise evident on his face. "But she's displayed no mastery."

"And she won't. She doesn't believe in herself." Her gaze turned to Alena. "Learn or leave. Tonight."

Sooni walked off then without another word.

Alena gritted her teeth, holding back a soft growl of frustration. There was much she admired about the Etari, but sometimes their belief in self-reliance went too far. If they were so convinced she had an affinity, she needed a teacher who wasn't a young boy, but a master. She didn't need another test, an ultimatum to prove herself to her adopted family.

Azaleth helped her put the bracer over her wrist, tying it tightly. She rubbed at it. "There's a part that's digging into my skin."

Azaleth gave her an affirmative hand sign. "It's normal."

Then he frowned, again looking as though he needed to solve a puzzle. Alena's heart sank when his eyes lit up. It made her think of Jace, when he had one of his "brilliant plans" that inevitably ended in disaster.

Azaleth picked out a handful of small stones from a bag at his hip. He grinned. "Turn around."

"What?" She stared at the first stone, already floating above his hand. Thankfully, it wasn't spinning. Azaleth wasn't planning on using it as a deadly weapon. Just as a stone.

"The training bracers only work when you already have some knowledge of what you are doing. But you don't." He gestured toward the floating stone. "I've seen you dodge projectiles, though. Maybe it will work."

"You want me to dodge a rock I can't see coming?"

He gave the affirmative hand sign.

This was a horrible idea.

A sudden and intense longing for her old academy instructors seized her. They never would have considered throwing rocks at her as an educational technique.

Still, she felt like a guest here, and what other choice did she have? It wasn't like she could propose a better idea for developing a skill she didn't possess.

So she turned, regretting the decision even as she did.

Azaleth gave no warning. The rock came straight for her left arm.

Alena twisted, but was distracted by the impossibility of *everything*.

The stone stopped, hovering in the air just beyond her.

Alena dropped to a knee, not trusting her balance. She blinked, but the sensations continued their subtle assault.

She felt the air. Not like the breeze against the skin, but as a presence. The air itself had a weight to it.

She felt the stone, too. The sensation wasn't as vivid as that of the air, but she noticed it all the same.

And more. So much more. Feelings she couldn't put a description to. When Azaleth walked to her, he wasn't just Azaleth. He was a collection of sensations. She felt the water within him, felt the air moving down his throat and through his lungs. For a moment, she thought she could see into his mind.

None of the feelings were overwhelming. Each was subtle, but it was far more than she was used to.

Azaleth bent down beside her and undid the bracer. He pulled it off gently, and the feelings subsided. She could still feel them, but they were whispered echoes of the sensations before.

Her young tutor checked on her, and it took her several tries to convince him that she was fine.

She curled up into herself then, pulling her knees tightly to her chest, looking out over the plains at nothing in particular.

Alena sometimes shot a glance at the bracer. It had caused her to feel this. This wasn't her.

But she knew that to be a lie.

Ryder had been right. Azaleth and the Etari were right.

She had an affinity. If she was interpreting her experience correctly, she had several.

Months ago, back in Landow, such a revelation might have broken her. She would have wandered for days, stunned at the knowledge.

But her mind had been battered by revelations in her travels. The mind adapted to stress, just like any other part of the body.

Alena stood up, picking up the bracer as she did. She turned it over and saw a small stone embedded in the leather. It appeared to be a small shard of diamond.

Azaleth tracked her gaze. "It's gatestone."

The same type of stone that had turned her life upside down in Landow. The same stone that had torn her from her family and sent her all the way here.

She wanted to hate it, but didn't find it within her. It was just a stone. A tool.

What she really hated was the man who had used the stone against her.

Alena looked at the bracer more closely. The leather was old, the way it appeared after hundreds of uses. Why did they use it for training?

Connections lit in her mind. They used it for training to

prepare for the rest of their lives. She looked up at Azaleth. "You have a stone on you, don't you?"

"All adult Etari do." He lifted up his shirt, where the stone was embedded near his navel.

Before the discussion could wander any further, Sooni returned. Her gaze was a question. Azaleth flashed a hand sign, letting her know the ultimatum had worked. Sooni smiled and looked to Alena.

"Welcome to the family."

41

B randt chased Ana up the mountain, his breath coming easy as he used his lightness to pull himself from stone to stone. He could keep her pace, but barely.

She crested the cliff and disappeared from sight.

Suspecting a trap, Brandt altered his direction, climbing a section of rock further to the right that provided solid enough holds. He crested the ridge less than a dozen heartbeats after Ana, unsurprised to see her waiting where she had finished her climb, wooden sword in hand. Had he followed her trail exactly, he expected that sword would be battering his ribs at the moment.

He landed softly, darting into a grove of trees as water condensed out of the air and formed a whip that snapped at him.

The trees protected him from Ana's water affinity. Out in the open, she had learned to use her water whip to great effect, but it wasn't quite as useful in the tight confines of the grove.

She came in with her sword, using lightness to bounce off of trees and attack from above.

Brandt parried her attack, leaping up to the trees and running along the branches.

She followed him on the ground below, leaping up to meet him when she spotted an opening. Their swords met and cracked together, each of them balanced upon a single tree branch.

Ana kicked at his shin, but Brandt jumped, the heel of her foot passing just underneath him.

He wasn't sure how her other foot reached him so fast, but the results weren't in dispute. He lost his balance, plummeting to the ground below. Even light, the landing hurt.

Ana laughed as she dropped down. She offered him her hand. He took it, but instead of letting her help him up, he pulled her down. Ana let herself fall, landing on top of him. Their lips met, and for a few moments, all was right in Brandt's world.

Ana pushed herself away. She sat down next to him as he rolled into a sitting position. They looked down at the valley below, one small corner of the monastery visible from where they sat.

"What's bothering you?" Ana asked.

"Maybe I just wanted to spend some time alone with you." Brandt tried to keep the concern out of his voice, but failed.

Ana waited for him to answer her question honestly.

He hadn't lied, exactly. He did want to spend time with her. Training filled most of his days, and what little time remained was dedicated to studying recent events within the empire. Being out here with Ana grounded his thoughts.

"It's nothing new," he said. "But the news keeps getting worse. I don't think we have much time left."

Just that morning, a new report had crossed his desk. It

had been from Tonno. A farmer outside of town, who lived near the border of Etar, had shot down a predatory bird. Unsure of the species, he had sent for an artist, who made several sketches of the bird and showed them around Tonno. Eventually the governor there had sent the news deeper into the empire, where it reached Brandt. The wolfblade wasn't even sure how old the information was. At least months had passed since the sighting. The bird could have even crossed the ocean last year.

No one in the empire knew the species of bird. At least, none of the naturalists had identified it yet. The farmer reported that the bird was willing to attack much larger creatures — behavior unusual for any known predatory bird.

By itself, the case was nothing but a curiosity. But such news seemed more common than ever. Hardly a week passed where Brandt didn't discover some new piece of information that didn't fit with the world they understood.

"Something is happening." Brandt searched for more specific words but failed. He didn't know enough to say more. "It feels like a storm is building off in the distance and I have no way to take shelter."

"Then don't. There was a time when you welcomed any storm that came. You even sought them out, as I recall."

"I was younger, and foolish."

"In some ways. But youth possesses a wisdom the elders don't always appreciate."

He supposed Ana spoke true. In the years he and Ana had spent in the monastery, he'd become comfortable. Once, he'd sought out conflict as a way to grow stronger. His desire to improve still motivated him, but what he wanted now was to live out his days in peace. He had grown to enjoy life within the confines of the monastery.

Being married to Ana helped.

He still couldn't believe his good fortune. Some called their union inevitable, but he refused to take their relationship for granted. They had been close friends, but their relationship grew unfettered within the monastery. Living with her no doubt fed his lack of desire to fight.

Their studies over the past six years had made them stronger. The martial skills of every monk in Highkeep were stronger than they had ever been. Brandt, along with the others, had developed fighting styles uniquely suited to their abilities, pushing the limits of their affinities and martial skills.

The knowledge was spreading, too. News that people could possess more than one affinity had entered the military, and there were already reports of soldiers with multiple affinities. Every day was a step in the right direction.

But those reports made him wonder if they had developed fast enough. No doubt, their enemy had also been preparing, and given how much of a head start they possessed, Brandt wasn't sure the empire could catch up.

The creatures, and the dangers they represented, threatened to put an end to Brandt's relatively peaceful life. The problem extended beyond the creatures, too. Though he never received a direct report, Brandt found the pattern whenever he looked. Buildings collapsed, fires spread, and storms struck, all in places the emperor just happened to be visiting. The incidents occurred far too often to be chance.

Brandt accepted the Emperor's explanation of Palagia, mostly because he had no other explanation. He wanted to blame the Etari, but the Etari were a simple people. They never had the knowledge or the ability to do something like this.

His world crumbled just as he desired comfort the most. "Do you feel it, too?"

She nodded again. "It feels like a change is coming. All we can do is be ready for it."

Brandt wished that she had different advice, but she spoke harsh truths. Maybe they would be prepared when disaster hit.

They sat in silence on top of the cliff for some time, enjoying the quiet peace of the secluded mountains. But all pleasant breaks had to come to an end. They took a trail from the grove of trees that led down to the monastery.

The monastery was the longest Brandt had stayed in one place since he was a child. Since joining the military, he'd never had a place he called home. He still wasn't sure if that was a title he wished to grant to the monastery, but he felt at ease here. This was as close to home as he'd ever gotten since leaving his family.

From the moment they stepped through the gates, Brandt knew something was amiss. The summons waiting for him at the gate confirmed his suspicion. "The abbot has requested your presence in her chambers," the guard reported.

There was a nervous energy among the monks, but no one spoke on what had happened.

It didn't take Brandt and Ana long to find themselves standing in front of the abbot. "What happened?" he asked.

She gestured for them to take a seat. Without a word she handed over a slip of paper. Brandt read it quickly and handed it to Ana. He noted that at one point it had been sealed with the black wax used only by the emperor. "What does he mean when he says that the storm broke?"

"The primary reason Palagia hasn't attacked us directly is because severe storms encircle our continent, once one gets far enough to sea," Kyla began. "The storms have been weakening for years, and it appears that this summer the storm broke for a little less than a month before reforming. The emperor fears that something has made it through."

"An invasion?"

Kyla shrugged. "Or an advance force. We don't know, but we need to find out. Hence the orders."

Brandt read the paper again. The emperor ordered parties of monks to spread out among the northern coast. Highkeep, because of its position, was to investigate from the Etari border to the small coastal port of Seagate. The monastery at Flan would investigate the rest of the northern coast.

Brandt imagined a map in his head, predicting Kyla's orders.

"I'm sending a group of monks up north. They'll travel to Landow, then spread out around the coast. I'd like you two to join the group, but I understand Landow carries a heavy toll. Will you go?"

Ana spoke for both of them. "We will."

Brandt stared off in the distance.

After all these years, he was returning to Landow.

42

A lena breathed softly through her nose as she gently parted the tall grass in front of her. Each of her movements was slow and measured. She remained alert to changes in the wind that might give away her position to the predator less than two hundred paces in front of her. She and Azaleth were close to their targets, but she wanted to be closer yet, wanted to guarantee that their shots would be true.

She froze when she saw the wolf poke its snout into the air, sniffing for clues. As much as she wanted to get closer, it might be a while before that happened.

Was it worth the risk to try now? A kill would be difficult, but Alena wasn't sure how much closer they could get, and it wasn't often that this creature provided them any opportunities.

She raised her left hand into the air and made a quick sign, questioning her partner.

Azaleth's response was immediate. Of course, confidence was never something that Azaleth lacked. Without better options, Alena agreed. They had to make the attempt.

Another few hand signs passed between them and then Alena pulled out a stone from the pouch at her hip. She held the stone in her hand for a few moments, admiring the deadly simplicity of the weapon. Then she floated it aloft and placed it between her and Azaleth. As the weaker of the two, she set the rock to spinning. She still remembered the first time that she had seen the technique in action, how amazed she had been by what she had witnessed.

But now that the secrets were unlocked, the technique seemed so easy, so mundane. Growing up, she had always thought of affinities as a result of strength alone, but the Etari showed her the error of her ways. Small changes, enacted one after the other, could create a tremendous effect. The rock was an excellent example. She set it to spinning, a small brush that required very little energy. Then another. And another, a series of ever-quickening brushes of will that sent it spinning dozens of times per heartbeat.

She still wasn't as fast as the native-born Etari. They had been practicing for longer than they could walk, and the difference in skill was considerable. But after a few moments she had the rock spinning quickly enough. She stopped brushing it and waited for Azaleth's push.

Azaleth could have completed the task on his own. But pairing up allowed for a little more power and accuracy. In this case, both were vital.

She didn't wait long. Less than two heartbeats after she stopped she felt his own strength push against the rock, sending it arcing into the air on a trajectory that should, if all went well, bring the stone piercing down on the wolf's head.

The responsibilities of both partners had been long etched in Etari tradition. So even when Alena thought that the shot was a little off, she made no motion. As soon as Azaleth had pushed on the rock, the shot was his responsibility. Any action she took would be a distraction. As the spinning rock began to fall, Alena became more and more certain that the miss was imminent. Azaleth, confident as he was, showed no doubt.

The rock missed, cutting through the outer fur of the wolf's neck without causing any meaningful damage. Alena cursed. It had taken them days to work up to the shot, and she didn't think the wolf was going to let them have another one.

Her guess became reality soon enough. But she had expected the wolf to escape, and she was proven very wrong.

The wolf stood up, glancing their way as it caught the flicker of movement that was Azaleth preparing another stone.

The wolf charged.

Every muscle in Alena's body screamed for her to run, her body's never-ending desire for life making itself known.

She ignored the reaction, fighting against her fear as her fingers fumbled in her pouch for another rock.

Beside her, Azaleth already had one spinning. He launched, but whether due to fear or error, the stone missed the wolf completely.

Alena pulled out a rock and spun it, her fear and lack of control causing the rock to wobble more than spin. With every heartbeat, the wolf grew closer. Panicked, she launched it, but her technique was horrible, and the shot was useless.

Except that it focused the wolf's attention on Alena.

Some small rational part of her knew that her only chance of survival was to kill the wolf. But that wasn't an option. Her body refused to obey her mind's wisdom. She turned and ran, listening to the shouts of Azaleth behind her, reminding her of how foolish she was acting.

Alena had no chance of winning a foot race against the wolf. She knew it, but she ran anyway, driven by fear.

She felt Azaleth's energy surge as he brought incredible focus to his next stone. It zipped out of Azaleth's grasp, catching the wolf cleanly through its torso.

It was a fatal shot, but not immediately so.

Alena felt the wolf jump for her. She dove to the side, rolling and coming to her feet while running at a right angle from the direction she had been. The wolf landed and turned, ready to pursue her, but not before Azaleth put a final stone through its head.

The wolf dropped, twitching and still, as Alena watched, fascinated. It only took Azaleth a few moments to come next to her. She gestured, letting him know that she was unharmed.

They stood together, looking down at the wolf's corpse. Dead, it looked so normal, like any of the other creatures she had hunted over the years. But in life, this wolf had been different.

Wolves didn't attack. Not like that. Startled by hunters, a wolf should retreat. Beyond that, wolves were pack animals, and this one was alone. And it had followed their family for days now.

The wolf's behavior was odd, but they had been seeing more odd phenomena lately. Animals didn't act in the manner they should. Clan leaders had been searching for explanations, but none were forthcoming.

The unusual behaviors weren't just limited to the animals, either. Rumors on the wind told of people behaving in ways that were distinctly not Etari. Murders and thievery had become growing problems, particularly for the clans out near the western shores.

The problems hadn't affected Sooni's family. After bringing Alena out of Tonno, they had avoided imperial lands for almost a year, running trade routes for larger clans.

Since then they had resumed trade with the empire, although further to the south, away from Landow and Tonno. They had been on their way to the Etari capital when they first spotted the wolf.

This wolf had stalked the family for several days. Azaleth, although no longer the youngest member of the family, still always jumped at an opportunity to prove himself. Alena had little say in her own appointment. Sooni still believed Alena didn't possess enough experience, and made her take every hunting opportunity that presented itself.

"It looks like a wolf," Azaleth said.

"You were expecting something different?"

A hand sign representing uncertainty. "I thought maybe it would be sick."

"It might be, just in ways we can't see."

They had instructions not to bring the meat back to camp.

That, by itself, was indication enough of how odd the Etari found the events happening around them. Food was never wasted. But Sooni didn't want anything from the wolf. She wanted it dead, which they had accomplished.

Azaleth, who still considered himself her teacher, even after all this time, turned to her. "You shouldn't have run."

"I know."

They spoke Etari now, the language second nature to Alena. She was grateful that they still made the trips into the empire. Without them, she worried her fluency with her native tongue would slowly disappear.

"I know you know, but you need to understand. Running put you in far more danger. It's not that there isn't a time to run, but it's still your first instinct when trouble happens."

"I know." Her voice dripped with venom. She loved Azaleth like a younger brother, but he could be overbearing at times. He acted as though her protection was his responsibility, even though it never had been.

Azaleth looked like he wanted to say more, but he wisely held his tongue. He turned in the direction of camp. "We should return. Sooni will want to know that the wolf is dead."

Alena followed him as he sulked his way back to the camp.

43

Walking the road to Landow twisted Brandt's emotions like wringing out a wet rag. In the years since he last visited, he had forgotten many of the details of the journey to the town. But some were familiar.

He recognized an inn they had stayed at, the sign above the door weathered by the intervening years. His wolfblades had drank too much that night, celebrating some minor event he no longer remembered. He and Ana walked past the inn without pause. He had no desire to relive those aching memories.

Despite the poignant nature of his remaining memories, he remembered nothing of their destination. Landow had changed the course of his life, but he felt as though he was visiting for the first time.

Brandt wondered if the one who had stolen his memories still lived in Landow. He often fantasized what revenge he would extract if he encountered the bandit again. At times, he caught himself grinning viciously at the possibilities.

Ana didn't share his feelings. For her, Landow was the site of her greatest failure. Brandt viewed it with a mixture of nervousness and curiosity. Ana viewed it with shame.

They were walking through the forest just south of Landow when Brandt heard Ana's sharp intake of breath. He turned to look back at her. She leaned up against a tree and appeared faint.

"What is it?" he asked.

"This is where we fought the bandit for the first time."

Brandt looked around and tried to hide the truth that one of his secret hopes had been dashed. Some small part of him had never believed the emperor, had always hoped that if he just returned to the area he'd encounter some sight that triggered his lost memories.

He felt nothing.

It was just a road through a forest.

He gave Ana some time to recover. When she did, they completed the trek to Landow's walls. They were part of a group of twenty monks. After a night in Landow, they would separate to different sections of the coast.

Brandt took note of the city watch that walked the walls. They appeared alert, and took their duty with the seriousness it deserved. Brandt considered such details evidence of strong leadership in the town.

Brandt's walk slowed to a stop when he neared the gates. He searched his memory, waiting for a flash of recollection.

None came.

Ana stopped next to him, grabbing his hand.

"I hoped I would remember."

"Nothing?"

He shook his head. "I feel like I've never been here before." He let go of her hand before he crushed it in his fist.

Without another word, he passed through the gate. Before long they were standing in Landow once again.

The streets were busy. Travelers came and went and the merchants positioned near the gate enjoyed brisk business. Brandt's mouth watered as the delicious scents of fresh food filled his nose. Other than a young boy trying to convince them to try a certain inn, though, no one paid them any mind.

Their arrival should mean something. Somebody should notice them. His friends had died here. Had any of it mattered?

Stealing memories was no different than stealing souls, Brandt decided. Without the lessons of the past to shape us, he thought, we are nothing.

Brandt ran his hand through his hair, clearing the melancholy thoughts away. He had hoped for different, but he hadn't expected much. The emperor himself had told him the memories were gone. Hope was foolish.

They had more important matters to deal with.

While most of the monks headed toward the inn, Brandt and Ana traveled to the town hall. The local governor, Kye, had promised the monks an updated set of maps to aid them on their journey. Secretly Brandt hoped the governor would have some information for him, some guidance regarding the events of seven years ago.

They announced themselves as visiting monks, and not long after a young man came to meet them. He walked with an easy grace and Brandt saw the young man's martial ability immediately. This was a man who had dedicated himself to his skills. They exchanged bows.

"The governor is honored by your presence. My name is Jace, and I am the governor's chief aide. We welcome you."

"Thank you for your kindness."

Jace led them deeper into the hall to a large receiving room. A man sat there, cross-legged on the floor. He rose with an easy grace, but Brandt swore he saw the man falter as he stepped forward and looked at Brandt for the first time.

"Governor Kye, these are—" Jace didn't have the opportunity to finish his sentence.

"Sergeant Brandt," the governor said.

Brandt felt as surprised as Jace looked. "Not sergeant anymore, but yes."

The governor looked from Brandt to Ana. "And you must be—"

Ana bowed. "Ana, sir."

The governor took a step back. "Brandt and Ana. I never thought I would see the two of you again."

The man looked surprised. But if he was the same governor who had known them seven years ago, Brandt supposed he had sufficient reason.

Brandt rushed to explain before the situation became awkward. "I'm sorry, sir. I know that I have been in Landow before, but I have no memory of the incident. If we've met before, I have no recollection."

Brandt thought he saw a flicker of relief pass over the governor's face. Or perhaps it was surprise. Very few people knew about the existence of mental affinities. Regardless, the governor recovered quickly.

Kye gestured for them all to take a seat. They joined him on a set of cushions, and Jace brought tea for them all. "I've prepared the updated maps, as promised. But I suspect you two have another purpose. How may I help?"

Ana glanced at Jace, who stood at loose attention near the entrance to the room. Brandt guessed he was a bodyguard in addition to an aide.

Kye answered her unspoken question. "You may say anything in front of Jace. He's my most trusted aide, and knows all that I do."

Brandt caught the pride on the young man's face before turning to focus on Kye.

"As you know, we are here on the emperor's request. But before we leave to scout the coast, I need to know if there is anything you can tell me about our last visit here, anything that isn't in the public record?"

Kye sipped at his tea. "There's little to tell that you probably haven't already learned. Your wolfblades fought with Zane Arrowood and a bandit. Three of your friends tragically lost their lives. Not long after, there was a fight in the woods south of town, unleashing incredible affinities no one had seen before. A fireball lit the entire sky. No bodies were found, but it was assumed, given the fire damage in the area, that both you and the bandit perished in the battle. I only heard a year or two ago that you were still alive, and I assumed you had been injured and were receiving care in the monastery."

Brandt started at that. He hadn't been injured when he came to the monastery, which meant that Kye had believed a lie. He leaned forward. "My memory was destroyed, which leads me to believe the bandit is still alive."

Kye gave him an apologetic look. "If he is, I assume he is no longer here. He was never seen again after the fight in the forest."

Brandt clenched his fist. Again, his hopes were dashed. He had hoped there would be a lead somewhere here in Landow. But it appeared the bandit had vanished.

Kye seemed to read his thoughts. "I'm sorry that I can't be of more help, but if I may, can I ask you a question?"

Ana nodded for both of them.

"The note I received from the emperor indicated he worries about a foreign invasion from a faraway continent. What more do you know? I confess that I worry. If the invasion comes from the north, Landow needs to be prepared, and I do not think our city guard is sufficient."

Ana answered. "We know little, except they possess a skill with affinities beyond our understanding. The emperor isn't sure the empire is at risk, but we must be sure."

Kye nodded. "The affinities are why he's relying on the monks instead of the military, isn't it?"

Brandt tore himself away from his dying hopes to rejoin the conversation. "I believe so."

Kye shook his head. "I've always wished for an affinity. I'm jealous of those of you with the strength to change the world."

Brandt frowned. "How so?"

Kye looked off in the distance. "When I was young, my family was part of a caravan that was ambushed by the Etari. The Etari, of course, claimed the caravan had trespassed on their territory. But most of my family died. I was the only one who survived, but most of our wealth had been invested in that caravan. I found myself a young man, alone and broke. I've always believed that if I just had more strength, I could reshape this world. Make it better."

"I'm sorry for your loss," Ana said.

Kye waved her sympathy away. "I think about them every day, and their memory still guides me, but it is long past. The emperor has rewarded my service, and I'm glad to continue offering it."

With that, Kye summoned the maps and offered them to the monks. "I wish you the best in your endeavor. Please, if you find anything, let me know. I vowed to protect Landow at all costs, and I take that vow seriously."

Brandt and Ana bowed and said their farewells. He was saddened he hadn't learned more, but he had more important problems to worry about.

Tomorrow they would begin their journey to the coast to see if the emperor's fears were justified.

44

Travelers could see the city from a long ways away. It rested on a rise in the land, providing a commanding view of the surrounding plains. For all the traveling she had done, Alena had never seen another city like it.

The Etari called it Cardon, and it was the closest thing to a city or capital they possessed.

Today marked Alena's third visit. Each of her previous ones had proven to be unique experiences, and this third promised much the same. Even from a distance, Alena guessed the city had swelled to over twice its normal size.

Sooni had told them to expect as much. News had traveled back and forth between the families about the odd events happening throughout the northern end of Etar. Most of the largest clans were gathering at Cardon to discuss what they might do. Sooni and her family were part of the influx of visitors.

They reached the outskirts of Cardon as the sun reached its peak.

Calling Cardon a city wasn't quite accurate. The location was permanent, but still consisted almost entirely of tents. It shrank or grew depending on circumstance, but it served as a central meeting place for all the clans. At least one clan always lived there, even though the responsibility shifted between clans.

Sooni guided her family to their larger clan's tents without problem, and her family joined with the others of the clan with shouts and embraces.

Alena wasn't left out. Though her acceptance into the clan had been a gradual process, she was now largely treated as one of their own. She embraced friends and caught up on news in a flurry of conversations and hand signs.

A few of her friends were pregnant, and one looked as though she might give birth any day. The women were congratulated by all. The size of their clan had diminished in the past few months. The strange events sweeping the land had killed a few, and the typical dangers of the world, including disease and age, had taken a number of the older members. Giving birth was a woman's choice, but even Alena, usually exempt from such matters, had been feeling pressure from her family to conceive.

Behind her, Azaleth followed. If given half the chance, she knew he would leap to the task. He'd made his affections public three years ago, but Alena hadn't bedded anyone since her arrival, a quirk that was frowned upon by most of the family.

It was the one step she couldn't allow herself to take, though. Most days, she now considered herself Etari. At night, however, alone, she couldn't bring herself to invite another into her bed. Bedding another, or worse, conceiving a child for the clan, felt like giving up on her past, like admitting that she would never return to the land of her birth. Despite her desire, she held strong.

And Azaleth suffered in silence. He bedded other women, and was considered quite a find by many. But his eyes were always fixed on her. He knew if he pushed too hard, she would push him away. So he contented himself with her companionship, a stalemate that left them both feeling uneasy.

She pushed thoughts of him aside. These reunions weren't about her, but her friends. She listened to their stories of pregnancy with as much grace as she could manage. Questions about partners were exchanged, and Alena noted how none of the questions were directed her way. She was Etari, and yet not.

Unfortunately, the reunions were cut short when Sooni found them and gestured for her and Azaleth to follow. As they fell in beside her, she explained. "Some of the elders are gathering to discuss the events of the past few weeks. It's nothing official, yet, but I've been asked to bring you two to the elders to tell the story of the wolf."

"Including me?" Alena asked. Her own clan was welcoming enough, but there were some who viewed the adoption of an imperial girl to be an offense to the rest of the Etari. The empire was a trading partner, but it was still an acrimonious relationship.

Sooni signed an affirmative. "You need to stop acting like you don't belong, Alena. The others seize on it and use it to drive a wedge between us. You're just as Etari as those of us born here."

Alena acknowledged, but wished she felt as confident as Sooni. Sooni didn't understand the sideways glances, the whispers and hand signs that passed between others when they thought Alena didn't notice. Just like a few moments ago, Alena was Etari, except she wasn't. She had no home.

Several large tents stood in the middle of Cardon, where

all the elders of the present clans held council together. Sooni arrived with her charges in the middle of another clan's testimony. They stopped near the outer ring of observers to listen.

"The birds attacked us!" the man in the center said. Alena's sharp eyes didn't miss the fading claw marks across his cheeks. "It didn't matter how many of them we killed. They kept attacking, until the last bird fell."

"And did you notice anything unusual about the birds when you examined them?"

The man shook his head. "They seemed unharmed, with no physical evidence of madness."

Alena ran her eyes over the crowd, picking up on the hand signs and whispers. Reason warred with trust among the elders.

The speaker was dismissed and another took his place. This Etari was a woman, who stood tall before the elders.

"Three months ago, I left our camp with my partner for the evening. We wished to be alone under the stars. On our walk, we startled a deer, who attacked us. My partner was speared by the deer's antlers, and he died soon after."

And so it went, a litany of stories of animals and nature acting in ways that were unfamiliar to the Etari. Each story, by itself, could be explained. But the larger pattern couldn't be ignored.

Alena and Azaleth were eventually summoned. Azaleth told their story while Alena watched the crowd. She saw several signs where she was called a traitor, but she kept her face neutral.

The elders questioned Azaleth. When they finished, they turned to her. "Do you have any explanation for the stories you have heard today?"

"None," she replied.

There was a snort of outrage behind her, but she refused to turn. "It's an imperial plot, a prelude to an invasion."

The elders didn't dismiss the idea, but focused it on her. "What do you think of that?"

Alena made the sign for uncertainty. "It doesn't feel right, but I don't know what abilities the empire possesses."

"You'd trust the word of an imperial?" The same voice, again behind her.

Such interruptions were rude, and an elder finally called it out. "She's lived among us for years. Sooni granted her a gatestone four years ago. By our traditions, she is one of us. Like it or not, it is true. I'll not suffer such disrespect."

Alena felt her cheeks go red, and she felt the gatestone, embedded near her navel. Sooni had granted her the stone after a long series of tests. When she'd received it, Alena had felt as proud as she had through any accomplishment in her life. It was the only reason she possessed the affinities she did. But now it felt like a weight. She didn't want to be here. Azaleth could have told the story just as well by himself, and wouldn't implicate the empire just by his presence.

They were dismissed, replaced by yet another testimony. Alena practically hid behind Azaleth as the afternoon continued. She still felt the angry glares of some of the other clans.

Anders I had waged war on the Etari during the War of Unification. Alena had never been clear on why he hadn't conquered the Etari. The empire had far more resources, far more people, far more *everything* than the Etari. Yet the land remained in Etari hands.

The war had devastated the Etari people. At least, that was what Alena's history books had taught her. The war had driven them to the barbaric existence they now lived.

Alena didn't believe the imperial histories anymore,

though. The Etari didn't like the empire, but in true Etari fashion, they only blamed themselves for their failure. Any imperial who crossed the border was killed, which led to no end of skirmishes. Bold traders often cut through Etar in a bid to deliver their goods more quickly to other parts of the empire. Beyond the resulting skirmishes, the Etari seemed to consider the empire something closer to an obnoxious older brother than an enemy. Alena had never quite figured the attitude out.

But they didn't live like savages. She knew that as a certainty, now. Their lifestyle was certainly different, but it was just as much a civilization as the empire.

The testimonies continued, strange event piling on top of strange event. The world was becoming an odd place, Alena decided. But it didn't look like the elders were going to make any decisions today. They were just collecting information.

Alena heard a commotion coming from outside the tent. She turned just in time to see a young man enter, a messenger. He was out of breath, sweat pouring from his forehead. The whole crowd gathered around the elders and went silent.

After a moment, the messenger stood up. "Elders, hear my news!"

He paused to catch his breath.

"Invasion!"

45

B randt, Ana, and the other monks left Landow the next day, separating just outside of town. Thanks to the horses and supplies, Brandt felt confident their mission could be completed quickly. He was certain that they would be able to scout their section of the northern shore and be back to Landow within a month.

He found that he was of two minds about the expedition. There was no doubt that strange events were occurring more regularly, and he did fear they were precursors to something worse. On the other hand, it seemed almost impossible to accept that not only was there a second continent on the planet, but that the people of that continent might be attempting to land an invasion force upon imperial land. His rational mind simply didn't accept it easily.

So he relaxed into his saddle and enjoyed the trip with his wife. He couldn't remember the last time he had been on a horse, but the skills he once earned in the military soon came back to him. The first day of riding was rough, but eventually they adjusted.

They traveled northwest, heading toward the Etari border. This far north, the Alna river was a wide border and largely unguarded. The Etari had always known when someone crossed the river, a feat no military strategist had ever explained. And the Etari never left their land this far north.

They found the river on the fourth day and followed it all the way to the coast. From there, their path took them further north, gradually curling toward the east. Riding filled their days, and at night they relaxed under the stars, eager for the time alone.

Brandt kept his senses alert, but he saw nothing in their journey that gave him any cause for alarm. They saw few people and enjoyed the quiet of their journey. At night, Brandt even allowed a fire so that they could stay warm as the nights grew colder.

The land they rode through was wild. The northern coast of the continent wasn't particularly friendly, supporting at best a light ranching operation. The ground was rocky and uneven, and little more than wild brush grew throughout the land.

Brandt didn't like the open spaces. He had grown up in cities and in forests, and the endless amount of open sky always concerned him. He kept feeling like he needed a place to hide, but there was no place to do so.

Six days after they started following the coast, they finally moved from the barren rugged grounds to a forested section of land. Brandt breathed a sigh of relief as they entered the trees.

They still rarely saw others. The land, as near as he could tell, was as empty as ever.

Until they came across a grouping of tracks.

Brandt swore. The party wasn't large, but the tracks told

him they had come from the shore and were making their way south. He glanced at Ana. Their decision was easy enough to make. They followed the tracks.

The pursuit lasted two days.

He and Ana were riding through a particularly dense growth when he called for a stop. Ana obeyed, and the two of them sat upon their horses in silence. Brandt listened, then spoke to Ana. "Do you hear that?"

She shook her head slowly. Then the same realization dawned on her. "It's too quiet," she whispered.

Brandt nodded. Far ahead, a group of birds scattered. Brandt traced the path ahead with his imagination. Where the birds had scattered seemed to be about the place where the path would lead.

Old instincts, dormant but not forgotten in his time at the monastery, reasserted themselves. It seemed very much like an ambush.

Brandt glanced over at Ana. He could tell from the look in her eyes that she was thinking the same. Which led him to a decision he hadn't thought he would have to make. Their mission dictated that they find out who had set the ambush. But he didn't want to risk Ana's life. He thought that he had lost her once, and he refused to endure that again. Especially now that they were closer than ever before.

She gave him no choice, though. She got off her horse and led it off of the road to where it wouldn't be easily discovered. Brandt followed suit.

From there, Brandt and Ana approached on foot. Their progress was slow. With every step Brandt would lift his foot, make sure the ground in front of him was safe to step on, then take the step. If there was a twig or something else in his way, he brushed it aside lightly before taking the step. Next to him, Ana did the same.

Their progress was slow, but Brandt was confident that their approach was unobserved. Every couple hundred paces they would stop and wait, studying their surroundings for the minutest detail that might indicate an enemy had spotted them.

They made a wide semicircle, attempting to sneak up behind whoever had set the ambush.

The forest around them remained too quiet. It sounded as though the trees themselves were holding their breath, waiting for the trap to be sprung. It was a giant game of hide and seek, with fatal consequences.

They won.

Ana spotted them first. She held up a hand to pause their slow advance, then pointed ahead. There, just ahead of them, were four figures lying still along the path their war party had made. Their clothing was unlike anything that Brandt had ever seen. It consisted of strips of fabric that mimicked natural patterns. If he focused too hard on them, he couldn't see them. It was only by keeping a light focus that he could catch the subtle movements that gave them away.

They held weapons he didn't recognize either. In a way, they looked like crossbows, but the design was unlike anything he'd seen before.

One of them shifted their head slightly, and Brandt knew in an instant that he had seen enough. Those features were unlike any that he had seen before. From this distance, there was little for him to make out, but there was just enough to know they weren't imperial, and they certainly weren't Etari. The skin was too pale for anyone on this continent.

He and Ana were outnumbered, but they had the element of surprise. If they could kill two immediately, they might have a chance at winning the fight. He was eager to test the skills he'd worked so hard for.

But that assumed the four were alone.

Brandt didn't like how the setup felt. They could make out the four, but there could very well be more hiding in wait. The risks were too high.

Besides that, they had found what they were looking for. Their mission, as far as Brandt was concerned, was complete. Their duty wasn't to fight, but to bring the word back to where it would do the most good. They needed to return to Landow and send word to the emperor.

Their ruler's worry had been right.

The invasion had arrived.

46

A lena closed her eyes and took a deep breath, willing the jitters coursing through her body to leave. She shook out her arms, one at a time, to no avail.

Up ahead, the Etari camp came into view. The collection of shelters wasn't nearly as large as Cardon, but was impressive all the same.

The last she had heard, over two dozen families were camped here, directly in the path of the mysterious invaders. While the invaders advanced, the Etari prepared for battle.

Beside her, Azaleth seemed to understand her thoughts. *It'll be okay*, he signed.

She wished she felt the same confidence. Every so often she found herself looking over her shoulder out east, toward the empire. Her homeland held many dangers, but none as immediate as the battle her family rode toward. It had been almost seven years. Surely her crimes had been forgotten by now?

That line of reasoning made her uncomfortable. She

wanted to believe that she had remained with the Etari because she felt some connection with them. That they had become her true family.

But now that her family was being tested, she wondered if she hadn't remained with them because it was the easiest path to take.

Hadn't she learned at all?

If her overwhelming desire to turn her horse around and ride for the organized armies of the empire was any indication, the answer was no.

While her thoughts ran to escape, she knew they would remain as thoughts alone. Tempting as the idea of running was, she couldn't do it. She couldn't betray the family that had risked so much for her, and even if she did, it was likely they would track her down before she got too far. The Etari were a secretive people. They couldn't allow their secrets to spread to the empire.

For the moment, her course was set.

She returned her gaze forward. From a distance, the sight of the camps didn't fill her with hope. As was usual when different clans came together, large open areas sat between the different clans' tents.

Such was tradition, but it also didn't bode well for the Etari. Reports claimed the invasion force numbered in the hundreds. To defeat them, the Etari would need to work together, a task which didn't come naturally to any of the clans. Within the families, coordination was excellent. But Alena had never seen multiple families fight together.

Which led to another thought. "Who is in charge?" she asked Azaleth.

"Of everything?" The question confused him.

"Who will lead the battle between the Etari and the invaders?"

Azaleth thought for a moment. "Rotger, most likely."

Alena raised an eyebrow. She remembered Rotger, not just from her arrival in Etar, but from a few meetings after. He had always been kind to her, which was more than she could say for many clan leaders. "Why?"

"He's been leading the northern defense of the Etari lands against the empire for years. He possesses the most relevant experience."

They reached the camp by early afternoon, and the family settled in at once, putting up their own shelters. Sooni's family was the only one of their clan present, so they set up a hundred paces away from the next nearest tents.

Alena wasn't entirely clear why their family was here. Their clan was a merchant clan, tasked with traveling vast distances to run supplies and to trade with the empire. The task of defending the land fell to others. And Sooni's family wasn't large. As Alena met more families, she realized Sooni's was one of the smallest. Also, the rest of their clan hadn't come, so it had to be something about Sooni's family in particular that brought them here.

That evening, around their family campfire, Rotger visited them. Alena thought he looked tired. They made space for him as he settled among them.

He sighed. "Thank you for coming, Sooni."

It was nothing, she signed.

"Not if you succeed. What do you need?"

So, Alena's guess had been correct. Sooni's family had been selected for a reason. One that hadn't been shared with her. Judging from the reactions around the campfire, it hadn't been shared with anyone. But the others took the news with a calm acceptance Alena couldn't match.

"A day, maybe two, to scout. That is all for now. Possibly goods to trade."

That is fine, Rotger signed. "A day I can offer you with no problem. A second might be challenging. They move quickly."

I understand, Sooni signed.

Alena wished she felt the same. Rotger, his task concluded, stood up and left the circle. The others waited for Sooni to speak. She sat alone with her thoughts for a while. Then she looked up and met the gaze of her family. "Rotger has asked that we treat with the invaders."

Alena almost asked why, until she answered the question herself. Sooni was one of the best negotiators Alena had ever seen, and she kept calm under all circumstances. Offhand, Alena couldn't think of a better candidate. If the Etari wanted to avoid war, Sooni was a superb choice, just as Rotger was an excellent choice to lead the clans if battle was unavoidable.

Still, she noticed the tremble in her fingertips as she lay down to sleep that night. A smart person would ride the other way. Though they were only going to scout tomorrow, the risk was real. Given the sounds of coupling she heard in the surrounding tents, she wasn't alone in her thoughts. The lovemaking had an uncommon intensity.

Azaleth had offered himself, but she denied him. He'd taken his desires elsewhere, giving her the privacy she wished for.

The next morning, Sooni found her well before they were set to ride. "I need your help today, Alena."

Alena didn't want to be singled out. Not today, of all days. But she swallowed her concern. "How?"

"I need to see with your eyes today. You see both as an imperial and an Etari."

Other days, the claim might have hurt. But hurtful or

not, Sooni spoke the truth. "And?" Alena couldn't quite keep the bitterness out of her voice.

Sooni noted her tone but ignored it. "Many of the rest of us will observe the same things today. We've been trained to look at the world a certain way. You've learned much of our ways, but you still see the world differently. Our success might hinge on your insight."

The repeated references to their separateness stung at her like angry bees, but she understood Sooni meant well. *Okay*, she signed.

Thank you.

Sooni's family was saddled and riding before the sun even broke the horizon, on a track to the northwest, where the invaders had last been seen.

They made no attempt at stealth. Sooni's family was far smaller than the invading force, and if Sooni's ultimate goal was to speak with the invaders, it did no harm for the invaders to notice them.

They rode hard for more than half the day before they reached the invaders.

Sooni's family spread out so as not to present a single target. Sooni herself brought her horse next to Alena's. They pulled out looking glasses and began studying the invaders.

Alena wasn't sure what she had expected, but her first glance of the invaders revealed little. They were pale compared to Alena and her family, but that seemed to be their only outwardly defining characteristic. It was hard to tell from a distance, but she thought they might be a bit taller, too.

"What do you think?" Sooni asked.

Alena kept watching through her looking glass. "If they weren't so pale, I would say they were Etari."

"What do you mean?"

"Look at the symbols on the tents. They are divided up into units, and the construction of their tents isn't much different than ours."

Sooni grunted. "This is why I needed you."

Alena noticed other details, too. The range of ages was less than among the families and clans. That made sense, she supposed. When invading, it wasn't wise to bring along the old or young.

"There aren't many women," Alena noted.

"I saw that, too," Sooni said. "I wonder if it is wise to send a woman to deal with them."

Alena didn't know the answer to that question. There were a few women in the enemy camp, and Alena didn't see any signs they were treated as less than the men, but it was hard to tell from a distance.

Alena stopped focusing on the camp and began studying the surrounding area. As she did, little details became much more interesting.

She caught sight of movement between them and the enemy camp. When she focused on it with her looking glass, she saw that it was a wolf, prowling outside the camp.

She frowned. Perhaps it was her memories of the wolf they had hunted on their way to Cardon, but something about the creature seemed unnatural. She continued to watch until she realized what bothered her.

The wolf wasn't acting like a wolf. It didn't wander back and forth, or stop and sniff the air. It walked in a straight line. She watched as it slowly made a circle around the enemy tents. It was a wolf moving like a human.

Further observation revealed it wasn't just the wolf, but other animals as well. A large bird circled constantly overhead.

The one sight that haunted Alena more than any other, though, was that of a deer, advancing demurely toward the enemy camp. It walked directly toward a group near the camp's edge, where a lone hunter stepped forward and cut the animal's throat with a knife.

The group was mostly men, but as Alena focused, her eye was drawn to one wearing brighter colors than the rest. It was a woman, older than the rest, although not by many years. The men appeared to defer to her, and as soon as the deer was killed, she slumped forward so suddenly Alena worried she had died.

The group of men went to work on the carcass, skinning it with practiced efficiency.

As they did, two others cared for the woman. They didn't seem too concerned about her health, and after Alena watched for a few moments, she saw the woman come to. Alena squinted. Did the woman look younger now?

She tilted her head away from the looking glass and blinked a few times. She was beginning to see things. When she looked again the woman was up, and now Alena was convinced she was younger than she had first appeared. The woman went back into the main camp. She was easy to track, her clothing brighter than anything else in camp.

After some more observation, Alena figured she had seen all she needed. She tore her eye from the looking glass.

"Did you see that deer?" she asked Sooni.

"I did."

"And the wolves and the birds?"

"Yes."

"What do you make of it?" Alena broke her gaze from the strange sights in front of her.

"Soulwalkers." Sooni replied. "And strong, too."

"What's a soulwalker?"

"An abomination."

"What does that mean for us?"

Sooni's voice was dry. "That if we fight, it'll be very interesting."

47

During officer training, Brandt had learned that few command challenges were as difficult as leading an orderly retreat. To many, a retreat simply meant putting your back to the enemy and running as fast as you could.

But such a retreat was even more dangerous than an advance. Archers could shoot you down with confidence, knowing they didn't have to watch the skies for a counterattack. Cavalry could run you down, and even basic infantry could give chase, secure in their victory. It was always easier to attack an opponent's back.

There was another, more insidious problem, though. The problem had been drilled into him time and time again. The mental focus of a retreating soldier is far different than an advancing one. An advancing soldier has a mission in front of them and danger approaching. A retreating soldier begins to think the battle is over, that all that is left is survival. It's too easy to lose focus.

It didn't take much to give away their position. A single twig, broken within earshot of the ambush they had avoided and observed.

For the space of three heartbeats, Brandt thought that perhaps his mistake had gone unnoticed.

His gut twisted when he saw movement behind him, indistinct, camouflaged by the strange clothing the invaders wore.

"Run."

She didn't need to be told twice. They sprinted like startled deer, Brandt following Ana.

After all these years, he was prepared to admit that her lightness was still better than his. She tapped her way through the forest, her footsteps so gentle they were almost as silent as they had been on their much slower approach.

Brandt could almost match her speed, but never her grace. His footsteps were heavier.

He considered separating. Most likely they would follow his loud footsteps.

But separation was no guarantee of Ana's safety. They had a better chance together.

His right shoulder suddenly went numb, and a small stone shot in front of his face.

So, they had affinities too, then. It would have been nice to discover that in a less painful way, but he supposed he should be grateful neither of the rocks had found his head.

He shifted directions, weaving through the trees, making himself as difficult to hit as possible.

Stones cracked into the trees around him. Their affinities were strong. Ahead of him, Ana gained ground. She wasn't weaving as vigorously as he was.

Off to the right Brandt thought he saw shadows shifting. He risked a glance.

On the trail, two more of the invaders, their cloaks making them almost impossible to make out. They gained on him and Ana thanks to the open path.

"Left," he shouted.

Ana didn't question. With the next tap of her foot, her momentum shifted perpendicular to its old path. Brandt followed suit, worried that his focus was already waning. He couldn't focus his internal energies forever.

They could keep running, or they could fight.

Brandt didn't like their odds either way.

So he kept running.

Besides the song of the stones, the forest remained strangely silent. The warriors behind them weren't shouting or coordinating in any way that Brandt recognized.

At the same time, judging from the directions the stones came from, he and Ana were being surrounded.

The invaders stripped Brandt's final decision from him. The two warriors from the path had pulled in front of them.

Ana stopped running, climbing straight up a tree instead, three footsteps that took her into the branches.

Stones came at him from all directions, and Brandt leaped into the air to avoid them. One caught his right calf, eliciting a grimace.

Brandt's leap carried him into the two who had cut them off. He drew his sword in midair, using his momentum to generate a powerful swing as he passed.

He landed lightly, ignoring the flare of pain in his right leg. The invaders dodged his cut easily enough, drawing swords as he passed. Brandt had never seen weapons quite like theirs. They were somewhere between a long knife and a sword.

Before Brandt could attack, a thin stream of water lashed out at one of the invaders, snapping across his eyes. The man let out a low grunt, swiping at his face.

Brandt didn't waste the opportunity. He lunged forward,

the point of his sword cutting through the odd clothing with ease.

The invaders might look different than anyone Brandt had ever seen, but they died the same. He removed the point of his sword as the man collapsed in a heap.

The water in the air writhed like an angry snake, but it didn't faze the second man at all. He snapped his arm into the air, and Brandt caught a flash of steel.

The water crashed to the ground, evidence that Ana had lost her focus. But she didn't fall to the ground with it, so she was well enough.

At least, he hoped so.

The invaders' swords were shorter than Brandt's, but the length was deceptive. Brandt tried to deflect a cut aimed at his neck, but the invader's sword was heavier than he anticipated. Their swords clanged together, an ugly sound. The impact forced Brandt a step back. His opponent was larger and stronger than him.

They circled one another, Brandt attempting to take advantage of his longer reach. The invader let him close, confident in the speed of his defense. For as heavy as the shorter sword must be, the man handled it like a knife.

More footsteps approached, and Brandt had to dodge another rock aimed for his head.

He backed up another step.

A few trees away, Ana leaped from the branches, throwing herself into the rest of their pursuit with reckless abandon. Her war cry put his to shame.

Something shifted in him, then.

Ana reminded him there was no safety in combat. Hesitation risked defeat.

Brandt's stance shifted. He saw the invader's eyes narrow at the change.

Brandt reached out with his sword, the steel an extension of his body. The invader shifted, trying to avoid the stab. But Brandt stepped in, angling his body low, and his sword snaked past the shorter one, cutting a gash in the man's stomach.

Painful, but not fatal.

The man took a step back, but Brandt had no plans to let him have a single heartbeat to recover. His first attack blended into a second, and then a third.

The warrior dropped, his eyes blank.

Brandt didn't even pause. A few paces away from him Ana fought a battle for her life, only her quick reflexes keeping her from a journey to the gates.

He picked up a few stones as he leaped toward her, hurling them with just a bit of aim. Even after years of practice, his stone affinity wasn't particularly strong. But it was enough to toss a few stones and disrupt the flow of a battle.

The rocks did little but distract two of the swordsmen, but that gave Ana the space to slay one of their enemies and let Brandt join the fight. Together their swords flashed.

The men they fought were talented warriors. They were each far stronger than an average imperial soldier.

But they weren't wolfblades. And they hadn't been training with the focus and dedication Brandt and Ana had brought to the monastery.

He was sure he had never fought better.

Two of the warriors turned their attention to Brandt, while the last focused on Ana.

He noticed a weakness as the battle evolved. Each of the warriors they fought was talented, but they didn't coordinate well with one another. They fought alone even though they were in a group.

Brandt seized the opportunity, shifting his position so that he kept one enemy close, and ideally between him and his second opponent. Against a better coordinated duo, the warrior closest to Brandt would have retreated, keeping both of them in striking distance. Instead, both of Brandt's opponents fought to be the first to kill him.

Brandt's sword slid through the first warrior's guard, finally sending him to the dirt. As the numbers evened, Brandt and Ana's advantage grew.

A few heartbeats later, the last of their opponents died.

Brandt's gaze wandered over to Ana, the familiar post-combat high seizing him. They had survived.

But they were still vastly outnumbered.

They needed to run.

48

Alena saddled her horse with the rest of her family. She dreaded another long day of riding.

But she feared the conclusion of that long ride even more.

Sooni had decided the night before that she had seen enough. There was nothing to be gained by delaying another day, and the speed of the invaders had to be taken into account. The rest of the clans remained rooted in their camps. The two forces would most likely meet the day after next, unless Sooni stopped them.

More strange phenomena had been reported at the camp when they returned, but now Sooni had the beginnings of an explanation to share with the others. Some among the invaders had formed a connection with the roving beasts of the plains. Sooni called it soulwalking, a term Alena had never heard before, but understood intuitively.

While Sooni and her family scouted the invaders, the Etari camp had also been observed, both by birds and wolves. There had been no attacks, but several creatures had been spotted. The assumption was that the invaders knew just as much about the Etari as the Etari knew about the invaders.

Regardless, Sooni's task remained the same: see if there was a way to avoid war and learn more about the mysterious invaders.

The family rode in silence, a nervous energy running between them.

Alena drew close to Azaleth. "Where do you think the invaders came from?"

It was a question she had been turning over in her mind since she had first heard of the invaders. At first, she had assumed it was some segment of the empire that had sailed around and attacked the Etari from behind. Her first glance the day before had put that idea to lie. Whoever the invaders were, they weren't from the empire.

Anders I had conquered the entire continent from end to end, with the exception of Etar and Falar. All lived under the empire's banner, but Alena had never seen such pale skin.

Which led to her most unsettling question. If they weren't imperial, Etari, or Falari, where did they come from?

The Etari didn't seem as disturbed by the discovery as she was. Last night there had been no talk of the question, and Alena wanted to know why.

Azaleth signed indifference. "Probably the Lolani."

"The who?"

"The Lolani. The great scourge."

I'm confused, she signed.

"It's an old story, one we learn as children. Long ago, the Lolani came and fought for control of the land."

"How long ago?"

A sign of uncertainty. "Long ago, well before the wars with the empire."

"We don't have any story like that." In fact, there weren't many stories at all from before the establishment of the empire. She had heard whispers of older stories, but not many. Most were tales of creatures no one had ever seen. In school there was the history of the empire and little else. She understood history didn't start with Anders I, but these seemed like stories that should have spread.

"What's the story of the Lolani?" she asked.

"There are a few, but they all agree on a few facts. Long ago, foreign invaders came to our land, and to yours as well. They were strong fighters, but a number of clans banned together to fight them off. It was before the Long Winter. After the Winter, they were never seen again."

"Long Winter?"

Now it was his turn to sign confusion. "Didn't you learn any history?"

Alena could name the meaningful events of every emperor since Anders I. She could tell the reasons behind every minor rebellion and what changes had resulted. But she didn't have the faintest idea what events Azaleth spoke of.

"The Long Winter was, well, a long winter." He spoke as though he was instructing a child.

"How long?"

"Several generations."

"What?"

"I forget exactly, but three or four, if my memory is right."

Alena thanked Azaleth for the information, then angled her horse away so she could think in silence. Had she been lied to by the empire?

It made her question her entire education. The Etari had never given her any reason to doubt their stories. No one particularly cared whether or not she believed them, which made her more willing to accept the tales as true. Azaleth considered the Long Winter to be a piece of common knowledge. And because Alena couldn't name a major historical event before Anders I, she didn't have a reason to argue. In academy, any questions about the far past resulted in the same story: the land of the empire had been filled with disparate, uncivilized, warring fiefdoms. No one worried about what took place before Anders I's reign because it hadn't mattered.

All Alena's thoughts of history and education fled when they came upon the Lolani. The invaders couldn't number more than two hundred, but a menace hung over their camp. Alena thought back to her last visit, to the deer who had walked demurely to the slaughter. The memory clung to her, no matter how she pushed it away.

Most of their family stopped, well in sight of the invaders. Sooni motioned, and a small party broke apart from the others. Without a shared symbol of peace, Sooni had elected to advance with only a small number of her family. Four of them rode forward. Sooni would negotiate, Alena observed, and two warriors flanked them if danger appeared.

They rode close, stopping over three hundred paces away from the invaders' outer perimeter.

Alena spotted two wolves, lying in the grass, watching her with eyes that seemed too alert not to be human. Her heart raced and her hands sweated as she held onto the reins.

For several long moments, she thought their friendly overtures would be ignored. The invaders continued walking forward, a loose collection of warriors that maintained no discernable order. And yet, as Alena watched, she wouldn't say they were disorganized. They reminded her of flocks of birds, flying together yet individual all the same. In places, two or three gathered together. Most seemed content to leave a couple of paces of distance between them and their nearest neighbor.

One man broke from near the center of the pack, turning toward Sooni's small contingent. Alena watched as the man seemed to part the tide of warriors walking past, moving perpendicular to the rest.

The man stepped away from the rest of the Lolani and Alena received her first real look at him. Her first impression reminded him of the Etari, of their effortless movement. As she noticed more features, she began to see the differences.

The Etari lived hard lives. Food needed to be hunted, and local plants needed to be harvested nearly every day just to survive. The resulting labor left them strong, able to run for leagues before experiencing even mild fatigue. But despite their readiness for warfare, the Etari were relatively peaceful. Alena knew small skirmishes happened regularly on the imperial border, but interclan fighting was almost nonexistent.

The Lolani warrior seemed to be a product of a similar lifestyle, with one notable difference: he was covered in pink scars. Some were long and thin, most likely the result of sharp steel cutting flesh. Others were round, scar tissue spidering out from a puncture wound. The man appeared to be of about thirty years, if age was judged the same among the Lolani. He approached with a confident swagger.

Alena immediately disliked him. Every movement spoke his contempt for Sooni and her family. Alena suspected the outcome of the discussion before it began.

"Greetings," said Sooni, her tone tentative.

Alena hadn't considered the problem of language.

The Lolani man studied each of them in turn. Alena refused to turn from his cold examination. He gave no other response.

"Do you understand our language?" Sooni tried again.

The awkward moment stretched between the two parties. The invader made no attempt to speak, but there was no disguising the intelligence behind his eyes.

Sooni sighed and tried again, speaking in a language Alena didn't understand.

It caused a reaction, though. The man in front of them grunted. "Don't try to speak our language ever again." His Etari was as fluent as Alena's.

Sooni's reaction was muted, a quick flicker of surprise over her otherwise impassive features. "Your Etari is impressive."

She left the question unspoken, hanging in the air. Where did the Lolani learn?

The warrior gave no answer.

"What is your purpose here?" Sooni asked.

Even though the Lolani was on foot and Sooni rode a horse, Alena felt as though Sooni was being looked down on. Like they all were.

After another long pause, he answered. "To make this land our own."

Sooni looked past the man to the crowd of Lolani, now mostly past their position. "You seem to have come poorly prepared."

The invader followed her gaze and gave a smile. "We were worried we had brought too many."

The quiet confidence in the man's tone unsettled Alena. It was a boast, but not the chest-beating claims of young warriors trying to catch her eye. It was the confidence of a man who knew his abilities.

What worried Alena more was that his perfect Etari meant he probably knew the abilities of his enemy as well.

And he still felt confident.

Alena forced herself to mentally step back, to become an observer of the situation.

"We are willing to trade, if it is goods that you seek," Sooni said.

Alena had always known Sooni as a confident, wise leader. But somehow, next to this man, she seemed uncertain and hesitant. She seemed small next to him, smaller than their difference in physical sizes alone would explain. Her offer, although a reasonable one, sounded weak to Alena's ears.

"Does the hawk trade with the squirrel?" the Lolani asked.

Alena felt, more than saw, their guardians tense up on either side of her. Such insults weren't tolerated well. Another wrong word, and they would have war on their hands.

But Sooni had been chosen for a reason. She gestured. *Relax.*

The guardians obeyed, but the tension remained.

"This land is ours. We will fight to defend it, and you are vastly outnumbered."

The Lolani waved his hand dismissively. "If you fight, you will die. This land has made you weak. Bend your knees and submit, or fight and die. It makes no difference to us."

Compared to the Etari, the Lolani warrior looked positively relaxed. Even here he was outnumbered. With no escort, Sooni could kill him easily and ride to safety.

What was she missing? How could this warrior be so confident?

When Sooni didn't immediately respond, the Lolani warrior pushed harder. "Do you speak for your people?"

"Yes."

"Then decide, now. Submission, or annihilation?"

Sooni stared hard at the man, as though her examination would unravel the layers of mystery surrounding him.

Then, without another word, she turned her horse and left.

Alena was surprised, but she turned her own horse and followed suit.

The Lolani laughed, a deep, grating sound that followed them as they retreated from the meeting.

49

"We need help," Brandt said.

Ana nodded.

Hidden safely, deep in the woods, the two warriors discussed their plans. Their initial panic had faded, and they debated heading straight to Landow or pursuing the invaders further and learning more about them.

Brandt took a deep breath, knowing how this next part would be received. "I think you should return to Landow and let Kye know."

Ana's eyes flared, and Brandt held up a hand to stall her retort. "Right now, Kye knows nothing. Even if you can't give him exact numbers, your warning should give him time to prepare some defense. That information is vital."

"We stay together, Brandt."

"Even if by splitting apart we could prepare the empire for an invasion?"

She shrugged. "Any plan comes with risks. If we separate and something happens to me, you would never know. There's no point in following them. We both need to return to Landow with as much haste as we can muster."

Brandt shook his head. "We don't know enough for Kye and the emperor to make wise decisions. We need to find the main body."

The argument had gone in circles since their fight. Which was why Brandt suggested splitting up. But he understood. They stood a better chance together, but they couldn't agree on which direction to head.

Ana threw up her hands. "Fine. We follow. But as soon as we know enough, we run."

Brandt agreed. They made their way back to the horses and to the trail, then continued their pursuit.

It was late in the afternoon when they found the rest of the invasion.

If it could even be called as much.

Brandt and Anna stood on ridge, protected by trees, watching the advance. Brandt counted less than ten warriors. Assuming other scouts roamed the area, Brandt guessed their total number still numbered less than a dozen.

The two wolfblades watched the group as they set up camp, their motions practiced and unhurried.

Brandt noticed one woman who seemed set apart from the rest of the group. No matter where she went, it looked as though the others made a circle around her, keeping her constantly protected. Few orders were given, but Brandt got the sense the others all deferred to her. Brandt memorized her features, but wished he could get closer to make out more details.

He glanced over at Ana, who met his gaze. He nodded. They had seen enough.

They moved silently away from the camp, pausing once they were well away. They put their heads together and whispered.

"Did you see how they treated the woman in the

center?" Brandt asked.

"I would guess she's their leader."

"Should we kill her?"

Ana bit her lower lip. "There's no point. No matter how strong they are, they can't do much damage to the empire. Not with so few people. We return to Kye, let him know what we've seen, and leave the rest to him."

Brandt thought a moment longer and agreed. If the situation seemed more dire, he might have tried an assassination, but with so few, it wasn't worth the risk. The entire force would be destroyed as soon as they approached Landow.

They continued their retreat, stopping only when a large gray wolf stepped out of the woods in front of them.

Every instinct in Brandt's body told him that something was wrong.

Wolves never traveled alone, and they never stopped in front of people.

Brandt reached for his sword, but his hand never reached the hilt.

The wolf whimpered and suddenly ran away, disappearing into the woods. At the same time, an overwhelming wave of fear crashed into Brandt, driving him to his knees.

He'd fought in many battles, and he had even seen the gates of death. But never had he felt a crippling panic like this. He gasped for breath and his eyes went wide as every shadow jumped at him.

He saw Ana's concerned face, and then he wasn't in the woods anymore.

Show me your fear.

He was on the road to Landow, years ago, with Lola and Ryder, Kyler and Ana.

He'd thought of this journey often, but it had never been so clear, so vivid.

It was a memory, but more.

Lola laughed at one of Kyler's raunchy jokes. Brandt thought he even saw a hint of a smile pass across Ryder's lips.

He missed them.

He had forgotten about Ryder's wry smile and Kyler's terrible humor. Tides of time washed away his memories, smoothing out the edges until little was left.

Then blackness swallowed him.

You have been touched before. A hint of surprise.

Ahh. Understanding.

Perfect blackness, then a memory of him on the road to Highkeep.

A crude working.

Brandt saw the wolfblades again, on the road, walking together toward Landow.

Then blackness.

Then walking again.

And darkness.

The images cycled, back and forth, and Brandt screamed. They were his friends, and he had forgotten their deaths. How could he honor them, if he didn't even remember how they had died? Had they died as heroes?

No. Show me your fear.

Darkness, followed by his life since Landow. His time at the monastery, the comfortable existence he had led there. His life with Ana, secure behind the thick walls. The voice put a name to the creeping uncertainty he always felt.

You're a coward.

The simple statement stabbed into his soul.

She ran and lived. If you live, it's because you ran as well.

The voice was female, but low and aggressive, dripping with malice and contempt.

A real commander dies with his troops. He doesn't run.

She was right, of course.

How else could he have lived through the events people had described to him? Ana had been clear enough about what she had done. She had been a coward. And he was, too.

He had abandoned his friends.

He felt a probing, like fingers massaging his soul, looking for something he didn't understand.

The pressure eased, and then he couldn't breathe, the sheer terror causing his heart to pound and his breath to catch.

Kill yourself.

Something in the woman's voice had changed. It was still assertive, but there was something else there, a quality his panicked mind couldn't identify.

Take your own life to honor your warriors. Join them on the other side of the gates. They are waiting for you.

"No!" a voice pulled at him.

His vision returned and he was back in the woods. He held a knife in his hand, and he was trying to cut his own neck. Only Ana's hands, wrapped around his wrist, prevented him.

She was infuriating. She was a coward, and she tried to make him one, too.

He wouldn't let her.

He growled and tried to free his wrist from her grasp, but her hands were like iron. "Stop!" she yelled.

She couldn't stop him. One small bit at a time, he pulled the blade closer. He could almost feel the cold, sharp steel against his throat.

Ana's eyes narrowed, and a wall of pure will slammed into him. Something inside of him broke, and he released the grip on the knife.

In one smooth motion Ana grabbed the blade and tossed it away from them. Then, for a few moments they both sat there, regaining their strength.

When she looked up, there were tears in her eyes. "What happened?"

He shook his head, not wanting to explain what he had just seen. Some thoughts were too close and too painful, even to share with Ana. "Compulsion," he claimed.

Her doubt was plain to see. "You said you can't compel someone to do something they don't already want to do."

He had no answer that would satisfy her. She watched him closely and understood.

"Brandt…"

Her voice shamed him. The pity and the pain were almost too much to bear.

A cloud of birds rising in the distance caught their attention. They rose from the trees Brandt and Ana had just come through, not too long ago.

They were being hunted.

Ana met his gaze. "Will you run?"

Had he given up? Had he finally been pushed too far?

That low voice called to him still, a seductive desire, an end to it all.

But he was too much of a coward to do so in front of Ana.

He stood. "Let's go."

She watched as he walked over, grabbed his knife, and sheathed it.

Then they ran, pursued by the invaders.

50

S ooni's return to the camp the next morning generated a commotion. Rotger was among the first to approach her. His expression was question enough.

No, Sooni signed.

Rotger made the gestures for battle, high above his head where everyone could see. The families, waiting for just such a signal, began their final preparations.

Sooni dismounted and Alena did the same. Sooni gestured for Alena to stay, but the others were to prepare with the rest of the family. The men did so, leaving Rotger alone with Sooni and Alena.

"They have no interest in negotiation," Sooni said.

Rotger frowned, his facial expression mirroring Alena's thoughts perfectly. "What do they hope to accomplish? They can't win."

"Their spokesman seemed confident," Sooni replied. "And so are we. One of us must be wrong, but I am not sure who." She paused. "Caution is warranted."

Agreed, Rotger signed. "We already know they soulwalk. We'll expect other internal manipulations."

Alena thought more discussion was warranted. They were marching off to battle, but Sooni and Rotger made the decision seem so easy.

The process jarred against her imagination. Shouldn't this be harder? Should she insist they try again for peace?

Sooni turned to Alena. "What did you notice?"

Alena froze. She hadn't expected to be questioned, but why else would Sooni have asked her to stay?

She thought of the cold confidence in the Lolani's face, the way he seemed taller than them even though they rode high on horses. "He believes they are stronger. Whatever they plan, they are not concerned by how we outnumber them. He looks down on us."

She didn't think her observations amounted to much, but Sooni signed her agreement, and Rotger looked thoughtful. He gave a sharp sign of agreement and turned to his other duties.

Rotger's trust in Sooni surprised Alena. He hadn't asked for details of their meeting, or questioned Sooni's decisions. He accepted her word and led the Etari to battle.

Alena followed Sooni, her mind caught in a loop. She was riding into battle.

With her family, yes, but before the sun set on this day, there would be war.

Now, more than ever, the Lolani's calm confidence shook her. He knew he was outnumbered, and he didn't care. Were they all reacting exactly as the Lolani expected?

She tried to focus her mind on the assumptions underlying the upcoming battle, but her mind was like a wild horse, running where it chose.

This was foolishness. Even after all the training, she was still one of the weakest members of the family. They would be better off without her.

Alena glanced over to the eastern horizon, where her true family lived. A thought tickled the back of her mind, but she ignored it.

How had their lives turned out? She had asked herself that question frequently in the first few months after her escape from the empire, but more rarely now. Jace would be a man, ready to fight for the empire. Did her father still work from sunrise to sundown, his eyes reflecting the blazing light of his forge? Alena's hand instinctively went to her knife, still sharp after all these years.

He had tried to show her how to care not just for her possessions, but for the world she lived in.

She missed them all, a deep ache in her chest. She longed to see them again.

It wouldn't be hard to ride away. Surely she'd earned the trust of the Etari by now. Surely they would let her ride.

Her thoughts were interrupted by Azaleth, riding up next to her. "Thinking of leaving?"

She smiled. "That obvious?"

Yes. He returned her smile, but there was no mirth there. "You will ride next to me. We have trained together the most, and we both know how the other fights. I will do my best to make sure you are safe."

The words were exactly what she needed to hear, and she suspected he knew that. He didn't promise her safety, like a soldier from the empire would. Azaleth couldn't promise that. But she knew he would die if it meant saving her life.

She couldn't turn her back on that devotion.

Perhaps it was time to claim her Etari family as her own. She could accept Azaleth and truly become a full part of the clan. No one had ever shown her the depth of kindness he had.

She would fight by his side. And after, who knew? Perhaps she would become Etari in truth.

Alena was surprised how little time it took the clans to prepare for battle. They were ready to ride in almost no time at all. Bows were strung, rocks were prepared, and steel examined.

Then they rode, their journey made largely in silence. Alena studied the faces of her family. A casual glance revealed little, but as she watched, she noticed the tics that revealed their true emotion. They were like her, terrified of what was to come, but pushing it down and riding forward anyway.

Azaleth's voice interrupted her, barely strong enough to be heard over the sound of the horses. "Soon, you will need to focus only on yourself. Distraction will be dangerous."

She signed her acknowledgement.

It was good advice, even if her innate desire was to watch. What little martial ability she had required constant focus.

The riders paused when they came within view of the Lolani once again. Alena saw them, off in the distance, walking east. The Lolani didn't react at first to the presence of the Etari.

Rotger relied only on hand signs now. He ordered families further east and west. They were to prepare attacks.

Alena had long ago discovered why the Etari relied on hand signs instead of expressions or language. Out in the open prairies, a clear hand sign could be seen for hundreds, if not thousands, of paces. With looking glasses, people could communicate over vast distances. Commanding a battle like this became much simpler because every family understood Rotger's hand signs.

As the Etari spread out, the Lolani began to react. They stopped, put down their packs, and faced the Etari.

Alena could not understand the Lolani's actions. How could less than two hundred warriors on foot possibly hope to defeat the nearly five hundred riders that Rotger had brought with him?

It was hopeless.

The only explanation she could imagine was if they thought they were that much stronger than the Etari. But Alena couldn't believe that. The Etari were some of the fiercest fighters to be found. Their clans had resisted the entire might of the empire for generations.

Whatever she thought, events had been set in motion that only moved forward.

A grunt from Azaleth returned her to the present. The Etari rode slowly. When Rotger deemed the distance ideal, he signed for a stop. Then another gesture, a definitive hand sign.

Ranged attack.

Up and down the line small rocks floated in front of the Etari.

Alena had seen the power of those stones once before, but over the years had come to realize just how important the Etari considered the weapons. Young warriors spent days precisely chipping away at the stones with their affinities. The stones were the most common currency traded between the warriors, often won or lost as the result of bets and feats of strength.

She understood the appeal of the small stones. Even she had a dozen in a small pouch on her belt, but at this distance she didn't bother to try. She felt the warriors spin their stones, then launch. Dark dots sped into the air, then disappeared from sight.

The first launch caught the Lolani by surprise. Alena couldn't see the stones, but she saw the bodies fall in the distance.

This far away, aim was imprecise. Even the Etari's skilled warriors could only aim for the general area.

But with hundreds of stones, some were guaranteed to hit. And they were too small to see coming.

Alena guessed almost a third of the Lolani fell in the first barrage. The second was already on the way by the time the Lolani realized what had happened and charged. Alena grabbed a spear, sized for her, and held it in hand.

A third and fourth salvo flew into the air. As the Lolani got closer, Alena realized she hadn't seen any of their warriors fall since the first attack. She frowned. The Etari couldn't miss that often, especially not as the distances closed.

Rotger must have observed the same a few moments before she did. As soon as the thought came to her, he signed for the charge.

She met Azaleth's glance. They hesitated just a moment, then kicked their horses forward, riding side by side.

Some of the Etari, skilled at mounted archery, released arrows at the incoming Lolani. Alena saw the arrows flung aside by powerful gusts of wind. There, at least, was one of the most potent uses of an air affinity. The strength behind such gusts was incredible, though.

A few Etari fell off their horses, bodies tumbling limply from their mounts. Alena didn't understand until she saw a small dark streak pass just in front of her eyes.

The Lolani were using the same technique the Etari used.

Affinities clashed first as the Etari and Lolani pushed the stones back and forth.

If the Etari were surprised by the Lolani's skills, they didn't show it.

But most didn't have time.

Despite Azaleth's advice, Alena couldn't help but observe as the battle unfolded around her. There, a few horses down the line, a stone wavered in midair for a moment, then slapped into an Etari's face.

Similar events happened up and down the line.

In a contest of affinities, it appeared the Lolani held the upper hand.

More Etari riders fell off their horses, too fast for Alena to keep track.

A wall of fire appeared, then vanished nearly as quickly.

The Etari charge never slowed.

Both sides were weakened, but when horse crashed into invader Alena's world became chaos.

She ran into one of the Lolani, a giant chiseled with muscle and baring teeth in a snarl. He swung at her with an oversized sword.

Alena brought her spear up, recognizing the gesture as futile even as she did so.

Then Azaleth was there, turning the sword away with a powerful stroke of his own, aided by the momentum of his horse.

Azaleth rode past, his momentum carrying him beyond the duel. He fought to turn his horse around in the press of the fight.

Alena didn't think. Years of training had instilled some instincts, and now that the sword wasn't coming at her, she stabbed at the enormous Lolani warrior.

She had aimed for his heart, but the warrior slapped the point of her spear away.

Alena's first thought was that Azaleth would be very disappointed in her technique.

The Lolani roared and raised his sword. With his free hand he seized Alena's spear and thrust it at her. The butt end of her own spear struck her in the chest. She wheezed at the impact.

Distracted, she didn't notice the Lolani move in for a killing strike until it was too late for her to do anything about it.

But she had bought herself just enough time with her ill-fated thrust. Azaleth was there, his own sword cutting down, embedding itself in the man's neck.

The Lolani howled, and for a single terrifying moment, Alena thought he would somehow survive the near-decapitation.

Then his eyes went dark and he collapsed.

Azaleth engaged another Lolani, his sword keeping both him and Alena safe. She didn't attempt to draw a weapon, afraid she was just as likely to hurt a friend as a foe.

Alena looked up, taking the measure of the battlefield. Their fight had cleared a small space, but it looked like the Etari charge had broken the Lolani. Riders wheeled and charged again, hacking and slashing with their blades. Pockets of resistance collapsed before her eyes.

But far fewer Etari rode on their mounts than before. Of the almost five hundred that had made the charge, it appeared that only half that number survived. At least, only that many remained mounted. Alena hoped more would be found behind, injured but alive.

They had won the battle, but the cost had been high.

51

Their pursuit remained relentless. Brandt and Ana jogged through the forest, sacrificing stealth for speed. When they needed to rest, they walked quickly, catching their breath and easing the burning pain in their legs.

Despite their exertion, they did not lose their pursuers. The invaders seemed to be every bit as determined to catch them as they were to escape.

Brandt led them south and east, toward Landow. They needed to get word to Kye, so he could prepare for the assault working its way toward the heart of the empire.

They ran and walked for a full day, never stopping. His belly gnawed at his ribs, demanding sustenance, and his throat felt cracked from a lack of water. But there was no time to stop. Brandt kept waiting for their pursuers to give up the chase. He and Ana had traveled leagues without stopping, a physical feat that would have destroyed many.

And yet they came.

The sun was falling and the trees cast long shadows. Below their feet the soft ground of the lowland forest was turning rocky, an early promise of the mountains that stood to the north of Landow.

He and Ana would need to find their way across those mountains if they were going to reach the town. Brandt knew a road lay to the east, but how far away he had no guess.

Their pace finally slowed as the sun set. Brandt's jog turned into a walk, and no amount of focus or lightness could convince his legs to run again. Ana slowed to keep pace with him.

Their pursuit closed, taking advantage of their weakness. Brandt stopped checking, pushing himself forward with every bit of focus he could muster.

"Should we ambush them?" Ana asked, the question coming in ragged gasps.

Brandt shook his head. The land was becoming more uneven, and their footsteps took them uphill. There would be caves ahead, places where they could hide and rest. An ambush would be their last desperate gamble, and from what he had seen of their warriors earlier, Brandt didn't think that chance favored him and Ana. The invaders were too strong.

The trees thinned as the land became more rugged. Glancing behind him, Brandt swore he saw shadows moving through the woods behind them. It spurred him to walk faster.

As the evening wore on, his mind emptied. He had no particular destination in mind. He found his own route through the rugged foothills, following whatever course looked best at a glance. So long as every step brought him closer to the distant city of Landow, he was satisfied.

The moons were high in the sky, hidden behind fluffy clouds, when Brandt reconsidered the ambush. He didn't think he could walk much further. His legs had stopped burning some time back, transforming into lifeless pillars that hardly moved. His head pounded with every beat of his heart, and his stomach had long ago given up its fight for food.

Beside him, Ana didn't look much better. They needed rest.

They came to the intersection of two small valleys, and Brandt chose the one on the left. He couldn't give a particular reason — his choices had become impulsive long ago.

As they crossed a small open ridge, Brandt looked down and saw other shapes struggling up the hill. The invaders were maybe a thousand paces away. Fortunately, they didn't appear to be moving much faster.

Brandt and Ana followed the small valley ever higher. Every step took a moment of concentration.

Brandt looked back again, but the land and a few lone trees blocked the view of their pursuit. Perhaps here they could find cover to launch an ambush?

His eyes found a crack in the land, a darkness blacker than the surrounding night. It had been hidden from view as they walked up, visible only to one looking down thanks to an outcropping of rock next to it.

That darkness called to him, beckoned for him to rest.

He grunted, which was enough for Ana to glance at him. He pointed. "There."

He thought a look of skepticism crossed her face, but they were both too tired to argue. Together, they approached the slit.

It wasn't wide. If he shuffled sideways, he barely fit, both his chest and shoulders scraping against the sides. He slid in, one hesitant step at a time.

After a full night of hiking, his eyes had adjusted to the dark. Even in the cave, he could make out the rough outlines of the walls illuminated by the trickle of light coming from the slit.

Had he been more awake, the tightness of the opening might have bothered him. Earth pressed on him from all sides. He heard the low hum of the element, barely audible even in the silence of the night. He was too tired to listen. It occurred to him that he could probably fall asleep right here, the walls narrow enough to prevent him from collapsing.

Then he stumbled, no longer supported by the walls, into an opening. After regaining his balance, he paused. A trickle of water could be heard nearby.

Ana came through a moment later, a soft grunt of surprise evidence of her own passage.

Brandt listened for the song of fire. Exhaustion made his eyes heavy, but he only needed to do this one last thing. He heard the song, faint to his sense.

But it was enough.

A small flame, pitifully weak, came to life in his hand. He could barely feel the warmth from it. Nor did it provide much light, but in the almost absolute darkness of the cave, it was enough.

They had stumbled into a cave with two chambers that he could see. The trickle sounded as though it came from the second. He wandered forward, finding a trickle of water dropping from the ceiling. He put his head underneath and filled his mouth several times.

The water was metallic, but it was water.

After a few drinks, he lit the way for Ana, who repeated his process.

Their thirst temporarily sated, they looked at each other. Words weren't necessary.

They couldn't fight. They couldn't move. Rest called to them both.

Brandt found a space to sit down in, and Ana came and squeezed herself next to him. Brandt let his fire die out, pitching them into nearly complete darkness.

Brandt pulled out his sword and lay it next to him. If the invaders came, he would do what he could. It was pitifully little, but he would die with a sword in hand. He would protect Ana until the end. He watched the direction they had come, looking for any slight variation of light and shadow that would indicate a visitor.

He didn't even notice when he fell asleep.

But he noticed when his dream world exploded in light and sound.

The world of his dream shifted from heartbeat to heartbeat. One moment he was looking down on a green and fertile land. The next he hovered above Highkeep, watching himself train with the other monks.

Then another land, stretches of endless desert that extended as far as his eye could see.

He saw the invaders in an unfamiliar forest.

Fights broke out between different groups of the invaders.

As the scenes passed in front of him, he began to sense a connection, as though he was being pulled along a series of invisible threads.

The landscapes shifted, and his dreams were memories. He and the other wolfblades approached Landow.

Then he was there, fighting against a bandit in the woods. He was in the streets of Landow, hovering above the battle like an indifferent god. Kyler died as a building collapsed on top of him, his life ended by one with his own affinity.

He watched Lola's life end, too. And he saw the moment Ana would regret for the rest of her life, when she gave in to fear for the first and last time as a wolfblade.

He watched his own brush with death, and this time he heard the different songs, the notes they played as he and the bandit battled with their elements. Still impassive, he observed his defeat.

Another shift, and Brandt saw Ryder and a young woman running away, pursued by a bandit far stronger than either of them. In the end, Ryder turned and fought, knowing the outcome was as good as inevitable.

That moment, perhaps more than any other, broke the emotional shield surrounding Brandt. The others had respected nobility. Their sacrifices were... expected, he guessed. Ryder hadn't suffered from the same outlook. Yet he had given his life for another.

A wolfblade, till the last beat of his heart.

The scenes sped by. Brandt recovered from his wounds and fell in with the same young woman Ryder had protected. He left town, followed by the woman, and his dream went dark.

Some part of him knew it was a dream, but some part argued that it wasn't, that this was true.

He heard a new song, richer than any he had heard before. It was elemental, but more.

He turned, searching for the sound in the darkness. Then he saw another man, standing still. He was dressed in rich robes, and his face was familiar, although Brandt couldn't quite place it.

"I'm sorry that I cannot show you more, but she has protected her agent too well."

Brandt frowned, not quite understanding, until he did. His eyes widened as realizations struck him, one after the other.

Emperor Anders I stood before him.

Dead over two hundred years, and yet somehow alive in his dream.

It couldn't be a dream.

"It is," Anders said. "It was a chance to pierce the veil, and a risk that needed to be taken. You must listen. Your answers are in Landow. Her agent has found the gate, and they seek to open it. If the invaders reach it, the empire may crumble."

Brandt didn't understand. He was just coming to terms with the idea that some manifestation of Anders I stood in front of him.

Until it didn't.

Anders I uttered a choked-off cry as a strong cold wind swept through the dream, sending everything to blackness once again.

When Brandt opened his eyes, he saw a sliver of light penetrating through the slit into the first cavern they had entered.

Somehow, he felt wonderful.

Which didn't make sense. He had rested, but he had just pushed his body harder than he ever had before. His muscles should be sore and exhausted. He hadn't even eaten, yet his stomach felt like it had just finished digesting a feast.

Ana stirred, and then her eyes came wide open. She blinked at him. "What?"

"How do you feel?" Brandt asked.

She wiped at her eyes. "I thought I heard bells waking

me up, as though alerting me to something." She paused, registering Brandt's question. "And I feel great."

She looked up at him, confusion and a hint of fear in her gaze. "What happened?"

Brandt shook his head. "I don't know. But I think we need to hurry to Landow."

52

T he only sight worse than battle was the aftermath of one. Alena wanted to be anyplace but here, but her obligation was here to her family. People she knew, people she had spent every day of the past several years with had made their journey to the gates.

Alena walked through the battlefield, searching for anyone she recognized from Sooni's family. The wounded had already been escorted off for whatever healing they could receive. Only the dead remained.

Alena missed Azaleth's presence. He had taken a deep cut during the fight and had been ordered to seek treatment so infection couldn't set in. His steady support would have eased her mind as she sought any final bodies.

She completed her search and returned to the main camp, set aside from the battlefield. She found Sooni there, fortunately uninjured. Sooni looked up from a piece of paper as Alena entered her tent. "I take it you didn't find anyone?"

No one, Alena signed. Sooni let out a small sigh of relief. "I think everyone has been counted, then."

Alena saw that the paper held all the names of their family, with markings beside each name. "How are the other families?"

Sooni gave her an exhausted glance. "The Lolani focused their defense near the center of the charge. Those families took the worst of it."

She didn't need to add that her family had been one of those families. Even if Alena hadn't seen the battle herself, the truth was written in Sooni's features. A glance at Sooni's list revealed that nearly half her family had died in the fighting. It would take a generation to recover from the battle.

Alena's exhausted mind couldn't comprehend the loss of life. Though the Etari had won a victory, the Lolani had given better than they had taken. Far better

Against the Etari, who could walk over empire forces that far outnumbered them.

Questions plagued her thoughts. How many Lolani existed on this other continent? Why had they returned? And why hadn't she known anything about either before now?

She left Sooni to her grim tasks. She needed rest. Muscles throughout her body ached, but she didn't think she would find sleep anytime soon. Her hands shook whenever she lifted them.

Without any particular purpose, she wandered through the battlefield again, this time to examine the Lolani. Perhaps some answers could be found among the dead.

An initial glance didn't reveal any remarkable details. On average, the Lolani were taller than imperials and Etari, but the difference wasn't great. They did have very pale skin, lighter than any Alena could remember seeing before.

The warriors all had dark tattoos around their forearms.

The markings were similar, but different enough that Alena assumed they represented something important in Lolani culture.

Something bothered her, worrying at the edges of her awareness. Where were the women?

Alena walked among the bodies, searching for a woman's brighter robes. She found none.

The women weren't there.

Alena swore.

She ran to Sooni, drawing stares as she did.

Fortunately, she found Sooni already meeting with Rotger. She burst in on them, not bothering with etiquette. "We didn't kill them all."

I don't understand, Rotger signed.

"There are no women among the dead."

Sooni understood first. She had seen the soulwalkers herself. She looked at Rotger. "The others were only a distraction. They were protecting their women."

Alena had reached the same conclusion. Why the Lolani would keep their women from battle was a mystery, but their reasons must be important. The Lolani women had to be at the center of whatever the tribes intended.

Rotger stared over the battlefield, watching his own people lick the wounds they had suffered.

Alena's thoughts jumped from one to the other. What destination did the Lolani women seek?

It occurred to Alena that ever since they had encountered the Lolani, the invaders had traveled almost due east. Their course had never deviated.

She thought of the confidence of the Lolani warrior Sooni had attempted to bargain with.

The guess was little more than intuition, but the pieces

fit. The Lolani were a people who made straight for whatever they targeted. "What is east of us?"

Rotger frowned at the question, then looked out to the east. "Nothing. Leagues of grassland, and then the border."

Sooni, more well-traveled than their commander, had a different answer. "Landow." She seemed to check her surroundings, then answered again with more confidence. "We're almost straight west of Landow at the moment."

A storm of emotions swirled through Alena.

Despite all her years of voluntary exile, Landow still felt like home to her.

And she felt certain the Lolani were heading there now.

ALENA WANTED HASTE, but the Etari refused to permit it. Rotger agreed the remaining Lolani headed toward Landow, which frustrated her even more. They had different priorities, though. Rotger didn't care if the Lolani made their way to Landow. As soon as the invaders left his land, they were no longer his problem. He had the dead to honor and an alliance of families and clans to lead.

Sooni, although more sympathetic, agreed with their commander. She reminded Alena that they had horses and the Lolani did not. If they decided to pursue the remaining invaders, they could afford to wait a day or two.

Alena built her arguments while she waited. Looking around, she agreed with Sooni and Rotger on one truth: the Etari weren't in any condition to ride today. Beyond physical exhaustion, a deeper weariness had settled upon the families. Everyone alive had lost a friend or loved one on the battlefield.

The surviving Etari dug graves for those who fell, backbreaking labor after a battle that had already demanded much of their strength. Alena lent what energy she had to the task.

She had observed the Etari death rites before. Unlike her own people, Etari wept openly. As in all aspects of their lives, their grief was physical and public. Years ago, such displays had discomfited her. But she had grown to appreciate them.

When her own family members were laid to rest, her tears finally came.

This had never been the life she dreamed of as a child.

Jace had been the one who wanted to fight, who wanted to see battles.

She had just craved some break from the safe routines of home. She traced cause and effect, all the way back to Landow, to the night she had decided to steal from the Arrowoods.

She had brought this all on herself.

Anger bloomed in her chest. She watched as the others began covering the dead with dirt. Now, of all times, all she thought of was herself?

She didn't deserve the company of the Etari.

She helped toss dirt on the bodies, the storm of emotions lending her one last burst of strength.

When the task was done, she collapsed.

Strong arms embraced her.

Azaleth.

She tried to push him away. She didn't deserve his affection.

Her efforts were in vain, and she surrendered, sinking into his embrace and returning it with one of her own. She buried her face in his chest, holding on to him as though he was the only thing keeping her alive.

Time lost meaning. The two of them might have

remained in that position for a few heartbeats or the rest of the late afternoon. Alena didn't know.

Eventually, the tumult inside her faded, leaving behind something solid and stable, a mountain of determination.

When she let go of him, he also released her. Their eyes met, and Alena felt understood. He nodded, the imperial gesture somehow seeming out of place.

It made her crack a smile.

She knew what she needed to do.

Alena searched the camp for Sooni, who was already beginning the celebration of the warriors' lives that had been lost. She and most of the rest of the family were gathered around a fire, swapping stories and drinks. Alena was glad she found her family head before the celebration had gotten too far.

"May I speak with you for a moment?" Alena asked.

Sooni cast her a wary look, but agreed.

Together they stepped away from the fire. Azaleth followed, and Alena found she didn't mind.

Once they had some privacy, Alena began. "Will Rotger send anyone after the women?" She kept her voice even, unwilling to start the conversation on the wrong foot.

"Unlikely." Sooni knew Alena was building to her real request.

"I would like to ride to Landow and warn them if I can."

Sooni's gaze was cool. "You wish to leave the family?"

Alena saw the hurt in Sooni's eyes. Whatever grief Alena felt in regards to the loss of family today was a single drop of water compared to the oceans of grief Sooni felt. Sooni had been born into this family and had been responsible for it for over a decade. The fallen weren't just her family, they were *hers*.

For the first time, Alena realized Sooni didn't look on

her as an adopted child, or an alliance of some sort. Their initial bargain had been a trade, but now Alena was as much Sooni's family as anyone that lay buried under the dark earth. The new understanding filled her with a rush of belonging. Sooni would take her loss just as hard as those she mourned tonight.

Still, Alena couldn't waver. Sooni was family, but she had another, and she couldn't ignore them either. She'd run long enough. It was time to face every mistake she had made. And it started here.

Alena stepped forward and held Sooni's hands. "I will never abandon this family." She'd never made such a promise before, but she intended to keep it. "But I must warn my first one."

She wondered if Sooni heard the determination in her voice, because the head of the family put up less of a fight than she expected. "I would bring the entire family to accompany you, if I could."

"You would start a war."

Yes, Sooni gestured. And she meant it, too. Sooni would go that far to protect her, if she could.

Alena's heart broke at that. She pulled the older woman into an embrace. "I will return."

Sooni returned the embrace.

When they broke apart, Sooni glanced at Azaleth. "I imagine you will join her?"

Yes.

"He's all the protection I can offer," Sooni said. "I hope that he is enough. Stay and celebrate our fallen tonight. In the morning, we shall see you off."

Just like that, it was done.

In the morning, she would begin her return to Landow.

53

B randt woke up well before the sun. He and Ana had slept within a depression the night before. It was slim protection, but it kept them out of sight. The caution was probably unwarranted. They hadn't seen a single sign of the invaders since they had entered the cave several days before.

That fact alone made him uneasy. He didn't know if the invaders were using the roads or if they avoided notice by traveling any of the trails that cut through the mountains. But he struggled to believe they had just given up their pursuit after the effort they'd expended. He struggled to believe a lot these days.

For all the answers his vision had provided, it had left him with more questions. The first, and perhaps the most important, was whether or not he should trust the vision at all. When he had woken, he told Ana all that he had seen. Her skepticism reinforced his own.

Still, he felt acutely aware of just how little he understood. What he had assumed was true ten years ago he now knew was false. He wouldn't follow the guidance of his vision blindly, but he didn't see any compelling reason not to accept the information. Someone in Landow sought to aid an enemy of the empire.

While Ana slept, Brandt trained.

In the monastery, his skills had improved. He possessed a basic affinity in each of the elements, a talent he wouldn't have believed possible as a youth. Fire remained his native element, but the vision had promised something else, a harmony between the elements he had yet to discover.

And he remained stymied by the cost. For all his new talents, he still wasn't stronger. The memories unveiled to him in the cave were yet another confirmation. Somehow, there had to be a way to escape the fundamental rules of affinities.

He just didn't know how yet.

So he trained, listening to the songs of each of the elements. He threw stones as high in the air as he could, catching them before they landed and woke Ana. He spun air in tighter and tighter circles until the dust caught within stung his hand. Fire blossomed and diminished within his gaze.

The elements obeyed his every command until his body felt spent.

The cost had been paid.

He finished his training as the sun rose, moving through his various sword forms.

Today they returned to Landow.

Finding Kye was the priority. He needed to be told about the agent Brandt's vision referred to. The governor was in the best position to take action against the invasion. He could order the city guard to intercept the invaders, hold them until reinforcements arrived. Given their small numbers, perhaps the city guard alone would be enough.

They reached the gates of Landow late in the morning.

Soon after, they stood before Landow's main hall, waiting for an audience with the governor.

It didn't take long for the young man they had met before, Jace, to greet them. He offered them a short bow. "I take it you found something?"

"We did," Brandt replied. "Is the governor in?"

"He is. He's finishing a meeting but should be done by the time we arrive." Jace led them with sure steps through building. They came to a small room with a low desk. Brandt noted that the room was incredibly neat, no doubt reflective of Kye's own personality.

Kye rose to greet them.

"What have you learned?"

Brandt took a deep breath, aware of how this would sound. "I believe Landow will be invaded within the week."

"The Etari?" Kye wore a puzzled frown on his face.

"Warriors from beyond our shores," Brandt clarified.

Kye sat down behind his desk, looking up at them. His look was skeptical. He turned to Ana. "Is this true?"

Ana nodded. "We were pursued by invaders here. They approach from the north."

Kye turned to Jace. "Send more scouts north. Double patrols around the wall."

Jace turned and left through the open door. Kye turned his attention to his guests. "What can you tell me?"

Brandt related what he knew, from their discovery of the small force to their pursuit. He held off on saying much about his visions. They were hard enough for him to accept. "They're dangerous," he concluded. "Just a few of them managed to give us trouble."

Kye leaned back, taking in all the information Brandt had just dumped on him. "Do you know when they will arrive?"

Brandt shook his head. "I'm not sure. They're looking for a gate of some sort, and are heading straight here. Have you ever seen or heard about a mysterious gate in the area?"

Now it was Kye's turn to shake his head. "I've never heard of anything like that."

Just then Jace came back, a single nod of his head indicating he'd passed Kye's orders along.

Kye stared off in the distance for a few moments. "We'll send birds to the emperor immediately. He'll need to know what is coming. But the nearest reinforcements are many days away at a hard ride. If we're going to stop this, we can only count on ourselves."

Brandt had assumed the same. The invading force was small, but he still worried. "Ana and I are willing to help. How can you use us?"

Kye thought for another moment. "We could use you at the city gate. If this gate you speak of is within the city, the invaders will try to enter. Your strength and eyes could both prove valuable."

"Very well." He glanced over at Ana to see if she had anything to add, but she was silent. "We will report to the captain of the city guard."

"There's no need," Kye answered. "I want you two easy to reach. Jace, will you accompany them and keep me updated on what they discover?"

A moment seemed to pass between the governor and his aide, some silent message Brandt could only guess at. Jace bowed and led the former wolfblades out of the government center.

Outside, Jace turned to the others. "Do you two have a place to stay?"

"No," Ana said.

"I can get you set up in the city watch barracks."

Brandt shook his head, giving Ana a meaningful glance. "I think I would prefer a place with a bit more privacy."

"Very well. How soon do you think you will need to take station on the wall?"

"Tomorrow morning," Brandt replied.

Jace bowed to them again and was off.

"Are you sure waiting until then is wise?" Ana asked once they were alone.

"No, but we've been on the run for days, sleeping in the wild. Kye is doing all that he can. We'll rest and recover, and tomorrow approach the problem with fresh eyes. We need the sleep."

Brandt looked off to the mountains in the distance. "Then we find the gate and stop whatever is coming."

54

T hey rode hard.

Their journey reminded Alena of her flight from Landow. They endured long days looking over their shoulders for any sign of the Lolani, either ahead of them or behind. She wasn't surprised their paths didn't cross. The plains were wide, and even a slight initial deviation could result in large distances over time. Azaleth's tracking skills were superb, but even he couldn't find their trail.

This part of Etar wasn't like the mountains around Landow, where only a few known trails existed. Anyone could cross the prairie anywhere, leaving far too much space to search.

Fortunately, she didn't need to find the Lolani. Knowing their destination, all she had to do was arrive there first. So they rode, pushing their horses to the brink.

The most difficult part of their journey was crossing the river. This far north it widened considerably, and they lost a day finding a ferry that would take them across. Azaleth wore his red cloak for the crossing, deflecting questions with vague answers about establishing a new trade route.

Then Alena was back in the imperial lands close to her home.

Once away from the ferry, Alena changed into imperial clothing, as did Azaleth. The farther they traveled in their red cloaks the more questions they would receive. Travel for imperials within the empire wasn't restricted, so hiding Azaleth's Etari features was easier than stopping to explain their trip to every passing soldier.

By the time they reached the woods south of Landow, Alena's thighs chafed, and if she didn't ride a horse for a year, she didn't think she would miss the experience. Even in the empire, Alena continued searching for the Lolani invaders, for any flash of unnaturally pale skin. She saw nothing, though.

Eventually they came upon the walls of Landow. There, for the first time, Alena pulled to a stop. She had returned to the town of her birth. Even after all these years, seeing those walls made her feel safe. She had spent most of her life inside them, protected from invaders and the outside world. Now she had come to ensure her home remained as she remembered it.

When they reached the gate, they encountered their first problem. In Alena's experience, passing through the gate was rarely difficult. The empire hadn't been at war in generations, and with safe passage almost guaranteed throughout the empire, there was little reason to guard the gates.

Either something had happened or traditions had changed since she had lived here. Many guards watched the gates, and everyone coming in or out endured severe scrutiny. Alena could enter without problem, but Azaleth was another matter. They retreated a ways to decide their strategy.

He could pull out his red cloak and pretend to be a trader passing through. But a lone Etari was incredibly uncommon. Azaleth would invite more questions and suspicion than they wanted.

Alena directed them to a small food stall outside the gates. They found seats and replenished their stomachs while she decided what to do. As she did, she studied the gates and the walls. If necessary, they could try to find a way over the top at night, as she had so long before. But the walls looked more heavily guarded than in the past.

Her watchful eye revealed several details as they ate. Most of the guards on the wall seemed bored. Even though there were many of them, most weren't paying close attention to their duties. Some talked freely, only sparing the occasional glance at the land surrounding them. Others stared off into the distance, slack expressions painted on their faces.

The guards at the gate suffered from similar maladies. Their examinations were thorough, enough so Alena was certain she couldn't bring Azaleth through without arousing suspicion. But the guards performed their duties without enthusiasm.

It all felt to her as though the guard had been increased, but wasn't given any specific reason to care.

Only one pair of guards seemed an exception to the rule. One man and one woman stood over the gates, their expressions serious. They exchanged occasional words, but they watched the road with sharp, unrelenting gazes.

She squinted, trying to make out their features. The man, at least, appeared familiar to her. But where had she seen him before? She hadn't known many city guards when she lived here. She spent most of her time trying to avoid their attention.

The guard shifted his weight, and something about the way the sunlight hit his face triggered her memory.

Sergeant Brandt.

But it couldn't be. The last time she saw him, he had wandered away. And he had been a wolfblade, not a member of the city guard.

She rubbed at her eyes and looked again. Perhaps she was only seeing what she wished to.

But the more she looked, the more convinced she was. The man standing guard over the gate was Brandt, the same man she had worked with so many years ago.

Alena couldn't even begin to guess how he had ended up as a guard for Landow, but the only way she would find out was by asking him. Perhaps he was their way into town.

She turned her full attention to him. While the other guards simply did their duty, Brandt's full attention was focused on the road and the people entering and leaving. He was looking for someone, or something. He knew more than the guards.

Did he know about the Lolani?

It was another question only he could answer.

She finally ended her study of the wall, unsurprised to see that Azaleth had eaten not just his food, but most of hers as well. She glared at him, but his only response was to smile.

"I need to go into town on my own. Will you remain in the area for the rest of the day?" Now that they were in public, they had switched back to imperial, the language feeling strange on Alena's tongue.

"Do I have much choice?"

"Not if you want me to come back for you."

"Then here I'll remain."

Alena ate what little Azaleth had left, then walked

toward the gate. She endured a few questions, the most interesting of which was the guards asking if she had seen anyone unusual on the road. Landow was searching for someone, but who?

Then she was through, returned to her home without a note of fanfare. She stood on the other side of the gates, nearly wrecked by memories. How many times had she run along these roofs, her youthful rebellion now a shallow and meaningless act?

A dozen desires pulled at her. She should visit her father's smithy, or the academy. She would even be interested in seeing what happened to Bayt's shop.

She should go home.

Soon, she would do all those things. But none of them would matter if she didn't stop the Lolani.

Alena found a place within the walls where she could keep an eye on Brandt and his companion. They held their posts as the afternoon wore on, only surrendering them as evening approached.

Following them felt like a return to her childhood. How often had she wandered these streets on Bayt's behalf, following strangers to discover what information they hid? Today she kept to the streets, waiting until they were alone to call for him.

"Sergeant Brandt."

They both turned at the mention of his name. When he saw her, his face was blank. But he and his companion waited for her to reach them.

Alena studied Brandt carefully. His face remained neutral but open. He didn't recognize her. She stopped about two paces from the pair. "You don't remember me, do you?"

He frowned, his eyes narrowing. "I don't."

"We worked together, many years ago. I was helping you find out what happened to the wolfblades who died here." Her own voice sounded awkward, but she didn't know what else to say. She wasn't sure what had happened after that fight with Kye.

A slow realization dawned on his face, a recognition of sorts. "You're the girl Ryder died to protect."

She gulped. "I am. And I watched your final fight with the bandit."

Brandt's face twisted into excitement then. "You know who I fought? You were there?"

"I was."

"Who was it?"

Alena looked around. The street was empty, but there were too many corners and shadows. "Is there a place we can go where we won't be overheard?"

A look passed between Brandt and his companion. She nodded and led them all to an inn. They climbed two flights of stairs to the top room, where the three of them locked themselves in what was apparently the couple's room.

Alena made herself comfortable in a chair, then answered Brandt's questions.

She told him all that she knew, leaving nothing out. She confessed to stealing the stone from Zane Arrowood, to being involved in the fight in the street that sent Brandt's friends to the gates.

And she told him how Kye was the bandit they had all been searching for.

Brandt let out a string of curses that lasted for several heartbeats. Ana, now introduced formally, also looked shaken. Alena didn't understand what worried them so much about the governor's secret identity.

Then Brandt told his side of the story, from the loss of

his memory to the training and learning he had undertaken in the monastery. By the time he finished, the sun was setting.

"So the man responsible for informing the emperor and calling for reinforcements is the very man who seems to be aiding the Lolani," Alena concluded.

Brandt nodded, and Alena saw the full extent of the problem before them.

There wouldn't be any help coming.

Every effort they had made thus far was meaningless. If Kye wanted to bring the Lolani into the city, no doubt he would have ample opportunity to do so. Brandt and Ana might be able to summon help, but any attempt would take weeks, if not longer.

The Lolani were near, and they had the help of the strongest warrior any of them had ever faced.

Alena asked the question they were all wondering. "So, what do we do now?"

Silence answered her question. She looked between the two warriors, hoping to find an answer there, but they had none. Brandt turned and stared out the window of his room while Ana fidgeted with her fingers.

Alena had hoped to find not just answers, but a solution here. Their lack of strategy struck her hard.

Then she realized part of their answer had been in front of them ever since they had met. They didn't need to find the gate, or the Lolani. They knew the identity of Brandt's mysterious agent. All they needed to do was follow Kye. In time, he would lead them where they needed to go. She presented the idea.

"It's a start," Brandt admitted, "but it still doesn't help us once we've found the gate. Against the Lolani and Kye, we don't stand a chance."

"Then we need to think of something before they get to the gate," Alena replied. "It's far better than doing nothing."

The two warriors were reluctant, but they agreed.

Only when Alena looked out at the darkening streets did she realize she had forgotten about Azaleth. Quickly, she told them she had brought an Etari. After their initial confusion abated, she convinced them to help her smuggle him in.

With Brandt and Ana's help, getting Azaleth into town was easy. The former wolfblades were known at the gate, and under their escort, Azaleth was allowed in without question.

As they stabled the horses and settled into the inn, Alena thought she saw the flash of a cloak in the street. Perhaps it was just her imagination, but she thought someone had been watching them.

She didn't want to dismiss the possibility, but after their long travel and the days ahead of them, she didn't pay much attention to it.

It had to be a figment of her imagination.

Because she thought she had seen a brief glimpse of a face.

Jace's.

55

The next morning Brandt and Ana returned to the wall. The group had argued about the decision for a bit. Brandt hated the idea of returning to a task that was almost certainly a waste of his time. If Kye had given them the duty, it seemed reasonable to assume the Lolani would not be coming through the main gate into town.

Alena argued against him, and he'd eventually come to see the strength of her logic. Kye's decision to have Jace frequently accompanying them held more ominous overtones than before. If they deviated too much from their stated plans, Kye would soon know, and they would lose the one advantage they currently enjoyed. Thanks to Alena, they knew more than Kye suspected.

Brandt paced the wall quickly. Ana watched him with a hint of a smile on her face. When Brandt noticed he stopped and turned on her. "What?"

The word came out harsher than he intended, but it only caused Ana's smile to widen. "You never had this much trouble letting the wolfblades out of your sight."

"Those kids aren't wolfblades."

"Those *kids* are older than we were when we fought here. If even half of what Alena told us last night was true, she's been through more than most."

"She doesn't have the training we had."

"And yet she's still alive and helping us."

Brandt shook his head and resumed pacing. He should be out there following Kye, not Alena. The danger was too great.

"You're going to exhaust yourself before we even find the Lolani." Brandt heard the sliver of laughter in her voice.

Brandt glared at her but continued pacing. Stopping now would acknowledge that Ana was right.

She wisely said nothing further. Brandt knew she meant well, but pacing helped keep him calm. If he tried to stand still, he felt as though he would jump off the wall and run toward the governor's offices.

Doing nothing simply wasn't in his nature. Kye's strength frightened him. How much stronger would the man be after years of training? And if he still held the gatestone, what chance did Brandt have? Fear and uncertainty only made the uselessness sting that much more.

He should be using this time to strategize, to figure out how to beat Kye. But his thoughts were untamed beasts, continually wandering back to Alena and the risks she took on their behalf.

Near mid-morning, Ana tried again. "Brandt, I've never seen you this nervous before a fight. What's wrong?"

Brandt snapped around, spinning on his heel. "What if something happens to Alena?"

Ana's eyes narrowed. "We'll find another way to follow Kye."

"That's not what I'm worried about."

Ana didn't respond for a moment, the realization coming to her slowly. She bowed slightly to him. "I'm sorry. My words were foolish."

He stopped pacing and approached her. He put his hand gently under her chin and raised it until they were looking directly at one another. "There's nothing to be sorry for. I'm just not the commander I used to be."

She smiled at that. "Some would say you're better."

The intensity of her gaze forced him to look away. "I hope so."

He turned slightly so he faced out over the wall. There were things Ana needed to know, but he wasn't sure he could meet her gaze and say them. "You know that I will gladly take the trip to the gates myself if it means that I can save any one of you?"

Ana nodded. "I admire your courage."

"I'm not sure if it's courage or cowardice. But the idea of losing more friends and allies here, it frightens me more than death. I can't stand the idea of losing anyone else."

Ana reached out and grabbed his hand. "And I don't want to run, ever again."

Brandt risked a glance at Ana. She shed no tears, but her eyes were rimmed with red. He felt himself a selfish oaf then. All morning he had been distracted by his own fear of loss, never considering that Landow held just as many terrors for Ana.

She'd told him often enough, especially back when they had just reunited at the monastery. Following Brandt as a wolfblade, she had always felt invincible. Of course, she felt fear. But Brandt's bravado had convinced her they could overcome any challenge.

When Kyler fell under the building, she had confessed, something inside of her shifted. Suddenly, the stakes of their battle had become all too real to her. In that moment, terror seized her heart and she ran.

She didn't speak about it often, and Brandt, self-obsessed, had forgotten about it. But Landow had broken her, too. He squeezed her hand. "You're still worried."

She nodded.

The offer pained him, but he had to make it. "You don't have to do this, you know."

Her distress turned to anger in less than a heartbeat. She kept her voice low, but it was laced with venom. "Yes I do. I was just as much a wolfblade as you. Their loss has haunted me every day. I ran once, but don't you dare imply that I can or should run again."

No words were sufficient apology. He squeezed her hand again. "I don't believe you'll run, Ana."

She returned the gesture, then gently pulled her hand away. "Thank you."

After a few moments, when Ana was more composed, she turned her head toward him. "Brandt, I know you'll do anything to protect those of us under you. I do. But what if you need to make the decision to sacrifice Alena, or me?"

Her words were like a knife slicing away the thin armor surrounding his heart. Some variety of that question had plagued him all morning. Even sending Alena to spy on Kye had tested his resolve.

Death was the end for them all. It was one of the few certainties in life. Sometimes, Brandt's instructors had taught him, death can mean something. As a wolfblade sergeant, he'd been expected to give the orders that sometimes killed the warriors underneath him.

Until Landow, he'd never had to make that choice.

But he might have to again.

He couldn't imagine the circumstances, but that was

exactly the point. A time might come where he would need to sacrifice one to save many.

And he wasn't sure he could.

He didn't know Alena or Azaleth well, but since last night, they had become *his,* just by virtue of their cooperation. He didn't think he could send them into danger any more easily than he could Ana.

"I'm not sure," he confessed.

"You need to be." Ana's eyes hardened. "Because it's not just our revenge at stake here. It's the lives of everyone in the empire."

56

Alena spent the morning following Kye. She woke before the sun rose and made her way out to his house, a walled estate nicer than any other property in Landow.

Part of her wondered if the Lolani were already here. If they were in Landow, there would be no better place to hide than within the governor's property. She saw no sign of them, though.

Kye left the property just as the sun began to rise. Alena dropped from her perch on the wall and followed him.

Years had passed since she last followed a human through a town, but she regained the knack of it quickly enough. It helped that Kye didn't seem to be concerned about being followed in the least. He stopped frequently to speak with passersby and merchants setting up their shops for the day, but he appeared remarkably carefree. Even though Alena had seen firsthand what Kye was capable of, she struggled to reconcile the deadly bandit with the political appointee she now observed.

She cleared those thoughts away. Kye was a two-faced

man, and had been for years. Of course he would seem nonthreatening.

Kye made a straight path from his house to the center of town where town hall was. Alena saw no need to follow him in. The building only had one entrance and exit, easily visible from a teahouse across the street. Alena stopped into the teahouse, found a table where she could keep an eye on the entrance, and relaxed.

It wasn't long before she saw Azaleth wandering down the street. She popped out of the teahouse, caught his attention, then ordered a fresh pot of tea as he joined her.

"How was it?"

He made a hand sign for confusion, then stopped himself mid-gesture. "I do not understand how your people do not go mad. Everything is so straight."

Alena softly chuckled. "The town was designed by Anders I after the war. He believed straight lines promoted order."

"As near as I can tell, there isn't a single road that curves within the walls."

Alena searched her memory. "That's probably true."

While she had kept an eye on Kye's house this morning, Azaleth took the time to understand the town of Landow better. The Etari placed a high value on understanding their terrain, and Azaleth felt uncomfortable not knowing his surroundings.

Azaleth muttered under his breath.

"What?"

He glanced up, as though just realizing he'd spoken out loud. "It just seems to be an imperial trend. You overpower your surroundings and force them into these unnatural shapes."

Alena acknowledged the point. "But such order comes

with benefits. It is easy to understand the whole town, to find places you haven't been before. Even your own exploration ended early because the town was so easy to understand. It is a far more predictable life."

Alena caught the beginning of a hand sign before Azaleth forced himself to nod. "I suppose I can see the benefit, but there is something about it that makes me feel uncomfortable."

Alena let the point slide. They weren't here to debate the town design.

Azaleth sensed the change in her attitude. "Any leads yet?"

Alena shook her head. "He left his house and came straight here. He's been inside most of the morning and hasn't left."

"So we wait?"

"We wait."

The first event of interest wasn't Kye, but another person, a young man who came down the road with a familiar saunter. Years of life apparently hadn't taken that away from him.

She hadn't been certain the night before, but today she was. That man, who struck quite a sight in his guard uniform, was Jace.

Her heart skipped and ached.

Through most of the morning she had managed to convince herself she was just in another town, a place that wasn't anything special. It helped that Landow had changed in the years since she fled. Shops she remembered had closed, replaced by new ones. She avoided her old neighborhood, the academy, Bayt's shop, and her father's smithy. The lie kept her focused on the task at hand.

Jace shattered the illusion.

Landow wasn't the home she remembered. Perhaps she wouldn't even call it home anymore. But it had been home for most of her life, and some of those people closest to her still called it such.

Alena was halfway out of her seat before she realized what she was doing. Azaleth looked concerned. "What is it?"

Alena pointed out the window toward Jace. "That's my brother."

Azaleth turned to look. "The warrior?"

"Yes."

"I see the resemblance."

Before Alena could take further action, Jace turned and walked into the town hall. From the manner of his walk, Alena suspected this was a journey he made frequently.

A sudden suspicion dawned on her. When she had escaped, Kye had known who she was. No doubt, Kye also knew that Jace was related to her. What were the odds that the traitorous governor would keep one of her family members close?

Alena didn't believe in coincidences, and it wasn't long before her suspicions were confirmed. Jace came back out of the building, but this time his back seemed straighter, his attention more focused.

He was acting like a proper bodyguard.

A few heartbeats later, Kye stepped out, now protected by her brother. Together they left the government hall.

Alena first noticed the difference in their bearings. Before entering the hall, Jace had appeared nonchalant and relaxed. Now his eyes ran over the street and his hand remained close to his sword. He looked ready to launch into battle at the slightest provocation.

Alena and Azaleth followed, keeping plenty of distance. The governor and Alena's brother traveled toward the north side of town, through the wage-earner's district. They even passed the house the Arrowoods had stayed in so long ago.

Alena couldn't help but wonder: what would her life have been like if she had decided not to steal the diamond from Zane? Would she have gone to university, or would she have followed Bayt's lifestyle?

Kye and Jace stopped at a small house less than a hundred paces from the wall. They disappeared inside, Jace scanning the area one last time before vanishing.

Alena's eyes narrowed. What could possibly be in that house? From the outside it seemed well-maintained. The paint was new.

Alena studied the house. The door appeared heavier than most, although she couldn't be sure from this distance. Something about the house bothered her, though.

Several heartbeats later, she figured it out. There weren't any curtains on the windows. Everybody had curtains to block the sun and prevent people from looking in.

Why would this house have a thick door and no curtains?

She wasn't sure, but the house wasn't what it appeared to be. Perhaps this was where Kye hid the Lolani within the town? The only way to know was to get closer.

Perhaps it was because they had just passed the Arrowoods' home, but Alena hesitated. How many times would her curiosity get the better of her? How many times would she look where she wasn't supposed to?

At least one more time, she supposed.

She made a series of hand signs to Azaleth, asking him to stay in place and watch for trouble. He agreed, and Alena ran across the street to examine the house more closely.

She ran around the house to the side, eyes and ears alert to anyone nearby. Then she crouched next to a dark window. She took a moment to catch her breath, then slowly raised her head to peer inside.

Alena had to press her face to the glass before she could see inside, but the room appeared empty. Not just of people, but of furniture and decoration as well.

She didn't think this was where the Lolani were staying.

Emboldened by the room's emptiness, Alena returned to the front of the house. A glance toward Azaleth confirmed the front had been quiet. Alena pushed gently on the front door, but it wouldn't budge. Her guess had been right, though. The door was far thicker than an average door. Alena went to work with her tools, only to realize the lock was already unlocked.

She pushed against the door, but it didn't give even a hair. She pushed harder, putting her shoulder into it, with the same result.

The door had opened easily for Kye and Jace, which meant it was barred from the inside.

Alena took a few steps back. She studied the building again. Why would an empty house in this neighborhood need such a thick door that could be barred from the inside? Then she noticed the city wall behind the house and cursed her stupidity.

The house was the entrance to another way out of the city.

Alena ran back to where Azaleth waited. "It's a tunnel out of town. I'm going to follow them. You need to get Brandt and Ana from the front gate as soon as possible. There will be a trail somewhere on the other side of this wall. I'll leave clues."

Azaleth argued. "I don't want to leave you alone."

He gave her pause. When this was over, she resolved she

would accept his unspoken offer. She had been a fool to push him aside as long as she had.

"There's no choice. I'll be fine. I'm only going to follow them. I won't do anything until you all arrive."

Though he didn't look convinced, Azaleth turned and ran, leaving Alena alone.

She returned her gaze to the house. She could either break into it and attempt to follow the tunnel herself, or she could make herself light, try to get over the wall without being seen, and find where the tunnel came out. Neither was a perfect idea.

She elected to try the tunnel. Getting over the wall without being observed in the middle of the day and managing to find the exit seemed the more difficult task.

First, she needed to break into the house. She returned to the building, walking around it quickly. The house had a back door that was barred as well. She turned her attention to the windows, quickly discovering that they were sealed shut. If it came to that, she would break a window, but she didn't want to leave evidence of her passing if she could avoid it.

Her eyes wandered up to the second floor. Perhaps their precautions hadn't applied through the entire building. She made herself light and climbed up the wall, holding onto the wall with one hand while she pulled out a slim file with the other. The tool slid between the window and the frame without a problem, and soon she was in, crouched down low, listening for any clue her entrance had been noticed.

When she was reasonably certain she was safe, she made her way downstairs. She couldn't hear a single sound in the house beyond her own breathing. A quick check of the ground floor confirmed she was alone in the house.

Alena opened all the doors, not surprised that none of

them led to a secret tunnel. But the floors were bare, so she started tapping on the wood, listening for hollow sounds underneath. It took her a few moments, but she eventually found the secret door under the floor.

Just like Bayt's.

Another few moments of searching revealed the latch, and less than thirty heartbeats later she was looking into a dark tunnel.

Her foot froze. Sending Azaleth away had been right. His tracking skills far surpassed hers, and with Ana and Brandt, he could leave the city without problem and find her.

The tunnel opening stretched in her imagination, threatening to swallow her whole. She took an involuntary step back, then shook her head at her own foolishness.

By now, Jace and Kye were certainly out the other side. But she had no light, and she would have to walk through the dark tunnel alone.

The temptation to run overpowered her. She glanced back at the front door of the house, the sunlight pouring through the windows. It wouldn't be hard. She could turn around, make some excuse, and return to the inn. When Azaleth didn't find her, they would return and they could try again.

She stepped away from the tunnel, returning to the steps she had come down from the second story. She bit her lip as her foot came down.

There might not be a second chance. Brandt believed that whatever the Lolani planned would devastate the empire. If Kye and her brother were on their way to meet the Lolani now, this might be the only opportunity she got. And her family still lived here, the first place disaster would strike.

Alena swore and returned to the tunnel opening. Her

arms and legs felt heavy, but she forced them to move, climbing down the ladder that led to the darkness below.

The tunnel was dark. Light trickled in from the opening, but after the tunnel took its first turn, the light vanished. Alena shuffled forward, her hands against the walls on either side. She tried not to think about the weight of stone above her.

Soon, she stopped. She kept bumping into walls and support beams cutting across the tunnel. No matter how she waved her hands about, there always seemed to be some obstacle she missed.

She closed her eyes, taking deep breaths in an attempt to calm her pounding heart. As she did, her air affinity became more pronounced. She realized that air moved through the tunnel, ever so slightly. She could feel the objects it brushed past.

Alena worked her way forward, mapping out the objects and creating a mental image of her surroundings. After five paces she was convinced her affinity could be used for the task. Within thirty paces she was comfortable moving in the dark.

Then the tunnel ended, thin slits of light visible above her. She could make out the faint outline of a ladder, which she climbed. The ladder ended with a wooden door above her. She pushed at it gently, breathing a sigh of relief when it moved easily.

Alena lifted the door just enough to poke her head through. The door opened into a tightly wooded grove of trees, and as far as she could tell, no one was near. She crawled out quickly, settling into a crouch outside the tunnel. The small wooden door had been covered with leaves. Alena debated, then left the door open. Hopefully it would help Azaleth and the others find her.

She studied the ground and the trees around. For a moment, she worried she had lost them. But then she spotted a broken branch and a footprint in soft ground. She followed, making sure to leave an obvious trail for Azaleth to track.

Alena followed the footsteps for some time. The task didn't come easy to her, but she refused to lose the trail.

She froze when she spotted movement ahead of her. She'd been crouching down, trying to determine where the tracks led. A shadow moved well ahead of her, drifting between the trees. When she focused on the movement, she saw the pale skin of a Lolani.

She had found them.

57

B randt imagined jumping off the wall simply to have something to do. Guard duty was a chore at the best of times, but the agony of boredom intensified when he knew there was work that needed to be done. Ana appeared to bear the strain of inactivity better, but Brandt knew disaster was coming. Somewhere nearby the Lolani lay in wait, ready to unleash whatever horror they had prepared.

And he stood on the edge of a wall, not knowing what else he could do.

When he heard his name being called he almost jumped.

He rushed to the other side of the wall, where Azaleth stood shouting his name. The youth's behavior drew the stares of other guards, but Brandt ignored them. Becoming light, he leaped from the wall, landing softly on the street below. "What?"

The young man's haste made his imperial harder to understand, but Brandt caught the gist of it. Alena had followed Kye out to a house near the edge of town, where she suspected a tunnel under the wall existed. She had followed.

Brandt couldn't decide if Alena was brave or foolish, but he hoped for the former. He turned and waved to Ana, who landed beside him. He repeated the story, and Azaleth told them he planned on tracking Alena.

A glance at Ana told Brandt that she knew his mind and agreed. They motioned for Azaleth to follow, and the boy was only a step behind them. They sprinted through the gates, earning more confused looks from the guards but no further response.

Azaleth took the lead heartbeats after they were beyond the gate. He ran the length of the wall. Though his lightness didn't come close to Brandt's or Ana's, his enthusiasm more than made up for the difference. He turned the corner, heading north.

Brandt and Ana followed as he ran the whole east length of the town, turning again and running west along the north wall.

They were nearly as far away from the main gate as they could be. Brandt supposed it made sense. If Kye had tunnels built underneath the town, having an escape far away from the road seemed sensible.

Finally, Azaleth slowed. "I believe the house is somewhere near the other side of that wall."

"How accurate are you?" Brandt didn't accuse, he just wanted some idea of how close the secret tunnel might be.

Azaleth's hands flashed in a sign Brandt didn't understand. "Maybe two hundred paces?"

That was better than Brandt expected. He strung them out in a line and they began searching for the tunnel exit.

Ana found it, far more quickly than Brandt expected.

Azaleth's sense of place had put them within fifty paces, and whoever had used the tunnel last hadn't covered it up. Brandt suspected Alena, a guess confirmed moments later by Azaleth, whose gaze ran over the dirt with a practiced eye. He pointed to a footprint. "That's her."

Brandt had little choice but to trust the Etari warrior. He saw the footprints, but couldn't have guessed whose was whose. Azaleth set off, almost at a run.

The young warrior tracked the trail with unnatural ease. Signs that Brandt barely noticed seemed obvious to Azaleth. Their pursuit rarely paused more than a heartbeat or two before they were off again.

Any lingering doubts Brandt held vanished when they came upon Alena's crouching form. Brandt hid a small smile. Azaleth's demeanor changed the moment he saw Alena. His shoulders relaxed and his pace slowed. Brandt wondered if Alena knew how strongly Azaleth felt about her.

Alena turned as they approached, relief evident on her face. They crouched next to her, and she pointed ahead.

Brandt's blood ran cold. The Lolani had gathered together around Kye, who was busy talking and pointing up to the mountains. Brandt couldn't make out the words from this distance, but Kye appeared very animated. Behind him, Jace looked nervous, his hand constantly wandering near his sword.

Kye argued with three women who appeared much calmer than him. Whenever he would pause, the women replied in short phrases that angered the governor.

Brandt had seen enough. The only reason he remained still was the group of Lolani warriors. He counted eleven men surrounding the discussion. Too many for him.

He reminded himself that Kye was also a threat. He had no memories of the bandit — only stories told to him by those he trusted. It colored his judgment. He accepted that Kye was strong, but the tales he heard strained his imagination. Time distorted memory.

Brandt didn't want to underestimate his enemy, but overestimation could lead to mistakes, too.

Regardless, there were too many enemies for him to attack.

"What do you want to do?" Alena whispered. "Should we return with city guards?"

Brandt studied the Lolani. Even at a distance, the pale warriors radiated menace. The extra numbers of the city guard might be useful, but they would die in droves against these warriors. Brandt understood their relative skills, and the guards would serve as little more than a distraction. What slim benefit they provided wouldn't be worth the time it took to summon them.

And that was assuming they would even attack a group that Kye had joined.

"No," he replied. "I'm afraid we're on our own here."

He saw her eyes widen at that, fear dancing in her gaze. He wouldn't have blamed her if she turned and ran. Instead, she gulped and nodded.

A brave girl.

Brandt studied the gathering of warriors he now commanded. He knew Ana's abilities nearly as well as he understood his own. He had some guess as to Azaleth's, but Alena's were a mystery. Commanding them with such limited knowledge begged for foolish mistakes.

They couldn't die today. Not if they listened to him. He would make sure of it.

"I wish I knew what they were arguing about," Brandt muttered to himself.

"The Lolani want directions to the gate, but Kye is refusing to tell them. He insists on taking them personally," Alena answered.

Brandt glanced over at her. "You can hear them?"

She nodded. "Bits and pieces."

"Anything else?"

She shook her head and nodded toward the invaders. "Kye just won the argument."

The Lolani became a hive of activity, forming into a line with Kye at the lead. They set off to the north, toward higher elevations.

Brandt turned to Azaleth. "Can you track them?"

The young man nodded. Once the Lolani were safely out of sight, Azaleth advanced to where they had met with Kye, making a careful study of the ground. He gestured with Etari hand signs, which Alena interpreted. "He says to follow."

"Remind him to stay out of sight," Brandt ordered.

Alena gave him an incredulous look. "He knows."

Brandt almost argued but bit his tongue. Azaleth's youth and confidence worried him, reminded him too much of his younger self.

Then Azaleth was off, leading them on the trail the Lolani had left. Brandt didn't like letting the Lolani have such a lead, but he didn't know their destination. He had no choice but to follow and wait for an opportunity to attack. He hoped it wouldn't come too late.

Their pursuit led them out of the woods and foothills surrounding Landow and climbed into the mountains. They hiked higher and higher, skirting around mountain lakes and fields of scree. Unfortunately, Brandt had no eye for the natural beauty that surrounded them. His only eye was for the Lolani. He kept asking Azaleth where he thought the invaders had gone, watching the terrain for places where he could rush ahead and set an ambush.

After a long, frustrating afternoon of hiking, Azaleth called them to a stop. The sun had already set behind the mountains, and while plenty of daylight remained, night was approaching. Brandt creeped forward to where Azaleth lay prone against the rocks. He pointed to the opening of a narrow valley ahead. Two Lolani were stationed there, keeping an eye on the surrounding area.

Brandt suspected the valley housed their final destination. The Lolani guarded the entrance.

He looked for any way to ambush them, finding nothing he liked. Only Azaleth's caution approaching a small ridge had saved the group from discovery. The Lolani had a clear view for hundreds of paces. Brandt could attempt to surprise them a hundred times and fail every time.

There had to be a way.

He noticed movement beside him as Ana and Alena joined them. Together they took in the situation.

After a few moments, Alena spoke. "They're too confident."

Brandt turned to her, his expression inviting her to explain further.

"When I met them. They hold this land and all within it with contempt. They underestimate us."

"How does that help us?"

"Send Azaleth. They won't be expecting an Etari, and he isn't dressed like one. They'll let him get close enough, and he can kill them."

Brandt gave her a skeptical look. "They aren't easy to kill."

"We know."

He didn't like it. He'd heard plenty of stories about Etari skill, but Brandt wasn't about to risk the future of the empire on one foreigner he'd never seen fight before. This risk was his. "I'll go," he proclaimed.

He ignored the protestations of the group. This was his task, and he was somewhat confident he could kill both Lolani. He stood up, solving the problem for good.

The Lolani noticed him right away, turning toward him the same way a man might study an insect that had made its way indoors. Alena's intuition was correct.

A heartbeat later, he heard the sound of footsteps behind him. He turned to see Azaleth there, a grin on his face. "Alena made me."

Brandt cursed, but there was nothing for it now. Both of them had been seen. The Etari had used Brandt's own strategy against him.

"Do you have a plan?" Azaleth asked.

"Get close and kill them."

"I should be able to surprise one and kill him before they understand what's happening. If I'm lucky, I can kill both, but it would help if I was within a hundred paces."

Brandt glanced over, unable to hide his disbelief. "You're sure of a kill within a hundred paces?"

"Yes. Unless they figure out what I am before I attack."

Brandt's confidence wasn't as high as the young man's, but they were committed now. He listened for the song of fire as he thumbed his sword loose of its sheath. If Azaleth attacked, Brandt would be right beside him.

Alena's assessment of their confidence held. If the Lolani had the ability to call for the others, they made no use of it.

When they were within a hundred paces, Azaleth fished

around the pouch that hung from his belt. He glanced at Brandt, who nodded.

Brandt didn't see Azaleth's attack. He thought he saw something small hovering in the air next to the young man, but then he blinked and it was gone. He glanced over toward the Lolani in time to see one of the warriors collapse.

Brandt turned back to Azaleth, his mind searching for an explanation of what he'd just seen.

Azaleth grimaced in concentration, and when Brandt looked toward the valley's mouth, both Lolani warriors were lying motionless upon the rocks.

Behind them, Alena and Ana stood and approached. Azaleth sagged for a moment before regaining his strength. "That was close. The second warrior realized what was happening a moment too late. He still almost stopped me."

Brandt tried to hide his surprise, but he wasn't sure he succeeded.

How?

A small voice in the back of his head complained. Those Lolani had been his responsibility. How dare Azaleth assume that burden?

When Ana and Alena reached them, a small celebration began. Alena, in particular, beamed at the young man.

The group traveled to the mouth of the valley, and Brandt looked down at the bodies motionless on the rocks. They each had small holes in their heads. One was perfectly centered, and the other looked like it had almost missed.

Brandt looked up at Azaleth.

So this was the power of the Etari.

Still, there was more work to be done.

Azaleth seemed to feel the same. He was crouched over a pile of stone. A moment after Brandt noticed the behavior, the Etari called them to him.

Azaleth brushed small stone to the side with his hand, and Brandt saw what had attracted his attention.

There was a path, buried by generations of neglect.

It led straight up the valley.

There were no coincidences.

Someone, long ago, had built a path to the gate.

58

A lena crouched, remaining well out of view of the mouth of the cave. About a dozen paces ahead, the other three were hiding behind a boulder, strategizing an approach to the cave where another four Lolani stood guard. Alena didn't possess a military mind, but she could guess the problem easily enough. Azaleth's same trick wouldn't work twice. Their very presence meant they had fought and killed the Lolani down the valley.

Alena had taken one glance at the cave entrance and retreated away from the others. The cave was a tall slit in an enormous granite wall. The darkness within seemed absolute, and the four Lolani men standing guard looked serious about their task.

All of that frightened her, but none of it bothered her as much as the paved stones they had followed up the valley. The path had been broken by roots and rubble, the ravages of time taking their toll, but its existence wasn't in doubt.

Someone, long ago, had built a path up to the cave they were seeking. That path had been destroyed, not just by time, but by someone.

The thought that itched at her, though, was that she had no idea who had built the path or why. She knew the history of this area. The academy had drilled it into her throughout her childhood.

They had always been taught no one had been here before the empire arrived around two hundred years ago. Anders I built Landow, which was said to be the first true civilization this far north.

But this path spoke another truth. A path like this required months, if not years, of effort. The sections of the path that remained unbroken revealed excellent craftsmanship, a care that echoed down through the years.

This path hadn't been made by the empire. Hunters and trappers traveled occasionally in these mountains, but that was about all. The terrain was too rough except for the pass the road out of Landow followed.

She had been lied to, and not for the first time.

When she had first learned of the Lolani and the second continent, she believed it was a mistake. After all, Azaleth made Palagia sound very far away. Perhaps even the emperor hadn't known about it.

But there was no excuse for this. There was no way the emperor hadn't known about whoever came here before. This wasn't a mistake, but a deliberate lie. And the lie had attracted the Lolani across an ocean. Her family was in danger, and Alena wasn't even sure why.

She had put together enough information to have some idea what transpired before her. Kye had found a gate in the mountains, the source of gatestones, which provided those with affinities some additional strength. But was that enough of a reason to risk crossing an ocean, to invade a foreign land with only a small force? It couldn't be. There had to be more, but she couldn't guess what.

Unlike the others, she looked down the valley they had climbed up. So she was the only one who saw the wolf padding toward them. It stared at them with undisguised curiosity, but it took Alena a few moments to realize the wolf's behavior wasn't natural.

"Azaleth." She spoke just loud enough for him to hear her. When he turned, she pointed to the wolf.

He understood faster than she did. He tapped Brandt on the shoulder. "We've been spotted by one of their soulwalkers." He dug a stone out of his bag just as the wolf sprinted forward.

Alena froze. Without preparation she had no way to defend herself. Her knife was a poor weapon against the wolf's fangs. She leaped out of the wolf's way as Azaleth launched a rock at the charging beast. In his hurry he missed.

The wolf turned to follow Alena, and Azaleth tried again as Alena scrambled back. The Etari hunter had a full view of the wolf, but his hurry again affected his aim, the rock spinning off high. But it still cut into the wolf, near its backbone.

The wolf went stiff, limbs flailing as it fell over, growling.

Slowly, Alena's senses returned to her. Though the wolf was dying, it stared at her with unnatural hatred. It was a wolf, and yet not a wolf.

The soulwalker remained in the wolf's body. But why? It was crippled and dying. Surely it didn't serve a purpose any longer.

A shout from Ana tore Alena's attention away from the animal. The Lolani were coming down from the cave. Somehow, they knew where Alena and the others hid.

Brandt swore. "At least four against four is a fair fight."

Azaleth made a negative hand gesture. "Alena should remain behind."

Brandt gave Azaleth a skeptical look, then glanced to Alena. She nodded. "I'm more a hindrance than a help in a fight."

He made the decision quickly. "Fine. Stay out of sight. If the worst comes to pass, maybe they'll forget you were here."

Alena didn't think that was likely, but she nodded. If it made him feel better, who was she to take that from him?

The three stepped out from behind the boulder. Alena thought she saw a rock pass back and forth between the Lolani and Azaleth, but they were prepared, and his Etari techniques wouldn't work. Swords were drawn, and the fight would be decided with steel.

Alena watched from cover for a few moments. Brandt was one of the best swordsmen she had ever seen. In her years with the Etari, she had seen any number of strong warriors, but Brandt's skill was something beyond those. Even the Lolani, strong as they were, fell back before the speed and accuracy of his blade.

She turned back to the wolf, her natural curiosity too strong to be ignored. The soulwalker was still in there, but the wolf had gone perfectly still. Alena assumed Azaleth's errant aim had shattered the animal's backbone.

Her curiosity pulled her forward. She took one hesitant step, then another. When she came within three paces the wolf snapped at her and growled, but it couldn't move its legs. She stepped around it until she was near its hindquarters. She took another step, growing more confident that it couldn't attack her.

Alena squatted down next to the wolf, laying her hand

on it. She couldn't say why she did. Curiosity, perhaps, or something deeper.

As soon as her hand touched the wolf's pelt, she felt her. The soulwalker.

The sensation was unfamiliar to Alena, but when she touched the wolf, the world unfolded like a flower before her, lines of interconnectedness spreading throughout the land. For a few heartbeats, she swore she could see the web with her eyes open.

One strand of the web was stronger than the others, more vivid to her senses. It ran from the wolf to the caves, deep within.

An invisible hand shoved at her, pushing her away from the wolf. The web between her and the wolf flared to life for a moment and she fell back, the connection severed.

But something still lingered, a knowledge she felt deep within her bones, an awareness she'd always had but never noticed. She blinked, catching movement in the corner of her eye.

One of the Lolani guards lay unmoving on the rocks, and another collapsed as Azaleth cut deep across his stomach. Her friends appeared to be winning, even though she saw several cuts on Azaleth's arms. They would be fine, she hoped.

Alena turned back to the wolf. She steeled herself and put her hand in the wolf's fur, grabbing tight.

Her world shifted again, the web reappearing. The attack came faster this time, a wave of pressure washing over her. Alena grimaced but imagined rooting herself like a tree. The wave passed.

For a moment, her mental landscape was silent. She still felt the Lolani soulwalker's presence, quiet and ominous somewhere in the distance. There was a third presence, completely unfamiliar. She turned to study it, reason failing her.

She allowed herself to approach the final presence, noticing a white-hot pain radiating from it.

It was the wolf.

In agony from Azaleth's weapon.

Alena's heart went out to the beast, and in that moment, the Lolani soulwalker attacked again.

This time, Alena was even more prepared. She felt herself rooted, then used those roots to push against the soulwalker. She knew how the attack felt and responded in kind. But while Alena couldn't be moved, she couldn't budge the other woman. She breathed deep, trying to push harder, but to no avail.

A faint warmth spread through her abdomen, gradually growing in intensity.

Her gatestone.

She focused her will on the stone, letting her inner energy flow through. As soon as she did, a new well of power opened itself to her. Effortless energy.

Still engaged in a mental battle, she gently shoved at the Lolani soulwalker. The other presence disappeared as quickly as she could snap her fingers. Alena hadn't expected that. Now it was just her and the wolf.

Tentatively, she reached out and touched the wolf's presence.

Her world shifted wildly. She was lying on her side, needles of pain stabbing up and down her body. Colors weren't what they should be, but the smells, the smells were richer than anything she'd ever experienced.

Alena tore herself away and let go of the wolf. She still felt that invisible web, but her awareness was her own. In front of her, the wolf let out a whimper.

Alena drew her knife across its throat. Better it not know pain any longer. She wiped the blade on the wolf's fur and sheathed it. She looked up and saw Brandt finish off the last of the Lolani.

The other three stood there, victorious and tired. They had hiked quickly all day, only to fight in vicious combat. But none of them knew what she had just been through.

Looking at Brandt, she suddenly felt ashamed. This skill was something similar to what had destroyed him for years, which still haunted him today. The Etari looked upon it as a curse.

She wouldn't tell them. What happened would never be repeated.

Azaleth motioned for her to join them, which she did eagerly. Her companions appeared tired but whole. Azaleth had taken the worst of it with a cut on his left arm and one on his back. Fortunately, neither were deep.

Brandt looked up to the cave. "We've killed over half their warriors. We need to find the rest before they can complete whatever ritual they plan. I'll take the lead." Without even leaving time for an argument, he walked up to the cave mouth and disappeared inside.

Ana looked worried, but she squared her shoulders and followed him.

Azaleth walked with her to the mouth of the cave. Brandt and Ana stood inside, each holding an ancient torch. They were shuffling forward, torches held high above their heads. The crack became so narrow it squeezed them on either side. Alena swore.

Her hands became slick with sweat and her heart pounded in her chest.

Her brother was in there, along with a man of unbelievable strength, five strong warriors, and three soulwalkers. They'd been fortunate thus far, but their luck couldn't hold forever. If she descended into that absolute darkness, she was certain she would never see the light again.

She closed her eyes and took a deep breath.

Then she opened them and stepped into the dark.

59

The crack widened after about a hundred paces, opening up into a dark tunnel of broken rock. The passage was barely tall enough for Brandt, and he had to carefully pick his way over the sharp stone. The path angled down, turning at random intervals. It didn't take long for him to feel completely lost. But there was only the one tunnel, so for now he could dismiss his disorientation.

The group remained silent except for their heavy breathing and the sound of their feet against the stone. An occasional curse washed over him as one of their party slipped or stubbed their toes against the uneven ground.

They needed rest. They'd gained elevation all day, and this path before them was anything but easy going. But they didn't have time. His only comfort was knowing that those they pursued had made the same hike. When they met, exhaustion would be a factor for them all.

The tunnel abruptly leveled out, surprising them. Brandt stumbled, caught himself, then noticed the darkness ahead of him had a different quality to what he had seen before. He kept walking, his torchlight finally finding the end of the tunnel.

When he stepped out of the tunnel, he stopped in surprise. The tunnel let out into a long chamber of smooth stone.

When Ana came through with the second torch, more details revealed themselves. The chamber wasn't a single room, but a hallway. The walls were smooth and even, demonstrating a skill even modern masons would be challenged to display.

For a few moments, their wonder halted their progress.

What was this?

He'd never heard any stories of people dwelling underneath the mountains, or any legends of this type of work. But the evidence was right in front of him.

He shook his head, clearing the thoughts away. The hallway opened up in both directions, and they needed to find the Lolani and Kye before they reached the gate. But which way did they go? He looked down the hallway, but the smooth floor evidenced no marks of passage.

Alena closed her eyes. Brandt wondered if she'd become too tired to continue. Then her eyes opened, a fresh determination within. She pointed. "This way."

Brandt didn't know how she was so certain, but he had trusted her this far. He would continue to do so. He took the lead, torch held off to the side so as not to completely blind him from any dangers ahead. Alena and Azaleth followed, with Ana taking the rear with the other torch.

The hallway opened up into another room, larger than the average room in a house. Like the hallway, the stone was smooth.

The greater problem was that several hallways were

connected to the room. Alena closed her eyes again and pointed.

Brandt didn't like being forced to trust someone this much, but lacking better options, he agreed. They turned down the hallway Alena indicated, their footsteps echoing in their ears.

When they turned a corner they came upon a woman, pale even in the light of the torches. She lay on her back, her eyes open and glassy, staring at the ceiling. She made no movement as they neared, even when they approached closer.

"She's one of the soulwalkers," Alena said.

Brandt turned to her, surprised. Something in Alena's tone implied she knew more than she said. He took a guess. "Did you do this?"

She nodded, tears welling up in her eyes.

The woman was breathing, and despite her complete stillness, seemed healthy enough.

But she was an enemy, too dangerous to leave behind them. Brandt didn't like his decision, but it was necessary. He ran his sword over her throat. She died without even a grimace.

They should all be so lucky to travel to the gates unburdened.

Alena gasped, but no one else made any comment. It was an ugly thing, but the risk was too high. He couldn't allow the soulwalker to wake behind them.

They continued on. His stomach felt queasy.

Killing someone who was actively trying to kill you was one thing. But slitting the throat of a woman lying prone on the floor? His body told him that was murder, no matter how he justified it.

He pushed the thoughts down. He could worry about his soul later, after the empire was safe.

However, the presence of the soulwalker did make one fact clear: Alena's information was good. Brandt still didn't know how, but she knew, or at least had some clue, about where they were going. That, at least, was one burden off his shoulders. Even if he couldn't explain it.

Wonder after wonder unfolded before them. Not every hallway or chamber was smooth stone. Whoever had built these structures also made use of a natural cave system. They came upon one room in particular where the ceiling stood far above them, so high the torches barely illuminated the stalactites hanging above. Another room had built a space for a natural pool. At times, slivers of light filtered down from high above.

The size of the place confounded his imagination. Either this had taken a great number of people many years, or several lifetimes had gone into this construction. The complex was a maze he could spend months exploring. Thankfully, Azaleth regularly left one of his stones behind, marking a path they could return on. He was grateful the Etari possessed such foresight. He hadn't thought about it until too late.

Alena kept guiding them, stopping on occasion to close her eyes and perform whatever technique she used to track them. Brandt guessed it had something to do with the dead soulwalker behind them, but couldn't say more.

He trusted her.

She led them out to an enormous cavern, their walkway suddenly becoming a bridge over a vast emptiness. The bridge was wide enough for three horses to walk abreast, but there was no railing. The bridge simply ended. A wrong step would be a last one, here.

A faint blue light emanated somewhere below. Brandt approached the edge, glancing over. Far below them another bridge crossed the chasm, ending in a room that was the source of the light. As Brandt peeked over, he saw a group walking across the bridge toward the opening.

The Lolani women. Kye and Jace accompanied them. Brandt could just make out their features from his position. Beside him, he heard the soft clacking of stones. He held out his hand to stop Azaleth from launching his deadly projectiles. Azaleth frowned, and Brandt whispered. "The governor has the strongest stone affinity I've ever seen. By far."

The Etari warrior still looked confused.

Brandt pointed to his feet. "We're standing on a stone bridge."

Understanding dawned on the younger man's face.

Brandt pointed to the other end of their bridge. Somewhere on the other side there had to be stairs to take them down. "We need to hurry."

Tired as they were, they ran.

They entered a large room with a spiral staircase. Brandt charged down the stairs, taking them as fast as the light of his torch allowed. Down and down they went, diving deeper into the bowels of the earth.

Brandt came out into yet another chamber, completely dark except for the light of his torch.

A soft grunt of effort was Brandt's only warning. He brought his sword up, taking a strong blow across the blade. He managed to keep from cutting himself, but just barely. The torch was cut out of his hand.

Then he saw them, the remaining Lolani warriors coming out of the shadows. Behind him, Azaleth and Alena came to a quick stop. Azaleth stepped to Brandt's side. The wolfblade appreciated the gesture, but he'd rather have the extra space to fight. Ana brought up the rear, tossing her torch into the middle of the room, hoping to provide slightly better illumination.

He didn't know how he survived the next ten heartbeats. His sword spun and deflected, driven entirely by instinct and reaction. Azaleth engaged the warriors on his side. The Etari was a skilled sword, but his shorter blades were a hindrance against the Lolani's heavier steel. When the invaders paired up, Azaleth couldn't get close enough to attack.

Brandt's sword was longer, and that additional length kept him alive through several passes, but he couldn't turn the table on the warriors. Their skill was superior to those he had fought earlier. The best, it seemed, had been saved as the last line of defense.

Ana joined the fight, pulling one of the three swords away from Brandt. The fight became more fair, but even Brandt couldn't quite turn the tables on his enemies. Whenever one attacked, the other kept their sword pointed at him, preventing him from closing.

Brandt lost track of the number of times he crossed swords with the Lolani without effect. He was unharmed, but his party hadn't killed a single Lolani standing in their way.

He was unharmed.

The fact struck him as odd. No fight went this long without a cut.

He yelled, pushing his two opponents back a few steps with a flurry of strikes. Then he disengaged, giving himself a chance to think. Beside him, Ana and Azaleth still fought, their movements light and easy. Alena hung back, keeping herself out of the way.

None of them had been injured, even though outnumbered.

That wasn't likely.

Of course.

The Lolani weren't fighting to win. They were fighting not to lose, to keep Brandt and the others from getting past them. He saw the dark outline of more stairs on the other side of the chamber. These Lolani were fighting a defensive battle, and they were skilled enough to hold Brandt and the others off indefinitely.

Alena noted the same. "You need to run," she shouted over the clang of echoing steel.

His gut sank. Memories of Kyler, Ryder, and Lola flashed through his thoughts.

"No," he yelled. "We fight together."

If he left, it would leave the other three without their strongest warrior. Against these five Lolani, it was as good as sentencing them to death.

One of the Lolani fighting Azaleth landed a strong kick to the Etari's stomach, driving him back. Those two warriors disengaged as well. A moment later, Ana stepped away from her opponent. The two sides stood facing one another.

Brandt could guess his opponents' minds well enough. Their ambush hadn't killed anyone, but fighting or not, they delayed the imperial warriors. That was all that was required.

He got the sense the Lolani across from him were very pragmatic.

"She's right," Ana said. "You have the best chance of stopping them. You need to get past them. We'll hold them here."

Alena stepped behind him, extinguishing his cut torch with her foot. The room darkened.

Brandt turned to Ana. "I'm not leaving."

"You must."

She was right. They all knew it.

But he couldn't leave them. Brandt looked around the room, searching for some answer. He couldn't stay, either. He was their best chance of stopping the Lolani from opening the gate.

But it meant leaving his command behind yet again.

Ana must have guessed at his thoughts, because she stepped closer. "I'm not going to run again, Brandt. I'm where I need to be. It's time for you to do the same."

It wasn't her words that convinced him so much as her tone. He heard the peace in her voice, the commitment.

Their eyes met, and he nodded.

What else was there to say?

Alena spoke. "Can you kill the torch in the middle of the room?"

"Yes."

Across from him, the Lolani shifted. From the expressions on their faces, they didn't understand what Alena said, but they sensed the plan being hatched against them.

"Do it when you're ready to leave. Run past them." Alena turned to their Etari ally. "Watch the stairs after he runs through. If anyone follows, kill them."

Azaleth made a sign and pulled the stones out of his pouch.

Brandt listened for the sound of the fire, familiar and faint in front of him. He pulled from the flame, enjoying the burst of energy it gave him. The room went dark except for the faint outline of blue light from the stairs. Brandt became light and jumped. He heard swords cutting below him, but he landed unharmed next to the door.

Then he ran, pursued by the sound of steel clanging against steel, the final fight of his abandoned friends.

60

D arkness fell over Alena like a protective shroud. In time, the faint blue glow coming from the stairs beyond might provide enough illumination to see more of their chamber, but that light was incredibly dim.

By the time their eyes became that sensitive, the battle would be over.

She closed her eyes, the difference almost meaningless. She felt the air, sensed its currents throughout the room, the way the constant breath of eight individuals kept the air circulating.

As she had hoped, she could also feel those small pockets where air moved around bodies. For a few moments, at least, she knew where the Lolani were, and they couldn't see her.

One of the Lolani moved toward the stairs Brandt had just taken. Alena issued a warning. "Azaleth!"

Then she shifted away. She was grateful she did. A small object, probably a throwing knife, cut through the air where she'd been standing a heartbeat ago.

Azaleth responded to her warning, a stone darting toward the stairs. The Lolani fell, dead.

Knife in hand, Alena stepped carefully through the room. The groans of the wounded Lolani sounded like shouts in the otherwise silent chamber.

In the space of a few heartbeats she was behind the Lolani closest to her. She needed her cut to be fatal.

Her heart pounded, so loud she worried it would give her position away. Her grip became slick on the knife, but she held tightly to it. Father had given her this blade, and while he had never imagined the uses she would put it to, she hoped he would be proud of her for protecting the family.

Alena felt where the Lolani's breath came from. The air moved down, so he was breathing through his nose, listening for any sound that would indicate where his enemies hid.

She imagined where his neck would be. If she had more time, she would have waited until she was certain. But her grip grew sweatier and her focus wavered with every passing moment. She couldn't imagine it would be long before the Lolani planned a coordinated reaction.

Alena stood and reached around the Lolani just as a torch flared to life near the center of the chamber. Alena saw her target for the first time, closer than she'd imagined. Before she could think, she finished her cut, drawing the blade across the Lolani's neck.

It was the first time she had cut into human flesh. She didn't know why, but she had always thought it would be harder.

But the skin protecting a human was little different than that of any animal she'd hunted while among the Etari. The

Lolani gurgled and collapsed, and the room erupted in chaos.

Ana leaped into battle, trailed by a thin whip of water. The water snapped at the face of the Lolani who stepped up to block her, distracting the warrior for a precious moment. Ana's blade carved into the Lolani, red gashes appearing across his pale torso.

The Lolani who had lit the torch charged Azaleth. The Etari warrior was caught unprepared. He had a stone already spinning, and he sent it into the Lolani, but the projectile wasn't fatal. The Lolani's short blade caught Azaleth in the side, and he collapsed to one knee.

Alena shouted, but there was nothing she could do. Azaleth turned to her and smiled as the Lolani completed his attack, driving his blade deeper into the man who had followed her so far from his home.

Alena screamed, a sound that echoed and grew within the walls of the small chamber. She fell to her knees, her mind and body frozen. She saw another Lolani step toward her, sword held high, ready to strike her head off and end her agony.

At that moment, she welcomed it.

Then the Lolani stopped moving, looking down in surprise at the sword point that had appeared in his chest. The blade vanished again, and the Lolani fell to his knees, now nearly eye to eye with Alena.

She hated him. She hated the Lolani and everything about them.

With a growl, Alena came to her feet and drove her own knife into the Lolani's chest. She knew the action carried no meaning of its own. Ana's blade had taken the Lolani's life, even if the man still had a handful of breaths left to take. But Alena didn't want him to have even that many.

Every breath the Lolani took was an affront to Azaleth's memory.

The Lolani's eyes lost their animating spark, and a fierce, hot flame of joy spread through her.

Alena looked up to see Ana engaged with the last Lolani, the one whose blade was covered in Azaleth's blood. The pale warrior dripped blood from where Azaleth's stone had hit him, but he seemed to ignore the damage with ease.

He was also one of the fastest warriors Alena had ever watched. Even though injured, he moved with nearly equal speed. Ana's skill didn't match Brandt's, but was far superior to most. Even she couldn't find an opening in the man's defense. She didn't have any time to employ her water affinity.

But the path to the door was open. Only the one warrior remained, and his attention was focused exclusively on Ana.

That plan disappeared the moment Ana suffered her first cut, a moderately deep wound in her side, the result of a deflected stab that hadn't been pushed off course enough. Ana fell back a step, but the Lolani didn't give her even a moment to recover. He pushed the advantage.

If Ana fell, Alena had no chance of advancing deeper into the caverns.

And anyway, Alena wanted blood.

She became light, sprinting toward the fight and leaping overhead. The Lolani's sword flashed toward her, but she sensed the attack and spun away from it.

Her distraction only gave Ana a moment, but the warrior took full advantage of the opportunity. Ana recovered and pushed forward. The Lolani blocked the strikes, but now Alena stood behind him, her long knife a worrying threat.

The Lolani tried to shift his position, bringing both threats into line of sight.

Alena refused to let that happen. She lacked the arm speed of either combatant, but she could run faster than either of them. She kept herself behind the Lolani, constantly making him turn.

The strategy worked for a few moments, but the Lolani didn't accept it for long. He turned and charged Alena. Alena gave up ground readily, but under his steady assault she was forced to turn her back to him, running away from him as fast as she could. He pursued, sword ready for a single killing strike.

Ana gave chase, but Alena quickly saw the brilliance of the Lolani. Ana wasn't quick enough to keep up with the others. The Lolani would isolate Alena, kill her easily, then finish Ana off.

Complicating matters, the room they were in wasn't large enough for Alena to ever get that much distance from the Lolani. He angled toward her, constantly forcing her toward a wall. He was fast enough and had a long enough reach that she found herself gradually corralled. Her options diminished with every moment, and she didn't have enough left for Ana to reach her.

She leaped at the wall, planting a foot on a crack, focusing on her lightness. For the space of a heartbeat the wall was now a floor, the Lolani closing the last few paces between them.

Alena gathered every scrap of internal energy she could find and pushed. She launched herself at the Lolani, knife blade leading the way.

The Lolani's reaction was lightning fast. She'd surprised him, but he still managed to flash his own steel, deflecting her knife. In midair, the impact turned her around, sending her uncontrollably spinning into the Lolani, which more or less been her hope. At the last moment she allowed her lightness to vanish, and she hit him with the full force of her weight.

They went down in a tangle of arms and legs. Alena sliced wildly at him as she untangled herself and tried to escape. The Lolani reached out and grabbed her ankle, locking her in place.

But Alena had created enough space and time. Ana reached them and brought her sword down at the Lolani. He had to release his grip to save his arm, and he did.

In another heartbeat he was on his feet again, Ana pressing the attack.

She had the advantage now, her water whip snapping at the Lolani's face again and again. The Lolani gave up ground, seeking to regain the advantage. Alena stumbled toward them, ignoring the bruises she'd earned in that last attack. Together they had to finish the Lolani.

The end happened before she even reached them. The Lolani sacrificed his guard attempting to finish Ana. The woman was too fast, though. The Lolani sword found Ana, slicing across arm and torso, but the cut wasn't the fatal blow the Lolani had needed.

Ana's own sword cut deep into the man's chest, missing the ribs and skewering the protected organs beneath. Ana pulled the sword out before the man could close the distance between them. She took another step back, then they both fell to their knees.

Alena felt the Lolani's breath stop. This fight, at least, was over.

Ana, though, didn't rise from her knees. Her breathing was labored. Alena rushed over to her. Before she could ask, Ana spoke. "Go. He'll need help."

"What about you?"

"If I go to the gates, I go to the gates. Otherwise, I'll be here when you return. Nothing you can do about it either way."

Alena heard the fierce pride in Ana's voice.

She wanted Ana to ask for help, to need her to stay. She was still alive, but the danger only increased the farther into the caves she went.

But it was also the only way. Alena nodded, then wiped her knife on the body of the last Lolani. She took a long look at Azaleth's body, but there was nothing she could do for him, either.

Alena ran. She flew down the stairs, reaching the bridge they had seen from above in little time. She poked her head out, looking for danger. The bridge, as near as she could tell, was empty. The blue light she'd seen before now blended with the familiar colors of fire. Someone had lit torches.

Before she could question herself, Alena ran onto the bridge and across it. Even down here, the cave appeared bottomless. She stopped when she came to the doorway on the other side. Again, she poked her head in, but she saw and heard no one else.

The room she had entered was a circular chamber, with thick pillars around the outside. It had the appearance of a sacred space, one dedicated to a purpose she couldn't begin to guess at.

She stepped through the door and into the chamber, pausing for a moment to study the inscriptions written on the wall. The symbols clearly meant something, but the words were unlike any language she'd encountered before.

But that wasn't why she was here. Brandt needed her help, in whatever way she could provide it. A doorway stood on the opposite side of the chamber, and Alena made her way toward it. She'd barely taken a handful of steps when there was movement from behind one of the pillars.

Her breath caught the moment she saw who it was.

He was taller than she remembered, even after seeing him in the street. Up close like this, there was no mistaking the years of training he had endured since they last met.

But it wasn't Jace's stature that caught her full attention. It was his eyes. They burned as they looked at her.

Jace drew his sword and pointed it at her.

"It's been a long time, big sister."

61

B randt forced himself to focus on the path ahead. As soon as he crossed the bridge, the sounds of his friends fighting behind him faded away, allowing his imagination to run wild.

On the opposite side of the bridge he came to a small circular chamber with pillars around the outside. Torches had been lit inside, but a quick glance didn't reveal anyone within. Brandt raced through, entering the hallway on the other side of the chamber.

He stopped when he thought he saw a flicker of movement in the corner of his vision. He glanced back, but the circular chamber appeared empty.

A trick of the imagination, he supposed.

Brandt ran down the hallway, the blue light growing more vivid with every step.

The hallway here was the same smooth stone they had seen so often in their descent through the mountain. The only difference was that here, inscriptions covered the walls. Brandt didn't recognize the script, but his only language was imperial, and these caves definitely weren't made by the empire.

He slowed again as he came to the end of the hallway. An arched doorway opened up to another chamber. The chamber appeared to be one large circular room. It was larger than the first chamber he'd passed through, and this room had no pillars.

Brandt checked behind him. The hallway remained empty. He turned back, giving his full attention to the lone man waiting for him in the chamber.

Kye held two short swords in an easy stance. Perhaps to an untrained eye, he might appear relaxed, but Brandt saw more. The man was in a position where he could react to almost any attack.

Brandt stepped into the chamber, then sidestepped until he could see past Kye. The blue light was nearly unbearable, and it came from the room beyond. Kye guarded the entrance. Brandt saw two women, kneeling before something out of his sight, something that was emitting the blue light.

It had to be the gate.

No matter what happened here, this was the end of his journey.

He was tired. The last day had exhausted him, and the fear that he had lost yet another group of warriors that trusted him whittled at his focus.

Still, he hated that he wasn't more scared. This was Kye, the bandit who had killed his wolfblades. He should be terrified. But he didn't remember.

Kye had been strong enough to defeat all five wolfblades fighting together years ago. Brandt was a stronger fighter now, but had he closed the gap between them?

The only way to find out would be to cross blades. He stepped forward, ready to put the question to rest forever.

Kye stopped him with a question. "You really don't remember me, do you?"

Brandt met the governor's gaze. He saw a stranger's eyes. "You took their deaths away from me."

Kye didn't respond for a moment, his gaze thoughtful. "One could say that I gave you a second chance at life. You became stronger. You and Ana found each other again and started a life together. If I hadn't taken their deaths from you, these last seven years never would have happened."

Brandt growled. After everything, Kye wanted him to be grateful?

What really burned, though, was the knowledge that Kye wasn't wrong. Because he hadn't killed Brandt, he'd led a longer and more interesting life.

How did he balance the memories of his friends and the years of his life?

"Why did you let me live?"

"Because I never wanted to kill you. I was only interested in becoming stronger. My story from a few days ago was true. I want to be strong. I want this empire to be strong. When you demonstrated the depths of your ability in the forest, I thought that someday you might become an ally. I wanted you to explore your powers, to understand what was coming."

Brandt pointed his sword at the Lolani women, still bowing and chanting beyond the doorway. "If you want the empire to be strong, why aid them?"

Kye gave a small shrug of his shoulders. "She will make us strong. Anders and his successors have made us weak."

Brandt didn't have time for Kye's madness. "Let me pass."

"No. But it isn't too late for you, Brandt, or your friends. You've again demonstrated your quality. Help us, and be a part of the new world we are building, stronger than anything that's come before."

Brandt's only answer was to step forward, his blade ready.

Kye almost looked saddened, but he didn't budge.

Brandt tested Kye's defenses, the point of his sword seeking gaps between Kye's twin blades.

With the shorter weapons, Kye was faster. Brandt attempted several attacks, but none of them came close to cutting the governor. Some small part of Brandt had always wondered if what he had learned about Kye were true. Without memory, doubt remained. But after three passes, Brandt knew Kye's skill surpassed his own. He broke off the attack.

The chanting of the women increased in volume. Whatever they planned, Brandt imagined they didn't have much longer in their ritual. Every moment of his life led to this act. This was where he made the sacrifice of his friends mean something.

Sounds and extraneous thoughts fell away. His sword became an extension of his body, a single sharpened limb designed to kill. His focus was only on Kye.

He glided forward, light on his feet. Their exchange wasn't the gentle exploration of a few heartbeats ago. Swords clashed in the blue light, waves of clanging sound echoing in the chamber, growing to a crescendo with each new impact.

Brandt barely noticed any of it. All that mattered was killing Kye, then killing the women beyond.

Brandt's sword came down and was deflected by one of Kye's. Kye stepped forward and attempted to impale Brandt. Brandt spun, keeping pressure on one blade while trying to land a quick spinning kick. Kye responded by stepping back, giving up less than a pace of ground.

Brandt used the momentum of his spin to bring his sword back around, stepping once again into Kye's guard.

His attack was fierce and sustained, but he couldn't break past Kye's impeccable defense. His two swords created a wall Brandt couldn't pass.

Brandt took two steps back to regain his focus, but Kye had no intention of letting him have that moment. The governor launched himself forward, taking the offensive for the first time.

Brandt had seen fighters good with two swords. Ryder had specialized in the technique and used it to great effect. But this was something else.

One cut led straight into another, an endless flurry of blows coming from different directions, nearly impossible to track. Brandt blocked, deflected, and dodged, but the only way to avoid the storm of steel was to give up ground.

Faster and faster, Brandt retreated, Kye's swords never more than a hand's width away, seeking to cut him open.

It was only a matter of time.

One of Kye's blades found his shoulder, another his hip. Neither cut was particularly dangerous, but pain ran through his body, causing him to falter and lose more ground. Kye stabbed him, catching him in the left shoulder again as Brandt desperately twisted out of the way. Another lance of pain exploded across his body. He didn't even see the kick that sent him stumbling to the ground.

His focus shattered as the back of his skull struck stone.

He'd given everything.

And it hadn't been nearly enough.

Kye stood above him, uninjured. The governor barely looked winded.

Brandt tried to stand, but Kye stepped forward, keeping to Brandt's left side, and kicked him in the stomach. Brandt gasped, his lungs screaming for air and unable to draw a breath.

Brandt refused to fail. He summoned every last bit of his strength and swung his sword with everything he could muster.

Kye deflected the blow with ease, blocking with such strength the sword flew out of Brandt's weakening hands. Kye stabbed down at Brandt. Brandt tried to roll away, the sword cutting through the side of his chest.

Brandt reached down and grabbed the knife at his belt. It was nothing special, an everyday knife he carried for cutting food and daily tasks. He swung wildly at Kye's legs, causing the governor to back up two steps.

A look of disgust passed over Kye's face as he looked down at Brandt. He took another few steps back, well out of Brandt's range. Then he relaxed into his defensive pose once again.

Brandt swore. "Are you too cowardly to kill me like a warrior?"

"There's cowardice and there's wisdom. I know the difference."

Brandt hated that Kye was right. Up close, Brandt had a chance, however small. But at a distance, there was little he could do. He would bleed out until he lost consciousness, and then Kye could finish him at his leisure. Kye didn't need to kill him. He only needed to stop him.

Brandt tried to stand, but exhaustion and despair caused him to crash back down.

There wasn't any point.

Kye had spared him once, but not again.

After everything, Brandt had failed.

62

How many times had she thought about this reunion? How many nights had she laid awake, wondering exactly what she would do if she ever came face to face with her brother again?

Alena took a step back. The fire in her brother's eyes frightened her.

He gave her no opportunity to reply. He flung himself at her, moving with unexpected speed. Her air affinity warned her of the sword, sweeping around for her neck.

Alena became light, leaping back and away from the slashing blade. The sword cut through the space her throat had been a moment before. Jace attacked without hesitation, the tip of his sword steady as it sought her heart.

Alena ran into a pillar, then ducked low as Jace's sword flashed toward her chest. The sword stopped short of the stone pillar. Jace cut down, forcing her to roll to the side.

She came to her feet and ran, lightly leaping and bouncing off a pillar. Jace remained right behind her, though, his sword never straying from its intended mark.

If she couldn't evade him, perhaps she could force him

to make a mistake. She darted around the pillars, managing to break Jace's line of sight for a moment at a time. Her speed and agility surpassed her brother's, and she slowly put more distance between them.

Until Jace stopped playing the game.

He gave up the chase and took position in front of the door leading toward the blue light. Alena stopped, too. Like the chamber with the Lolani, Jace didn't need to kill her. All he needed was to prevent her from advancing.

"Why?"

Jace scoffed. "You were always the bright one. Did you really think I'd welcome a murderer and Etari lover with open arms?"

Murderer? Alena was so surprised she took a step back. It took her a moment to make the connection.

Bayt.

Her brother thought she had killed Bayt.

The denial died on her lips. What could she say here that would counteract seven years of hatred? If her family thought her guilty of Bayt's death, she could only imagine how it would have torn them apart.

But perhaps he didn't know what ends his master served. "Kye is giving the Lolani a powerful artifact, Jace. We need to stop him!"

"I know, and we don't. The Lolani will make everything right, Alena. I've seen it."

Words weren't going to work. Alena saw the immovable steel of belief in his eyes. If she was going to stop the Lolani, her brother had to fall.

She drew her knife and stepped forward, closing the distance to five paces. She took another step. He still didn't react.

Another step brought her three paces away. She saw the tension running through his body.

The indecision.

He might hate her, but he had still spent most of his life looking up to her. He wouldn't kill her, not when the time came. She had to believe that.

Alena sheathed her knife.

She stepped forward again, closing the distance to two paces. His sword snapped up, the point leveled straight at her neck. Despite the apparent tension in his body, the point was perfectly still.

Alena took a deep breath. Another step would bring her within Jace's reach.

She took it, angling to the side so that she didn't impale herself. She saw through the door Jace guarded. Beyond a long hallway, two shapes fought. Brandt was there, and he still lived.

Alena lifted her foot to take another step, to draw even with her brother and then pass him.

Then she found herself lying on the ground, gasping for air. She looked down, afraid for a moment that all her trust had been misplaced, that he had killed her.

But no blood flowed from her stomach. She looked up, her breath slowly returning. Jace sheathed his weapon. The tension in his body was gone. He had decided.

"You're right," he said. "I don't want to kill you. But I won't let you pass, either."

Alena sat up, then found her way to her feet. "He'll destroy the empire."

"Then it deserved its fate."

She didn't have time to argue with her brother, even if she thought it would work. Kye's thinking had shaped Jace's.

Her brother believed, and belief wasn't so easily swayed as reason.

But the fight was no longer lethal, which gave Alena a chance. She'd lived among the Etari for years. She wasn't the weak martial artist her brother remembered.

Alena caught her breath and stepped forward, launching a few tentative jabs at her younger brother.

As she expected, he batted them aside with ease.

So she attacked in earnest, unleashing a flurry of jabs, elbows and kicks. Her assault surprised Jace, driving him back a few paces while he collected himself. She was almost in reach of the door.

Then his foot snuck through her guard and ended her hope. His kick caught her in the chest, pushing her away from him. He took full advantage of the extra space, launching an attack of his own.

For a heartbeat Alena thought they were evenly matched.

But Jace was too fast. She fell for one of his feints, and his fist found her face, snapping her head around and sending her spinning to the floor again.

Alena tasted blood. She spit and ran her finger across her lip where it had been cut. Anger blossomed in her. She hadn't come all this way to be stopped by her own brother. She pushed herself up, spinning around to face Jace.

Her attacks were more cautious this time. She kept her weight balanced, ready to retreat against his next onslaught. They traded blows. Jace was fast, but only a little more so than her. She grinned as two of her punches found their target.

She'd hoped a few hits would make him angry. Anger led to mistakes she could take advantage of.

Half her plan worked.

Jace exploded toward her with a roar, the ferocity of his anger astonishing her. He caught hold of her, shrugging off her surprised counters as though he didn't feel them. His left arm wrapped around her neck and shoulders while his right drove into her side.

Once.

Twice.

Three times.

After the third, the only reason she stood was because Jace supported her. Then he twisted his hips and threw her. What the move lacked in technique it made up for in sheer strength. Her body flipped in the air and she landed on her right shoulder and rolled to her back, where she skidded across the stone floor.

The agony was exquisite. Every breath she took set a new wave of pain up her spine. She tried moving her right arm. It moved, but painfully. When she had landed on her shoulder, something had shifted into a place it didn't belong.

Alena rolled over onto her stomach and forced herself to hands and knees.

"Stay down, Alena."

Despite the pain he'd already caused her, she didn't detect a hint of sorrow or distress in his voice. It sounded closer to exasperation, like he was a teacher drilling a lesson into a student too stubborn to learn.

And she was too stubborn to learn. She'd already failed her family, and she'd failed Azaleth. This would not be another failure.

Before she could even reach her feet, Jace stepped in and delivered a crushing kick to her stomach.

Her world exploded and turned black.

She came to, blinking. Jace had his back to her. She must have lost consciousness for two or three heartbeats. When he heard her struggle to her feet, he turned to watch.

If she had hoped to impress him with her determination, though, it didn't work. He shook his head. "You can't win, Alena. Even if you somehow made it past me, my master is the strongest warrior on this world. I've seen his affinity with my own eyes."

Alena thought about telling her brother that Kye's power wasn't his own, that it was only through the use of a gatestone that he achieved so much. But it would do no good. Jace believed his master would change the world.

She feared he was right.

Her only chance to get past him was to kill him. He stood, his sword still sheathed, confident.

It wasn't honorable.

But what did honor matter when so much was at stake?

She worked her way back to her feet, the world spinning wildly around her. Blood dripped from her chin, but she ignored it. She stepped forward, raising her fists high.

Jace sighed and stepped closer. He reached out with his left arm, intending to repeat the same move he had before. Alena let him. He might land one punch, but it would be enough time for her to make a killing strike. Her vision blurred as she committed herself.

Jace wrapped her in and brought his right arm back. As he did, she went for her knife, drawing it from its sheath and punching up into his torso.

Except somewhere in that motion, her world shifted. Jace wasn't in front of her anymore, but was behind her, his iron grip around her right wrist, yanking the arm up.

She recognized the technique, but too late to do anything about it. He drove her down, face first into stone. She managed to shift her body and take most of the impact against the left side, but it did little except protect her head.

Jace's knee drove into her spine, pinning her painfully in place. Between his knee and the overextension of her arm, she was locked in place.

Jace's attention seemed to be on the knife. "This is one of Father's blades." Anger creeped deeper into his voice. "And you meant to kill me with it."

She heard the disgust in that sentence. Jace wasn't mad she had made an attempt on his life. He was disappointed.

All he had feared to be true, was. His sister was the murderous thief Kye had probably painted her as.

"Is this what you used to kill your master? I heard that when the city watch found him he had been tortured. Did you use Father's steel for that, too?" The anger in his voice was a living thing.

She wanted to argue, but the pain was too great. She cried out, but Jace only tightened the hold, extending her arm just a hair more. It felt like her shoulder was being torn out of its socket.

He ripped the knife away from her with his free hand. He tossed it away, and she watched it clatter along the stone, well out of reach.

"You don't deserve our father's work," Jace said.

If Alena could have sagged, she would have. Jace was right. She didn't deserve that blade, but how many times had its presence kept her going?

She didn't deserve it, but it was all she had.

And Jace had taken it away.

It broke the last of her will. She had fought as hard as she could, but it wasn't enough. She couldn't get past Jace, and her brother was right. What chance did she have against Kye?

Her best hadn't been good enough.

She closed her eyes, their tears dropping down and wetting the stone beneath her.

I'm sorry.

63

Brandt felt his life draining from him. None of his wounds bled rapidly, but taken together, he didn't think he had much consciousness left. He lay on his back, staring at the perfectly smooth stone ceiling.

"What is this place?"

He wasn't expecting an answer, but Kye provided one. "A home of our ancestors."

"This is imperial?"

Kye laughed. "No. These caves are many hundred years old. They predate the empire by many generations."

"I didn't think anyone had this level of ability." Brandt hadn't been a very attentive history student, but before the empire all that had existed were small warring states. None had been as advanced as the state which grew to become the empire.

"Anders I wanted you to think that way."

Brandt suppressed a groan. Whenever he tried to move, his body protested. He looked up at Kye, studying the governor, who still stood in his defensive posture. Brandt wondered if he would hold that position until the soulwalkers completed their task in the next room.

Then he noticed something from this angle. From his position on the floor, he saw a small bulge in Kye's shirt, right in the center of his chest.

The gatestone.

The diamond that Ana told him had caused all this trouble years ago.

Kye still kept it close to his chest.

Literally.

The effort of holding his head up exhausted him, and he rested it back on the stone floor.

Kye stood six paces away. Brandt didn't have a hope of reaching him before the governor reacted. Brandt still had his knife, but it only worked if Kye came closer.

"Why are they right?" Brandt asked.

"What?"

"Why are the Lolani right?"

"Because they will make us stronger."

"That doesn't make any sense."

"It doesn't have to. You'll journey to the gates soon enough. Then you can watch from the other side, and you will understand."

Brandt laughed. "You sound like a madman."

Kye didn't rise to the bait. "Perhaps. But you know little compared to me. If you saw what I've seen, you would believe the same."

"I would never kill the very people I swore to protect."

Kye stepped forward, Brandt's knife forgotten for a moment. He came within a few paces, and Brandt heard the agitation in his voice. "Oh, but you have. You don't remember, but when we fought the last time in Landow, you killed your friends."

"You killed them."

"No. I would have let them be. I had acquired the gatestone and was eager to finish Zane Arrowood and be gone. But you gave the order to attack, even though you already knew your squad wasn't strong enough to fight me. You sent them against an enemy they couldn't hope to win against. You killed them."

Kye paused, then took another step in. "Your orders killed the people you were supposed to protect."

Kye was almost close enough. Brandt didn't need to feign a lack of energy. He fought even to keep his eyes open.

Brandt didn't want to believe Kye's words, but he did, because they echoed his own thoughts. He didn't remember Landow for himself, but he knew the man he had been. He would have fought, no matter the odds. And the wolfblades would have followed him.

"I gave those orders because you needed to be stopped."

"And I made my choice because the Lolani bring something to the empire that it desperately needs. We both act based on need."

Brandt heard the resignation in Kye's voice. For the governor, this conversation had reached its conclusion. Brandt still needed to draw the man a pace or two closer. He made himself light, forcing his internal energies into alignment. He just needed to focus long enough for one move.

"My warriors had a choice," he said. "Many choices. They knew I wasn't a perfect commander. But they chose to follow. It doesn't absolve my responsibility, but I wasn't alone. This thing you do, you do without the knowledge of those whose lives will change forever."

Brandt took a deep breath. It was getting harder to speak. "You aren't a leader. You're a tyrant."

His guess about Kye's character proved correct. The governor took another couple of steps forward, a snarl on his face. He brought his sword up to strike the killing blow.

Brandt slammed his fist down, sending his light body flying into the air.

Brandt reached out with his left arm, wrapping his hand around the diamond even as Kye's blades pierced him once again. Pain blossomed within, a new layer of agony sharper than the last. Black spots swam at the edge of Brandt's vision, but he brought his knife up and sliced through Kye's shirt. His cut wasn't clean. Broken as he was, his strength gave out.

But Brandt allowed his lightness to fade. The weight of his body falling ripped the last shreds of fabric away. Brandt collapsed.

The rough edges of the diamond cut into his palm.

Brandt had hoped the disorientation of being cut off from his diamond would open Kye up for an attack.

It worked. Kye's eyes went unfocused and he collapsed to his knees next to Brandt.

The only problem was that Brandt didn't have any strength left to fight. His body refused to listen to his commands.

But he held the stone. Against every instinct he possessed, Brandt closed his eyes and channeled his affinity through the diamond.

It unlocked a new world. He heard only fire, but the songs were louder than any he had heard before. He was buffeted by waves of chaotic noise.

He found Kye.

He'd never tried the technique, but he had heard about it. He imagined wrapping his hands into Kye's body's heat, and he pulled, the same way he sometimes pulled heat from his own body.

Kye resisted. On some level, he understood what was happening. But Kye's primary affinity was stone, not fire. And Brandt had the diamond. When he pulled, no human could resist. The ability intoxicated him. He pulled and pulled, destroying Kye's meager resistance.

And just like that, it was over. Kye's resistance snapped and Brandt pulled. It almost felt too easy. When Brandt opened his eyes, Kye still knelt before him, but his eyes held no life. His face was literally frozen in fear. Brandt reached out a tentative hand, then pulled it away again when he felt how cold Kye's skin was.

His wolfblades were revenged.

He closed his eyes, knowing there was one more fight that remained.

His life flowed from him freely, though. Kye's last cuts would kill him, and quick. No matter what, he would make another trip to the gates today, and he didn't think he'd be returning from this visit.

But he was going to die well.

He still had an empire to save.

64

Every time Alena thought Jace's hold slipped she tried to break it. But whenever she tried, he simply resumed the hold, pushing her that much further. She was certain that her arm was near useless.

Her left arm scratched the stone, seeking anything she could use as a weapon. But her body was locked in place by Jace's hold.

The world as she knew it was about to end, and she could do nothing but lie here, helplessly. She couldn't beat her brother.

Alena sagged, every muscle in her body finally giving up the fight. There wasn't anything left to do. She closed her eyes and rested her head against the stone floor. Tears dripped from her eyes. When they hit the stone they splashed on her cheek.

Then she felt a presence, an awareness her panicked struggles had hidden from her. She felt Jace, his presence, the same way she had sensed the wolf and the soulwalker back in the valley.

Possibilities unfolded within her mind. Could she

soulwalk into her brother? His presence was right there. She was certain she could reach out to it and join it.

But did she dare?

Kye must have possessed some small degree of soulwalking ability, and his use of it had nearly destroyed Brandt's life. If she did the same to her brother, would she be able to live with herself?

Did she even have a choice? Her brother served Kye with his whole heart. The damage they intended to unleash upon the empire would cost countless lives. If she had the power to stop it, why wouldn't she?

Because it was her brother. Hurting him might shatter her.

Indecision tore her in two.

He tightened his grip on her arm, causing her to scream.

She plunged into his soul.

Alena wasn't prepared for the journey. She passed through his memories, each laced with the emotions he'd felt at the time.

The anger and confusion when Kye had come to their door, telling the family that Alena was a murderer.

The gratitude when Kye had found him later at the academy. Kye had put his hand on Jace's shoulder, had told him that Jace wasn't his sister, that he could do great things.

Murky darkness swirled around memories of home. Jace believed Kye's story, no matter how their parents argued in favor of Alena.

Gratitude filled Alena's thoughts for a moment. Her parents still believed in her, even after she'd abused their trust so sorely.

But that wasn't how Jace saw it. He saw them choosing her over him, the same way they always had. They even chose her after she had murdered her master.

He'd turned away from them then. Left the house for good.

He declined university track, joining the military as soon as he was able. There his feats attracted Kye's attention.

There had been a stint with the city watch. He'd made a name for himself singlehandedly finding and destroying a smuggling ring.

Alena saw the memories through Jace's own eyes, the skill and cold ease he'd possessed as he cut the smugglers down.

Her brother's rage was cold and unyielding.

Then Kye's personal tutelage. The importance of strength. An overwhelming warmth and loyalty to the man who had never given up on him, who had given him exactly what he believed he deserved.

Alena focused her will, stopping the flood of memories. She saw, now, how she could do what had happened to Brandt. She could wipe those memories away. A small effort of will brought her back to the moment Kye had knocked on the door of their home to deliver the news. She could wipe years away, like a wave washing away writing on the beach. Then Jace would only have his childhood memories of her, when he had looked up to her the way he now looked up to Kye.

She couldn't bring herself to do it, though.

Doing so wouldn't be killing his physical body, but it still felt like murder. Memories shaped identity. Brandt had lost weeks. She considered wiping away years. If she took those years away, would he return to being a child in a man's body?

Too many questions plagued her mind. She took a step away, separating herself from Jace's past.

Alena still felt her brother's soul. She imagined it as a glowing sphere, a hardened but brittle shell around it.

As she imagined it, so it was. Her thoughts and will had power in this plane.

She imagined her father's knife in her hand, and there it was. It would be so easy to reach out and cut that shell away from her brother's soul. But if she did, what would result? She was no soulwalker. She had no idea how to manipulate a person's actions.

She stood there, floating in a place she couldn't describe or understand, before making a decision. Her instincts had guided her well thus far, and she had no other tutelage. With luck, she wouldn't cause permanent harm to her brother.

And if she wasn't lucky, the cost was still worth paying.

Alena returned to Jace's memories, going back, back before Kye had any bearing on their lives. She searched for times when the two of them had been together, when she had earned his adoration.

The moments were far fewer than she would have liked. As she saw herself in his memories, she saw how little time she had given him, how little she had respected his enthusiasm. He had looked up to her and she had barely noticed him.

The thought pained her, but she kept searching, finding suitable memories. The time she carried him to the infirmary after he'd injured himself at academy. When she had volunteered to complete some of his chores so he could play with friends.

The moments were rare, but whenever she found one, she pulled on it, enlarging it. Memory after memory, all the times she had acted like the big sister he believed her to be.

Then she backed out of his memories. She held out her hands and a blanket appeared.

Alena looked at her brother's soul, then down at the blanket, imbuing it with what will she could.

I would never harm my sister.

The deception tore at her. As her arm could currently attest, he had no problem hurting his sister. But some part of him still thought of her as family. Hopefully this would be enough.

She tossed the blanket over the construct she'd created of his soul, tying the blanket shut with a thin rope.

Then she stepped away.

Somewhere, far away, she felt the pressure on her arm disappear.

And then she was back in the chamber, her face pressed against the stone. She heard an unfamiliar sound. She looked up.

Jace had retreated and was curled up in a tight ball, his arms wrapped around his knees. He rocked back and forth, staring at his hands as though they had committed an atrocity.

It had worked.

She wanted to run to him and hold him in her arms. Though he was now taller and larger than her, curled up as he was, he looked like a young boy. And he was terrified of what he had done.

Alena worked her way to her feet. As she had feared, her right arm was nearly useless. She walked over to where Jace had thrown her father's knife, gripping it tightly in her left hand.

Jace didn't move from his position.

She hated herself for what she had done.

But it was necessary.

If she could, she would fix it. But the blue glow coming from down the hall was a constant reminder that a more terrible threat remained.

Alena took a step toward Jace and he scooted back. She held out her hand. "Stay here, Jace. I'll be back for you soon."

He didn't reply, but there wasn't time for her to comfort him. She turned and ran toward the blue light.

65

Brandt rolled onto his stomach, then immediately regretted the decision. Every movement unleashed a new flood of pain, and he thought he could feel the blood leaving. He didn't have many heartbeats left. Every one needed to matter.

With a groan, he pushed himself to hands and knees, his bloody clothes peeling away from the stone.

He gasped as he came to his knees. The final door was only about five paces away, but it might as well have been a hundred leagues. There was no way he could get to his feet.

Brandt grimaced. He would not give up. When he died and joined the other wolfblades, the only way he could meet their gazes was if he had given everything.

He couldn't stand, but he could crawl.

On hands and knees, he made his way toward the door, more of the final chamber becoming visible. He held Kye's diamond in his hand, the edges cutting deeper into his hand as he crawled.

The two soulwalkers still knelt in front of the gate. Their

eyes were open but unseeing. Brandt didn't know what they hoped to accomplish, but he would take every moment they offered him.

When he got to the door, he finally saw the gate for the first time. It was an arch, made of glowing blue diamonds.

It reminded him of the gate he had seen so many years ago, when infection had almost killed him. The stones appeared uncut, but fit together perfectly.

And within the arch?

Nothing.

Just air, with the stone walls of the chamber visible behind it.

Brandt collapsed. His body couldn't go any farther. But hopefully it would be close enough. He closed his eyes and let his affinity flow through the diamond he still clutched.

He wasn't prepared for the power that battered him. The moment he allowed his affinity to flow through the diamond in his hand, his world exploded in sensation, a music that seemed to reverberate in his bones.

Since his training in the monastery, he had become used to the different music of the elements. Fire remained the easiest for him to discern, but years of training had unlocked all four elements to various degrees.

He'd never heard anything like this.

The gate sang, a chorus of elements echoing with untold power. The intensity of it rolled over him, a pressure he barely understood. Fire, stone, water, and air joined, the notes of each forming complex chords, the joining of the elements something far sweeter than any one alone.

Brandt let go of the diamond and the song vanished. He was sprawled on the ground, panting with the effort of simply listening to the gate.

What was it?

Without the diamond, he sensed next to nothing. He heard the soft song of fire emanating from the two soulwalkers in front of him, and if he focused, he could feel the lower hum of rock below that. But that was all.

If he thought he had the strength to fight the soulwalkers on his own, he would have let the diamond lie next to him, untouched. But he lacked confidence. He didn't even have the strength to move.

Brandt reached out and clasped the diamond again. With a deep breath, he funneled his affinity through the stone.

As before, the chamber pressed against his senses.

This time, Brandt was better prepared. He didn't try to fight the power, but instead allow himself to be carried away by it.

As he did, more details revealed themselves. Brandt felt the soulwalkers, a combination of elements with a new song laid on top of them. A fifth element.

A soul.

He sensed faint tendrils extending from the soulwalkers to the gate. They were tying themselves to the object in a ritual he couldn't begin to guess at.

There was something else, as well. As Brandt continued to ride the currents, he understood these underground passages better. They had been formed with the aid of the gate, and they weren't just passages of stone. All the elements had played some role in their construction. He couldn't say how he knew, but he was certain that even if the mountains themselves collapsed, these structures would remain.

The gate had made the passages immortal.

Brandt focused on the soulwalkers. Even though the currents of power from the gate threatened to overwhelm him, he believed he could use his affinity.

Just as he had with Kye, Brandt reached out and called for the fire from one of the soulwalkers. He found the element and pulled.

For a heartbeat, the process went as it should. Someplace far away, where his physical body resided, he could feel the heat building within him, providing comfort as he bled out on the cold stone.

Then it stopped. He pulled, as though he pulled on a stuck climbing rope. But nothing gave. No matter how great his effort, he could pull no more. Another force prevented his.

Then he felt tendrils reaching out toward him, the same way the soulwalkers were reaching toward the gate. In this place, he wasn't sure how to defend himself. He imagined slapping one away, but it wrapped around him.

Exhaustion crashed over him. He had failed. He'd come all this way to die just a few paces away from his goal.

As a last ditch effort, he pushed some of the fire he'd stolen at the tendril. It burned away from his arm.

And he suddenly felt encouraged. He was still tired, sore, and dying, but the exhaustion and despair was gone.

The tendril.

He was fighting against soulwalkers, owners of the same techniques that had caused him to lose his memory. One of the soulwalkers was trying to compel him to give up.

More strands of power reached toward him, more aggressive than the first. He sent fire toward them, burning them up. More came, and faster. Whenever one so much as brushed against him he felt that same overwhelming despair.

Soul met fire, the two elements giving and losing territory as quick as thought. Brandt clutched the diamond, pulling heat through it. If he had to rely on his own strength alone, he would have lost after the first exchange.

But even with his borrowed strength, Brandt was losing ground. The tendrils whipped and snapped ever closer. As fast as he burned one, another two took its place. How could the soulwalker be so strong?

Brandt had more to give, but his skill didn't match the soulwalker's. Eventually the tendrils encircled him. Acting through a will that wasn't his own, Brandt broke his connection with the diamond. He still held it, but he felt no desire to channel his affinity through it.

His connection broken, Brandt found himself back within his dying body, unable to move.

He didn't want to, either. This task had always been hopeless. Again, he had brought a group of warriors to their deaths. He welcomed his next trip to the gate. Even death was better than he deserved.

As he lay there, wallowing in self-pity, he watched as one of the soulwalkers opened her eyes and stood up. It wasn't the same soulwalker that held him tightly in her grip. That one was the slightly younger woman, still kneeling with her eyes closed.

The elder soulwalker stepped toward the gate, her stride purposeful. She stopped less than a pace away. Then she turned to Brandt and smiled, a grin as malicious as any he'd ever seen. The soulwalker gloated for a moment, then reached out and touched the gate.

The blue stone flared, brightening until the light was almost pure white. Despite the intensity, Brandt found that he had no problem watching. The light didn't hurt his eyes, although it seemed as though he stared into the sun itself.

Now he couldn't be sure if the despair he felt was the soulwalker's or his. The sense of failure he felt moments before had become true.

The Lolani soulwalker had completed her mission.

66

Alena couldn't run. She kept herself light, just to ensure she remained upright, but her control over her internal energies was fading. Jace might not have killed her, but he had beaten her harder than she first thought.

With every step she became increasingly certain she would die in these tunnels, never to be seen again, except perhaps by some future explorer. Even if, by some chance, they won, Alena wasn't sure she could make the trek back to the surface.

She found the acceptance of certain death offered a certain clarity. If living wasn't possible, all that remained was to die well.

The hallway from the first chamber seemed to stretch on forever. She shuffled forward, knife gripped tightly in her left hand. She suddenly laughed, the sound echoing in the silent tunnel. When she found the battle, she realized she wouldn't exactly cut an imposing figure.

Perhaps there was a hint of madness growing in her.

She didn't care. Anyone who had gone through what she had today would suffer the same. A mind could only accept so much newness, and she had found that limit before even entering the impossible structure she now wandered through.

The door to the next chamber grew ever larger, illuminated by a blue light from deeper within. When she stumbled through the door, ready to fight, she was surprised by what she found.

The room was empty except for Kye, who lay motionless in a horrifying position, his face frozen in a look of terror. Alena paused, taking the scene in. Kye's blades lay on the stone floor, both of them covered in blood.

Somehow, Brandt had won.

Her cheeks flushed with pride. She'd seen what Kye was capable of years ago. She imagined his power had only grown stronger.

But Brandt had killed him. He had revenged his wolfblades and the loss of his memory.

Her eye fell on the trail of blood that ran around Kye's body and into the next chamber.

It was a lot of blood.

More than anyone could afford to lose.

She closed her eyes and took a deep breath. None of them had been certain they would survive.

But they would finish this as well as they were able.

The light from the next room suddenly increased in intensity. The blue became almost white. The gate was in there, and something had happened.

Alena shuffled as quickly as she could, skirting around the edges of Brandt's blood.

She froze when the tableau revealed itself to her. Brandt lay on the floor, blood pooling around his body. She could sense him breathing, but his breath came in ragged gasps.

He didn't have long to live. One of his hands was clenched tightly around something.

It had to be Kye's gatestone.

Two soulwalkers were in the room. One was on her knees, eyes closed, concentrating. The other had her hand on the gate, her face contorting in ecstasy.

She couldn't take on two soulwalkers on her own.

A pit of despair suddenly opened up below her. She collapsed to her knees, the power of the emotion holding her in thrall. But even as the feeling crashed over her, she recognized it as foreign.

Alena closed her eyes and activated her gatestone. There was a resistance there, a pressure she'd never felt before. But she visualized her father's knife, cutting through the murky blackness. Then she felt the connection with the gatestone.

The connection unlocked another wave of sensation, but not all of these came from the soulwalker. The room itself exploded with power. Alena surrendered to it. She allowed herself to simply observe the currents.

And then she was in a desert. She noticed Brandt, wrapped up tightly in a weave the soulwalker had snared him in. The other soulwalker dove deep into the power of the gate, their energies linked in a complex web.

Alena turned her attention to the soulwalker who ensnared Brandt and sought to do the same with her. Threads of will extended from the woman, reaching toward Alena.

Alena observed them.

And she hated them.

As they reached toward her she voiced a mental command, uttered with all the strength she could draw from her own will and that of the gatestone.

No.

The strands stopped in midair and died. The soulwalker rocked back, her eyes wide. She flung out black darts, but like the strands, they died before coming close to Alena.

Alena turned her attention to Brandt. The wolfblade was dying, but he deserved a better death. Her father's knife appeared in her hand, and she stabbed at the web surrounding him. The strands peeled away, the net decaying with her touch.

The soulwalker screamed, a piercing shriek of agony.

Alena realized that she wasn't just cutting into the strands. In this place, the strands and the darts were a part of the soulwalker.

Alena reinforced her will, then opened her eyes. Brandt still lay unmoving, but his breath came much easier. The soulwalker on her knees had fallen over, but was coming to her feet, a long knife in her hand. Alena knew she didn't have a chance against the woman. All she had was her left arm.

She kneeled down, reaching down to touch Brandt. "I need you, Brandt. I can't do this on my own."

Brandt groaned, but that was all. She imagined she could feel the life draining from him, his soul preparing for its journey to the gate.

She couldn't let that happen. Brandt could die, but only when they had stopped the Lolani.

The soulwalker was on her feet now, stepping toward them, knife raised above her head, ready to finish the fight with cold steel.

Alena closed her eyes. Her only useful weapon was her soul.

Holding on to Brandt, she pushed her will through the gatestone, the connection and the passage to a different plane easier with every attempt.

She and Brandt stood on the rooftops of Landow, the soulwalker appearing confused a few paces away.

Brandt appeared to share her confusion.

Alena thought she understood. "This is my home," she said. Movement caught her eye. A wave of strands rushed at them, but with a thought, Alena stopped them. As they fell, Alena noticed many more on the ground. She even saw those she had cut from Brandt. So much the same as the desert, and yet this environment was hers.

The rooftops faded, and for a moment Alena thought she felt sand beneath her toes, a return to the desert. She focused, and the rooftops of Landow snapped back.

Another scream tore from the Lolani soulwalker. It was voice and will, all entwined in this place. Landow shook and buildings crumbled as the soulwalker tore at Alena. The land buckled and swayed as though Alena's home had been built on an undulating ocean.

The waves of destruction faded as they approached her, but with every wave the destruction came closer. Alena sank to her knees, overwhelmed by the sight of her home suffering such a fate. It wasn't reality, but the veil between reality and this dream plane was hard to remember.

Black strands raced from the Lolani to the two of them. Brandt was still weak. His breath grew stronger, but Alena didn't think she could hold on long enough for him to recover.

The walls of Landow crumbled while the black strands sought for a crack in the bubble of power that remained around Alena. For every strand that died as it explored for a weakness, two took its place. She could feel them. With every contact her bubble retreated. Perhaps it was just the width of a hair every time, but as dozens of strands impacted every heartbeat, they didn't have long. She just wasn't strong enough to fight the soulwalker on her plane.

Tears blurred her vision as more buildings collapsed into rubble.

She had never been strong enough.

She hadn't stopped Kye.

She'd relied on the Etari to keep her safe from her enemies.

Whatever small victories she had earned, they had been by chance. Not through any skill of her own. For all the gifts she'd been born with, she'd wasted them all.

Alena looked down at the knife in her hand. It was her father's knife, down to the smallest details, even in this place.

I'm sorry, Father.

One of the black strands finally broke through the bubble, wrapping itself tightly around her neck.

Alena almost lost her connection with her gatestone then. Her despair magnified a hundred times and she closed her eyes.

She would wait on the other side of the gate for her family. There, she hoped she would find forgiveness. More strands wrapped around her arms and legs and she fell to hands and knees. Even breathing seemed like too much effort.

At least her death would come quickly.

She lost all track of time, her thoughts a maelstrom of loss and self-pity.

Then she felt a hand on her shoulder. Before she understood, there was sudden movement, and the crushing weight that had possessed her vanished.

Alena opened her eyes. Brandt knelt beside her, his sword held in a reverse grip. He had sliced through many of the strands, but she saw their relief would be temporary at best. More strands gathered, peeling apart the last layers of her defense.

Beyond the roof the three combatants shared, Landow was nearly gone.

"Look at me," Brandt said.

She did, seeing the fire still in his eyes.

"We're not dead yet."

His words were true, but they still didn't matter. The soulwalker would finish them soon enough.

Brandt pounded his fist into the ground. Stone shattered around it. Alena blinked, trying to separate reality from the plane where she and the soulwalker did battle.

"I can't do it alone."

Brandt's words held the weight of confession, of a man unveiling the truth he hid from the world.

Brandt reached up with one hand and held her chin. His hands were rough and callused, yet were as gentle as any touch she had ever felt. He held her gaze. "I need your help."

Brandt's confession galvanized her. She thought of her family. She thought of Jace and Azaleth. It felt like her entire life had been nothing but a long string of failures.

But not Brandt. Following the invaders down into these caves might have been a one-way trip to the gates, but she would not fail Brandt. She would die with that much dignity at least.

She nodded and brought her father's knife up.

How often had she looked to that knife for inspiration?

Even after all these years the knife still held its edge with a minimum of upkeep. It had weathered all the storms with her, a constant companion and silent witness.

Her family was still with her. Brandt was still with her.

She closed her eyes and imagined her soul consisting of

that same steel, made with the same craftsmanship that her father put into every one of his pieces. She refused to bend or lose her edge, no matter what obstacles sought to destroy her.

She channeled every scrap of will she possessed into the stone that reminded her of her Etari family. Then she opened her eyes and pushed her will against that of the soulwalker.

The clash of powers disoriented her. In one moment she was on the rooftops of Landow, and the next she was within the cave glowing with a fierce brightness. In both places the very air between them twisted and writhed with the energy expended.

The disturbance in the air pressed toward her. Both warriors fought with their entire strength. Alena could feel the desperation in her opponent's actions.

But the soulwalker was stronger. No matter how hard Alena fought, she simply wasn't skilled enough to go up against a woman who had no doubt trained these skills for many years.

But she didn't need to. She wasn't alone.

As the battle raged between the women, Brandt crawled on hands and knees toward the soulwalker. The Lolani woman noticed him when he was about halfway to her, but she was giving everything she had to fight Alena. Her eyes widened with surprise and Alena felt the intensity of her attacks immediately diminish as she attempted to stop Brandt.

No you don't.

Alena forced herself to return to the rooftops of Landow. She pushed, not caring if she spent the last of her life's energy. She ran toward the soulwalker, knife ready to strike. She didn't know what such an attack represented on this plane, but she assumed the soulwalker would have to defend.

Her assumption proved correct. Once again, Alena felt the full attention of the soulwalker fall upon her. A wave of pressure stopped Alena from advancing, but both women needed to commit their entire attention to the war between them.

Then the soulwalker vanished from Alena's world. Her presence was gone.

Alena returned to the cavern.

Now, two bodies lay in front of her. From the looks of it, Brandt had reached the soulwalker and killed her. His knife was in his hand, coated in blood. His eyes were open and their gazes met. He nodded and closed his eyes for a moment.

Alena turned her attention to the final soulwalker, her eyes closed and her hand on the gate. From the look on her face it appeared that her attention was somewhere far away.

They had to stop her before she completed her task. In the midst of the battle Alena had lost all sense of time. Regardless, they didn't have any to waste.

Brandt felt the same. "Help me up."

Alena stumbled toward him. Every part of her body felt weak, every step a monumental effort. But they would step forward together.

67

Brandt didn't understand exactly what had just transpired. At one point, he swore he saw the air ripple between the two women, but they had fought a battle beyond his skill, and perhaps even beyond his comprehension. The soulwalker hadn't even looked down at him as he drove his knife cleanly through her heart.

Alena looked dead on her feet, but being as he looked dead on his back, she was still the better off of the two of them. She helped him to his feet.

She looked concerned, and for good reason. His head felt faint. He'd lost a lot of blood and didn't have long before he reached the final gate. But first, he had to deal with the gate in front of him.

If it was possible, the gate seemed to be even brighter than it had been before. He feared that whatever task the soulwalker sought to complete was nearly so.

"What do we do?" Alena asked.

"I don't know," Brandt confessed. His only plan had been to kill everyone before the gate was fully opened. He supposed the plan still held.

Using Alena for support, Brandt shuffled toward the final Lolani soulwalker. Like the last, his advance wasn't even noticed. He almost felt guilty for killing them like this.

Almost.

He stabbed his knife out, the bloody point aimed straight for the heart.

It stopped about two hands away from her chest.

Brandt tried again, stabbing from a slightly different angle. Nothing changed.

He looked to Alena. Perhaps this was yet another task for her. She reached out with her hand until it too stopped. She closed her eyes for a moment, then gasped.

"What is it?"

"It's a wall, woven of elements. I don't know how to breach it."

Brandt frowned. He looked at the hand that held Kye's gatestone. This close to the gate, he feared what would happen if he channeled his affinity through the stone. He would take Alena's word for now.

He looked at the stone in his hand. It only worked through contact. The soulwalker touched the gate. Perhaps he needed to do the same. He nodded toward the other arch of the glowing gate. "Help me over there."

"What are you going to do?"

"Touch it."

"Are you sure?"

He shook his head. "I'm very open to other ideas if you have any."

She remained silent.

Just as he'd feared.

Together, they shuffled over. Brandt wasn't sure how much longer he could stand even with her support.

He quivered with exhaustion and fear. The soulwalker

had kneeled in front of the gate for some time before daring to touch it. The power coming from the stones was palpable. But Brandt didn't know what the soulwalker had done to prepare, so he saw little point in waiting.

He turned to Alena. "I think you should let go."

She looked doubtful.

"I can stand for a few moments. But you've done all you can. Live, Alena. Return to your parents. We all take our last journey alone."

She still looked uncertain, but she gently ducked under his arm, making sure he was balanced before letting go completely.

He wished he had more time with her. He wished for more time with his wolfblades, and with Ana. Soon, though, he would have plenty of time with them all.

"Thank you," he said.

Before she could reply, he reached out and touched the gate.

His world exploded into color and sound, a vivid, kaleidoscopic nightmare. The sounds of the elements pounded against his skull, threatening to shatter it. Primal forces battered at him.

He pushed forward, skin torn from his limbs, coruscating energy slicing through his body. Three more steps brought him to his knees. This was beyond comprehension, beyond his ability to control and shape. He covered his ears, but the deafening sound still rattled his head.

It was too much power. No matter how he tried, he couldn't even begin to control it. His body came apart, tearing itself limb from limb.

Then he felt a hand on his shoulder. With a flash, the pressure decreased. He remained whole.

"Don't try to control it. Flow with it."

He looked up to see Alena standing beside him. Grateful as he was for her presence, it could only mean one thing. His heart sank. He'd hoped, if nothing else, she would survive these caves. "You touched the stone?"

"I touched you. You didn't look like you were doing so well."

Alena guided them. They broke out of the torrent of power and floated above it, like skimming over fast-moving rapids.

"How are you doing this?"

Alena shook her head. "The same as the soulwalking. It feels right."

"That's... vague."

She shrugged. "I wish I had a system, too. But it is what it is." She looked around. "Where are we?"

Brandt looked at her. "If you don't know, I certainly don't."

This plane seemed alive with energy. Brandt had the sensation of incredible speed, but his vision provided no clues.

"There's a pattern here, something underneath the chaos." Alena's curiosity sounded piqued. "Hold on."

Then Brandt's reality snapped. He was still in the other plane, but now he saw images, hints of a horizon. "What's happening?"

"It's your mind," Alena answered. "Here, the power of the mind is even more real than in our world. Give yourself a few moments. Nothing you see is real, exactly, but is a representation your mind creates."

"So this is a dream?"

"Of a sort. Except actions have consequences here."

The images in his brain suddenly solidified, but what he

saw was completely beyond his comprehension. He and Alena stood in a large open space, the ground lined with bricks.

In front of them, hundreds, if not thousands, of pale soldiers were lined up in formation.

Lolani warriors.

As startled as Brandt was by the warriors, though, his attention was drawn to two women standing about a dozen paces away from them. One of the Lolani was familiar.

The soulwalker from the cave. She was the one in contact with the gate. As Alena and Brandt watched helplessly, the soulwalker reached out her hand and grasped the outstretched hand of the other woman.

A shock ran through every bone in Brandt's body. Though he couldn't understand the source of his knowledge, he knew that a connection had just been made.

Alena understood before he did. "The gate is open." She looked out over the assembled warriors. "She intends to lead them through. We're too late."

The second Lolani woman turned to them, somehow towering over them even though Brandt swore they were the same height.

The woman possessed an otherworldly beauty. Brandt found himself attracted to her in ways that he didn't understand. She drew him toward her until he felt a pull on his arm. He glanced back and saw Alena grimacing with effort.

The woman waved her hand and Alena collapsed, hands to her chest. Though she made no sound, she looked to be in terrible agony. Brandt wanted to help her, but he wanted to be closer to the woman more. He turned and realized he was already in front of her, bending the knee.

He didn't remember getting here, but it felt right.

The woman reached out and cupped his chin in her hand, pulling his gaze up until their eyes met. Her eyes were like deep still pools. Brandt knew he could dive into this woman's soul and spend eternity there. He'd never met a woman like her.

Then she spoke, her voice creating a shiver that ran up his spine. He almost moaned in ecstasy. "It was foolish for you two to come to this place."

Her gaze broke from Brandt's, looking beyond him. She frowned. Brandt glanced behind him. Alena struggled to her knees.

Brandt's heart pounded with sudden fear. He understood, for the first time, the danger they were in. With the speed of thought he had a knife in his hand. He stabbed out at the Lolani woman.

A scream broke from Alena's throat and she collapsed again. She kicked wildly, apparently struggling for air.

But Brandt didn't care. He was with the only person in the world that mattered.

Something in the Lolani woman's demeanor changed, though. She watched them with an appraising eye. "I see why he let you live. Your will is admirable. Perhaps there is a place for you in my new world. Swear fealty and live."

Brandt wanted to please her, but she needed to know the truth. Even in this place, he could feel his body dying. "I do not have long to live, my queen."

"You are the one in contact with the gate, are you not? A problem easily remedied."

For a moment, his world went white, a sharp blinding pain beyond any agony he'd ever experienced.

Then it was gone. He still kneeled in front of his queen, but his body was healed. It was weak but intact.

"A gift for you, a rare treasure given in honor of the strength you have displayed. Now, do I have your word?"

ALENA GASPED FOR AIR, the invisible, unbreakable grip on her throat gone. The woman's attention had left her for the moment.

She didn't dare move. Ever since she had stolen the gatestone from Zane Arrowood, she had been exposed to powers that stretched the limits of her comprehension. But here, in this place, she realized that all she had seen and experienced before were the acts of children beginning to explore their world. The woman that Brandt kneeled in front of exuded will, a boundless strength that dwarfed even Alena's connection with her gatestone.

Such a power was inconceivable.

Whoever this woman was, she was the one behind every action. She had guided Kye and brought the Lolani to the shores of the empire.

The woman was the queen of the Lolani people. Perhaps they used a different title, but she ruled them absolutely. Even though the queen's attention wasn't on her, it took nearly every scrap of focus Alena possessed to keep her thoughts safe from the woman's will. If Alena lost her struggle, she would find herself on her knees beside Brandt.

This wasn't compulsion, not as she had seen it before.

It was one's soul conceding dominion to another.

Such strength terrified her and sapped her will to fight. What was the point against such a strength? The whole empire would crumble against this woman.

She summoned her father's knife. For a heartbeat, it wavered in her grasp, then became solid. She didn't swing it or stab at anything. If she could get close enough to the queen she might try, but she doubted the queen would allow that.

And there was nothing here to cut. No threads of compulsion weaved their way around her.

But the knife served as a focus. So long as her gaze was on her father's steel, she remembered what she was fighting for.

Sometimes, she knew, there was no chance of victory. But the fight still mattered.

Alena rose to her feet.

Beyond Brandt, Alena saw she had gotten the queen's attention once more. The woman gestured, and the last soulwalker stood in front of Alena, blocking her path to Brandt.

A dozen strands of compulsion leaped from the woman, all aimed for Alena's heart.

BRANDT'S MOUTH worked over the words, but he could not voice his commitment to the queen. He wanted to, desperately, but couldn't.

He feared his failure would anger the queen.

It did the opposite.

She smiled, lighting up his world. "Such strength. Even here, I cannot quite tame your spirit. He was right, indeed, to save you for me."

"Kye?"

She nodded. "Yes, Kye. I imagine that if you are here, he is dead?"

"I am sorry to say that I killed him, my queen."

"Don't be sorry. The strong survive. If he could not stand against you, even after the gifts he'd been given, he did not deserve the place I promised at my side."

She came closer to him and a soft floral scent filled his nostrils. He hoped to never forget that smell. "That place is now yours, if you wish it."

Sounds of a struggle behind them reached his ears. He found it frustrating, as it interfered with his conversation.

"You helped him?"

"Of course. When he first explored the gatestone he'd taken from Zane Arrowood, he inadvertently created a connection to me. I brought him here and showed him the future. He pledged his sword, and in return, I taught him some small tricks."

Understanding crashed over Brandt. The queen had taught Kye how to wipe memories and compel people.

She was responsible.

He felt something in his mind shifting, like a child trying to crawl out from an enormous pile of blankets. It awakened, but slowly.

"And what is the future?"

She licked her lips. "I can feel you struggle, Brandt, even if you don't realize it. No one has held out so long in this plane. Every moment here weakens you, and still you resist."

She leaned in until her mouth was next to his ear. She bit his earlobe, gently, then whispered, "Your will is intoxicating."

Another wave of pleasure rolled over Brandt. He would do anything for her. Anything at all.

And yet he couldn't swear her his fealty.

The queen gestured at the rows of soldiers staring blankly ahead. "This, Brandt. This is your future. The gate has been opened. Once you pledge yourself and you and your friend cease your struggles, I will be able to send my warriors through the gate." She gestured to the side, where an enormous archway stood.

In many ways, it was like the gate he had seen in the cave. It was just much larger. But the makers had clearly been the same.

"And once they are through?"

"They will wreak havoc on your empire, as they should have done hundreds of years ago."

THE STRANDS WRAPPED around Alena's neck, arms, and legs. They attempted to force her once again to her knees.

Alena cut at the strands, but it felt as though she was trying to cut steel. Her knife was useless.

She almost let it go.

But she refused. If she was going to die, she wanted her father's knife in her hands. As the strands increased their pressure, she stared at the knife.

Her father had made that for her.

Had told her that he trusted her.

The pressure surrounding her lessened.

The strands broke, cut by a bubble of energy that surrounded her. Alena stood tall and proud. She could still become the daughter that her father believed her to be.

Another set of strands reached for Alena's heart, but the energy surrounding her let nothing through. The soulwalker let the strands die. A long knife appeared in her hand and she stepped forward, driving her knife at Alena's chest.

The knife cut into Alena's shield, slicing through it and reaching slowly toward her heart.

The Lolani had killed Azaleth. Perhaps the kindest soul she had ever met.

Anger grew in her, and she fought against the soulwalker, grabbing the woman's wrist with one hand and pushing against the attack. But the knife blade kept advancing, inexorably, toward her. When the point penetrated her chest, a sweet agony rolled over her.

Alena screamed, then drove her own knife into the woman's chest.

The soulwalker's malicious grin vanished as Alena's blade searched for her heart.

Their fight was one of incremental progress. Each stabbed into their opponent with one hand while trying to stop their opponent's stab with the other.

Pain dropped Alena to her knees, the soulwalker following suit. The torment of the soulwalker's knife cutting through her flesh was beyond bearing.

For her family.

For Azaleth's broken dreams.

She bore the unbearable.

Their souls intertwined as they fought, the knives a representation of a more abstract battle. Alena saw the soulwalker's childhood, a series of torturous events that left her broken but devoted to the queen.

Alena wondered what the soulwalker saw in her own past.

Would she see the family dinners and the quiet conversations she had with her father? Would she see the way the Etari patiently taught her their ways, after risking everything to adopt her?

Alena didn't understand the flashes of memory she saw within the soulwalker. But she saw enough suffering in just a few glimpses that she could predict the results of a successful Lolani invasion.

It couldn't happen. She wouldn't let it happen.

With a scream, Alena put everything she had left into her knife, breaking past the soulwalker's defense and slicing the tip of the knife into the woman's heart.

The soulwalker died, and Alena's soul, intertwined, traveled with her.

She found herself in a different place. Here, all was calm. There was no fight and no strife.

Those were only found within the domain of the living.

She looked up, then took a step back.

The gates.

Not the powerful portals of rock and stone that they fought the Lolani queen over.

The actual gates, a legend she had grown up with and yet never believed.

The soulwalker was here, too. She looked different somehow, with all the cares stripped from her. She smiled at Alena and walked toward the gate.

Although the gate looked to be nothing more than an arch, as soon as the soulwalker stepped through she vanished. Into what, Alena could only guess.

Alena felt a deep well of power grow within her then. She looked down at her navel, where she felt the power now resided. She tested it, manipulating her internal energies.

She felt powerful.

There was a soft laugh next to her.

She spun, surprised. A man stood there. He looked to be in his sixties and seemed strangely familiar. But Alena couldn't quite place him. His grin was wide.

"You begin to understand."

"I don't think I do."

"You will."

"What happens if I go through that gate?"

"You die."

Though she hated to admit it, she felt the pull toward the gate. There was peace on the other side.

"I would ask that you don't."

She hadn't even realized she'd taken a step towards the gate. She turned back to the older man. "Why not?"

"Because Brandt needs you. My empire needs you."

Alena thought of the suffering she had caused. The death of Brandt's wolfblades, the distress within her family. Azaleth. "Nobody needs me."

The man held a knife in his hand by the point, extending the grip to her.

It was her father's knife.

"Do you truly believe that?"

Alena looked at the gate. Its promise of everlasting peace called to her. She wouldn't disappoint anyone ever again if she stepped through.

Then she looked at the knife.

She also wouldn't have any chance of making things right. She had left Jace alone in those caverns. If she died, her family would lose both children in one day.

The man smiled, as though he was privy to her thoughts. She snatched the knife from him.

Turning away from the gate was the hardest thing she had ever done.

BRANDT HAD QUESTIONS. With every answer his queen gave him, he wanted to know more. Her tone, once patient, became strained. She didn't want him asking questions. She wanted submission. He felt ashamed he couldn't offer it to her. How he wanted to, though!

"What happened hundreds of years ago?" he asked instead.

"Nothing that concerns you!" she growled. Her gaze was no longer fixed on Brandt, but on something behind him. The sounds of battle had ended, and the result appeared to displease his queen.

When her gaze returned to him, it held ferocious intensity, the gaze of a stalking predator preparing to leap upon its prey. His queen was a fierce ruler, and he loved her even for that.

"Swear to me, now!" she demanded.

But the words wouldn't come from his lips. He couldn't force them past.

"Fine, then." A sword appeared in her hand, a style Brandt had never seen. She raised it high, ready to take his life. His heart pounded with ecstasy as he bared his neck.

Then a cool breeze washed over him, restoring his sanity in this place of madness. His heart pounded not with expectation, but with fear. He rolled out of the way as the sword came down, cracking the stone that had been beneath him.

Brandt came to his feet, glancing back to see Alena, wreathed in power.

The Lolani queen's look toward Alena was full of venom. "You took her to the gate, didn't you?" Her eyes flashed. "You begin to understand. Too late, though."

The skies above darkened and lightning crashed down, reminding Brandt of the attack on the monastery.

Alena stepped toward them, knife in hand. The queen snarled, "Enough. If you will not bow, get out of my way."

A dozen spears appeared in the middle of nowhere, half a dozen aimed at each of the imperials. They launched. Brandt felt for the familiar hilt of his sword but grasped only air. Where was his sword?

The spears stopped before they reached him, though he heard the impacts of the spears aimed at Alena.

When he turned back, he saw three of them embedded deeply within her. Alena looked down, a look of surprise on her face. She sank to her knees, and again Brandt felt that now-familiar tug of desire towards the queen.

The skies went from dark to black, a starless night that bowed to the queen. Slowly, inexorably, Brandt felt himself falling to his knees again.

His queen smiled, a beautiful, vicious smile.

PAIN FORMED the entirety of Alena's world. Every breath she took moved the spears, causing a fresh wave of torment to wash through her body.

Even with her newfound power and the gatestone, Alena was no match for the Lolani queen. At best, she had caused the queen to stumble for a moment.

Alena wasn't sure the queen had a limit. No matter what they did, she and Brandt had no chance. They couldn't beat the queen.

Her body shuddered uncontrollably. Soon she'd make the trip to the gate herself.

Her eyes wandered over her surroundings. She stared at the rows of troops, eyes locked forward, oblivious to the fight in front of them. They looked only toward the gate.

The gate.

Alena followed their empty gazes.

They didn't have to beat the queen.

They just needed to close the gate. The soulwalker who had opened it was now dead. If they closed it, the queen had no way of coming through.

But Alena couldn't do it. The agony of movement was too much.

Brandt could, though.

Hating herself, Alena reached out with a single strand of thought, resting it on Brandt's shoulder with the gentleness of a butterfly.

Brandt.

She felt him respond, his body tensing at the sound of her voice.

Break the gate.

Brandt fought to push himself to his feet. In this place, where the queen held such control, even such a small defiance took everything he had. Then she felt an answering thought. *I have no weapon.*

Alena almost laughed to herself. He still didn't see. She pushed her understanding into his mind. *Here, you are the weapon.*

Then she summoned every scrap of strength she had and pushed it at him. She channeled the energy of the dead soulwalker, the gatestone, and her own flagging energy. She gave it all, because there was no point in holding back.

Blackness crowded the edges of her vision, but she continued to push.

She vowed to push until her last breath.

BRANDT FELT the queen's hold on him diminish. He stood, well-balanced between his feet.

Alena fed him her own knowledge. Her own life.

Once again, those around him sacrificed themselves for him.

He sensed the queen's attacks, her sword cutting at him. Energized by Alena's efforts, his sword appeared in his hand. He deflected the queen's strikes, but every parry sapped his strength.

Even if Alena died to save him, he couldn't beat the queen.

He slid under one of her attacks. The gate was thirty paces away, too far away for him to reach before the queen killed him.

But Alena's understandings held the clue. What did distance matter, here, in a place ruled by the mind and the will? Brandt lifted his sword high.

He knew the queen's attack was coming. He twisted, causing the queen's sword to cut across his torso. Burning pain almost blinded him, but it didn't matter now.

His sword, held high above him, grew. Soon it reached fifty paces into the air, balanced precariously above him.

Brandt swung. The enormous sword moved slowly at first, but as it fell it gained speed. He put all his strength, all Alena's strength, into the cut.

"No!" the queen screamed.

He felt two dozen spears impale him, but it was too late. He finished the swing, and the impossibly huge sword cut into the gate.

His sword cut clean through, the stone shattering with an earth-rending crack.

A cry of despair tore from the queen's throat as Brandt's blade gouged a vicious wound into the ground.

Alena's strength flowing into him vanished, and he feared the worst. Then a blinding light emanated from the broken gate, and everything went white.

68

When Alena opened her eyes, she saw nothing. Eyes opened or closed, all was dark.

She brought her hand to her torso, feeling for the spears she was convinced still impaled her. She felt them rending her flesh, but the feeling was like an echo of memory. Her hand found nothing except for her clothing. It caught slightly on the gatestone embedded near her navel, just as it always did.

Alena heard movement beside her.

"I'm here."

Brandt.

A hand reached out to join hers.

As her eyes adjusted, she noticed that the room wasn't perfectly dark. Faint light from far away penetrated the gloom. It wasn't much, but she could just make out Brandt's figure. He sat cross-legged beside her.

"What happened?"

"I'm not sure. But I think we closed the gate."

Memories assaulted her. But she remembered Brandt

struggling to even reach the gate. "Are you—" She couldn't finish the question.

"Healed?" She heard a hint of bitterness in his voice. "Yes. She didn't lie about that."

"I don't understand."

He chuckled, a low sound that barely carried even in the small chamber. "I'm not sure I do, either. I think she truly believed I would serve her." He paused. "I might have, too. Thank you."

She shook her head. "You wouldn't have, and I should be thanking you."

"She'll try again." Resignation dulled his voice.

"And hopefully, we'll be better prepared."

They sat there in silence for a while, each of them wrapped up in their own thoughts and memories.

Alena broke first. "Brandt?"

"Yes?"

"Can we leave now?"

"Absolutely."

Brandt pulled some fire from far away, lighting their way as they stepped around the Lolani corpses and into the chamber where Brandt and Kye had fought. Brandt moved well, proof enough the Lolani queen possessed a healing skill the empire didn't. Alena was in much the same shape she had been when she stumbled into the gate chamber. Her right arm barely functioned, and she was certain Jace had cracked some of her ribs. But the damage the queen had done lasted only in her soul.

Alena couldn't help but glance at Kye's frozen form as they passed. "How many of his actions, do you think, were compelled by the queen?"

Brandt shook his head. "It doesn't matter. Some part of

him wanted to obey. He's responsible for all the pain he's caused."

Alena laughed.

"What?"

"You should meet my Etari family. I think they would like you."

It didn't take long for them to reach Jace. He was still sitting, his arms wrapped around his knees, rocking gently. Alena held out her left hand. "Come on, Jace. Let's get out of here."

He followed her like an eager puppy.

Brandt gave her a questioning look, but Alena simply shook her head. She already felt terrible enough as it was. She'd compelled Jace, and she wasn't sure there would be forgiveness. But that matter could be dealt with after they left these caverns.

They crossed the first bridge and climbed the stairs back to the chamber where the Lolani had first ambushed them.

Ana still lived. Her breathing was ragged, but she lived.

When Brandt saw her, he rushed to her, taking her in his arms.

Though Alena had known how close they were, she had to turn away from the scene. Her own tears blurred her vision.

As Ana and Brandt reunited, Alena turned to Azaleth's corpse. His eyes were wide, staring at nothing. Somehow, they seemed even softer than when he was alive.

He shouldn't have followed her here.

She kneeled down next to him and let herself cry.

Eventually, she felt a strong hand on her shoulder. She looked up to see Brandt. "We need to bring him with us. I need to bury him."

Their going was slow. They bandaged up Ana as well as

they were able, and Brandt gave her Kye's gatestone as a source of energy. Then he put Alena's arm back in place.

Alena couldn't stand having Jace help her, so he supported Ana while Alena and Brandt struggled with Azaleth's body.

They stopped in a chamber about halfway up. The day had taken an enormous toll on all of them, and they needed rest. They took turns on watch, as none of them completely trusted the compulsion on Jace.

But when they had all slept their fill, they stood and continued the arduous journey out of the caves. Alena lost track of time. There was no sun in this place, and she didn't see natural daylight until they found the crack they had entered through. If not for Azaleth's stones, Alena wasn't sure they would have found their way back. Even in death, he saved her. The thought brought even more tears to her eyes.

Ana and Jace were the first to step out into the open sky. Brandt, carrying Azaleth, followed. The last stretch was the most difficult, the shape of the crack forcing them to carry and drag Azaleth in awkward ways. She hoped he would understand.

She was the last one to step into the fading light of the day. They all rested, and Alena laid Azaleth out on a stone. She took her knife and removed the gatestone embedded in his flesh, the same way she had seen it done in Etar. She grabbed his stones and his sword, surprised that the remains of his life amounted to so little.

Then she built a cairn around him. It wasn't as good as a grave, but it would satisfy Etari customs. She worked until the sun had fallen in the sky, refusing help from anyone. This was her task alone. He had followed her.

When she was done, she collapsed into Brandt's arms.

"Did you have any final words?" Brandt asked.

Alena shook her head. "He always knew my heart. I wish I had understood his sooner."

They hiked a little ways down into the valley before resting for the night. When the sun rose, Brandt turned his attention to Alena.

"Come. Let's get you home."

THEY DIDN'T ARRIVE in Landow until the following day. Brandt set them up in an inn, as Alena was too nervous to approach her family, and Brandt had tasks he needed to complete. A bird needed to be sent to the emperor, and the commander of the city guard needed to take control of the city until a new governor could be appointed.

Alena ate her fill, bathed, then ate again. She collapsed while a healer looked in on Ana, falling asleep and not waking up until most of the day had passed. Then she ate again, her body constantly demanding more food.

It wasn't until breakfast the next day they all came together again. Their spirits were up, but they each carried the cost of their actions. Jace still followed Alena around without complaint, and Brandt waited on pins and needles to hear back from the emperor.

As they ate, Brandt turned his attention to Alena. "You will remove that compulsion, right?"

Alena nodded. "I suppose it's time. I'm afraid, though. Will you remain between us, in case he attacks?"

Brandt nodded and stationed himself.

Alena had thought about this moment since they had made it successfully out of the caves. Through the connection soulwalking created, she had seen his memories. Perhaps it was possible to share her memories with him the same way.

She closed her eyes, then reached out and held his hand. After a moment of focus, she found herself again standing in front of her representation of his soul. She created a thin golden strand of light and reached out to him to connect their souls.

The strand cut through the weave of compulsion she had placed over him.

It was met with pure, unbridled fury.

He knew what she had done, and he wanted to kill her.

Acting on impulse, Alena dropped the compulsion. The weave broke, and a moment later, Jace was standing in front of her, hand on his sword.

"You killed him!"

Jace drew his sword and attacked, murder in his eyes.

In the physical world, Alena would have run.

But she had faced the Lolani queen, a power she still didn't fully comprehend. On this plane, she was far stronger than Jace. She imagined an invisible wall of force between her and her brother. His sword glanced off it, his blows ineffective.

She let his anger rage. Time had a different meaning here, but it also didn't matter. Brandt would keep her physical body safe. Her patience would be rewarded.

Jace swung wildly, but none of his strikes even came close to breaking through her wall. Eventually, his rage burned out and he fell to his knees, tears in his eyes.

Keeping the wall between them, Alena kneeled down next to him. She fought to keep her voice from cracking. "I'm sorry, Jace. I'm sorry for everything."

For several long moments, she wasn't sure what to do. She had hoped this wouldn't be so difficult, but she feared that if she dropped her wall Jace would attack. He had years of reasons to hate her.

Alena took a deep breath, then dropped the wall. She reached out and touched him, allowing her memories to flow from her mind, through her arm, to him.

She didn't send him the memories of their happy moments together. After her compulsion, he might view such an attempt as another manipulation.

Instead, she sent the memories that represented the beginning of their separation. The fight with Niles in the street, her curiosity about the boy. She let the events spool out.

Had she once been so foolish? The signs had always been there, and Bayt provided plenty of warning.

"What is this?" Jace asked.

"What happened to me," she replied.

They came to the night when she made her fateful choice. Jace watched her run across the rooftops, stealing the diamond from Zane.

"They told me you were a thief." Jace's voice was flat and empty. "For the longest time, I didn't believe. But you were, weren't you?"

"I thought I was."

Knowing what thieving had cost her, Alena found she could barely understand her younger self. She had a family that loved her, and opportunities to succeed. She had thrown it all away, and why?

Because she thought she was bored.

She knew Jace could feel her regret, but she let the memories continue.

Together, her and Jace came upon Bayt's body. She felt her brother recoil. She paused the memory when she spotted the message written in Bayt's blood.

"You didn't kill him," Jace said.

"Zane wielded the knife, but it was my decisions that killed him."

The memories resumed. Jace watched the chase, the fight between Zane, the bandit, and the wolfblades. Jace didn't speak as he watched his childhood idols fall one by one.

"Who was the bandit?" Jace asked. He sounded as though he had a guess, but was afraid to voice it.

Alena didn't answer. Her memories could speak for her, and were far more powerful.

She came to her and Brandt in the teahouse.

Jace's breath caught. Connected as they were, she had a sense of his thoughts. His sister had worked side-by-side with a wolfblade. What he saw warred against the story he had believed for the better part of a decade.

She didn't speak, allowing her memories to tell the story for her.

Alena told Brandt she figured out who the bandit was.

Jace resisted, even though some part of him had already guessed the truth. Brandt revealed his plans to fight the bandit alone in the woods outside of town.

It was then Alena realized that using this technique, she actually could reveal to Brandt much of what he had forgotten.

But for now she focused on Jace. She let him watch the battle in the woods. She felt his heart sink as he saw Kye defeat and then manipulate Brandt.

Alena flashed through the rest of her memories. The most important pieces for Jace had happened in Landow, but she wanted him to know. He watched her as she fled to Tonno, then into Etar. She allowed him glimpses of her life there.

Then she showed him what caused her to return, and what happened when she did.

When it was done, she broke contact with him. Being so close to another's soul made her uncomfortable.

Whatever desire for revenge he'd held had been shattered. He saw how he had been lied to for years.

For a while, he feared the truth would shatter him.

She couldn't imagine his suffering. He had built his life around her betrayal. He had built his life around a lie.

He collapsed into her arms, and she held him tightly.

She severed the connection between them, thrusting them back into the real world. Her cheeks were damp from tears, but at the moment she couldn't care less.

Before Brandt could react, she ran to Jace, still fighting disorientation after the soulwalk. She embraced him, holding tightly onto him. He tensed, and for a moment she worried.

Then he relaxed and returned her embrace.

"I'm sorry," he said.

Alena shushed him. They were both sorry. It didn't need to be said.

Brandt cleared his throat. "I'm going to have a drink."

Alena didn't know how much time she spent holding on to Jace. She didn't want to let him go, not ever again. From the way he clutched onto her, she wondered if he felt the same.

Eventually, though, they broke apart. Jace sat on the chair in the room while Alena sat on the edge of the bed.

"What happens next?" he asked.

"The emperor is coming. He wants to see the gate himself. After that, I don't know."

Jace chuckled and shook his head. "Not in the empire. With us."

"Ah." Alena paused. "I — I want to go home."

She couldn't speak her question, but Jace understood. After their soulwalk, she wasn't sure it would be possible to keep secrets from one another.

"They would love to see you," Jace said. "Your leaving broke their hearts, but I don't think they ever really believed the stories Kye told about you. Especially Father. I always suspected he knew more than he said, but all he would ever say was that you were innocent. It angered me."

Alena nodded. "I always was his favorite."

Jace shook his head, wiping away his final tears. "Even after you left." He stood up. "Let's go, then. It's been too long since I've been home, too."

Alena wasn't ready, but she took his proffered hand, and they went downstairs. Brandt, true to his word, was enjoying a morning mug of beer. When he saw Alena's judgmental look, he shrugged. "They don't have beer at the monastery. You're going home?"

"We are. I'll return."

"I'm glad for you, Alena."

Jace and Alena left the inn, walking the familiar paths to their family home. Alena had many questions, but she found it difficult to speak. All she could think about was seeing her house once again. Seeing her parents.

Despite Jace's assurance, she worried about their reaction. She had run, had put the family through more difficulty than they had ever deserved. So much blame could be laid at her feet. Would they still welcome her?

When they came close, Alena gave a low laugh.

"What?" Jace asked.

"This is the same route we took when we came home from academy."

Jace looked down the street, then laughed as well. "Huh."

"I feel like you're the one escorting me, now," Alena admitted.

"I was escorting you back then, too."

She heard the pride in his voice. Even though he'd been younger, he'd always considered himself her protector. She'd taken that away from him, too. "I'm so sorry, Jace."

He shook his head. "No more apologies. Let's only look forward."

Alena nodded, a weight slipping off her shoulders. The road ahead wouldn't be easy, but she would walk it with Jace and her family by her side.

Alena paused when their house came into view. In all these years, it had barely changed.

Jace gently pulled her forward. As they came close, he reached out and held her hand.

They came to the door, standing awkwardly outside it.

Alena looked at Jace. "Do we just go in?"

He smiled. "I think you better knock."

Alena raised her hand, hesitating just for a moment. This whole event felt unreal, like a dream finally coming true.

She knocked.

It took a while, but she heard movement on the other side of the door, and soon it opened, revealing her mother's face.

They all stood there in silence for a moment. Then Jace spoke. "Look who I found."

Her mother took one look at her children, both in front of her. Alena saw how she noticed them holding hands. For one long heartbeat, she worried her mother would turn away.

Then Mother threw herself into them, wrapping them both in an embrace far stronger than Alena expected. She sobbed as she pulled them all to their knees.

Alena heard the sounds of someone else moving in the house, and then she saw him.

Father, coming to investigate the commotion.

When he saw everyone, he paused midstride, as though he couldn't believe his eyes. Then he ran forward, crushing them all in his thick arms.

Alena cried.

It was good to be home.

EPILOGUE

Alena knocked on the door to Brandt and Ana's room. It opened quickly and Ana gestured her in. "How are you?"

"Good," she said. "Excited to be out of the house for a few days."

Ana gave her a questioning look. Alena waved away her concern. "It's nothing serious. But my mother, in particular, is worried that something will happen to me again. She checks on me about fifty times a day, and if I even want to go to a teahouse, she insists on coming with me."

From deeper in the room, Brandt laughed. "It's hard to blame her."

"I don't, but I'm glad the emperor himself summoned us today. I'm not sure anything less would have convinced her to let me out of her sight."

Brandt stood up from the table he'd been sitting at and joined the women. "How's it been?"

Alena shrugged. "It's been hard, but good. Years of absence, especially mine, left wounds. They're healing, but they'll take time. We all understand that."

"I'm glad," Brandt said.

"Speaking of wounds," Alena said, eager to change the subject, "how are yours?"

Brandt looked himself over. "When the queen healed me, it was complete. I don't even have the aches I had before."

Ana rolled her eyes. "He won't stop talking about it. Not only did he save the empire, he came out of it healthier than before."

Alena laughed. She hadn't known the wolfblades for long, but they felt as close as family.

The mood turned somber when Alena broached the question that had brought her here so early. "Are you sure you want this?"

Brandt nodded. "Their loss still eats at me."

"Very well. You still want both?"

"Yes."

"Lie down, then. Ana, if you could stand on the other side and hold his hand." Alena did the same for Brandt's other free hand.

She closed her eyes and began the soulwalk. In preparation, she'd practiced a bit with her family. Alena wasn't sure that sharing memories was the best way of catching up with friends and family. What people saw during a soulwalk was unvarnished memory, a soul-baring experience. Everyone preferred to put their own feelings and interpretation on stories they told. Despite the advantages of soulwalking, Alena figured old-fashioned conversation was still best for most relationships.

But Brandt wanted his memory of his friends' deaths. Alena couldn't do that, but she could give him hers, and Ana's. Hopefully then he could rest easier.

The three of them appeared in the soul plane. Alena

fashioned it after the physical room they were in, minimizing disorientation. Then she opened the gates of her memory, sharing hers first, then Ana's. Brandt absorbed it all silently.

When the task was done, she severed the connection and stepped away from the bed. Ana still held onto Brandt's hand, and together they wept. Alena gave them space, turning to the window. The sun was coming up on a cold autumn morning, but the skies were clear.

LATER, Brandt led the women out of Landow and into the mountains. He rode ahead of the others, wanting to be alone with his thoughts.

Alena's ability had given him something he had been missing for years. Anders I had hinted at it, but the dead emperor's vision wasn't the same as a living human's. The fix wasn't perfect. Some part of him still recognized the memories weren't his. But they were better than nothing. He knew how his wolfblades had died.

The knowledge wasn't easy. He'd been mistaken to send them into that battle. Between the wolfblades and Zane, they'd pushed Kye into a corner, and nothing was more dangerous than a predator without an escape.

Behind him, he heard scraps of conversation between Ana and Alena. The two women got along well, and they spoke at length about Alena's reunion with her family.

He supposed he should be grateful. They had stopped the Lolani from invading, reunited Alena with her family, and earned the gratitude of the emperor. But the victories felt too costly.

Kyler.

Lola.

Ryder.

Azaleth.

And more. He knew the Etari had lost warriors fighting against the Lolani. They'd achieved a respite, but it didn't feel like enough.

He pushed the thoughts aside. The sky was mostly clear, and although the air was crisp, it was a gorgeous autumn day. The emperor had summoned them up to the caves where they had found the gate. He slowed down so the women could catch up to him.

As they did, Brandt overheard them talking about Jace and his new responsibilities. As chief aide to Kye, he knew more about the workings of the region than any other person. Apparently, he'd been offered a temporary governorship, but he'd refused, instead helping the emperor's new appointee.

All conversation stopped when they came in view of the valley leading up to the cave. Now a garrison of soldiers built a wall in the valley, sealing it. Brandt saw no small number of wolfblades among them.

The emperor's seal got them through the lines without problem, and they made straight for the crack.

Someone with a stone affinity had made the crack wider since they'd last entered. The way was also lit with torches, making the whole complex much more welcoming than it had been the last time they'd visited.

Welcoming or not, the journey still took most of the day. They were told the emperor was in the bottom chamber that held the gate, so they had no choice but to walk all the way down again.

The feeling of descending through the mountain couldn't have been more different. The caves were now filled with people. The emperor had brought scholars, masons, and soldiers to protect them all. Every corner they turned, they were greeted by friendly faces. They didn't quite erase the horror of that first descent, but they came close.

Eventually they reached the chamber of the gate. Here, the cave was quiet. Guards stood over the bridges, and it appeared very few were allowed past. Brandt recognized some of the warriors from their visit to the monastery. When they came into the final chamber, the emperor was alone.

They all bowed, but the emperor waved them away. "None of that nonsense, not here. If anyone should be bowing, it should be me. I had an inkling of the danger we faced, but I had no idea her plans had progressed so far. You saved the empire from a foolish emperor."

"There was no way you could have known—" Brandt began.

The emperor cut him off angrily. "There are always ways of knowing, and if I didn't see far enough ahead, the failure is my own. Had this gate remained open, the empire would have fallen within two years." He turned to them. "Tell me what happened."

So Brandt and Alena told their story, frequently stopped by the emperor. He wanted every detail, from the soulwalkers' abilities to their fight with the queen.

Brandt interrupted when Alena told of her visit to the other gate, the one she saw when the soulwalker died. "You saw the gate?"

She nodded, clearly discomfited by the experience.

"And you saw an old man there?"

"Yes. But I don't know who he was."

Brandt fished in the pockets of his robe. "Like this?" He held out a coin. Alena's eyes widened when she realized who she had seen.

Hanns, by contrast, didn't. Brandt noticed his lack of reaction and turned to him. "You knew?"

The emperor gave a small shrug. "It appears my predecessor has been more helpful than I realized."

"But he's dead!" Brandt exclaimed.

Hanns laughed. "He never did want to give up the throne."

Brandt's jaw moved, but no words came out. He didn't even know where to begin. But Hanns didn't seem too interested in the assistance of Anders I. He asked them to continue their story, and there was no denying an emperor's request. By the time they finished, Brandt was certain the emperor knew more about their encounter than they did. Hanns stared silently at the gate as he considered their story.

"I don't suppose either of you have any clue how to destroy it, do you?"

Brandt frowned. "I thought I did."

The emperor shook his head. He reached out and touched the gate. When he did, a soft blue glow emanated from the diamond. "You closed it, but I'm not sure these gates can be broken by us. Whoever fashioned them possessed far more power and skill than we can dream of."

"But aren't gatestones just fragments of gates? If so, there must be a way to break them," Alena said.

"They are," Hanns agreed. "I know of four gates on this continent, each tuned to different groups of affinities. The Etari possess two, one of which is shattered, and the source of the gatestones they use. There are two within the empire."

Brandt couldn't help but ask the question. "Where's the other one?"

"The palace is built over it," Hanns answered. "It's

through the power of that gate I work to maintain the storms that keep this continent isolated and safe."

"How much do you know," Brandt asked, waving his hand around to encompass the chamber, "about all of this?"

"More than anyone else, but not nearly enough," Hanns said. "I suspect the Lolani queen wants this land, not to conquer it, exactly, but to have access to the gates. A connection with one provides the wielder with immense power. I can only guess what a connection to more would do."

"You're going to attempt it, aren't you?"

"I would like to. But there are risks. The power within these gates resists command. That is why, Brandt, you nearly died when you touched the gate."

"Why didn't I have the same problem?" Alena asked.

"Because your strongest affinity is mental. Unlike the elemental affinities, yours is comfortable with chaos. Those like Brandt and I seek to control the elements. You ride them. It is also why it is almost impossible to instruct mental affinities. Their manifestations are so wild and varied, teaching is nearly useless."

Now that she had asked her first question, Brandt knew Alena was going to ask the next one that had plagued her since their adventure. "Why all the lies?"

The emperor sighed. "They are a legacy of Anders I. No one has ever been more powerful than him on this continent, and his knowledge led him to decisions we all question. One of which is the secrecy surrounding the past and the world we live on. I can't speak for my predecessor, but I believe he thought secrets were necessary to bring order to the continent."

Alena didn't look happy with the answer, but the emperor gave her no more.

Brandt took it all in. His years of study in the monastery made him comfortable with questions, but as he stood alongside the emperor, he realized just how little they knew. "What happens next?"

The emperor turned to look at the gates. "We must prepare. Your actions saved us this time, and no doubt the queen was surprised by the resistance she faced. We may have a year or two of safety, but this has been her quest for hundreds of years. She is patient, and her next attempt will be that much more of a threat."

Hanns looked at them both, a sadness in his eyes.

"We must be ready for war."

WANT MORE FANTASY?

As always, thank you so much for reading this story. There's an amazing number of great fantasy stories today, and it means so much to me that you picked this book up.

If you enjoyed this story, I also have two other fantasy series, filled with memorable characters. My first fantasy series is called *Nightblade*.

Links to all of my books can be found at www.waterstonemedia.net

THANK YOU

Before you take off, I really wanted to say thank you for taking the time to read my work. Being able to write stories for a living is one of the greatest gifts I've been given, and it wouldn't be possible without readers.

So thank you.

Also, it's almost impossible to overstate how important reviews are for authors in this age of internet bookstores. If you enjoyed this book, it would mean the world to me if you could take the time to leave a review wherever you purchased this book.

And finally, if you really enjoyed this book and want to hear more from me, I'd encourage you to sign up for my emails. I don't send them too often - usually only once or twice a month at most, but they are the best place to learn about free giveaways, contests, sales, and more.

I sometimes also send out surprise short stories, absolutely free, that expand the fantasy worlds I've built. If you're interested, please go to https://www.waterstonemedia.net/newsletter/.

With gratitude,

Ryan

ALSO BY RYAN KIRK

The Nightblade Series

Nightblade

World's Edge

The Wind and the Void

Blades of the Fallen

Nightblade's Vengeance

Nightblade's Honor

Nightblade's End

Relentless

Relentless Souls

Heart of Defiance

Their Spirit Unbroken

The Primal Series

Primal Dawn

Primal Darkness

Primal Destiny

Primal Trilogy

The Code Series

Code of Vengeance

Code of Pride

Code of Justice

ABOUT THE AUTHOR

Ryan Kirk is the bestselling author of the *Nightblade* series of books. When he isn't writing, you can probably find him playing disc golf or hiking through the woods.

www.waterstonemedia.net
contact@waterstonemedia.net

 facebook.com/waterstonemedia
twitter.com/waterstonebooks
instagram.com/waterstonebooks